Ever After

JUDE DEVERAUX

Ever After

headline
ETERNAL

First published in Great Britain in 2015
by HEADLINE ETERNAL
An imprint of HEADLINE PUBLISHING GROUP

Published by arrangement with Ballantine Books,
an imprint of Random House,
a division of Penguin Random House LLC, New York.

1

Cataloguing in Publication Data is available from the British Library

ISBN 978 1 4722 1144 6 (Hardback)
ISBN 978 1 4722 1145 3 (Trade Paperback)

Offset in Sabon by Avon DataSet Ltd, Bidford-on-Avon, Warwickshire

Printed and bound by CPI Group (UK) Ltd, Croydon, CR0 4YY

Headline's policy is to use papers that are natural, renewable and
recyclable products and made from wood grown in well-managed forests
and other controlled sources. The logging and manufacturing processes are
expected to conform to the environmental regulations of the country of origin.

HEADLINE PUBLISHING GROUP
An Hachette UK Company
Carmelite House
50 Victoria Embankment
London EC4Y 0DZ

www.headlineeternal.com
www.headline.co.uk
www.hachette.co.uk

By Jude Deveraux

Nantucket Brides Series
True Love
For All Time
Ever After

Ever After

Prologue

Hallie couldn't find the packet of papers she needed to give her boss. She remembered putting them in a big white envelope, then slipping it into her tote bag. Although the bag was in the trunk of her car, the envelope wasn't in it.

As she stood in the mall parking lot, she went over everywhere she'd been that morning. To the pharmacy to pick up her stepsister's favorite hair conditioner, to the dry cleaners to get the skirt Shelly had stained. And she'd stopped by the garage to ask yet again when Shelly's car was going to be ready so she could run her own damned errands.

Hallie took a breath to calm herself. There were also six plastic bags in the trunk—all of them full of her stepsister's clothes, unopened bills, shoes, and beauty products—but none of them contained the envelope full of papers.

She closed the trunk and turned away. Too much! she thought. It was all getting to be too much for her. Since Shelly had returned six weeks ago, everything had been chaos. Hallie was a morning person; her stepsister liked to stay up all night. Hallie needed quiet to study for her exams; Shelly didn't seem alive unless some machine was emitting noise. The car Shelly had driven back from California was in such bad condition that she'd wanted to have it towed away. "I'll just borrow yours," she said, then left the room before Hallie could protest.

But then Shelly had made it clear why she was staying. She wanted Hallie to sell the house and split the money. The fact that Hallie's father hadn't changed his will after he'd married Shelly's mother made no difference. Shelly said that *legally* the house might not be half hers, but it certainly was *morally*.

"He was my father too," Shelly said, tears in her thickly lashed eyes. As a pretty little girl, she'd perfected the look of sadness that made people give her whatever she wanted. When she grew up to be an even prettier young woman, she saw no reason to stop using her looks to manage people.

But Hallie had never fallen for her act. "Cut it out!" she said. "It's *me*, remember? Not some casting director you're try-ing to seduce."

With a sigh, Shelly sat up straight and the tears instantly ceased. "Okay, so let's talk about *you*. Think what you could do with your half of the money. You could travel, see the world."

Hallie leaned back against the car and turned her face up to the sun. It was spring and the trees of New England were burst-ing into bud.

Her stepsister's attitude of here's-something-else-you-can-do-for-me wore a person down. Shelly's incessant talking, bad-gering, pleading, and at times anger made Hallie want to throw up her hands and call a Realtor. She'd shown on paper that if she sold the house, by the time she paid off the mortgage she'd had to get to buy a new roof and repair the plumbing and electrics, they would barely break even. But Shelly had just waved her hand and said houses in L.A. sold for millions.

But in the last two weeks Shelly had been calmer, almost as though she'd given up. She'd been asking Hallie about her work as a physical therapist, saying, "What would you recommend for a man with a torn-up knee?"

"Describe the injury to me," Hallie said, and Shelly had read about it from an email she'd received. Pleased by her stepsister's interest, Hallie had outlined the lengthy rehabilitation the man would need.

Although Shelly wasn't forthcoming with the details, Hallie assumed that her stepsister had a friend who'd been injured. Whatever the reason, it had been nice to have some relief from Shelly's relentless pursuit of her goal. Hallie began to think that her life was at last coming together. She'd finally finished her coursework, passed her exams, and received her Massachusetts physical therapy license. And next week she was going to start a job at a small local hospital.

She glanced at her watch. She had just enough time to run home to get the papers and make it to the office before Dr. Curtis left for the weekend. As she drove, she thought it was exhilarating to imagine having a whole new life. New career, new job, new *world*. Only it wasn't actually new. Her job was close to the house she'd lived in all her life, and she'd be working with people she'd gone to school with. And her stepsister also planned to stay in the area. "You're the only family I have left," Shelly said. Hallie knew that meant her stepsister would be at her house for every holiday, weekend, and catastrophe in Shelly's very dramatic life.

Hallie believed in looking on the positive side of life, but sometimes she felt like applying for a job in some faraway, exotic place.

When Hallie turned down her street, she immediately noticed the blue BMW parked in front of her house. It stood out from the Chevys and Toyotas like a jewel in a pile of gravel.

Across the road, Mrs. Westbrook was opening her mailbox. "Braden's home," she called before Hallie could pull into the driveway. "You should come over and say hello."

At the mention of the lawyer son, Hallie's heart did a little flip. "I look forward to it," she said honestly. Since she was a child, Hallie had often gone to the older woman—a substitute mother—when Shelly's give-me-give-me attitude got to be too much. Chocolate lava cake did wonders to soothe Hallie's tears.

She parked the car, got out, and closed the door quietly. She didn't want to meet whoever was visiting Shelly. But as Hallie glanced at the shiny car, she did wonder who it could be.

Hallie opened the back door slowly so it didn't squeak. As soon as she was inside, she saw the envelope on the table on the far side of the kitchen—and she could hear voices. Since there was an open doorway leading into the living room between her and the package, she didn't know how she was going to get across without being seen.

But the man's voice took her mind off the papers. She'd heard it before but couldn't place it. When she peeped around the doorway to look into the living room, what she saw startled her.

Shelly, seen in profile, had on one of Hallie's suits. She was taller and thinner than Hallie, so the skirt was shorter and the jacket too big, but she did look businesslike.

On the coffee table were a cake and cookies, and what Hallie knew was Mrs. Westbrook's best tea set. Obviously, Shelly had known the visitor was coming, but she'd said nothing.

The man on the couch was facing the kitchen, but his attention was fully on Shelly. He was talking in a low voice, something about a house, and for a moment Hallie thought he was a Realtor. But, no, she had seen him before.

When Hallie turned back to the kitchen, she remembered.

He was Jared Montgomery, the famous architect. In school she'd dated an architecture student who'd wanted her to go to a lecture with him. The guy had raved about the architect who was speaking. Hallie had expected to be bored—and she was by what he said, but the speaker was very good-looking: tall, slim but muscular, with dark hair and eyes.

She hadn't been surprised to see that most of the audience was female. The girl next to her whispered, "I hope he's doing that thing of imagining his audience naked." Hallie couldn't help but laugh.

So what in the world was the famous Jared Montgomery doing sitting in *her* living room?

Hallie tried to hear what they were saying, but their voices were too low. She didn't know if she should step forward and introduce herself or tiptoe out and leave them alone.

She had just turned to leave when she heard Mr. Montgomery say, "Now, Hallie, if you'll just sign here, the house will be yours."

Hallie froze in place. Shelly was pretending to be her and selling the house to this man?!

She stepped into the living room. Shelly, pen in hand, had just finished signing a paper. "May I see that?" Hallie asked softly, her voice controlled in spite of the anger she could feel bubbling inside her.

Shelly, her face draining of color, handed the paper to her stepsister. It had the small print of a contract, and on the bottom was Hallie's full legal name written in a rather good imitation of her handwriting.

"Just let me explain," Shelly said, her voice near to panic. "It's only fair that I get a house too. It's not fair that you get *all* of the inheritance, is it? I'm sure Dad would want me to have half of whatever he owned. He would—"

"Excuse me," the man said, "but would someone please explain what's going on?"

Hallie's anger was rising to the surface. She held out the paper toward him. "You're Jared Montgomery, the architect, aren't you? I can assure you that if you plan to put a skyscraper in here, the neighborhood association will fight you to the very limit of the law."

Her statement seemed to amuse him. "I will do my best to repress my tendency to build skyscrapers wherever I go. Are you Hallie's stepsister?"

"No. *I am Hallie.*"

The smile left the man's handsome face and for a second he looked from one young woman to the other. Without speaking, he pulled a paper from inside his briefcase and handed it to her.

Taking it, Hallie was shocked to see that it was a photocopy of her passport—only in place of her photo was one of Shelly. When she looked closely, she could see where her stepsister had carefully cut around the edges of the picture to make it fit. If you were looking at the actual passport, what she'd done would be obvious, but the photocopy hid what Hallie knew was criminal fraud.

"I *had* to do this," Shelly said, her voice frantic. "You wouldn't listen to me, so I did what I had to. If you would only *listen,* I wouldn't have been forced to—"

Her look made Shelly stop talking. Silently, Hallie went to her bedroom, opened the top drawer of her bureau, and took out her passport. She went back to the living room and handed it to Mr. Montgomery.

He studied the two documents, then looked at Hallie, who was still standing. "This is my fault," he said. "I didn't examine this carefully enough. Now I see what's been done." He looked at Shelly, his dark eyes narrowed and angry. "I don't like being part of something illegal. My lawyers will contact you."

"I didn't mean anything bad," Shelly said, tears welling in her pretty eyes. "I was only trying to be fair, that's all. Why should Hallie get so much while I get nothing? Dad would have wanted me to have—"

"Quiet!" Jared said. "Sit there and don't say another word." He looked back at Hallie. "I'm beginning to see the enormity of this and I can't apologize enough. I take it I haven't been emailing *you* for the past two weeks?"

"No." Hallie was glaring at Shelly, who had her head down, tears dropping onto her hands clasped in her lap. "I only know who you are because I attended one of your lectures at Harvard."

Jared ran his hand across his face. "What a mess this is!" He looked back at Hallie. "Since I don't know what's true and what isn't"—he glared at Shelly—"I'd better start at the beginning. You are a physical therapist and you just got your Mass license?"

"Yes."

"That's a relief! What do you know of your father's relatives?"

"Very little," Hallie said. "He was orphaned young and raised in foster homes. He had no living relatives that he knew of."

"Right," Jared said. "That's what I was told. It seems that—" He glanced at Shelly. Her tears were now accompanied by sobs growing increasingly loud.

Shelly raised her head and looked at her stepsister. Her eyes were pleading. Pleading for what, Hallie didn't know. Forgiveness? Or to prove her "fairness" by doing what Shelly wanted?

"Shelly," she said quietly but very firmly. "I want you to deliver the envelope of papers on the kitchen table to Dr. Curtis's office. I know you have no idea where I work, but the address is on the envelope. Do I make myself clear?"

"Yes, Hallie, of course you do, but when I get back, you and I must talk. And this time you have to listen to me so you'll understand—"

"No!" Hallie said firmly. "Shelly, *this* time I am *not* going to forgive you. Now get the extra keys, take my car, and leave."

Shelly had the self-righteous look of someone who had been falsely accused of a crime, but she did what Hallie told her to.

When she was out of the house, Jared said, "If you want to prosecute, I'll bear all the financial responsibility. I feel really stupid about this."

"It's not your fault, Mr. Montgomery," Hallie said in dismissal, and he told her to call him Jared. She glanced down at the forged signature on the paper on her lap. With this as evidence, she knew she could prosecute. But she also knew it wasn't in her nature to do so.

"Hallie," he said as he looked at her, "I have a lot to tell you, explain to you—and even more to make up to you. Hallie— I mean Shelly—was going to leave with me today."

"I see," Hallie said, and for the first time she noticed her own luggage piled in a corner. Her tone told what she thought of that liaison.

"It's not like that," Jared said. "My wife and I live on Nantucket, and in about an hour I have to leave to board a friend's plane and return home. Shelly was to go back with me, but I can assure you that it was purely business."

Hallie wasn't understanding anything. "But what about the house? Why are you trying to buy it?"

"*This* house?" He glanced around at it. "No offense, but—" He broke off when he realized how badly he was explaining things. "Your stepsister wasn't trying to steal *this* house from you. I'm the executor of the will of the late Henry Bell and he left his house on Nantucket to *you*."

This news so shocked Hallie that she was barely able to reply. "I don't know any Henry Bell."

"I know." He tapped his briefcase. "It's all in here, and I sent copies of the documents to your stepsister. It will take some time for you to read them all. And . . ." He let out his breath.

"There's something else you should know." He paused for a moment. "Hallie and I," Jared said, "I mean, Shelly and I have been corresponding, but she's also been writing to a cousin of mine. She said she was a physical therapist and since he—"

"Tore all four ligaments of his right knee while skiing," Hallie said as puzzle pieces began to fall into place. "Shelly grilled me about how to rehabilitate that specific injury."

"Uh . . . Yeah, well . . ." Jared said. "How do I say this? She gave permission for the old workshop on your property to be equipped as a gym." He hesitated. "And she invited my injured cousin to move into the downstairs living room of your house. She was to have the upstairs to herself. The plan was that her job for the next few months would be to get Jamie back on his feet." His eyes widened. "If this, uh . . . exchange hadn't been found out, how could she have done your job?"

"I have no idea," Hallie said. "But then I never second-guess my stepsister." For a few moments she looked at him in silence as she tried to take in what he was saying. The first thing was to clear her mind or else anger would take over. As far as she could tell, right now she had two choices. She could stay here, start a job that was stable but offered little in the way of advancement, and live in her childhood home. But that would mean that she'd have to deal with Shelly's never-ending whining about the injustices of her life—all of which could be solved if Hallie just gave more, did more, cared more for her stepsister.

Or, Hallie thought, she could go to Nantucket and . . . She didn't know what was waiting there for her and right now that sounded heavenly.

She took a breath. "Are you saying that I have a house and a job waiting for me on the beautiful island of Nantucket?"

Jared smiled at her tone. She sounded like she was on the receiving end of a magic wish. Considering what he'd just seen of her stepsister, that's what she was being offered. "If you want them, that is. You could leave with me now, or come later. Or I could sell the house for you and send you the proceeds. It's your choice. I'll help you, whatever you want to do. I certainly owe you."

For the first time since she'd come home, Hallie smiled. "Can I have twenty minutes to pack?"

Jared grinned. "I'll call the pilot, delay the flight, and you can have thirty."

Hallie went to her luggage, which Shelly had filled with her own clothes, emptied the contents onto the floor, and pulled out her things that her stepsister had "borrowed." She looked at Jared. "If Shelly wanted to do this, that means your cousin Jamie must be either gorgeous or rich—or both."

Jared shrugged. "I don't know about gorgeous. He's short and stocky, just a kid, really, but his stepmother is the writer Cale Anderson."

Hallie nodded. "Rich. I thought so. I'll be ready in twenty-five minutes."

Chapter One

Even the sight of the private jet she was to take to the island of Nantucket didn't cheer Hallie up. The interior was tan leather and dark wood, beautifully elegant, and she and Jared were the only passengers. She hoped that the trip would distract her from her thoughts. Before a few hours ago she would have sworn that her stepsister was incapable of doing something so treacherous, as well as illegal. The forged passport, the planned meeting with the famous architect, and the contract signed in an imitation of Hallie's handwriting all ran through her mind.

On the way to the airport she'd asked Jared how he'd first contacted her, and he said he'd sent an overnight package. Hallie's guess was that Shelly accepted delivery, opened the envelope, read the contents, and decided to take what wasn't hers.

Hallie thought about what would have happened if she hadn't returned home unexpectedly. Would she have come home from work to find an empty house and a note from her stepsister saying she'd decided to leave town? How long would it have taken her to find out about her stolen inheritance?

When they were on the plane, Jared made sure she was belted into a seat, the thick folder of papers on her lap and a glass of champagne beside her. As soon as they were aloft, he stepped away to make some calls, and Hallie started reading about why she'd been left property by a stranger. It seemed that she had an ancestor, Leland Hartley, who had been married to Juliana Bell, whose family—including her sister, Hyacinth—originally owned the house. At the sight of her own unusual name, her interest was piqued. Was this her ancestor? But, no, poor Juliana and her sister had died before either of them had children. Leland Hartley had returned to Boston, remarried, and had one son. Hallie was descended from him. Henry, the man who'd willed the house to Hallie, was descended from the Bell side. He had no immediate family so he'd left everything to Miss Hyacinth Lauren Hartley, aka Hallie.

Henry had composed a genealogy chart that traced Leland down to Hallie. She unfolded the long paper and read the names and dates. There was her mother's death when Hallie was four, and her father's remarriage when she was eleven. It ended with the death of her father and Ruby—Shelly's mother—in a car accident when Hallie was in her second year of college and Shelly was still in high school.

Jared returned to his seat. "Do you understand about the inheritance?"

"I think so," Hallie answered. "But I'm not a blood relative of Henry Bell."

"I know," Jared said, "but on Nantucket we take relationships—however tenuous—seriously. And by the way, Henry left his house to you specifically, not to your father. No matter what your stepsister claims, she has *no* right to it. I was sincere when I said that if you want to take legal action for her attempted theft, I'll pay all costs." He took a breath. "I'm especially sorry that I helped put a patient in the house without your actual permission. Shelly had given her permission in your name, of course, but now I know she isn't you. If you want me to send him away, just let me know. I'll make a call and he won't be there when we land."

"Thank you," Hallie said.

She looked down at the folder. In the back were some medical notes about her patient, James Michael Taggert, nicknamed Jamie, but they were brief and not very informative. But then Hallie had heard everything before when Shelly was quizzing her about her injured friend. Hallie didn't want to imagine what would have happened to the man without proper care.

Mostly the papers were about the excellent financial terms being offered to her for rehabilitating this one young man. She'd be able to make her mortgage payments on the house her father had left her outside Boston as well as put food on the table in Nantucket.

When she glanced up at Jared, he seemed to be hard at work, either with the papers or tapping out messages on his phone. At one point he said, "My wife, Alix, says hi and that she very much wants to meet you."

"Me too," Hallie said, and wondered what his wife was like. He was famous, so he probably had married some elegant blonde who spent all his money maintaining her beauty.

It was at lunch—perfectly cooked chicken and salad served by a young woman attendant—that she asked Jared who owned the jet they were on. When he said "Jamie's family," Hallie nodded. It looked like her patient was indeed some rich kid. He'd gone skiing, probably in some exotic locale, and torn his knee. Since his family could afford anything on earth, he was being given his own private therapist. Jared had told her that his family had even put in a private gym for the rehabilitation work. No being one of many for him!

"What's this guy like?" she asked. "I mean his personality."

Jared shrugged. "He's a distant cousin of mine, but I don't really know him. I've dealt with his father. I only saw the boy from a distance. He seems to always be surrounded by his family."

Hallie nodded and thought, Rich and spoiled. Everything always handed to him.

"There's still time to call," Jared said.

"I think I'll give it a try and see how it works out."

They talked about the physical therapist job Hallie was due to start at a small local hospital, and she told Jared that she'd call and turn it down. Since they had a waiting list, she didn't feel guilty about it. He said he'd have his super-efficient secretary take care of it for her, and she thanked him.

"You're taking all of this very well," Jared said. "With great sportsmanship."

She smiled at the compliment. A lifetime with her stepmother and Shelly had taught Hallie how to hide her emotions.

When they landed, in spite of her bravado, Hallie began to feel nervous about what was coming. While it was exciting to think of the adventure before her, it was also terrifying. At twenty-six years old, she'd lived in one house all her life, had gone to college nearby, and had been about to accept a job that was close to her home. She was leaving behind people she'd known since she was born—and that included Braden. She reminded herself that it was her choice whether or not this was permanent.

In the little Nantucket airport, she stood to one side and waited for Jared to finish talking to people. Whereas the experience of flying on a private jet was awe-inspiring to her, it didn't seem to be unusual on the island. In fact, three other privately owned jets had arrived at nearly the same time, and Jared and

Hallie's flight had needed to wait for permission to land. Jared was talking to passengers from the other planes, to the baggage handlers, to the pilots, and to a man who seemed to be the manager of the airport. As far as Hallie could tell, he knew every person within sight. This was certainly different from Boston!

Abruptly, Jared turned from them and walked quickly to Hallie. "Come on, let's go. A tourist plane is landing." He sounded as though a tsunami was about to hit. He put his hand at her lower back and ushered her out of the airport into bright sunshine and the clean, salty air of Nantucket.

It wasn't until they were in Jared's truck that reality began to hit Hallie. The vehicle was old and beat-up, and something about it seemed *real*. The world of the leather-upholstered BMW Jared drove and the private jet was too foreign to her to allow her to think clearly. But now she was grasping the truth of all of it. She was on her way to a house she'd never seen but that belonged to her. And for the time being, she was going to be living with a young man she had never met.

As they drove from the airport to the downtown area, Hallie marveled at the houses they passed. They were nearly all clad in untreated wooden shingles that had turned a beautiful, misty gray. It was almost as though she were traveling back in time, to when Nantucket was known for its whaling. It wouldn't have surprised her to see men in jackboots carrying harpoons over their shoulders.

Jared drove down a frighteningly narrow lane and stopped in front of a small two-story house with a pretty blue door. The house had pink roses growing up a trellis and lushly green bushes along the front. "This is it?"

"Yes," Jared said as he opened the truck door for her. "You like it?"

"It's like a fairy tale."

Jared shrugged. "The roof is good and I had the windows repaired. Later I want to check some foundation cracks."

Hallie smiled at him. "Spoken like an architect."

He opened the front door for her. "You think I'm bad, wait until you meet my wife."

As she stepped inside a little entryway with a staircase in front of her, she didn't reply. The house was beautiful! It had a feeling of age and memory and coziness that she'd never felt before. "This is *mine?*" she whispered.

"It is." He was pleased by her reaction. "Why don't you have a look around while I find Jamie?"

Eyes wide, Hallie only nodded in agreement. As he went through the door to the right, she climbed the stairs. At the top was a small landing with open doors on opposite sides, both of them leading into large, furnished bedrooms, each with its own bathroom. Behind them was a little sitting room with a big window looking out to the back.

Since the house had belonged to a lifelong bachelor, she was surprised that it looked warm and inviting down to the smallest details. The wallpaper was of pretty woodland flowers, and the antique beds were draped in soft blues and greens, with big downy pillows against the headboards. The window seat had cushions of pale pink and peach, and tassels were on the curtain tiebacks.

She went to the window and looked down into the garden—and gasped. Since the front of the house had very little land, she was shocked at what was in the back. There was a big square area, with branches leading off both ways to form a T-shape. There were several huge old trees, and flower beds were outlined. That the beds were nearly empty made her long to get her hands on them. Unbidden, the thought came to her that with Shelly and her mother out of the picture, *this* garden would never be in danger of being bulldozed.

She wondered where she could find the workshop with the gym that Jared had spoken of. Pushing the window up, she looked out to see past the tall fence that surrounded the entire garden.

When she heard voices, she pulled back from the window. Walking together were two people. One was a small, older woman and facing her was a man on crutches—and he was close enough that she could see he was beautiful. Not like some model out of a magazine, but in the way of a man who turns and smiles at you and your knees go weak. He had thick black hair, a stubble of whiskers over a strong jaw, and lips of such softness they made Hallie dizzy.

When the man smiled at the little gray-haired woman, Hallie could see lines at his eyes. She guessed that he was at least thirty. As for being short, he wasn't under six feet, and the "stocky" looked to be about two hundred pounds of pure muscle. He was wearing a long-sleeved shirt that couldn't conceal the curves of the powerful muscles underneath. Below that were sweatpants that draped over heavy quads, and she could see the outline of a big leg brace beneath.

That's who I'm to work on? she thought. But that couldn't be! Jared had said he was a "kid" and "short and stocky." But that certainly didn't describe *this* man!

Hallie moved back to lean against the wall. To say that he was her type was an understatement. She'd always liked athletic, muscular men.

"This is a problem," she whispered. Her teachers, first in massage school and later in physical therapy, had repeated over and over the importance of professionalism. A therapist was never to get personally involved with a client. She'd been warned that some of them would flirt and tease. With her massages and later in her many student sessions, she'd found out that was true. But it had been easy to laugh those guys off. She'd been so concentrated on her work that she'd thought of little else. Besides, she wasn't particularly attracted to any of them.

But this man, this Jamie Taggert, was different. She saw that her hands were shaking, and she could feel beads of perspiration on her upper lip.

"Control!" she said as she pushed away from the wall. She took a few deep breaths to calm herself, then went through a bedroom to get to the stairs.

At the bottom were two beautiful old doors. One was locked, but the other one led into the living room. The ceiling was fairly low, with great overhead beams that spoke of the age of the house and added to the calm, peaceful feeling of it. A wide, deep fireplace was along the wall, with pretty windows on the far side. The couch and two big chairs were soft and comfortable looking. They had been moved to the far end to make space for a narrow bed and a desk.

As Hallie looked at the bed, she wondered how a man with shoulders like his could sleep on it. Did his feet and arms hang over the sides? The thought almost made her giggle.

On impulse, she went to the desk. It was old and scarred from many years of use. On top of it were a few neatly stacked paperbacks—murder mysteries written by men—and a big leather date book with a matching pencil holder.

Hallie sat down on the little wooden chair, and after a quick glance about the empty room to make sure she was alone, she opened the date book.

What she saw made her gasp. Inside were large, glossy photographs of Shelly. On top was one of those professional-looking head shots. Shelly just out of the shower was beautiful, but fully made up, her hair swept to one side, a seductive little smile on her perfect lips, she was a stunner.

Beneath that were composites of other shots. There was Shelly riding in a convertible, her hair tousled, her face turned up to the sun. It looked as though it had been taken on a movie set. Another one was of Shelly in a red silk blouse, open to show her black bra, on what looked like a stage. There was a photo of her holding a bar of soap to her cheek. An ad, maybe?

The last picture was a full-length shot of Shelly in a bikini. All five feet eleven of her, not an ounce of fat anywhere, long blonde hair pulled into a high ponytail, and looking like the all-American girl. Every man's dream.

Hallie leaned back in the chair, feeling like she'd just deflated.

In all the turmoil of what was turning into a very long day, it hadn't registered with her when Jared said that Shelly had exchanged emails with the prospective client. But then Hallie's mind had been reeling from the news that her stepsister had faked her passport and tried to steal a house.

Hallie held up the bikini shot. She'd never been able to understand how Shelly and her mother could live on a diet of greasy burgers, fries, and cola and never gain weight. After they'd come into her life, Hallie went from her grandparents' fresh vegetable diet to endless carry-out and she'd begun to pack on the pounds. In school, playing soccer had kept most of the weight off, but after her father and stepmother died, Hallie'd had the job of supporting Shelly. She didn't have time to cook. It had been work and nothing else. Coming home late at night and eating Big Macs and drinking big colas had left her with an extra twenty-five pounds. Add that to the fact that she was only five foot four and . . .

She didn't want to think of a physical comparison between her and Shelly. She'd lived with it for too many years. "*Both* of these girls are your daughters?" people would ask her father. Tall, willowy Shelly and short, childishly round Hallie the product of the same parents? Not possible!

One time Ruby had answered the question by saying, "But Hallie is *real* smart."

Hallie knew Ruby had meant well, but it still hurt. In her

family, Hallie was the smart, responsible one who always did the sane, sensible thing, while Shelly was the pretty one who always screwed up and was always forgiven. "Hallie, you need to help Shelly" was something she'd heard on a daily basis.

Hallie stood up and carefully put the photos back inside the book. That's what she got for snooping!

She put the chair back under the desk and went into the kitchen—and the charm of it helped to clear her mind. How her grandparents would have loved the old-fashioned appearance of it! The sink was huge, as were the gas stove and the refrigerator. In the center was a square table that looked as old as the house, and it was in front of yet another fireplace.

Two of the doors leading out of the kitchen were locked, but a third one led to a pretty little glassed-in porch that was full of white wicker with pink and green cushions. There was a piece of white linen in an embroidery hoop and she picked it up. It had a design of two birds and half of it had been beautifully sewn. She wondered if the late Henry Bell had done it.

When she heard the click of a door, then two male voices, she froze in place. One was Jared's and the other was a deep, rich rumble that made Hallie's breath catch in her throat.

Damnation! she thought. This guy is expecting Shelly and he's going to be deeply disappointed. Have some sympathy for him.

"Hallie?" Jared called. "Are you here?"

With her shoulders back, she walked into the kitchen and saw him. Heaven help her, but he was even better looking close up. Worse, there seemed to be an energy around him that was like some powerful magnet pulling her to him. Part of her wanted to leap the distance between them and lose herself inside his big, strong arms.

But years of practice at hiding her true feelings kept Hallie glued in place, her expression pleasant but neutral.

"This is—" Jared began, but Jamie cut him off.

"*You're* Hallie?" Jamie asked, his eyes wide. "But you're not—" He broke off to look her up and down in a way that every woman hopes some gorgeous man will look at her. Not in that lecherous way that can make a woman feel exposed and vulnerable, but in a way that made her feel beautiful and so very, very desirable.

Jamie grasped the side of the sink, as though if he didn't support himself he'd fall down. "I thought someone else was coming, but you . . . You're . . ." He didn't seem able to say any more. When he leaned against the cabinet, his crutches fell backward, and Jared caught them.

Hallie straightened her shoulders. It looked like to him, one female was as good as another. If he couldn't have the divine Shelly, he'd take this one.

But Hallie'd had too many years of guys trying to get near *her* so they could be close to Shelly. All she knew for sure was that this had to stop *now*!

She took a step toward him and when he smiled broader, she frowned deeply. "Look, Mr. Taggert—at least I assume that's who you are—I don't know what you're thinking about me, but it's wrong. You're here in *my* house so I can help you recover and that's *all*. Do I make myself clear?"

"Yes, ma'am," he said softly, his eyes widening even farther.

She took a step closer to him, her finger pointed at his chest. "If you *ever* make an advance toward me that is the least bit unprofessional, you're out of here. Do you understand?"

Jamie was blinking at her as he nodded.

"Professional!" She tapped her finger on his very hard chest. "Touch me and you leave. Got it?"

When he said "Yes," Hallie could feel his breath on her face. He smelled of *man*. Abruptly, she took a step back, then walked all the way around the table, around both men, and paused at the back door. She glared at Jared. "Short, stocky kid, huh?" She went outside, closing the door firmly behind her.

Jared was the first to speak. "Now *I'm* going to be in the doghouse. What the hell were you thinking, coming on to her like that?" he half shouted. "This isn't going to work! If you knew what that girl has been through . . ." He glared at Jamie. "That sister of hers—with *my* help—tried to steal this house from her."

Jamie hobbled over to a chair and sat down. "She's beautiful, isn't she?"

"If you mean the stepsister, no, I don't think she is. To tell you the truth, I didn't like her from the moment I saw her. She's too much like the girls I used to date."

"Who is the stepsister?" Jamie's puzzlement showed on his face.

"The blonde," Jared said, sounding like Jamie had no brain. "The photo on the passport, remember? The one who said *she* was Hallie."

"Oh," Jamie said. "Her. I like this one better. She's got beautiful eyes, and she is *built,* isn't she?"

Jared groaned. "Deliver me from the days of youth. What I want to know is if it's safe to leave you here with her. She's in this mess because of *me* and I plan to look out for her."

There was no smile on Jamie's face. "Are you asking me if I'll take what she doesn't want to give?"

Jared was taller and older than Jamie, but the younger man had the muscles of a bull. Jared didn't back down. "Yeah, that's exactly what I'm asking."

Jamie's face softened. "It looks like there will be two of us protecting her. I apologize to you now and I will apologize to her for my behavior. It's just that I wasn't expecting . . . her. Tall skinny blondes aren't appealing to me, but this one I like."

Jared grimaced. "I'm going home to my wife. The next time I talk to Hallie she'd better tell me that you've treated her well or I'll call your dad to bring a cattle truck to haul you away."

"Spoken like a true Montgomery," Jamie said, his eyes laughing. "Did you *really* tell her I'm a kid?"

"You are to me."

Jamie was still smiling. "Go on. You can leave. She's safe with me. She stands up for herself well, doesn't she?"

Jared had the idea that if he remained there he might have to listen to hours of whatever this young man was feeling, which he had no doubt was nothing but lust. "I'll be back in an hour and I'll ask Hallie whether or not you can stay here. If she even hints that you've come on to her, you're moving into my house."

"Yes, sir," Jamie said, his eyes sparkling.

Chapter Two

*A*s soon as Hallie was outside, she realized that her anger was more about what her stepsister had tried to do than about the young man who needed her help. And her anger had increased when she realized she was attracted to a man who had hidden away photos of Shelly.

Before her was a large grassy area crisscrossed by old brick pathways. There were high walls on each side and what looked to be beds for plants. The weeds had been cut, so someone was taking care of the garden, but it still had a barren look to it. There were a few scraggly bushes, but not much else.

She walked to the end of the wall and saw a long, narrow strip of land that ran perpendicular. It too was walled. At one end was a big red gate, but at the other end of the garden was a building with a vine-covered arbor attached to one side.

She went down the old brick path to the small building. The

door was open, and inside was a lot of shiny new gym equipment. When Shelly had asked about rehabilitating an injury such as Jamie had, Hallie had been flattered. She'd been pleased to make a list of necessary equipment. Inside the little building Hallie found everything she had put on the list. Machines and free weights were in the center, and the walls were hung with rubber tubes and yoga equipment. When she went out the side door to the arbor, she saw a seating area and a lean-to that housed the massage table she would need. Overhead, grape vines had pretty, pale leaves that were beginning to unfurl. Massages under the arbor would be perfect.

When she heard a cough to her left, she knew the man was letting her know of his approach.

He stopped just under the edge of the arbor and leaned heavily on his crutches. "I apologize for my behavior," he said. "I'm very sorry."

"And I for mine," she answered. "It's been a tough day and I took my anger out on you. Why don't you take your clothes off and let's start over?"

Jamie lifted his eyebrows high.

Hallie's mind was so much on all that had happened that it took a moment to realize what she'd said. "I meant for a massage. To begin work on your knee." She could feel her face turning red.

"Darn!" he said with such feeling that Hallie couldn't help but laugh, and he joined her.

But he didn't begin to disrobe. Instead, he made his way to a chair and sat down heavily. "That's better." He smiled at her as she took the other seat. "I would like to start over. I'm James, generally called Jamie." He held out his hand across the little table separating them.

"My name is Hyacinth, but thankfully I'm called Hallie." When she shook his hand, his eyes seemed to be offering only friendship, and she was glad of it.

Leaning back in their chairs, they looked out at the garden.

"Isn't Hyacinth the name of one of the original owners of the house?" he asked.

"Yes. My father had only a small box of papers about his family. He didn't talk about them, but my mother found them in the attic of the house I grew up in. She saw the name Hyacinth and gave it to me."

"And your mother's name was Ruby, right?"

"No. She was Shelly's mother," Hallie said tightly.

"Sorry," Jamie said. "I'm afraid I'm a bit confused about it all. I don't know if Jared told you, but I exchanged some emails with a woman I thought was you. She said her mother was named Ruby and that Ruby had died when Hallie—or Shelly, I guess—was four."

"Part of that's correct. My mother died when I was four, but her name was Lauren."

"My biological mother died when I was a baby," Jamie said softly.

We have that in common, Hallie thought but didn't say, and for a few minutes the air was heavy between them. Shared tragedy did not make for happy conversation, she thought, and wanted to change the subject. "So where does that gate at the end lead?"

"I have no idea. I just got here last night and I slept late this morning. When I got up, I looked around a bit, then came out here to see the gym. I was just returning when Jared found me."

"But I saw you with an older woman. You looked like friends."

"That was Edith and we'd just met. She lives in the B&B next door, so the gate probably leads there. Her son and daughter-in-law run the place, but I think she visits here often."

"Maybe she was a friend of Mr. Bell's and misses him."

"Could be, but she didn't say so. Tell me exactly what your stepsister did."

"No," Hallie said. "I'd rather not go into that. I really would like to have a look at your knee. And from the way you're holding your shoulders, I think you're carrying a lot of tension. I'd like for you to get on the table and let me see what's going on with your body."

"As tempting as that sounds, I'm hungry and you must be starving. Did Montgomery feed you?"

"We ate on the plane." Hallie watched as he awkwardly stood up. It looked like she wasn't going to get him on the table today. His leg was encased in the heavy brace and she knew that the slightest movement of his knee without it would cause him intense pain.

"Let me help you," she said.

"Gladly," he answered. He stood on one foot while she got the crutches and helped him put them under his arms, and they began to walk back to the house.

"So tell me about your injury."

"Skiing. Being stupid. Nothing unique." He paused. "It's going to take me a while to remember all the things I told Shelly and that you don't know. My aunt Jilly is getting married here on Nantucket soon and Edith was telling me that my family has booked all the rooms of the B&B for that week." He stopped on the walkway. "I have a lot of relatives and they'll be all over this place. Hordes of them. Like fire ants covering their territory." He looked at her. "If that idea horrifies you, let me know now and I'll keep them out."

"I don't think it will bother me, but I've never had a large family so I don't know for sure."

"Okay, but when they get here, if at any time they're too much for you, tell me and I'll send them away." Jamie looked around at the garden. In front of them was an enormous oak tree with an old bench under it. "What are you going to do with this place?"

"I haven't had time to think about it. When I woke up this

morning my only concern was getting some papers to my boss
before he left for the weekend. It was my last assignment for
him. Next week I was supposed to start a new job. Anyway,
when the papers weren't in my bag, I had to go back home to
get them. Minutes later I was being told I owned a house on
Nantucket and soon after that I was on a private jet." She
looked up at him. "Which I believe is owned by your family."

"True," he said, "but not by me. My dad believes kids should
pay their own way."

Hallie knew he meant to sound like an average guy, but not
many people had their own private physical therapist. And
from the healthy look of him, almost anyone could have helped
him. His injury wasn't unusual, and certainly not life threatening. She could see no reason for him to be isolated with a therapist. He could have stayed at home with his family and been
driven to an hour-long session five times a week and he would
have done well. "Why do you want to be here?" she asked.
"Rehabilitation of your knee could be done anywhere. You
don't have to—"

"Oh, look, Jared has already come to check on me. If you
don't give me a good report, he's threatened to beat me up."

"I'd settle for lifting you onto the massage table," Hallie said
and went forward to greet Jared and reassure him that Jamie
Taggert had been a perfect gentleman.

Jared listened, glared in warning at Jamie—who smiled back
at him—then left, and they went into the kitchen.

Hallie opened the refrigerator door and looked inside. It was
packed full of containers of food, all carefully labeled. Fruit and
salad greens were in the crisper, and the freezer was also full.
"Who did this?"

"My mother sent someone to fill it."

"I thought your mother was . . . gone."

"Stepmom, then," he said. "But she's always been my
mother, so . . ." Trailing off, he saw the weariness in her eyes.

He led her to the old kitchen table. "You've done enough today, so you sit and I'll microwave us a meal."

"But it's—"

"Your house and you're the boss? You can claim all the power tomorrow, but tonight I'll take care of you. What food do you like?"

"Obviously, anything." She was referring to the extra pounds she had on her. Her plan had been that she would start a regular exercise program as soon as she was in her new job.

"What's obvious is that every ounce has gone to exactly the right places." He gave her such a warm look that Hallie almost blushed. "Sorry, please don't tell Jared on me."

Hallie searched for another point of conversation. "Jared told me your mother is the mystery writer Cale Anderson."

"She is. She and my widower dad married when my brother Todd and I were just kids." It wasn't easy for him with the crutches, but Jamie was managing to get packages out of the fridge and carry them to the counter by the sink. He was beginning to like this woman. Yes, he was *very* physically attracted to her, but there was more than that. How many people would unexpectedly inherit a house in one day yet still put her patient first? As far as he knew, she hadn't even looked at all the rooms. Instead, his welfare seemed to have been her first thought.

"What was it like, growing up with someone so famous?"

Jamie smiled. "Fame has never meant much to Mom. She writes because she likes doing it. When we were kids she used to have my brother and me act out scenes of her books so she could see how they'd work. Todd and I never thought anything about it until one day when we were in the third grade and some candy went missing. At recess we set up an interrogation room and asked some hard questions. That ended up with three kids crying in the principal's office. And later, little Chrissy McNamara stepped up onto a pile of books and gave me a bloody nose."

"You're kidding!"

"I'm not. I was in love with her until I entered high school."

Hallie smiled. "How much trouble did you get into?"

"After the dust settled, everyone agreed it was all Mom's fault. Dad was mad at her for an entire twenty-four hours. That may have been a record."

"So you had to stop acting out police procedurals?"

"Not at all," Jamie said. "Todd and I just learned to keep our mouths shut."

Hallie laughed hard. "I can see it all. She sounds like fun."

"She is. Dad is the disciplinarian, but Mom believes childhood should be a joy and that's how she made it."

"How nice for you," Hallie said, with feeling in her voice.

Jamie put a plate of sliced roast beef, two warmed vegetables, and salad in front of her. "What about you? What was your childhood like?"

"My dad sold pharmaceuticals and he traveled constantly. After my mother died, her parents moved in with us and Dad traveled even more."

"I'm sorry," Jamie said. "You must have missed him a great deal."

"No, actually, we didn't. My grandparents were wonderful. We had a huge backyard and Grams and Gramps were fabulous gardeners. We grew all our own vegetables and most of the fruit. I—" She broke off, seeming to be embarrassed.

"You what?" He put his plate on the table and sat down across from her.

"I was the center of their lives. What I did, who I liked and didn't like, girlfriend fights, boys—they wanted to hear about all of it. I had slumber parties and big birthday parties. And when Dad came home we treated him like visiting royalty. We were thrilled to see him arrive and breathed a sigh of relief when he left." She paused. "I think maybe I was the happiest child on earth. But they moved to Florida a year after Dad married Ruby."

"Do you see them often now?"

"They passed away before my dad died, within months of each other. I still miss them." She took a bite of green beans. "These are good. Where did your mom get all this?"

"She's no cook, but she's great at finding where good food is sold. So where did your stepsister come in?"

Hallie waved her fork about. "That was later. Dad married Ruby when I was eleven, and she and her daughter moved into the house. We need to start on your treatment first thing tomorrow."

"All right," Jamie said. He could tell that she didn't want to talk about her life after her stepmother's arrival. "What exactly are you planning to do to me?"

"I have to see your injury first." The shirt he had on was big and concealing, but it couldn't hide the muscle underneath. "You look like you know how to pick up a dumbbell."

"Oh, yeah. That's from Dad and his brother. When they were young they competed in power-lifting matches."

"Did you compete?"

"Never had the time," he said.

"What took up your time?" She saw his face change, as though he was about to tell her something but decided not to.

"Would you like some cheesecake?" He had eaten three helpings of everything.

Hallie looked away to hide her expression. Rich kid, she thought. He didn't want to tell her that his time was taken up by skiing and other pleasures. So be it, she thought. She wouldn't push him to tell what he didn't want to.

She moved her nearly empty plate away and stood up. "I'm worn out and I think I'll go to my room. Will you be all right?"

"I'm fine. I swear that I can bathe and dress myself."

There was a bit of tension in his voice, but she ignored it. She was too tired to wonder what was bothering him. She reached for her plate to take it to the sink, but he took it from her.

"I'll clean up, and I'll see you tomorrow."

"And I'll look at your leg." She covered her yawn. "Mmmm. Sorry. See you in the morning." The house was so new to her that she had to think about where the stairs were. She had to go through the living room and past Jamie's narrow bed to get to the front stairs.

At the top she looked right and left. Each doorway led to a bedroom. She wished that when she first saw the rooms she had chosen which was to be hers. She stepped left, but it was almost as though she heard two female voices say, "No."

She went to the right and felt a sense of calm, as though the old house was smiling at her. There was a pretty chorus of voices who whispered, "Hyacinth." Maybe she should have been frightened, but it was almost as though she was being welcomed. Smiling, she thought how she needed to undress, take a shower, and find her nightclothes in her suitcase. For that matter, she needed to find her luggage.

It was still daylight out, but between the eventful day and overwhelming emotion, she was worn out. The big bed beckoned and she threw back the covers to expose crisp white sheets. The bed was high off the floor and she had to throw her leg up to get on it. She told herself that she was just going to test the mattress. Were the pillows any good?

She put her head down and was instantly asleep.

CO

Jamie finished putting the kitchen back in order and had just sat down in the chair at his desk when his cell buzzed.

"I've been trying to get you all day!" his brother said. "Can't you carry the damned phone with you?"

"I came here to get away," Jamie said, unperturbed by his brother's anger.

"From them, but not from *me*," Todd said and when Jamie was silent, he backed down. "All right, do whatever you want. What's she like? Other than too beautiful to be real?"

"It's not the girl you saw in those photos," Jamie said. "The blonde is the stepsister. Jared didn't tell me the details, but she pulled a con and tried to steal the house."

"That's illegal," Todd said, his voice stern.

"Yeah, Detective Chief Inspector, it is. Why don't you drive down to Boston and find out the truth of it all?"

"I can't now. I'm dealing with a string of armed robberies and what may turn out to be a homicide case. What I want to know is how *you* are."

"Fine."

"Don't give me that crap! How *are* you?!"

Jamie took a breath. "Good. I still don't like how you got me here, but . . . it's okay."

"Ah," Todd said.

"What the hell does that mean?"

"It means that Jared called Aunt Jilly who called Mom who called me. Seems you made a fool of yourself over your physical therapist."

Jamie rolled his eyes. "And here I thought I got away from the family hovering over me. Yeah, when I first saw her, I did have a moment of weakness. She's pretty and built and . . . I don't know. There's something about her that I like. She's smart and— Stop laughing!"

"I'm not," Todd said. "Well, maybe I am, but not in the way you think. I—"

Jamie cut him off. "She wants to start on my leg tomorrow."

Todd lowered his voice. "How much are you going to let her know?"

"As little as I can get away with. She thinks I'm some rich

playboy. I think she believes I jet around the world from one fun place to another."

"And you're going to let her keep thinking that, aren't you?"

"I'm going to encourage it," Jamie said. "It'll be a relief not to have to deal with pity. I gotta go. I need sleep."

"Take your pills," Todd said.

"I won't forget. Do me a favor, will you? Call Mom and tell her to back off for a few days. Tell her I'm all grown up and can feed myself. I'm worried she'll helicopter in baskets of groceries."

"Then you're planning on leaving the grounds to get food?" There was hope in Todd's voice.

"Not yet!" Jamie snapped. "And stay off my back about it! Understand?!"

"I hear you," Todd said softly. "So go to bed and I'll deal with Mom. And Jamie . . . I, uh . . ."

"Yeah, me too," he said, then clicked off.

Hallie awoke abruptly. The inside of her mouth was fuzzy and she had that swollen feeling of having slept in her clothes.

She turned on the bedside light and looked at her watch. It was just after two A.M. She got up, went to the bathroom, and rinsed her mouth. The first thing she was going to do in daylight was find her bags and unpack them.

As she was walking toward the bed, she heard what sounded like a moan. "Oh, great," she mumbled. "More evidence that I've inherited a haunted house. Maybe I should give it to Shelly. I'd like to see how *they* would deal with her!"

With a yawn, she started to unfasten her jeans so she wouldn't have to spend the rest of the night in them. But then she heard the sound again, only this time it was louder.

It's him, she thought and ran toward the stairs. By the time she got down to his room, she could hear him making noises, sounding as though he were trying to escape from someone. There was a nightlight, the kind used for children, on the desk and in front of it was an orange plastic pill bottle. From the time she could read she'd helped her father with the drugs he sold. By the time she was in high school, she was reading the brochures about the latest medicines and paraphrasing them for her dad so he could sell them.

When Hallie read the prescription label, she knew it was a very strong sleep aid. If he'd taken two of these, a tractor could run over him and he wouldn't wake up.

She looked at Jamie on the bed. He was rolling his head from side to side and his body was beginning to move. The bed was narrow and he was big. All it would take was one toss to the side and he'd be on the floor. Even though he had on his leg brace, a hard impact could re-injure him.

She went to his head and began to massage his temples. "Ssssh. Be quiet. Everything is all right," she said softly, soothingly.

He calmed a bit, but the moment she took her hands away he began to turn in the bed.

"No, no," she said. "Don't do that."

When he kept moving, she went to his side and made an attempt to hold him on the bed. She had to plant her feet firmly on the floor and push against his chest with both her hands. It worked and he didn't fall out of bed. He rolled onto his back, and for a moment he was so calm that Hallie moved toward the door.

But when a shout came, she ran back to him. His whole body was shaking, as though in fear, and he lifted his arms as if he were reaching out for someone.

"I'm here," Hallie said. "You're safe." When she leaned toward him, he put his arms around her and pulled her down to him, holding her close.

It was an awkward position that nearly twisted Hallie in half. She knew she wasn't strong enough to break his hold, and she doubted if she could wake him to make him let her go. Whatever was the basis of his nightmare, right now he needed comfort.

It wasn't easy to stretch out beside him on the little bed, but as soon as she did, he turned to his side and pulled her to him. He tucked her into his body as though she'd always been there, and he quieted instantly.

"So now I'm your teddy bear?" she said, her face against his chest.

But for all her sarcasm, it felt good to be held, even if the man doing it was sound asleep.

She could feel herself drifting off, but as she did, her mind began going over the events of the day. Seeing the contract Shelly had signed and the passport she had redone had hurt more than she wanted to admit. A week earlier, Shelly had asked Hallie to stop by an office supply store after work to buy her some glue and a new pair of scissors. "They need to cut cleanly," Shelly had said. "So no edges are showing." It seemed that Hallie had helped her stepsister defraud her.

When Jamie kissed the top of her head, Hallie started crying. He might be asleep, but he seemed to sense that the woman he was holding needed help. His body quit twitching, and he was quiet and relaxed. It was almost as if he were waiting for her to tell him what was wrong.

"I didn't deserve it," Hallie whispered. "I've never done anything bad to Shelly. She and her mother took over my life, but I stood for it. When Dad and Ruby died, I had no time to grieve. I had to take care of Shelly. I don't know how I did it, but I did. So why did she try to steal from me?"

Hallie looked up at him, saw that his eyes were still closed, and put her head back down. "If I'd been told about this house, maybe I would have given her the one in Boston. That's what she wanted. She said it wasn't fair that I own two houses and she has none. I don't know what I would have done, but I certainly would like to have been given the choice."

Her tears were fading, even if the pain wasn't. "I don't know what to do now, either legally or ethically. Should I reward Shelly by giving her a house? But I know that won't be enough for her." She looked up at him.

There was enough light that she could see his sleeping face. He looked so sweet, so calm. But then suddenly, he began to thrash about again. She could see movement under his eyelids, as though another nightmare was beginning.

"Oh, no, you don't!" she said. "You start rolling again and I'll be crushed. Be quiet! You're safe."

But Jamie didn't quit moving, and when he threw his big leg over her hips, she pushed hard to get out from under him and stood up. As she looked down at him, she saw that he seemed to be gearing up for another round of thrashing.

Bending, she put her hands on the sides of his head. "You are *safe*! You hear me? There are no demons chasing you." His face was so near hers, his lips so very close, that she couldn't resist kissing him. It wasn't a kiss of passion, but one of reassurance. A kiss of friendship and understanding. Two people who had deep problems were sharing them.

The kiss lingered for a while, as though they were receiving strength and reassurance from each other. They deeply and truly *needed* each other.

When Hallie pulled away and looked at him, Jamie's face was calmer, more relaxed. Taking her hands away, she let him lean back on the pillow, and at last he seemed to sink down into a restful sleep.

She watched him for a few moments, then turned to go back upstairs. But she got only as far as the couch at the end of the room. What if he had another nightmare? He could fall off the bed and damage his torn knee.

Looking at the old couch, she sighed. Upstairs was a bed with crisp, clean sheets and a down comforter. The couch had nothing on it but one small pillow.

She hesitated, but with a sigh, she stretched out on the couch. If Jamie again became restless, she'd hear him and would be able to keep him from falling.

I'll settle him with sleeping kisses, she thought, smiling as she began to fall asleep. As barren as the couch was, it felt better not to be alone in a strange house.

Chapter Three

"So you decided to get up, did you?" Jamie said when Hallie walked into the gym.

He was teasing, but his words implied that she was someone who lolled about in the mornings. It was tempting to tell him the truth about her night of wrestling with him. At five she'd awakened on the couch, her body stiff, her teeth chattering from the cold, and made her way upstairs to her bedroom. She'd staggered to the bed and flopped down on it, awoke hours later, took a shower and washed her hair, then went downstairs. On the kitchen table was a lovely breakfast of boiled eggs, little apricot turnovers, sausages with bits of apple inside, and cut fruit. Jamie must have just prepared it because the dark tea in the pretty ceramic pot was still hot.

But Hallie didn't tell him about last night. Using kisses to calm him from a nightmare wasn't exactly professional behavior. "Thanks for breakfast," she said. He was straddling a bench and doing lat pull-downs. Her eyes widened at the amount of weight he was using.

He finished his set before speaking, then picked up a towel to wipe his face. His thick shirt was soaked with sweat. "I'll tell Mom thanks for you."

"I want to see your leg."

"It's fine today. No need to go poking around." He gave her a smile of such promise that she was sure it had made many women forget their resolve.

Hallie smiled back at him with the sweetest look she could manage. "Do you have your cell phone with you?"

"Sure. Want to check your emails?"

"No. I want to call Jared and tell him that you're not allowing me to treat you."

After a moment's hesitation, Jamie laughed. "All right, you win. But we keep it to the leg."

She didn't know what he meant by that, but she went outside to get the big massage table and set it up. When Jamie came out on his crutches, he was still wearing his heavy clothes.

"Everything off," she said as she began coating her hands and forearms in almond oil. "Or if you're modest, leave your undies on. I'll keep you covered."

He was frowning at her, as though trying to decide what to do.

She knew that people varied in their sense of modesty. Some people quickly stripped down to their skin while she was in the room; others wouldn't remove their shoes without absolute privacy. It looked like he was the latter version. Excusing herself, she went into the gym for a few minutes.

When she returned, Jamie was on the table, but he'd only partially undressed. He still had on his heavy sweatclothes, but on the right side, he'd slipped out of the pants and rolled their leg to one side. Except for his brace, he was nude from waist to toes. But his left leg and the upper half of his body were completely covered by his heavy gym clothes. "This isn't what I meant," she said. "You need to—"

He didn't let her finish. "This is what you get," he said in a tone she'd not heard him use before. His usual manner was teasing, as though he were on the verge of laughter, but now he looked as though he were daring her to take what he was offering—and if she didn't, he'd leave.

Angering an injured client was not something she was going to do. "This will be all right," she said in a cheerful voice. "Want to lie back?"

He was leaning on his hands, his arms rigid behind him. "This works for me." That tone was still there.

Smiling, she began to unfasten the Velcro bindings of the big brace. "Whatever you do, don't move. I want to see how your leg is healing and I'm going to do some gentle massage. Okay?"

He didn't answer, and his face seemed to be settling into a deeper frown.

His knee was very swollen, but worse, every one of the big muscles of his leg seemed to be tied into a knot. Hallie had long ago learned that a person's body often told a different story from what could be seen on the outside. It looked like Jamie's easygoing manner was hiding a great deal of stress.

"Will I pass?" His voice had an edge to it, as though he were challenging her.

She kept smiling. "I can't answer that until I get my hands on you." She picked up the bottle of oil. The thickness of his leg muscles meant they would take some work.

"You've seen my leg, so that's it," he said. "I'll do some leg extensions and we'll be done." He started to get off the table.

She put her hand on his chest. "You move that leg with the brace off and I really will call . . ." She narrowed her eyes. "I will call your mother."

Jamie blinked a few times, then the frown left and he genuinely smiled. "And she'll tell Dad. You do know how to terrify a man. All right. One leg and that's it."

"You are kindness personified."

Hallie coated her hands in the oil, then set to work. She'd worked on a few bodybuilders and it took a lot to dig into their muscles, but Jamie was the worst she'd ever encountered. There was so much tension in his body that his muscles were the consistency of hard rubber tires. As her fingers dug deep, she thought she might be hurting him, but she could feel him beginning to relax, and finally, he lay back on the table.

At his knee she moved the skin around gently, trying to get the blood and fluids to start to flow again. She attacked his thigh and calf, digging as deeply as she could manage.

It took over an hour on his leg before she felt that she'd done as much as she could. As she refastened the brace, she wished she could get at the rest of his body, but since he had left most of his clothes on, it was covered. He didn't move, just lay quietly on his back on the table, his eyes closed.

Tentatively, she went to his left foot. It was bare so maybe he'd allow her to work on it. When he didn't protest at her hands, she massaged pressure points in his feet, flexing his ankle back and forth. She thought he had fallen asleep, but when she slipped her hands under his sweatpants at the ankle, he immediately tensed and she withdrew.

She massaged his hands. He had beautiful fingers, long and strongly made. From there she began on his head. The amount of tension he was holding in his neck was horrible to feel. There were lumps of lactic acid at the base of his trapezius muscles. She went over his head, feeling his short, dark hair. Her hands roamed over his face, massaging, caressing. Cheekbones, his nose, his lips. Her fingertips touched them all.

She kept remembering the kiss of early this morning. But

from the way he'd greeted her, he didn't seem to remember any of it.

He had an extraordinarily beautiful body! As her hands slid over his skin, she remembered being held in his arms, kissing him.

Maybe she was losing herself more than she realized in the pleasure of touching him because when she put her hands on his shoulders, she started to move down his shirt and over his chest. But Jamie caught her hands before she could pass his collarbone. He held on to her wrists for a moment, then released them. It looked like she wasn't to touch the areas covered by his clothing.

Embarrassed, Hallie stood up straight. "Sorry," she murmured and stepped away from him. There was a water spigot nearby with a hose attached and she thought about turning it on. She would like to douse herself in icy water. Just hold the hose over her head and let it flow.

Behind her, Jamie sat up on the table.

"Do you feel better?" she asked, forcing herself to smile but thinking, I need a boyfriend!

"I do," he said. "Thank you." He started to get off the table but then halted and looked at her.

It took Hallie a few moments to realize that he was waiting for her to leave before he stepped down. Why? Because he was afraid that his movement would allow her to see more of his nude body? What an odd man, she thought as she walked into the garden.

When Jamie was again fully covered, he joined her. They walked around together, speculating on how the garden had once looked. At the big oak tree, they found a little brass plaque that said, *In memory of my beautiful ladies, Hyacinth Bell and Juliana Hartley. Henry Bell.*

"Your namesake," Jamie said.

As they sat down on the bench under the tree, Hallie told

what she'd learned: that she wasn't related to the Bell family at all but to Leland through his second marriage. "It makes no sense that Henry Bell would leave the house to *me.*"

"Maybe he really was in love with women who died long ago and you're the closest person he could find," Jamie said.

"Which would mean that Henry had no relatives of his own. But then . . ." She shrugged. "My question is, did he decorate the upstairs for them?"

Since Jamie hadn't seen the second floor, they went back to the house and up to the two bedrooms. It wasn't easy for him to go up the stairs on crutches, but he did it. Only when they were in the bedroom did Hallie remember seeing her few pieces of luggage downstairs. Jamie insisted on hauling them up the steep, narrow stairs, and that caused some hilarity. He kept pretending he was about to fall, so Hallie got behind him and pushed on his lower back.

While she unpacked and put her toiletries in the bathroom, Jamie looked around. "Very girly. You're right that these rooms were decorated for women." He sat in her bedroom on a chair covered in blue and pink chintz and watched her. "Whose bedroom was whose, do you think?"

Before she thought, she said, "This one belonged to Hyacinth."

"How do you know that?"

There was no way she was going to tell him that she kind of, sort of, maybe, possibly heard two female voices telling her which bedroom to use. "I like this one better, so I'm sure it belonged to the sister with my name."

"Makes sense to me." He looked over his shoulder into the sitting room. "I bet you can see the garden from that window." It was as though he momentarily forgot about his injured knee. Leaving his crutches leaning against the bureau, he made almost a leap across the little sitting room to the window seat.

"So help me, if you hurt your knee, I'll—"

He waited. "Come on, what's the threat now? You've used Jared and my mother. Who's next?"

As she sat on the opposite end of the seat, she gave him a little smile. "The next time I massage your head, I won't lean over you so very far."

After a quick look at Hallie's ample breasts, Jamie put his hand to his heart and fell back against the wall. "Bring me the hemlock. My life is over. I have nothing more to live for. Even the prospect of losing that soft but very firm, luscious treat will take away all that I have left in life. I will—"

Hallie's face was turning redder by the second. His very intimate description was too much! "Will you stop it? You're my client, not my—"

"Patience is what I have. I will wait forever if it means that I may—"

"Look!" Hallie said loudly as she nodded toward the window.

"I can only see you. I can see no one else but—"

"Okay! I'll smash my entire chest up against you for head massages! Now will you look?"

With one more glance at Hallie's bosom, he looked out the window. Edith was leaving the side of the house and walking quickly toward the red gate.

Jamie pushed up the window and leaned out. "Edith!" he shouted in a voice so loud that the force of it nearly knocked Hallie backward. She had an idea that he may have been heard in Boston.

Hearing it, the little woman halted and smiled up at them. "Jamie? Is that you? I can't stay, but the Tea Ladies left something for the both of you. Is that Hyacinth with you?"

Hallie was a bit startled at being called that, but then she leaned close to Jamie and put her head out the window. "It is me," she called down. "It's very nice to meet you. Stay and we'll come down and have something to eat."

"Thank you, dear, but no," Edith said, her hand up to shield her eyes. "I'm full now. At least for a few minutes." For some reason she seemed to find this statement highly amusing. "Maybe tomorrow. Kiss Jamie for me." Turning away, she began to hurry toward the gate.

"Good idea," Jamie said.

Hallie realized that she was practically lying against him, his face close to hers.

"I think you should kiss Jamie," he said in a low, seductive voice.

Ignoring his words, she moved back to the opposite side of the seat. "I thought you just met her, but she's sending you kisses?"

"What can I say? Women fall for me."

She narrowed her eyes at him. "And do they manage to get your clothes off you?"

"Only if it's very, very dark."

Laughing, Hallie stood up and got his crutches. "What did she mean that the Tea Ladies left us something? And who are they?"

"I have no idea. Maybe they work for the B&B." When he took the crutches, he acted as though he'd forgotten how to use them. "I'm going to need help getting down the stairs."

"What if I remind you that the food is downstairs and you can't have it unless you get down there?"

"I think part of being a good physical therapist is making sure your patient is fed." He sounded serious.

"No, it's not. In fact, even the massages aren't part of it." Smiling, she was walking backward toward the staircase. "I learned that art form in totally different classes that I took before I became a physical therapist. Used massage sessions to pay for school. In fact, they were—"

She broke off because she tripped on a loose corner of the big floor rug and was about to fall. But in a lightning-fast move,

Jamie dropped his crutches and reached out to grab her. They went down together. He hit the floor hard, with Hallie on top of him, his braced leg to one side.

Hallie's head hit his chest almost as hard as his back slammed into the floor. "Jamie! Are you all right?"

He lay on the rug, utterly still, his eyes closed.

She clutched his head in her hands. "Stay here." Her voice was frantic. "I'll call an ambulance." She started to roll off him, but his arm held her tightly against him. "Let go! I have to—"

When she realized that he wasn't even near being unconscious, she lay where she was, her upper body on his wide chest. "Let me guess. High school football taught you how to take down your opponent." She saw the tiniest of smiles on his lips. "What were you? The entire defense team?"

His smile grew and she felt his stomach move in laughter.

"Let me up or I'll—" Since she couldn't think of anything to threaten him with, she put her elbows in the two spots on his chest where she knew she'd cause the most pain and pushed down.

"Yeow!" Jamie yelped, his eyes flying open.

Hallie rolled off him and stood up. "Can you get up by yourself or do I need to get a crane?"

"I think my back is broken," he said, smiling up at her.

"That's too bad. I guess I'll have to get scissors to cut your shirt off and have a look at your bare back."

Jamie gave a sigh, rolled over, grabbed a crutch, and stood up.

"It's a miracle," Hallie said and went down the stairs, Jamie not far behind her.

Waiting for them on the kitchen table was an afternoon tea so lavish it would have pleased King Edward VII. There were two tiered stands with three pretty plates on each one, all of them loaded with food in miniature—two of each item. One stand had savory dishes: crustless sandwiches cut into shapes, miniature quiches, tiny pickled quail eggs, and dumplings tied up like little purses. The other stand held desserts: scones, tarts, pies the size of silver dollars, tiny bowls of creamy coconut pudding. From the look of it all, it was a smorgasbord of food from around the world.

There was also a steaming hot pot of tea, a jug of milk, a bowl of sugar cubes, and pretty cups and plates. To the side were glasses of champagne with raspberries in them.

"Beautiful," Hallie said.

"I don't know about you, but I'm starving."

They sat down at the table and Hallie poured the strong black tea and added milk to their cups, while Jamie filled their plates.

"How do you think Edith got all this here?" Hallie asked. She was eating a dumpling filled with vegetables and chicken.

"Probably someone from the B&B brought it over in one of those electric golf carts." He had just finished a little lobster roll. "Best lobster I've ever had and I've spent a lot of my life in Maine. Wonder where they got it."

"This cheese is fabulous."

Jamie smiled, his mouth full.

"I'd like to see some of Nantucket," Hallie said as she bit into a cupcake that tasted of oranges. "Try this. It's really good." She'd meant for him to take the other cupcake off the plate, but he took the half she'd bitten into from her hand and ate it.

"Fuzzy navel," he said.

"What does that mean?"

"It's a drink of orange and peach juice and that's what it tastes like. My guess is that it's made with peach schnapps and if so, it's fairly lethal. Here, try it again." He bit into the second cupcake, then handed her the other half.

Hallie hesitated, but there was a look of challenge in his eyes. Daringly, she bent and took the cake from his hand with her lips. "Mmmmm. Quite delicious."

Jamie was smiling broadly. "It's named fuzzy for the peach and—"

"Navel for the orange. Now, as I was saying, I'd like to see some of the island. Jared drove through town and I saw some nice shops. Maybe you'd like to go too."

"No, thanks," Jamie said. "I have enough trouble with these blasted crutches without tackling streets and sidewalks."

She'd already learned that half of what Jamie said was teasing, so she played along. She mentioned beaches and a meal out. No, he didn't want to do that. Drinks at sunset? No. A boat ride? He said he'd had enough of that with his Montgomery relatives. "They *live* on the damned things. I like the earth." No matter what she came up with to try to entice him to go into town, he said no.

"I guess I'll have to go alone," she said as she picked up a piece of what looked to be poppy seed cake. For a tiny bit of a second, she saw something flash across his eyes, some emotion, but she wasn't sure what it was. If it weren't coming from such a strong, healthy young man, she would have thought she'd seen fear. But that was, of course, ridiculous.

Whatever it was, it was gone in an instant and Jamie's handsome face was back to smiling. "What I want to know is where Edith came from," he said.

"You mean where she grew up?"

"No. Here. Twice now I've seen her walking out from the side of the house. Yesterday when I woke up, I went looking for my brother with the intention of telling him what I thought about what he'd done to me."

"And what was that?"

Jamie waved a sweet, sticky ball of rice around before popping it into his mouth. "It's a long story, but my point is that on the far side of this house are two big doors and they're locked. I thought maybe my brother was hiding in there so I used a bit of force to try to open them, but they didn't budge."

Hallie licked coconut off her fingers. "Let me see if I get this straight. You woke up angry at your brother—for a reason that you won't tell me—and tried to batter down a couple of *my* doors to get to him? Possibly with the intention of murdering him?"

Jamie nearly choked on a square made of carrots and honey but managed to recover himself and said, "Pretty much." His eyes were laughing. "I wonder if Edith has a key and what's—"

"In there?" Hallie finished for him.

"My thoughts exactly. What would you say about searching for the key? Whoever finds it gets to kiss the other one."

"And what does the loser get?" Hallie asked.

"Two kisses?"

She laughed. "Go on and start searching. I'm going to clean this up and have it ready in case Edith returns for the dishes."

"I'll help," he said.

After they cleaned up the kitchen, they went out to the side of the house and inspected the doors, but as Jamie had said, they were locked tight. He wanted to try again to use his considerable strength to open them, but Hallie persuaded him not to. Inside the house, all the doors that led into the hidden room were also locked. They began to search for the key, but even though they looked through every drawer, under every piece of furniture, they didn't find any stray keys. They did, however, find brochures and tickets dated from the 1970s to two years ago.

As they made a pile of what they found, they speculated about Henry Bell. He seemed to have been very interested in the history of Nantucket. Twice he'd won the annual *Jeopardy*-like Nantucket trivia contest. There were a couple of newspaper articles with photos of him with Nat Philbrick, who wrote so well about Nantucket.

What they saw made Hallie and Jamie say they were going to learn more about the island. But when Hallie repeated her invitation to go exploring, Jamie's face closed. He said that he'd be the researcher and she could do the footwork.

By ten Hallie was yawning, but Jamie looked wide awake, as though he never planned to go to sleep. She wanted to ask him about the medication he was taking, but she didn't. Instead, she bid him goodnight and went upstairs to bed.

Maybe some part of her mind was on alert because just as she'd done the night before, she awoke at two A.M. She lay there for a while, staring up at the silk rosette on the underside of the bed canopy, and listening. But the house seemed quiet.

She was just about to go back to sleep when she heard a far-away sound, something like a groan. If it hadn't been for what happened the night before, she wouldn't have paid any attention to it.

Without a second thought, she leaped out of the bed and ran down the dark stairs. She stubbed her toe on a table leg, but she kept going toward Jamie.

The nightlight was on, but this time there was no pill bottle on the desk. Jamie was in the bed, rolling back and forth, making soft sounds of panic.

"I'm here," she whispered as she put her hands on the sides of his head. He calmed somewhat, but his legs were moving, his brace hitting the side of the bed.

Keeping her hands on his face, she stretched out beside him. As before, he drew her close. He settled for a while, but when he again started thrashing, she lifted her head up to his and kissed him.

This kiss, their second one, had a bit more passion than the first one. When Hallie felt herself moving her leg between his, she pushed away from him. "Sleeping kisses are one thing," she said softly, "but no sleeping screws."

But the kiss did settle him and before Hallie knew what happened, she fell asleep in his arms.

Chapter Four

When Hallie awoke the next morning, daylight was beginning to come through the window. She and Jamie were spooned together on the narrow bed like they were one person.

Peeling his arms from around her body was no easy feat. When she stood up, she had a crick in her neck and one in her lower back. The bed was too small for one person, much less a former football player and her.

She tiptoed up the stairs to her own bedroom and took a shower. When she went back down, Jamie was in the kitchen, his hair damp. As usual, he was covered in clothing from neck to ankles. Hallie had on a sleeveless top, cutoff jeans, and sandals.

"I think I'm going to go into town this morning," she said, avoiding his eyes, as the memory of last night was too clear in her mind. She needed some distance from him. On the other hand, exploring a new town on her own wasn't going to be a lot of fun. "Want to go with me?"

"No," he said, his voice firm, as though he didn't want to be questioned any more. He ran his hand across the back of his neck.

She put a plate of scrambled eggs in front of him. "Are you all right?"

"Just . . . dreams," he said as he picked up his cup of coffee.

She sat down across from him. "What kind of dreams?"

He hesitated, but then looked at her. His eyes were hot, intense. "If you must know, they're about you."

"Oh," Hallie said and got up to refill a cup that was already full. "Hazards of working together," she mumbled. Or sleeping together, she thought. All in all, it probably would be better if they spent some time apart. "Tell me again when your relatives will begin to arrive."

"I'm not sure what day. If I know the sprouts, they'll come running as soon as the ferry docks."

"And who are the sprouts?"

"I have a brother and sister, twins, who are seven years old."

"How wonderful!" Hallie said. "What are their names? Tell me about them."

The tension that had been caused by Jamie's mention of his dreams was broken and they ate breakfast while he told of his family. The twins, Cory—a nickname for Cordelia—and Max, were going to be in the upcoming wedding and they were very excited about it.

As Hallie watched him talk of his family in such a loving way, she again wondered why he hadn't stayed with them for his therapy. Why go to Nantucket where he knew so few people? Why isolate himself with a stranger? Hallie knew that if she had a loving family, nothing on earth would get her away from them.

When she said she needed to change to go to town, Jamie

said he had another story to tell about the twins. She listened, then said she was going. But when Jamie came up with yet another story, she realized he didn't want her to leave.

How flattering! she thought, but she still excused herself and went upstairs to change. She put on a pretty flowered dress with a matching cardigan and her pink sandals.

When she went downstairs, Jamie was waiting for her. "Wow! You look very pretty. I was thinking that we should keep looking for the key to that room. We didn't check the attic. Or maybe we should spend the day in the garden and plan how to improve it."

"When I get back, we'll search some more and talk about the garden. Anything you need from town? And it's not too late to go with me."

"No, nothing," Jamie said and stepped away from her. "Go. Have a good time. I'll call my brother or something."

He sounded so sad that Hallie almost said she wouldn't go, but that was ridiculous. If he was a man who hated to be alone, *why* had he left the company of his extensive family?

But no matter how much his eyes seemed to be pleading, she didn't give in to him and left the house. She walked to the end of the lane, took a left, and went to beautiful downtown Nantucket. The old buildings, the wonderful little shops, were all fascinating to her.

As she wandered about, in and out of the stores, she kept thinking of Jamie. She went up the stairs to a shop called Zero Main and looked around. The clothes were beautiful, but as she started to leave, it hit her that she could afford some new garments. Ever since her father and stepmother had died, Hallie'd had to work, sometimes at three jobs. She'd had to support Shelly, then when Shelly had left for California to try her hand at acting, Hallie had put herself through school. And the house she'd inherited from her father had needed a lot of repairs.

As she looked about the shop, she realized that that was all done. She had graduated from school and could now earn money.

With a smile, she took her time looking at the beautiful merchandise and ended up buying an entire outfit. She got a pretty white knit top, a dark blue jacket, black silk trousers, and a long necklace with a purple glass ball on the end of it.

As she left, she thought that even though her relationship with Jamie was professional, it didn't hurt to look good.

At Sweet Inspirations she bought him candy she thought he'd like. At the Whaling Museum she bought four books on the history of Nantucket and put the titles of eight more into her phone's notepad. The museum was a historian's dream.

After lunch at Arno's, she walked home. She put her shopping bags down in the kitchen, removed the sack of candy, and went through the house, searching for Jamie. She found him outside, sitting on the bench under the oak tree—and he looked almost forlorn. When he saw Hallie, his face lit up. Having someone glad to see you was a soul-lifting feeling. It was how her grandparents greeted her when she was a child. But after Shelly and her mother moved in, she got looks that seemed to say, Oh, it's you.

Smiling, Hallie brushed the thoughts from her mind and went to sit beside him, holding out the bag of chocolate-covered cranberries.

"Tell me everything you did," he said as he took the candy, and she did.

They were still on the bench when a woman burst through the gate. Jamie was holding his phone out to show Hallie photos of the "sprouts," so they didn't at first see her. His family lived in Colorado and he had just shown her a picture of the children racing scooters down the hallway of what looked like a marble mansion. Immediately, Hallie asked him to tell her more about the house.

"It was built by my robber baron ancestor, Kane Taggert,"

Jamie said. "My dad is named after him. He was responsible for a lot of reforms in mining—the first Kane, that is, not Dad. He—" When the big gate made a sudden, explosively loud sound as it slammed behind the woman who came running through it, Jamie jumped to his feet. He grabbed a crutch and held it in a way that looked like he was ready to use it as a club.

Hallie was torn between her astonishment at Jamie's reaction and what appeared to be rage on the face of the woman. She was short and stout, with iron-gray hair, and she looked like she wanted to tear someone apart.

"Is my mother-in-law here?" she demanded.

When Hallie stood up beside Jamie, he took a half step in front of her, as though to protect her. "Who is your mother-in-law?"

"Edith!" the woman said, then took a breath. "I'm sorry. I'm Betty Powell from Sea Haven, the B&B next door, and she is my husband Howard's mother. If he doesn't know where she is for even a few minutes, he gets frantic. I told him she's probably over here, but he said I have to make sure. She's not inside, is she?" She nodded toward the house.

"I was in there just minutes ago and it's empty," Hallie said.

"What about in the tea room? Is she hiding in there?"

"If you mean the room on the side of the house, it's locked," Jamie said. "We've been looking for the key."

"There *is* no key!" Betty said. "According to my crazy mother-in-law, only *they* can open the doors." She looked back toward the gate. "Why can't that woman stay where she's put?" She turned to Jamie and Hallie. "If she shows up, send her home, would you? Tell her Howard wants her. Heaven knows she won't return for *me*. I'm sorry I bothered you." She started for the gate at a rapid pace.

Jamie and Hallie, both wide-eyed, looked at each other, then back at the woman.

"Wait!" Hallie called.

With a look of impatience, Betty stopped and turned back to them. "Yes?"

"Who are 'they'?" Jamie asked. "Who can open the doors?"

Betty looked shocked. "Don't tell me you bought this house and no one told you about them?"

"Hallie inherited it," Jamie said.

"Ah. Right. Makes sense. Old Henry Bell wouldn't want just anyone around his precious ladies." She looked at her watch. "I have to get back, but 'they' are the Tea Ladies. The Bell sisters who died. They're ghosts. I don't know much about them. All I know is that my crazy mother-in-law comes over here, goes into what she calls the tea room, and spends hours talking to them— or she thinks she does. I'm trying to get Howard to lock her away somewhere, but he won't do it. I really do have to go. I have fifteen people coming for afternoon tea." She left, slamming the gate hard behind her.

For a moment Jamie and Hallie stood side by side in silence.

At last Hallie said, "We should have told her we love her fuzzy navel cupcakes."

"And the lobster. But then my guess is that she has no idea Edith brought us the food."

"I can understand that," Hallie said. "I wouldn't want to confront that woman." She looked at Jamie. "It seems that I own a haunted house."

"I think so. Does that scare you?"

She thought for a moment. "No, it doesn't."

"Wanna go knock on the tea room door and see who answers?"

"Definitely!"

Jamie smiled at her. "Hallie, baby, I like you more with every passing minute. Race you there!"

Hallie won the race, but she knew it was only because Jamie

was on crutches. She hadn't been to that side of the house and was surprised to see a narrow driveway and a double gate. If she had her car on the island, this was where she'd park it.

In front of her was a set of tall, wide double doors that looked very solid. She tried the knob, but it didn't turn.

She waited for Jamie to come along on his crutches, and the way he pretended to have a tough time walking made her laugh.

When he reached her, he said seriously, "I think I need another massage to loosen me up."

"Full body?" she shot back at him.

"Lights off?"

"Ten candles," she said.

"One candle in the next room. With the door closed," he answered.

"No deal, and it's your loss." Hallie looked back at the doors. "Are you going to knock?"

"I'm still thinking about a candlelight massage and besides, it's your house."

She took a step forward and after an encouraging nod from Jamie, she knocked on the door. Both of them held their breaths, but nothing happened.

Jamie stepped forward and knocked louder. Nothing.

"Maybe tomorrow we should call a locksmith," she said.

"Yeah, maybe." Jamie raised his voice. "We're friends of Edith and we'd like to meet you. I'm James Taggert and this beautiful young woman with me is named Hyacinth, after one of you two. She's called Hallie and she's descended from—" He looked at her.

"Leland Hartley. He was married to Juliana."

Jamie loudly repeated what she'd said. "Hallie is a cousin of yours by marriage and if there's one thing I know about in this world, it's cousins." Looking back at Hallie, he lowered his voice. "I have thousands of cousins. My dad has eleven brothers and sisters and they all have kids."

"Really?" Hallie asked.

"Yeah." He looked at her. "That big marble house you saw? You wouldn't believe it at Christmas. It's pure chaos."

He looked back at the door. His tone implied that it was a horrible time, but Hallie thought it sounded like fun. In her experience, Christmas had been a fairly solemn occasion. There had been pleasantries but nothing even near chaos—unless Shelly didn't get enough gifts.

Jamie banged on the door again, but still nothing happened. "So maybe Edith *is* crazy."

" 'Fraid so," Hallie said. The truth was, she was looking at the way he leaned on his crutches. His body was tilting toward one side, and she was planning his next treatment. Besides that, she was dreading the coming night. She was getting tired of running up and down a dark staircase. One of her toes still ached from where she'd stubbed it this morning. The nighttime turmoil had happened twice now and a third time would make it a habit. It needed to stop *now*! "I can't believe that after all we ate just a couple of hours ago, I'm hungry again."

"Me too," Jamie said and they started back to enter the house through the sunporch. Hallie picked up the unfinished embroidery she'd seen the first day. "I could swear that more of this has been completed."

Reaching into his pocket, Jamie pulled out his cell phone and took a photo of the embroidery. "If it changes again, we'll have a record of it." As Hallie put the hoop back on the sofa, he quickly snapped a couple of photos of her.

"What was that for?"

"To send home to the relatives. You're the woman who keeps begging me to take my clothes off."

"You aren't really going to say that, are you? Your mother will think I'm—"

"Trying to help me recover and she'll thank you." He was smiling.

As they went into the kitchen, she said, "Why didn't you stay at home with your family and do your therapy there?"

"What can I say? They wanted to get rid of me."

Hallie started to ask more, but he strode ahead of her, opened the fridge, and began to talk rapidly. "How about giant sandwiches and four kinds of salad? You know how to make lemonade? I like mine with less sugar and maybe we can find some club soda to add. Ah! Here's—"

She didn't listen to the rest of what he said because she knew he was just filling the air with words. Obviously, he didn't want to answer her question, so she backed off.

While they made the sandwiches they chatted easily, laughing at themselves for believing there were ghosts living in the house.

"If they were here, they wouldn't need locked doors," Hallie said. "They could float through the walls."

"So what do you think ol' Henry Bell has locked away in that room that he didn't want anyone to see?" Jamie bit into his sandwich.

"Oh, please, I hope it's not porn."

"What's secret about that? It's all over the Internet. Any kind you can imagine, it's all there. I've seen—" He broke off. "Not that I know for sure, but my brother Todd—he's a law enforcement officer—told me about it."

Hallie laughed. "Todd the Educator and Jamie the Pure. But maybe Henry was old school and thought porn was something to be hidden away. I haven't checked if there's Wi-Fi in the house."

"What about cross-dressing?" Jamie said. "The room could be full of his dress-up clothes."

Hallie frowned. "When we get the doors open, I really hope we don't find anything hideous and especially not illegal in there. Why do you sleep downstairs?"

Because Jamie was still thinking of the possible contents of the locked room, he almost blurted out the truth. But he caught himself. "It seemed the right thing to do. I was going to be alone in the house with a young lady. It wouldn't be good for her reputation for us to be so close."

"Reputation. I haven't heard that word since I last saw my grandparents. In this world of one-night stands, who worries about a woman's reputation?"

"All those girls who get nude photos of themselves posted on the Internet. I think they're starting to make laws about that. I read that . . ."

Hallie blinked at him. And are you changing the subject again? she thought. It looked like she'd hit on yet another one of his secrets. How many was that? About a hundred? She reminded herself that he was her patient, not her boyfriend.

She picked up her empty plate and carried it to the sink. If he kept secrets, so could she. For one thing, she wasn't going to tell him what went on between them during the night. Nor was she going to mention that she knew his sleep was drug-induced. What she wanted to do was try to stop both the drugs and the night terrors. "I want you to move upstairs," she said.

"And why would you want that?" He was still sitting at the table.

She'd expected him to do more sexual teasing, but he didn't. Instead, he sounded as though he was about to refuse—and she could guess why. He knew about his nightmares, but he didn't want her to know. He wanted to keep his male ego intact and make her think there was nothing wrong with him.

She wanted to be near him so she could soothe him during the night, then get back to her own bed. There would be no more sleeping on the couch or with him. And the bigger bed upstairs would eliminate the danger of his falling onto the floor.

But Hallie was sure that if she told him the truth, he might . . . What? Leave? That was possible. Any man who had nightmares like his needed help and Hallie planned to give it to him.

She turned back to him. "I, uh, well . . . I, uh . . ."

He looked at her. "What are you trying to say?"

"This ghost thing kind of . . . Well, it scares me. Earlier you said that my lack of fear made you like me more, so now I'm worried that you'll like me less."

Jamie stood up and reached out to pull her to him. It was a brother-sister hug and he rubbed her back comfortingly. "I'm sure there's nothing in the ghost story. Betty is probably right and her mother-in-law should be put under care. I don't agree that she should be locked away, but she should get some help."

He held Hallie at arm's length and looked into her eyes. "My guess is that old man Bell did something he didn't want people to know about. And he probably spread the ghost rumor to keep people away."

"I'm sure you're right." Hallie lowered her eyes so she'd look properly frightened.

Jamie drew her back against him. "Tomorrow we'll call a locksmith and I'll go in and look around."

Hallie wanted to say, Not without me! but couldn't since she was pretending to be afraid. "So you'll move upstairs into the other bedroom and I won't be alone in this strange house?"

"I don't think that's a good idea." His tone went back to being stern.

Hallie pushed away from him. "Okay. I'll move downstairs. But, no, that couch down there is too small to sleep on. I know. I'll call Jared and see if I can stay in his house for a few nights. I know it's empty. You'll be all right here by yourself, won't you?" She batted her lashes at him in innocence.

Jamie looked like he was torn between anger and helplessness. "All right, I'll move upstairs." His teeth were clenched together.

"That's great!" Hallie said. "I'll help you pack your things, and tonight I want to do some breathing exercises with you." She headed toward his room.

"Look only in the bathroom and the closet!" Jamie called after her. "I'll take care of the desk." He glared at the locked door that led into the tea room. "Whatever you've got hidden away in there, Henry Bell, I'm going to expose it, 'cause look what you've done to *me*."

He moved as fast as he could to get to the living room and dragged his duffel bag from under the bed. While Hallie was gathering toiletries from the bathroom, he slipped eight bottles of medication into the side pocket and zipped it.

Chapter Five

*J*amie was lying on his back on the floor of his new bedroom, his hands clasped and raised above his head. Hallie was seated beside him, leaning over his midsection, her hand just below his navel. Not that she could *see* his belly button, but she could guess at it. "I want to feel your breath coming from here," she said. "Now deeper and slower."

"Are you sure this is going to do anything?"

"Shhhh," she said. "Don't talk. Just breathe." She watched him slowly raise and lower his hands and take long, deep breaths. He was such a contradiction! she thought. On the surface he seemed to not have a serious thought in his mind, always teasing and laughing, but his body felt like a tightly coiled spring. If she could just get him to fully relax, maybe he wouldn't need pills to help him sleep.

She couldn't help wondering what had made him so tense.

Was there a recent tragedy in his life? A brush with death for him? But she knew better than to flat out ask him. He'd change the subject.

They spent an hour together doing exercises. Jamie called them "girly" and frowned, but she could tell that the breathing movements were helping him. At one point she saw his eyes flicker as though he were sleepy. The thought that she'd helped enough that he might not need pills for sleep made her feel good.

When she finished with him, he lay on the thick rug, his eyes closed, and smiling. "Feel better?" she asked.

"I do, actually." He sounded surprised.

She stood up and looked down at him. He'd said that he was truly beginning to *like* her and she felt the same way about him. She'd never before felt so comfortable with a man. Sometimes they even seemed to have the same thoughts at the same time.

With the few boyfriends she'd had in the past, she usually couldn't wait to get away from them. Growing up, her neighbor Mrs. Westbrook, Braden's mother, had been a best friend to her. She used to say that Hallie's problem was that she chose men like the people she knew. Hallie asked what she meant. "Larry was slow and easy like your grandfather, and Kyle was never available, just like your father. And Craig sat in a chair and let you wait on him. He was a male Shelly." At the time, she'd laughed at the very accurate description of her past relationships, but she knew she didn't want to repeat herself.

Of course there was one man they hadn't spoken of: Braden. They both wanted the same thing, for her and Braden to get together, but that didn't look like it was going to happen.

As Hallie looked at Jamie Taggert, still lying on the floor, she wondered if it was possible that they could have a future together.

Slowly, Jamie opened his eyes and looked up at her. Some of what she was thinking must have been showing because his expression changed from sleepy to an invitation. He held up his hand for her to join him on the floor—and Hallie knew where that would lead. A quickie with him in his big sweatsuit. It would probably be wonderful, but in the morning she'd be angry at herself for mixing business with pleasure.

She had to turn away or she'd let the pleasure side win. "Can you get up by yourself?" Her back was to him.

"Sure," he said, his voice flat. He sounded like a man who'd just been rejected—which, in a way, he was.

She heard him as he held on to the bedpost and got up. When he was standing, she looked back at him and gave a smile as though nothing had happened. "I'll see you in the morning."

"All right," Jamie said, his voice cool and distant. But then his head came up. "How do *you* work out?"

"The usual way," she said. The truth was that between taking care of Shelly, multiple jobs, going to school, and, well, taking care of Shelly, gym time had been left out. She'd told herself that the practice sessions where she'd learned the proper form for rehabilitation had been enough.

The wary expression left Jamie's handsome face and the tension between them was gone. "Tomorrow morning you're going to work out with me."

"No, I'm not," Hallie said quickly. She'd seen him in the gym. He'd probably hand her fifty-pound dumbbells and say, "Now, let's see what you can do with them."

"I'll see you at six A.M. Goodnight."

"I don't think that would be a good idea."

With an almost menacing look, he came toward her on one crutch and Hallie backed up. She didn't realize she was in the hall until he closed the door in her face.

She started to open the door and protest, but she didn't. Instead, yawning, she went into her own room and got into bed. She'd deal with that in the morning.

Hours later, when the groans woke Hallie, she came alert

instantly, and in seconds she was in Jamie's bedroom. It was very dark, with no nightlight, and she had to use her memory to get to the bed. He was thrashing about, rolling from one side to the other, and when Hallie touched his shoulder he grabbed her to him. Her feet were still on the floor and she was so twisted that she was close to breaking.

She threw a leg up onto the bed. He'd tossed the covers off so her body was next to his. She wore only a big T-shirt and underpants, but even at night he was covered by sweatpants and a long-sleeved cotton shirt.

He pulled her to him, snuggling them so her legs were held between his. As soon as her hips were pressed to his she knew he was ready for her.

"Jamie?" she whispered, but there was no answer.

His hand slowly moved over her body, down to her nearly bare backside, caressing her flesh all the way down.

Hallie's eyes closed. He was such a beautiful man and his hard body against hers was making her heart beat quickly. "I can't— We can't—" she began, but he bent his head and kissed her.

It wasn't like the other two kisses. This one was full of passion and desire. When his tongue touched hers, Hallie forgot about the forbidden aspect and kissed him back. She'd wanted him from the moment she'd first seen him and days of being near him had intensified that desire.

She kissed him back as though she were desperate, needed him past desire. With her knee nudging his maleness, when her foot touched the mattress, she dug in so that he turned onto his back. A groan came from him. It wasn't his usual nighttime sound of fear, but raw, unbridled passion.

Hallie straddled him, feeling his hard desire between her legs. The room was so dark she couldn't see his face, but when she kissed his eyes they were closed.

Sitting back, she flung her T-shirt to the floor and leaned

over him, her naked breasts in his face. There was another sound from him, this one almost of pain. There was deep yearning in his voice.

In one quick, strong movement, he flipped her onto her back. She felt him pulling the drawstring on his pants and lowering them. Her arms were around him, feeling the muscles in his body, the deep curves of them, the ridges and valleys. Naked, he must be a sight to behold, she thought.

She still had on her underpants, so when he started to enter her, there was a barrier. "Wait," she whispered as she reached down to remove them.

"I will wait for you forever, Valery," he said, his lips on her ear.

Hallie froze beneath him. In an instant her mind went from being blind with lust to crystal clear. She was about to have sex with a man who was in a drug-induced sleep! Was she *crazy*?! Not only would he not remember it in the morning but he'd think he'd dreamed of making love with another woman.

For a moment, the feel of his magnificent body, his breath on her cheek, and his sheer masculinity made her think, Who cares?

But she had more pride than that. It wasn't easy, but she rolled out from under him and stood up. Her heart was still pounding, her breath coming fast and loud, and it took minutes to get herself under control.

The darkness of the room had annoyed her, but now she was glad for it because she was nearly nude.

When she heard Jamie moving his arms, she knew he was searching for her.

She felt her way around to the far side of the bed, found her T-shirt, and put it on. The noise he was making had stopped and for a moment she thought maybe he'd awakened, but she heard the soft sound of his breathing and she knew he was still asleep.

She made her way to the door and through to her own bed. As she lay there—alone—part of her regretted her decision to leave him. Sex with a sleeping man. When you thought about it, it wasn't such a bad idea.

But Hallie knew herself well enough to realize that it wouldn't have stopped there—not for her, anyway. She wasn't the type of person who could sue her stepsister when she tried to steal from her, and she wasn't one to have sex without feelings attached. Like Jamie had said, she was growing to like him more every day. Would they have easy, pleasant companionship during the day and sex at night? Sex that he didn't remember?

"So what happens when Valery shows up?" she whispered aloud. Would Hallie just step aside and think it was fun while it lasted? Smile at the two of them as they walked around the garden and kissed and snuggled?

No, she knew she wouldn't be able to do that. Before she finally went back to sleep, she renewed her vow to keep the relationship between them professional.

"Hartley!" came a voice like a drill sergeant.

Hallie, on her stomach under the covers, moved farther down.

Jamie tossed back the coverlet, exposing her T-shirt-clad upper half. "It's time to go to the gym."

"Who is Valery?" she asked.

She didn't see the shock on his face that was followed by anger. But he got his emotions under control. "She's the love of my life. Jealous?"

"Does she put up with your moans and groans and calling her name at night?" Hallie still hadn't turned over, and she was berating herself for having asked about the woman. But it was better than not knowing.

"I'm lovable as I am," Jamie answered. "Now get up and let's go to the gym. I'm going to toughen you up."

"Oh?" she said and turned over in the bed to look up at him. Her braless upper half was barely hidden under the thin T-shirt. "You don't like the softness of women?"

She had the pleasure of seeing his eyes widen. Putting his crutches aside, he sat down on the side of the bed.

"If you want to . . ." He trailed off and when his hand reached for her, she flung back the cover on the opposite side of the bed, rolled out, and walked around toward him. Her T-shirt hung only to her hips so her bare legs were exposed.

She had the great satisfaction of seeing Jamie's face turn nearly white. "Holy crap, Hallie! I'm only human."

"You're the one who told me to get up."

"And now we both are."

She didn't know what he meant, but a quick glance downward explained it. While trying to suppress a giggle, she hurried to the bathroom and closed the door.

Over two hours later they left the gym and walked back to the house. Hallie was sure that every muscle in her body was going to be sore. Jamie had put her on a program on the treadmill that went back and forth from easy to fast and difficult. Then he'd had her sit on a bench while he guided her arms as she did variations of flys and curls.

In return, she got him off the weights and into exercises that were part Pilates, part yoga, with a lot of meditation added. Her goal was to get the tension out of his giant muscles.

For all that the long, hard workout nearly killed her, Hallie had enjoyed it. They'd laughed and talked throughout the time. Jamie told her stories of his family, a lot of them about his brother Todd, who Jamie seemed to think was the best guy on the earth. "He does undercover work with the police and sometimes I don't hear from him for months." Jamie sounded as though when he and his brother were separated, they missed each other to the point of pain.

His talk of his family was so happy that Hallie wanted to respond in kind, so she told him more about living with her grandparents. She described the big garden they had and how her school friends loved to come to sleepovers and pick berries. "My grandfather would set up a screen in the garden and we'd watch movies outside. It sounds tame now, but to a bunch of nine-year-olds it was wildly exciting."

"But later your grandparents moved out?"

"Yes," Hallie said and her voice changed. "When Dad showed up with his new wife and her cute little blonde daughter, my grandparents ran to Florida."

"So the only relative you have left is Shelly?"

"Yes," Hallie said and she could feel her back teeth clenching.

Jamie saw in her eyes what he guessed was years of repressed anger. He could give her sympathy, but he knew from experience that was often what a person needed least. "You want some? Relatives, I mean. I have what feels like millions of them. Just last year a whole new branch of them found us. Jared Montgomery Kingsley showed up and we found out we're related to half of Nantucket. So tell me what kind of relatives you want. You could go by age, sex, personality, profession, or location. Just tell me and I can find whatever you want."

By the time he finished, Hallie was laughing. "I'll take a tall, dark, and handsome male."

"Here I am."

She laughed harder. "You and your ego! Get down on the floor and start breathing."

"Is this the one where you use both hands to search for my belly button? Just so you know, last night it moved six inches lower."

"Get on the floor!" She was shaking her head at him and still laughing.

When they finally quit working out and got back to the house, they were pleased to see that the kitchen table was loaded with food.

"Looks like Edith has been here," Jamie said.

"And she's trying to win us over to her side."

Jamie picked up a little triangle of crisp strudel, broke it in half, and gave the larger piece to Hallie. "Let's see. Angry woman who slams gates versus Edith who brings us food. Hard to decide, huh?"

"Edith has won me. This is delicious. Apricots?"

"I think so. What's your favorite berry?" He picked up a square cookie with a design of a rabbit on it.

"Lingonberry. They grow on little bushes. When I was little, Grams made a killer jam from them. Is that tea hot?"

Jamie touched the pot. "Scalding."

By the next minute they were seated at the table and helping themselves. Before they finished, Jamie's phone rang. He looked at the ID. "A cousin. What a surprise." He touched "answer." "Jared, good to hear from you. I just came up from the basement, where I have Hallie chained to a wall. She—"

"Give me that!" Hallie said as she took the phone from him. "Hi, Jared. Everything here is okay. What about you?"

"Fine," he said. "Alix and I are in Texas right now, but I wanted you to know that I haven't forgotten about you. I'm going to get a lawyer on this case against your stepsister."

"I don't think that's necessary," she said. "I'm sure you made your point clear enough that Shelly won't do anything like that again."

"Hallie," Jared said with patience, "we left your stepsister alone in a house that you own. For all we know, by now she's put it up for sale."

"I don't think she'd do that. She—"

Jamie took his phone back and put it on speaker. "I agree with you," he said to Jared. "You have a lawyer? If not, I'm related to some."

"That's why I'm calling. Alix wondered if Hallie knew an attorney who is aware of the family situation. It might save time explaining."

Jamie looked at her in question.

"My neighbor's son, Braden Westbrook, is a lawyer," Hallie said. "But he's with Hadley-Braithwaite in Boston. They're a big-deal law firm and I'm sure this case would be too small for them."

"Does your friend know Shelly?" Jared asked.

"Oh, yes. He's known her since she was a child."

"Perfect. I'm going to call him."

"Do you want his phone numbers and addresses?" Hallie asked. "I know them by heart."

"Let me get a pen," Jared said. "Okay. Shoot."

She recited Braden's cell number, office number, the addresses of his law firm and his apartment in Boston. Then she gave the cell number and address of his mother, who lived across the road from Hallie's house.

"This is great," Jared said. "Thanks, and I'll get back to you as soon as I know anything."

"Ask about the tea room," Jamie said.

"Uh, Jared?" Hallie asked. "Uh, something happened. I don't know how to say this exactly, but . . . Well, actually, nothing really *happened*, but—"

Jamie picked up the phone. "Did you know this house is haunted by a couple of tea-serving ladies?"

"Oh, Lord," Jared said. "I forgot about them." He let out a sigh. "Nantucket has . . ." He trailed off. "How scared are the two of you?"

"Not scared at all," Jamie said. "Well, Hallie is a bit, but she had me move upstairs to be near her and she's okay now."

"Did she?" Jared said in a way that left no doubt that he thought the "moving upstairs" had nothing to do with a couple of ghosts.

Jamie looked at Hallie, whose face was turning red. "Actually, we're intrigued and would like to know more about the ladies, but that room is locked. We thought we'd call a locksmith and—"

"No," Jared said. "I know someone who can open the doors. I'll call him and he can probably answer any questions you both have. His official title is Dr. Caleb Huntley, director of the Nantucket Historical Society. Are you two going to be home today?"

When Jamie looked at Hallie, she nodded. "We'll be here." As he hung up, he picked up another of the square cookies, this one with a rose on it.

"It'll be interesting to find out the history of the Tea Ladies, won't it?" Hallie said.

Jamie was staring at the food on the tiered tray. "What's your stepsister's cell number?"

"I'll look on my phone and give it to you."

"You don't know the number off the top of your head?"

"No, I don't."

"So you're not one of those savants who can remember everybody's numbers and addresses?"

"Of course not. What gave you that idea? Oh. Braden. It's just that I've known him a very long time and his mother and I are close. She helped me after my grandparents moved out, when I was left alone with Ruby and Shelly. And he—"

"How old is this Braden?"

When she realized what he was getting at, she couldn't help a little smile. "Thirty-two. Jealous?" She was teasing, just as he'd done this morning, but there was no laughter on Jamie's face.

"Of an old lawyer? Not at all." He got up from the table. "I have some emails to answer." He left the room.

In spite of his denial, his attitude made her smile.

Jared called Caleb Huntley, his wife's stepfather—though past that, the two of them had a very long history together. He didn't bother with preliminaries. "You have to go to the Hartley-Bell house today and tell Jamie and Hallie about the ghosts. And be gentle. They don't understand Nantucket."

"Ah," Caleb said, his voice soft. "Those beautiful young ladies. I'd like to see them again."

"Forget that. I don't want you talking to ghosts and scaring a couple of off-islanders to death. Go as Dr. Huntley, the director of the NHS, and tell them the facts."

Caleb chuckled. "You mean tell them how every male on the island under the age of seventy used to climb the walls to get to those women? Actually, old Arnie was seventy-two, so make that every man under eighty."

"I don't have time to reminisce with you about the good ol' days. Just please go over to the house and tell them some nice, quiet story that will keep them from jumping on the next ferry and leaving the island. I especially want Hallie to stay calm. She can't leave until I get this business about her stepsister straightened out."

"I'll take care of it," Caleb said. "You handle your buildings and leave the ghosts to me." As soon as Caleb hung up, he buzzed for his assistant. When she entered he said, "If I draw a map of the attic of Kingsley House, could you go there and get something for me?"

Like all historians, her eyes lit up at the prospect. Kingsley House had been owned by the same family since it was built in the early 1800s. It was rumored that the attic was full of treasures that should be in museums: journals, clothes, historic artifacts, things historians could only dream about. "Yes," she managed to say.

Caleb quickly drew a map of the arrangement of the attic. Third row from the door, all the way to the back, under four crates full of China imports, inside an old trunk, on the bottom left side, was a little cinnabar box that contained a key. He wanted that key.

Chapter Six

*W*hen Caleb got to the Hartley-Bell house, he knew he should go to the front door and knock, but he didn't. Instead, he went around to the back gate. It wasn't the big double gate by the B&B but the small one hidden behind shrubs and the old chicken coop. It took some muscle to open the gate, but in the last year Caleb had spent a lot of time in a gym. At first he'd protested what was, to his eye, an artificial form of exercise. He believed men got muscles from climbing rigging and hauling anchors. Jared had scoffed at that idea and hired him a personal trainer. Caleb hated to say it, but it had worked.

The first thing he saw was that the chicken coop had been remade into a home gym. The yard where the chickens had scratched and fluttered in their mud baths had a pretty grape arbor over it and two chairs beneath it.

He sat down in one and looked out over the long view of the garden. It was awful! It had once been lush to the point where it looked like the Garden of Eden. Now it was nearly bare, the flower beds still outlined but empty.

The big pergola was gone. The girls had served tea under it, and he remembered pink and white rose petals dropping onto the tablecloth. He'd always thought the petals matched the perfect skin of those beautiful girls.

As he envisioned those soft summer days, the food, the laughter, and most of all, the perfection of the girls, he could feel tears coming to his eyes. So many years had passed, but today it all seemed fresh.

He heard a door close, then a woman's laughter, and he knew he should leave. If he went back out the gate and around to knock on the front door, they'd never know he'd been there.

He was about to get up, but when he saw them, he sat back down. He was always curious about people. They were a young, handsome couple and Hallie looked like Leland. How many generations separated her from her ancestor? he wondered. But no matter the time, the resemblance was still there.

For a moment Caleb closed his eyes in memory. They had all envied Leland so very much. Every man on Nantucket had tried to make the girls fall in love with him. They'd brought back gifts from their sailing voyages to far-off places, poems written on scrimshaw, busks made of ivory to slip into their corsets, buttons. The risks they'd taken to get recipes for the girls! Around Nantucket it became a saying, "What did you bring back for the Bell girls?" Their father made his daughters return silks and jewelry, but they were allowed to keep plants nurtured on long voyages, pretty pieces of china, and their favorite, recipes from foreign lands.

When the young men were home from their long voyages, they hung around the house constantly. The girls' father used to run them off with an oar, threatening them. But it didn't deter any of them. They were back again before daylight, with a new gift and a new hope.

But none of them came close to receiving that look of love. The girls were the same to all the men who visited. They were gracious, kind, generous. But there was no spark.

Until Leland Hartley arrived. He had come over from Boston, a young man who wanted time away from his blue-blood family, away from his endless studies. One of the Starbuck boys invited him to tea at the Bell house to meet the sisters. They were young and at the height of their beauty.

Caleb hadn't been there that day, but he'd heard about it—as had everyone on the island. Hyacinth opened the door, smiling as always, and was introduced.

Then Juliana came into the room. She and Leland looked at each other and . . . Well, that was that. They were married six months later. A week after that . . .

Caleb didn't want to think about the end of the story, of when he'd been told of their deaths. None of the Nantucketers could imagine the island without the Bell girls, and for days everyone was silent in grief.

Afterward, the girls' father lived alone, willing himself to join his cherished daughters in Heaven. The garden became a mass of weeds and the house was always dark. As for Leland, Caleb was told that his deep sorrow had made him suicidal, and he'd been put under watch to prevent him from harming himself.

As Caleb watched the young couple, he could see Leland in the girl, and he couldn't help marveling at how characteristics were passed down through the centuries. The way the girl moved her hands was like Leland. The tilt of her head was like him. Even her laugh sounded like his.

She was walking with a big, muscular young man on crutches,

and their heads were very close together. He could hear quiet laughter between them. Like Leland and Juliana, he thought. They had eyes only for each other.

Oh, my poor, poor Juliana, Caleb thought. How it must hurt her to see this young woman who was so like the man she loved. Or did it make her feel good to see that he'd lived on in this pretty girl?

The couple were coming closer and even as absorbed in each other as they were, they'd soon see him and that would be embarrassing. He started to get up, but then that odious woman from the inn next door threw open the big red gates and came storming toward the couple. The gate slammed behind her, loud enough to be cannon fire.

The young man, Jamie, was a bit behind the girl so she didn't see his reaction—but Caleb did. Jamie dropped to one knee, reached out to grab the girl, but then seemed to remember where he was and let his hand fall away. His action was something that Caleb had seen many, many times and he knew what caused it.

When the young man was using his crutches to get himself up, he saw Caleb sitting in the chair. Instantly, his face took on a look of aggression.

"Jamie!" Hallie called. She was with the angry woman. "Have you seen Edith today?"

He hardly turned around, but kept his eyes on Caleb. "No, I haven't," he said over his shoulder as he made his way to the older man. His face was glowering, menacing, even. "May I ask who you are and why you sneaked onto this property?"

"I'm Caleb Huntley," he said, "and I shouldn't have come unannounced. I apologize for my lack of manners."

Jamie recovered himself, his face relaxed, and he sat down in the other chair. "Sorry for the . . ." He waved his hand, not knowing how to explain his actions, then nodded toward the older woman standing in front of the gate. "I take it you know who we are, but that's Betty, and her mother-in-law, Edith, constantly runs away."

"Do you blame her?" Caleb asked. They could hear the angry tone of Betty's voice.

"Not at all. I think that even if Edith were here, we'd not tell on her. She sneaks us food from the inn, so we have these wonderful afternoon teas, or a lavish breakfast after an early workout."

"Does she?" Caleb asked, smiling, his eyes sparkling as though from some mischief. "Does she still serve those little anise seed biscuits?"

"Oh, yeah. And cookies with bits of fruit buried in them. And fuzzy navel cupcakes."

"From the 1960s," Caleb said, nodding. "I remember them well. That recipe was from a woman trying to find a man she'd met years before."

"You mean someone who stayed at the inn?" Jamie asked.

Caleb was trying to think of a way to answer that when he saw Hallie coming toward them. He got up, introduced himself, and offered her his chair.

"I couldn't take your seat," she said to the very handsome older man.

"I'll get a bench," Jamie said and went into the gym.

Hallie sat down in his chair. "I'm sorry I didn't greet you when you arrived, but Betty showed up and . . ." She shrugged.

"I'm afraid I came in through the gate behind your new gym. I was trespassing and I apologize. I haven't been here in years and I wanted to see the place."

Hallie looked through the open door into the gym. For Jamie to carry a bench and manage his crutches by himself was going to be difficult. She started to get up to help him, but Caleb put his hand on her arm.

"Let your young man impress you," he said. "Help him when there's no other male around."

"Good advice." Hallie looked back at the garden.

"Have you had many visitors?" he asked.

"None, unless you count angry Betty. Edith has been here, but I've never had a conversation with her."

"But I hear you've eaten her food," Caleb said, smiling. "Fill you up, did it?"

What an odd question, Hallie thought but didn't say.

"Tell me about your young man. Jared said you're treating him for his injured knee."

"Yes, I am." She glanced toward the gym at Jamie. He had his cell phone to his ear and when he caught her eye, he mouthed, "Todd."

"Any problems?" Caleb asked.

"No," Hallie said. "Jamie is pleasant to be around and laughs easily. I enjoy his company very much."

"But . . . ?" Caleb asked. When Hallie didn't say anything, he lowered his voice. "If something's bothering you, you can tell me. I have a lot of grandchildren so maybe I can help."

"It's nothing," Hallie said, but just the idea of "grandfather" seemed to open doors. When she was growing up, her grand-parents were her best friends. "He won't take his clothes off."

"Oh," Caleb said.

"No, not like that. For massages. I've never seen a body hold as much tension as his does and I could help him, but he won't let me." She gave a sigh. "It's just one of his quirks, that's all."

"Does he have many of these odd behaviors?"

Hallie laughed. "About a dozen of them. I can't get him to leave this place for a moment. He won't even walk down the lane with me. And there's some big mystery about why he's here. If his family can afford a private jet, why didn't they send him to some exclusive place in Switzerland or somewhere? Why here, to me, to someone they don't even know?"

"Whatever their reason, from what I've seen of you two to-gether, I think they made a wise decision."

Hallie waved her hand. "It's not what it seems. We laugh and tease and . . ." She broke off with a grimace. "Anyway, he's in love with some girl named Valery. He says she's the love of his life."

Caleb looked toward the gym. Jamie was still on the phone. "From the look of him, I think you're doing an excellent job."

"I hope so. The truth is, it doesn't seem like work. Jamie said his family will be arriving in a few days. Have you met them?"

"Not many of them, no." Caleb leaned closer to her. "When your young man gets off the phone, why don't you leave him with me for a while? I'll see what I can find out. Petticoat Row Bakery has marvelous pastries. I'd love to have tea here in this garden."

"I will," she said. "And thank you." After Jamie put his phone away, she went to the door and told him she was going into town and that Dr. Huntley was staying for tea.

"Maybe Edith will bring us something," Jamie said.

"No, I think we'll try something different today. I'll be back in about an hour." For a second she hesitated, as his eyes seemed to be asking her not to leave. Heaven help her, but she almost kissed him in reassurance. Like she did at night. *I need* to get away, she thought. She waved to both men and left.

Jamie took the chair by Dr. Huntley and for a while they sat in silence, looking at the barren garden.

"She has no idea what you've been through, does she?" Caleb asked quietly.

For a moment Jamie seemed to be trying to decide whether or not to tell the truth. "None."

Caleb nodded. "I hear you won't take your clothes off."

"Too many nicks and holes in this old body," he said. "People see them and I get the 'poor Jamie' routine. Then they start with questions about how I'm feeling. What I've learned is that they just want to hear that I'm fine."

Caleb understood what he was saying. "Who is Valery?"

Jamie took a deep breath. "A fellow soldier. We were all half in love with her and envied her husband back home. She kept our spirits up, made us laugh, kept us from being too scared to move." He paused. "She was in the Humvee that blew up when I was in it. I was the only one who survived with all my limbs."

"And Valery?"

Jamie had to swallow the tears that were beginning to come. "She didn't make it."

"Something like that leaves a man feeling guilty, doesn't it?"

"Beyond what you can imagine."

"Actually, I believe I can," Caleb said softly, then changed tone. "When are you going to tell young Hyacinth about all this?"

"Never!" Jamie said fiercely. "Since I got back, she's the first person who hasn't looked at me with pity in her eyes. My whole family tiptoes around me. They tell the kids to be quiet, not to drop things, not to yell because Uncle Jamie is . . . is half a man." Closing his eyes, he tried to calm his temper. "But what really hurts is that I need all of it."

"How did you get here on Nantucket with Hallie?"

He took a moment to answer. "When we heard about a physical therapist inheriting this house, it seemed like a solution. It was a chance to get me away from my family. Let me have some peace. I was all for it. I even exchanged some emails with a girl I thought was Hallie. But the night before I was to leave I chickened out. I did *not* want to dump my fears and terrors on some innocent female. You saw that I can't even hear a gate slam without going into a defensive position! Who deserves that? Who—"

Jamie's hands were clenching the arms of the chair, his knuckles white. "My brother drugged me. Mom and Dad knew nothing about it. I went to sleep at home and woke up here, and I met Hallie."

At the mention of her name, he started to relax. "She's been the best thing for me. She doesn't pity me. She just thinks I'm a bit weird." He gave a little smile. "But that's okay with her. I get the idea that she's used to dealing with people who aren't exactly normal human beings."

"And you don't want to risk losing that," Caleb said. He knew a lot about being scared of losing something. Long ago he'd been afraid that if he weren't a very wealthy man, he'd lose the woman he loved. His penalty for that vanity had come down from Heaven itself. "You should tell her," he said. "Strip down to your skivvies and show her the truth."

"And watch her eyes change?" Jamie said. "I've seen that too many times. No, thank you. I like her ordering me to do her exercises. I even like her thinking I'm some rich playboy. Better that than feeling sorry for me."

Caleb shook his head. "You do know, don't you, that when women find out a man has lied to them that they are *not* amused." When he looked at Jamie, he saw that he didn't seem to be concerned. "I can tell that you have never been on the receiving end of a woman's rage over a man's prevarications— no matter how well intentioned they were."

Jamie's eyes were twinkling. "I'm not sure yet, but I think Hallie might forgive me."

Caleb laughed. "Ah, the vanity of youth. You make me glad I'm an old man." He stood up. "Come on and I'll tell you how the garden used to be. You can use the knowledge to impress your pretty girlfriend."

"She *is* pretty, isn't she? I like the shape of her. She—"

Rolling his eyes, Caleb pointed out where a row of blueberry bushes had been.

When Hallie returned, she had a bag full of muffins and cookies—and a new pair of navy-blue flats. "Sorry," she said.

"There's a beautiful clothing shop by the bakery and I had to make an emergency purchase."

Jamie, leaning on his crutches, was standing at the back door. Caleb, beside him, wondered what he'd say. Would he try to prove his masculinity by saying she shouldn't have made them wait?

"Wise decision," Jamie said solemnly. "Do you think they have them in my size?"

"If they did, they'd have to be tied to the dock." She looked at Caleb. "Where do you think the ladies served tea?"

"There," he said, pointing. "There was a pergola covered by roses."

There were only a few stones left to mark where the structure had been. Hallie pointed out the shade near the wall. "What if we bring some furniture out and have our tea there?"

"I'd like that very much," Caleb said.

"Come on," she said to Jamie, "help me set this up and maybe I'll let you try on my new shoes."

"With or without you in them?" he asked as he followed her to the house. At the doorway he paused to look back at Caleb. "See? No pity," he said and went inside.

It didn't take long to bring out three chairs, a little table, and a tray full of tea things.

"I want to hear every word of the story of the Tea Ladies," Hallie said as she poured the tea. "Although I fear that if they ended up ghosts, there isn't a happy ending."

"There is usually good in every story," Caleb said and began to tell of the two sisters who had been born less than a year apart. They had been pretty little girls, but by the time they reached sixteen, they were extraordinary. "Nantucket men traveled the world over, but all of them agreed that they'd never seen beauty to compare with that of Hyacinth and Juliana Bell."

Their mother died when the girls were quite young. Their

father—who had a store that sold tea and coffee—dedicated his life to providing for them and protecting them.

Caleb was a good storyteller and he had them laughing as he described what the men of Nantucket did to try to court the gorgeous young women, from gifts to secret visits. "See this high wall? Old man Bell put it up to try to keep the men out. But it didn't even slow us—them—down. Night and day, men and boys vaulted over the wall and fell to the ground. Doc Watson said his practice was based solely on what he called the Bell Fools. Broken ankles, arms, collarbones, twisted necks. Half the males on the island were on crutches."

Jamie and Hallie were laughing.

"What we all loved about them"—Caleb again caught himself—"I mean *they* loved is that the girls never let the attention or their own beauty go to their heads. They were kindness personified. They . . ." He had to pause to get control of himself. Hallie was right: This story did *not* have a happy ending.

He looked back at the eager young faces waiting to hear more. "They were the town's matchmakers."

"As in putting couples together?" Hallie asked.

"Yes, and they were quite brilliant at it. They were the ones who got Captain Caleb Kingsley and the lovely Valentina Montgomery to stop arguing and admit they were mad about each other." He looked at Jamie. "If they hadn't done that, your Kingsley ancestor wouldn't have been born and you wouldn't now be sitting here with this lovely young lady."

"I love them very much," Jamie said with such seriousness that he made Caleb laugh and Hallie's face turn red.

Caleb continued. "The girls invited people, young and old, to tea nearly every afternoon, and what they served was beyond delicious. It was said that they could take barnacles and bilge water and bake them into ambrosia. Between the beauty, the food, and the matchmaking, you can see why all the sailors brought back gifts for the girls." He told of their father's taboo on keeping expensive personal items, so the sailors offered gifts for the tea parties. "The girls especially liked recipes that came from all over the globe."

"That's like our teas!" Hallie said. "The B&B seems to be carrying on the tradition because Edith brings us food from everywhere."

"Does she?" Caleb said, smiling, then continued. "Over the years, the Bell sisters got to know their guests and saw who interacted well. Then they contrived ways to get prospective couples together at church, at socials, wherever they could. And they had a knack for breaking up unsuitable engagements and putting people together who actually liked each other." Caleb chuckled. "Sometimes they met with resistance, like the time they put the daughter of a tavern owner with one of the rich Coffin boys. It took a while, but his family grew to love her."

"Weren't they too young to do something like that?" Hallie asked.

"Old souls," Caleb said softly. "Sometimes when people intuitively know that they aren't to be on the earth long, they seem older than their ages. I think in this case those beautiful young ladies wanted to leave behind what they instinctively knew they were never going to have for themselves. They gave people love and families."

"I don't think I want to hear the end of this story," Hallie said.

Reaching across the little table, Jamie put his hand over hers and gave it a reassuring squeeze. "Didn't Hallie's ancestor change everything?"

"Yes, he did," Caleb said and began to describe the instant love between Juliana and Leland. "Once those two saw each other, everyone else ceased to exist."

Caleb saw the quick glance that Hallie and Jamie exchanged, as though they knew the feeling. It wasn't easy for him to suppress his smile. In his long lifetime he'd seen many people fall in love the moment they saw each other.

"Juliana and Leland got married, didn't they?" Hallie asked.

"Yes. Just six months after they met, they married."

"Was it a nice wedding?" Hallie didn't want to sound too girly around the men.

"By all accounts, it was glorious. I heard that Juliana wore a dress the color of the sky just before a storm, and her sister wore one like early dawn at sea."

"Oh," Hallie said, letting out her breath. "I'm not sure what those colors are, but I like the sound of them. Were there lots of flowers?"

"The islanders denuded half of the gardens on Nantucket. But then there were few families who didn't owe the girls something, including children who wouldn't have existed except for them. Someone called them the Princesses of Blissful Tomorrows."

"That's lovely," Hallie said. "I've always dreamed of—" She stopped herself. "Anyway, did the newlyweds have time for a happy life before . . . you know?"

"No," Caleb said flatly. "At the party after the wedding, the sisters' father collapsed. Everyone had been so preoccupied that no one had noticed he was ill." Caleb took a breath. "He had a fever that he probably caught from one of the ships that had recently returned with a cargo of tea. His daughters insisted on taking care of him, so Juliana postponed her wedding trip—and her wedding night."

When Caleb looked at the young couple, his eyes were bleak. "The girls caught the fever. Their father recovered, but they did not."

He took a moment to calm himself. "The whole island grieved. In less than a week they went from joyous celebration to deep mourning."

"And what about Leland, the bridegroom?" Hallie asked.

"He was inconsolable. His relatives came from Boston to get him and took him home. He never returned to the island. Many years later he married again and had a son, your ancestor."

The three of them sat in silence for a while, listening to the birds and the wind, the tragic story hanging over them.

Jamie broke the sadness. "You know, if I'm going to be in a haunted house, I'm glad the ghosts are two hot babes."

Hallie and Caleb couldn't help laughing.

Caleb reached into his pocket, withdrew an old key, and put it on the table. "That should open the side door."

Jamie picked up the key. "And we'll see them inside?"

"Only if you've not yet met your True Love."

"What?" Hallie asked.

"Jared didn't tell you that part?" Caleb had to feign innocence, as he well knew that Jared wouldn't have told them the old story.

"No, he didn't," Hallie and Jamie said together.

"The legend is that the Bell girls still like to match people and the only ones who can see them are ones who need their help. If the door opens, they're allowed to go into a beautiful room, and the dear young ladies will be there waiting for them."

"And if they aren't needed?"

Caleb shrugged. "Then they'll see a room that has been closed up for a very long time. Henry kept all the doors locked after he bought the house. I'm not sure he ever went in there after the first time. By now, it must be a very dusty room." There was a lot more to that story, but Caleb wasn't going to tell it, at least not now.

Jamie gave a little snort. "Wait a minute! If Edith can see them, does that mean she's looking for her True Love? Isn't she a little, you know, past that?"

Caleb didn't smile. "Are you asking if she's too *old* to find love?" His voice was louder and deeper.

"I'm just trying to put some reality into this fairy tale, that's all." Jamie's voice was also rising.

Hallie glared at him. "If you get into a fight and hurt your knee, I swear I will cut your clothes off *before* I call an ambulance." She turned back to Dr. Huntley. "So why wouldn't the door open for *me*? I know Jamie has someone, but I don't."

"Who do I have?" Jamie asked quickly, but when Hallie gave him a look, he said, "Oh, yeah."

"You'll have to figure that out on your own." Caleb looked at his watch. "I'm afraid I have to go. My lovely wife is waiting for me." He stood up. "Perhaps you two could come to dinner some night." A look at Jamie's frown stopped him. "But with the coming commotion of the wedding, it might be too much."

Jamie and Hallie walked with Dr. Huntley to the front gate and watched him go to the end of the lane. When he was out of sight, they looked at each other.

Hallie had the key in her hand. "So now what do we do?"

"We go see a dirty old room that has been locked up for who knows how long?" Jamie said.

"If we see it as dusty, that means you and I have already met our True Loves."

"No," he said. "It means that the place hasn't been cleaned."

"But Edith—"

"Obviously has a key," he said. "The next time I see her I'm going to put her in a stranglehold and make her talk."

"You do that and she might stop stealing Betty's food and delivering it to us," Hallie said.

"Good point. So? You ready to open the door?"

"Maybe we should wait until the morning when the light is better and we can—" She broke off when Jamie started toward the side of the house. He was getting quite fast on his crutches! By the time she got there, he was standing in front of the double doors.

"You want to open it or do you want me to do it?" he asked.

Hallie held the key on her outstretched palm. "What happens if we open the door and two beautiful ghosts are standing there?"

"We'll say hello." Jamie took the key and put it in the lock. It turned easily. "Ready?" When she nodded, he turned the knob.

Inside was a room covered in dust and cobwebs, with dried leaves on the dirty floor. But no ghosts.

"See?" Jamie said and she knew he was laughing at her.

"I guess this means I've met the love of my life." She began to walk around. It was a large room and although everything was thickly coated in gray, she could see that under it was beauty. In a corner was a seating area with a little couch and some chairs. Two tables were by the dirty windows. Against one wall was a huge old-fashioned Welsh dresser heavily laden with china. She picked up a plate and wiped her hand through the dirt. "Look. This is the pattern of the dishes we've been eating off of."

"If Edith has a key, based on her actions at the B&B, she probably 'borrowed' some." He was at a door in the corner. "Wonder where this leads?"

Hallie went to him as he opened it. Inside was a big pantry, with floor-to-ceiling shelves—and they were packed with objects. There was a window, but little light could get through the dirt.

"What is all this stuff?" Hallie asked.

Jamie swung past her to a door at the far end and opened it to see into the kitchen. "Now, that's weird. This door has a lock on this side but not on that one."

"You don't think ghosts are strange, but a door that locks on only one side is?"

"So far I haven't seen any proof of ghosts." In the kitchen, he got a flashlight out of a drawer, then returned to shine it on the shelves in the pantry. Before them was cooking paraphernalia that seemed to cover the centuries. A rusty cast-iron waffle grill was next to a hand eggbeater from the 1950s. There was a pile of blackened copper molds connected by thick cobwebs. Boxes of products, ranging from elixirs to Swans Down Cake Flour, filled two shelves. Bottles, vials, containers made of marble, pewter, glass, and unidentifiable substances were fit into every space.

"I feel like I'm looking at a sunken ship." She tried to take a breath but they'd stirred up enough dust that she started coughing.

"Come on, let's get out of here." They went into the kitchen and closed the door behind them. "Are you all right?" he asked.

"Sure, but it is a bit depressing, isn't it? Whether there are ghosts or not, Henry Bell closed off part of his house and didn't go in it. And all those things in there! Do you think they were given to those poor women who died so long ago? By people who saw the room as clean?" Her head came up. "Did the Tea Ladies put them away? In hope for a future they were never going to have?"

"Let's go outside and I'll tell you what Dr. Huntley told me about the garden."

She knew he was trying to take her mind off the tragic story and she was glad of it. The truth was that she'd been surrounded by so much death in her life that the merest mention of it took her back there. When her father and Ruby died in a car crash, Shelly had fallen apart. She was just a teenager then, so most of the responsibilities had landed on Hallie's shoulders. Choosing burial clothes and caskets—all of it had been left to Hallie.

Once they were outside, Jamie stopped and looked at her. He didn't have to be told what was in her mind. He let his crutches fall to the ground, then pulled her into his arms. "It's okay to grieve," he said softly. "They all deserve it, but don't get it mixed up with here and now."

Hallie held on to him, her cheek against his heart. It was good to feel the comfort. She would have stayed that way if he hadn't broken them apart.

"Come on," he said, "let's go to the gym and work up a sweat. It'll make you feel better."

Hallie groaned. "Why did I get stuck with a jock? I'm more of a reader. Why don't we check the Internet to find out about the Tea Ladies? We could—"

"I'll fix that," he said as he picked up his crutches, leaned on them, and began to tap his phone. He was fast and he showed Hallie the message he was sending to his mother: THIS HOUSE IS BELIEVED TO BE HAUNTED BY TWO BEAUTIFUL YOUNG WOMEN. THEY FIND PEOPLE'S TRUE LOVES. CAN YOU TELL US ANYTHING ABOUT THEM? YOUR LOVING SON, JAMES.

"That should do it," Jamie said. "Mom will call some of her friends and the lot of them will be up all night searching. The minute she has anything, she'll send us everything there is to know about your ghosts."

Hallie smiled. "Curious, is she?"

"Insatiable. Now can we work out? My knee is aching."

A look of alarm ran across Hallie's face but then stopped. "If I worked on your whole body, you'd be more balanced. You certainly wouldn't be slumping to one side and causing yourself pain, as you are now."

"I do not slump!"

"Yes, you do. You move like this." She did an exaggerated walk with the left side of her six inches lower than the right. "If you'd let me, I could straighten that out."

Jamie was frowning. "Do it again. I like the view from the back."

"You!" Hallie said but then laughed. "Come on and I'll work on your leg."

Grinning, he followed her to the gym.

Chapter Seven

"Are you going to take the case?" Mrs. Westbrook asked her son, Braden. Her tone was impatient, annoyed even. But then her ambitious, hardworking son looked like he was auditioning for the role of a hobo in a 1930s movie. He was stretched out on the couch, eating potato chips and watching endless reruns of *Charmed*. He hadn't shaved in days. Actually, he hadn't even taken a shower in the week he'd been home.

"I don't know," he mumbled. "I hate family law. All those tears and hurt feelings."

She made herself count to ten. "It's for Hallie. She needs help. Her stepsister did yet another lowdown rotten thing to her, but this time she doesn't just need a shoulder to cry on. She needs *legal* help."

"Hallie would never go to court, so some first-year student can draw up the papers. She doesn't need someone who's almost a partner to do it." He gave a little snort. "Or Hallie could grow a pair and tell Shelly to get out."

Mrs. Westbrook didn't know when in her entire life such anger had run through her. She went to stand before him, looking down as she snatched the bag of chips out of his hands. "You may talk like that in the big city but not here and not to *me*. Do I make myself clear?"

Braden sat up straight on the couch and turned off the TV. "Sorry, Mom. Really, I am. I know I've been a burden to you this last week, but—"

She held up her hand to stop him. "I understand why you're wallowing in self-pity. Your girlfriend dumped you."

"Zara was more than a girlfriend. She was—"

"The girl who wouldn't commit to *you*." Mrs. Westbrook threw up her hands. "Braden, you are the smartest person I've ever met, but sometimes I wonder if you have any sense at all."

"Mom!" he said, sounding hurt.

She sat down on the edge of the sofa. "My dear son, Zara is a two-faced lying snake. The one and only time you ever brought her home I saw her flirting with the Wilsons' oldest boy."

"Tommy? I hardly think Zara would go for someone like him."

"If you ever bothered to look past her shapeless, skinny body, you'd have seen that young Tommy has grown into a real stud."

"Mom!" He was genuinely shocked.

She lowered her voice. "Braden, my dear child, if you want actual *love,* why don't you look around you? Maybe somewhere closer to home?"

He let his head fall back against the couch cushion. "Not Hallie. Please tell me you aren't going to start that *again*! Hallie is a nice girl. A hard worker. She has a high pain tolerance to stand that family of hers. I'm sure she's going to make some man a wonderful wife and produce a bunch of kids who will walk all over her."

"Better that than a wife who will walk all over *you*!" his mother said and started to get up, but he caught her arm.

"Mom, I'm sorry. I apologize for this." He motioned to the mess of empty bags around him. But he also meant his inability to make himself return to the office where he'd have to see the woman he loved with one of the partners. He'd heard that she was now wearing a five-carat engagement ring.

"I know you love Hallie," he said. "She's been the daughter you never had, and maybe that's the problem. She's like a sister to me."

His mother narrowed her eyes at him. "Is that so? Yesterday when Shelly was outside wearing less fabric than it takes to make a handkerchief, that was the only time you got off the couch in a week. Is *she* also your sister?"

"Mom, please be reasonable. Shelly is so hot she stops traffic."

"Hallie is a very pretty girl, but more than that, she has a *heart*. She cares about people."

"Yes, she does." He gave a little smile. "I just wish I could put Hallie's heart in Shelly's body."

His mother did not return his smile. "I'll tell you what you're going to do—and I'm not asking for this. You are going to get up, shower and shave, then you're going to negotiate, mediate, take it to the courtroom, whatever you have to do, to solve this for Hallie."

Braden opened his mouth to protest, but his mother kept talking.

"And furthermore, you're not going to charge her a penny for any of it."

He was looking at his mother's face. It was the one she wore after she had repeatedly told him to pick up his toys and he still hadn't done it. He didn't know what would happen if he defied that look because he'd never dared to do it. "Yes" was all he managed to say.

She gave a curt nod and got up. "I got your father's brand of shampoo. Don't use that fancy stuff of yours. It's going to take work to get you clean." She went into the kitchen.

Rolling his eyes, Braden got off the couch and headed upstairs to the bathroom, all the while muttering, "Damn it, Hallie!" He dreaded the way she looked at him, with adoring eyes that begged him to say even one kind word to her. And his mother's insinuation that he didn't look out for Hallie was totally unfair! For all Hallie's life, he'd looked after her.

As he turned on the water, he couldn't help smiling at the image of Shelly in her bikini. Yesterday half the neighborhood had turned out to see her bending over the flowers. Braden wasn't sure what had happened this time between the stepsisters but he had no doubt that it was Shelly's fault. She'd always been a conniving little brat, always planning something devious, usually with poor Hallie on the receiving end.

The day he'd arrived home after Zara had—as his mother so inelegantly put it—"dumped" him, he'd guessed that Shelly was up to no good. She'd been in the kitchen with his mother, sweet-talking her into lending Shelly a tea set and asking where she could buy some bakery items. It seemed that she had an important guest coming.

At the time, Braden had been too miserable to show himself, but even through his deep unhappiness, he'd realized that something was amiss. For one thing, Shelly seemed to think men were put on the earth to do things for her, not the other way around. So why was she going to so much trouble for this one? When she told his mother the man's name, only Braden had heard of the famous architect. Why in the world was that man visiting Shelly? he wondered.

The last thing Braden wanted to do was get involved in whatever Shelly was up to, but he did think that Hallie should know what was going on. On the day the man was supposed to show up, Braden was rolling the garbage can to the curb when he saw Hallie rushing in and out of the house and putting things in the open trunk of her car. Maybe he shouldn't have interfered, but he did. He walked across the road, meaning to warn her but dreading it. Instead, on impulse, he pulled an important-looking envelope out of her tote bag and slipped it behind the storm door. When Hallie got to where she was going and found it missing, maybe she'd have to return to get it. And maybe she'd find out what Shelly was up to.

When Braden got out of the shower, he thought that, first, he should go over and visit Shelly. He'd hear her side of whatever it was that happened—but he dreaded all the drama. If Shelly didn't look the way she did, no one would put up with her. On the other hand, he couldn't help thinking of what Zara would say if he showed up at the office with a girl who looked like Shelly. When she was in heels, wouldn't she be about six feet? Nice heels, and a suit. Maybe something in Chanel.

The more he thought about the idea, the more he liked it. If whatever Shelly had done this time could possibly get her put in jail, she'd owe Braden for keeping her out.

Two birds with one stone, he thought as he began to shave. Or was this I scratch your back, you scratch mine? Whatever it was, he looked forward to Zara's face when she saw Shelly on his arm.

When Hallie awoke, she looked at the clock. It was five minutes before two A.M. Time for Jamie's nightly demon wrestling. As she got out of bed, she thought that when she had children she'd be prepared for sleepless nights.

She'd put his nightlight in the bathroom so at least she could see him. Right on time, he began to thrash. She put her hands on his shoulders, but she wasn't strong enough to hold him in place. Thinking of what they'd been told about the ghosts, maybe the name of his True Love would calm him down. Maybe his nightmares were because he missed her. But when she said the name "Valery," Jamie's rolling got worse. He began moaning, then threw his hands up as though to shield his face.

"It's me, Hallie," she said loudly. "Remember? Hallie and Nantucket and working on your leg. And Todd. Don't forget him."

Her words seemed to calm him, as he stopped thrashing, but he was still tense. Leaning over him, she smoothed his hair back from his forehead. "You're safe now," she whispered. "Go back to sleep."

When he'd settled, she started to step away, but his hand grabbed her bare leg. "Oh, no, you don't," she said, but then smiled. It looked like he wasn't going to release her without his goodnight kiss.

She took his face in her hands and kissed him. When it started to deepen and he began pulling her into bed with him, she stepped back and looked at him. With every minute of every day she liked him more—and she knew it wouldn't take much for her to fall in love with him. But then what? When his leg healed would he go jetting off with a girl who looked like Shelly? Tall, gorgeous rich boys who spent their lives going from one pleasure to another didn't commit to short, pudgy physical therapists. They had flings, then left.

No, Hallie thought. She'd already given her heart to a man who couldn't seem to see her as anything other than the kid across the street.

Jamie was sleeping, so she could go back to her own bed. As she walked through the dark house, she considered the idea that the ghosts hadn't appeared to her because she'd already met her True Love. She thought of Braden, of being around him as she was growing up. He was six years older than she and she'd adored him from afar. He'd always been . . . well, spectacular. A star athlete, top grades, king of the high school prom. He got into Harvard on a partial scholarship, made great grades, and was hired by a top law firm. A true Golden Boy.

As Hallie got into bed, she thought of Braden as the man she most wanted—a sentiment encouraged by his mother. But she knew he had never seen her as anything but the kid who was always hanging around his house.

Hallie saw him as smart and kind. Sometimes he'd come home from sports practice and she'd be in the kitchen with his mother, eating cookies, her eyes red from crying. "So what'd she do to you *this* time?" he'd ask as he grabbed a handful of cookies to take to his room. He knew that Shelly was *always* the cause of Hallie's unhappiness.

"Crashed my computer," Hallie would say. Or, "Spent the money I was saving." Or the most common one, "I can't go so and so place because I have to help Shelly with something." Braden—who had always known he wanted to be a lawyer—would say something like, "You want me to draw up a contract and send her off to work for the Snow Queen?"

His questions and his funny "punishments" always drew her out of her misery. Over the years they'd worked to come up with things they could do to Shelly.

"I'll have her put into the body of an avatar," he said once.

"She'd never get used to being that short," Hallie shot back.

Braden had laughed, as avatars were over eleven feet tall.

If Hallie had possibly already met her True Love, she was sure that had to be Braden.

⁓

The next morning, her cell phone ringing woke Hallie. Sleepily, she answered it to hear Jared's voice. "I'm sorry for calling so early, but I'm catching a plane out of the country." Quickly, he told her that her friend Braden was going to handle the case.

"Braden agreed?" Hallie asked, then she sat up, listened, and asked a few more questions.

Jamie came clumping into the room and stood at the foot of the bed.

"Sure," Hallie said. "I'll be here. You don't have a car I could borrow, do you? I need to run some errands, and where do I buy cleaning supplies?" She listened in silence for several minutes. "Okay. Thank you very much! And I hope you have a great flight." She clicked off and looked at Jamie.

"My friend Braden is going to handle everything with my stepsister. He wants to draw up some papers so it's made clear to Shelly who owns what. And Braden is going to fix it so she never again hassles me for money." Hallie let out her breath. "For me, it's going to be a sort of Declaration of Independence."

Jamie sat down on the side of the bed. "And this Braden guy gets to be the hero. So how does he look in that big, flowing cape?"

"Braden looks good in anything." She threw back the covers and got out of bed. "And Jared said I could use the car of a man named Toby." Hallie went to the bathroom and shut the door. When she came out, Jamie was stretched out on her bed, hands behind his head, and staring up at the ceiling.

"Toby is a girl and she's going to marry my cousin Graydon," he said.

"Are you invited to the wedding?" Hallie asked as she grabbed a pair of jeans.

"No, but Aunt Jilly is. It's in another country, but my uncle Mike rigged up some TVs so the wedding can be streamed in live. I could get him to connect it here if you want to see it. I think it's going to be a fairly big wedding."

"That would be nice," Hallie said. She stepped behind the bathroom door to put on underwear, the jeans, and a T-shirt, then went back into the bedroom. "You want to get up so I can make the bed?"

"No," Jamie said, still looking up. "Tell me more about this guy Braden. Can you trust him?"

"Absolutely. He knows Shelly and the things she's done over the years, so that's an advantage to me. He won't be falling for her like you and all the other men in the world do."

"What?!" Jamie sat up on the bed. "How did I become the villain in this? I've never even met your stepsister."

"No, but you keep her photos in your date book. Why? So you can drool over them?" Hallie said before she thought, then added quickly, "None of that matters. I need to get the car so I can go to a store called Marine Home. I have a lot of things to get."

When Jamie got off the bed, he grabbed his crutches so fast he nearly fell, but he managed to head Hallie off before she reached the stairs. "You can't accuse me of something, then walk out before I can defend myself."

"You'd only need a defense if you were being attacked—which you're not. All men make fools of themselves over Shelly." Hallie stopped trying to get around him and glared. "Why aren't you in the gym trying to put even more muscle on your body?"

"I slept well and late," he said. "And now I'm being falsely accused of some crime I didn't commit. Yes, I exchanged emails with your stepsister, but I thought she was *you*."

"And you have some gorgeous photos of her. Great. Now please move so I can leave. I have a lot of work to do today."

"On me? My leg is doing well, aches some, but I know you can fix that." He gave her a suggestive little smile.

She glared at him. "For your information, there is more in my life than just *you*. In a few days, my friend Braden Westbrook is going to come here and I want this place to look good. I'm going to buy a lot of cleaning supplies, then return here and scrub the tea room. Braden isn't the type of man to like anything as filthy as that place is. Now, are you satisfied, and can I go?"

Jamie didn't move. "You're going to do all this for *him*? By yourself?"

"Yes." She looked at him hard—and could swear there was jealousy in his eyes. "I'd ask you to go with me, but you won't leave the grounds, so I guess the entire project is mine alone." She turned sideways to get past him and started down the stairs.

"I'll go with you," he said.

Hallie paused halfway down the stairs but didn't look back. "You'll drive?"

"Don't push it," he said.

Smiling, she continued down the stairs.

In the store, Hallie concentrated on what she needed to get the cleaning done, and did her best to ignore Jamie's nervousness.

Before they left, she'd made a list. When she was ready to go, she fully expected Jamie to chicken out. In fact, he seemed to be sweating at the prospect of going. But she said, "Don't let me forget to call Braden's mother and get her recipe for oatmeal raisin cookies. They're his favorite."

That comment seemed to strengthen Jamie's resolve so much that he went with her across Kingsley Lane to Jared's big house. He waited outside while she got the car keys, then they walked down the lane to a small house to get the car. On the drive, he grasped the armrest at the two roundabouts, but he did well.

By the time they got to the store, Hallie was thinking, James Michael Taggert, what in the world *happened* to you?!

The cleaning supplies were in a far corner and as soon as they were away from other people and the open space, Jamie calmed considerably and they filled the big cart to the brim. On the way to the register, they bought a vacuum cleaner and many dust bags for it.

When Jamie insisted on paying for it all, Hallie protested. "Let me win *something* over Braden the Magnificent," he mumbled as he handed over his credit card.

By the time they left, Hallie was dizzy with hunger and she pulled into the parking lot of a restaurant called Downyflake. Jamie almost refused to go in, and when he did, he wouldn't sit at a table near a window. He took one in a closed corner.

They had thick tuna melt sandwiches and Jamie ordered a dozen doughnuts to go. On the way to the car, he offered her one. "Braden doesn't like fat women," Hallie said.

"You're not fat," Jamie said, "and any man who doesn't like the look of you doesn't like *women.*"

"You're sweet." She was smiling, but then said, "Oh, no! How do I get out of here?" Two pickup trucks were on either side of the borrowed car, both parked at an angle. There was little space on the driver's side for her to get in the door. "We'll have to wait for one of them to move."

"Give me the keys," Jamie said as he handed her his crutches. He hopped his way between the car and a pickup, opened the door as wide as possible, and managed to wedge his big body inside.

Hallie stepped back as he deftly maneuvered the car out. She tossed his crutches in the back, then got in the passenger seat. "Do you remember the way home?"

"I do," he said, but when he reached the road, he turned right instead of left.

"Where are you going?"

"Actually, it feels good to drive. Do you mind?"

"Not at all," she said and leaned back in the seat. There was a map of Nantucket in the glove box so she was able to tell him where to turn as they spent the morning exploring the island. Jamie had to drive using his left leg, but he did it with ease.

On the way back, they stopped at Bartlett's Farm to load up

on groceries. Jamie didn't want to go in, but when Hallie said she couldn't remember Braden's favorite cheese, he went with her.

"You're doing this on purpose, aren't you?" he said.

"Oh, yeah. Next time we're going there." She nodded to the huge nursery full of plants.

"Let me guess, Braden loves flowers. Do they have any to match his superhero cape?"

"I was thinking more of matching his eyes." She laughed at Jamie's grimace. She'd never had a jealous boyfriend before and she was enjoying it. Not that Jamie was her boyfriend, of course, but whatever he was, she was liking this teasing.

When they got back to the house, the kitchen table was covered with one of Edith's glorious teas, this one all sweets. On the bottom plate of the tiered stack were little coconut tarts with tiny wild strawberries on top and three-inch apple pies with cheese oozing from the crust. On the top were squares of gingerbread with bits of apples and grapes sticking out.

"I bet she heard how her daughter-in-law has been bothering us and this is her apology," Hallie said.

"Whatever the reason, I love the woman. I'm starving. Try this." He held out a mini cupcake with bits of red, ripe cherries on top.

Hallie turned away. "I think I'll just have a salad."

Jamie groaned. "Not the caped crusader again! Did you know that you've lost weight since you got here?"

"That's ridiculous. Edith's pastries are nothing but calories."

"So what's this?" He stuck his finger into the waistband of her jeans and pinched a couple of inches of empty space.

The truth was that her clothes were a bit loose on her. She'd thought she wasn't drinking enough water, but maybe that wasn't it.

"Look, Hartley," Jamie said, "between two workouts a day and all the energy you expend digging into me, you're using more calories than you take in. And when you consider the work we're going to do this afternoon—"

"I'm sold," Hallie said as she took the chocolate cupcake and ate it in one bite. "Divine." She sat down and began to pour the tea.

As always, they ate it all. After they washed the dishes, they made a little drama of beginning the project and went outside to the double doors that led into the old tea room.

"Maybe your ghosts cleaned it up during the night," Jamie said, but it was exactly as they'd left it. In fact, the light was brighter so the place looked worse. Cobwebs, grime as thick as shoe leather, the air gloomy with floating dust.

"Okay," Hallie said, "I think we should take everything washable outside and start hosing it down. What's left inside, we'll vacuum, then hand dust."

"Good plan," Jamie said and after they'd hauled the supplies from the car, they began. They put on white cup masks and opened all the windows and doors. Hallie began taking load after load of dishes into the kitchen to wash them, while Jamie tackled the pantry.

At first they worked in silence, but gradually they began to talk. Jamie asked her a lot of questions about her life. As she had earlier, she talked only about before her father married Ruby.

"I don't understand something," he said as he raised his mask. "If your dad was gone most of the time and you just said that a lot of his work was in Florida, when your grandparents left, why didn't you go with them? Why did you stay with your stepmother, who you hardly even knew?"

"I wanted to go with them and my grandparents begged Dad to let me go, but Ruby said Shelly needed her big sister. Dad was still crazy about Ruby then, so he agreed and said I couldn't leave." She gave a little laugh. "Sometimes I felt like I was being used for body parts. My function in life became to 'help Shelly.' Helping my stepsister took precedence over school-work, my social life, et cetera." When she looked at him, she saw the concern on his face. "Feel sorry for me now?"

"I don't believe in pity," he said. "I don't take it and I don't give it out."

"Good philosophy," she said. "Sometimes you just have to accept what is and live with it."

"I agree completely," he said and they smiled at each other.

Chapter Eight

At six o'clock Hallie had an unpleasant run-in with one of the many spiders in the room and Jamie gallantly saved her life—or at least that's the way he described it. When he said he had earned a hero cape, she laughed.

They were both dirty and tired, but a half day's work had made a big dent in cleaning the place. When they went through the pantry to the sparkling clean, well-lit kitchen and looked at the dirt on each other, they laughed.

"We should go upstairs, take showers, put on clean clothes, then come back down here and have a civilized dinner," Hallie said.

"What are you? A Montgomery?" Jamie said as he went to the kitchen sink, pushed up his sleeves, and began to lather his hands and face.

"You're going to have to explain to me about your relatives

so I can understand these comments." Hallie went to the other side of the big sink and took the soap from him. For all that she wanted some part of her to be clean, her job was always in her mind. She hadn't seen his bare forearms before and she couldn't help sneaking glances at them. There was a long scar running up his left arm and three small ones crossing his right wrist.

When he saw her looking, he turned away and grabbed a towel.

"Montgomerys," he said, as though the little incident hadn't happened, "were born with a salad fork in their hands." He pulled a container of chicken out of the fridge. "At home they use real napkins that somebody has washed and even ironed."

"They sound like monsters," Hallie said without a smile.

"They're too delicate for that. Mom said the two families are Beauty and the Beast. Guess who is who?"

Jamie's hands and face were clean, but his hair and neck were coated with sweat-drenched dirt, and his heavy clothing was filthy.

"I don't know," she said as she frowned in decision, "you're kind of pretty."

Laughing, Jamie bent over and kissed her neck. "You're—" He stopped because he was sputtering. "I think I got a mouthful of cobwebs."

"That'll teach you," she said as she ran a towel over her neck. "Are you going to share some of that chicken?"

After they ate, Todd called and as always, Jamie sought privacy to talk to him. But as he walked away, Hallie heard him say that he'd driven a car. "Yeah, Hallie did it," Jamie added.

Smiling and feeling like all her late nights of studying were paying off, she cleaned up the kitchen.

Later, after a long, hot shower, Hallie turned in early and, as was becoming her habit, she awoke at two A.M. For a moment she thought Jamie was going to forgo his nightly terrors, but at the first groan, she was by his side. She was beginning to develop a routine for calming him. Telling him he was safe and saying her name and Todd's helped. But most of all, sleeping kisses settled him.

Within minutes he'd calmed down, turned on his side, and began to sleep peacefully.

She started back to her own room, but instead she paused to stroke his clean hair. "Tell me what happened to you," she said softly. "Tell me what you went through that did this to you." But there was only silence from him, and she went back to bed.

When she awoke the next morning Jamie was already at work. She dressed and went to the kitchen, where a beautiful breakfast of cheese, pastries, and hard-boiled eggs was on the table. It looked like Edith had been there early.

She opened the door into the pantry, but that was a mistake. Dust filled the air. Coughing, she waved her hand about. "How long have you been at this?" she asked Jamie, who had his arms full of animal-shaped pewter molds.

"I started before daylight," he said. "About four, I guess."

She was about to express astonishment but saw the twinkle in his eyes. "Got here ten minutes ago, did you?" she said, laughing.

"More like eight. Did you eat?"

"Just starting. Come on, the tea is hot."

After they'd eaten, they went back to cleaning. What they found in the pantry was fascinating. Items were three rows deep and they seemed to cover all the years since the young women had died. There were iron pots and wooden implements in the back, and what looked to be Victorian gadgets in the middle. In the front was cookware from after World War II. There were even a few ration cards.

"I guess we should contact the Whaling Museum and get someone to come look at these things." Before them, spread out on the sheets they'd put on the grass, were a lot of the artifacts they'd cleaned, many of which they had no idea what they were. "Or maybe we should call Dr. Huntley at the NHS."

"Are you sure?" Jamie asked. "Didn't he say the sailors brought the Tea Ladies gifts? If that's true, then all of this belongs to them."

"You think we should put it all back in there, don't you?"

"It's an option," Jamie said.

She was watching him. "You pretend that you don't believe in them, but you do think they exist as ghosts, don't you?"

"I'd like to think there is more than just the finality of death, yes." When he looked at her, there was something in his eyes, an emptiness, a hollow place that ran through them. It was there and gone in an instant.

He knows about death, has felt it, she thought. But in the next second Jamie gave his devil-may-care grin and he was back to being the guy who jetted around the world from one party to the next.

"What's made you—?" she began, but he cut her off.

"You ready to hit it again?" he asked.

Obviously, he didn't want to talk about anything serious. "Shall we take on the last layer of the pantry?" She looked him up and down. The heavy sweatsuit he had on was covered in dirt and drying sweat. "If I can stand the smell of you, that is."

Jamie looked down at himself. "You're right. I'll be back in a few minutes." She watched him disappear into the house, then sat on the grass and began to clean some more of the old kitchen items. There were half a dozen pretty white ceramic molds that she thought were for ice cream. They had designs of fruit and flowers on the bottom. She dunked one into a bucket of warm, soapy water and began to wash it.

She wondered if her ancestor Leland Hartley had touched the molds. Had he eaten ice cream made from them? The

thought led her to that wedding day long ago, when two beautiful young women had caught a fever and died within a week.

What were they like? she wondered. Did they have dreams
for the future? Were Juliana and Leland planning on living on
Nantucket? Or were they going to his home in Boston? If they
were leaving, what about Hyacinth? Was she going too?

No, Hallie thought, Hyacinth would stay with their father—
which would make the wedding day sad as well as happy.

Hallie was so absorbed in her thoughts that she didn't hear
Jamie approach.

"Better?" he asked from a few feet away.

Smiling, she looked up at him, but her face froze. He had
changed clothes. He was still covered, but he had on a thin outfit meant for jogging. The long-sleeved shirt fit him snugly—and
showed off muscles that curved over his body. He also wore
pants loose enough to go over his brace but tight enough to
show off his heavy leg muscles. Superman would envy his body.

When she looked up at his face, she saw his smug expression. He certainly knew how good he looked!

Hallie made herself turn away long enough to recover from
her awe, then put her professional face back on. "You'll be
cooler in that," she said seriously. "Ready to go back to work?"

Jamie's smirk turned into a frown as he stepped back. "Yeah,
sure." Looking a bit disappointed, he went into the house.

Hallie got up to follow him, but when she stood up, she
found her knees were weak, and her skin was overheating. She
leaned against the side of the building and tried to calm herself.
Jamie Taggert looked like every movie star and professional
athlete she'd ever been awed by, ever giggled about. His beautiful face was over a body that made her ache to touch him. She
could feel her lips on those abs!

Jamie looked out the door to see her leaning against the
building. "If you're too tired to do this, I can finish by myself."

"No, no," she said as she pushed away from the wall. "What should we do next?"

"You could climb on the stepladder and hand down things from the top shelf."

"Sure," Hallie said and he went back inside. She took a step toward the door, but then she saw the new hose and hand sprayer they'd just bought. She picked it up and sprayed herself in the face with ice-cold water. The way she felt, she could have dived into a glacial pool and turned it into a hot spring.

"Come on, Hartley," he yelled from inside, and she went back into the house.

∞

When Jamie's phone vibrated, he took it out of his pocket and looked at the text message. I HAVE INFO, Todd had written.

He glanced at Hallie. She was sitting on the floor washing the legs of the tea tables. When he told her he needed to call his brother, she didn't look up, just waved her hand.

Once he was outside, he called. "What have you found out?"

"I may lose my job because I took time off to go to Boston and do some investigating for you."

"Who did you talk to?" Jamie asked.

"What happened to 'Thanks, Todd, you're the best brother anyone's ever had'?"

"Give me grief later. Right now I need to get back to Hallie."

"Is that need or want?" When Jamie was silent, Todd knew he'd pushed his brother far enough. "I talked to Braden West-brook's mother. The woman is a fount of information. Has Hallie told you what her stepsister did?"

"No," Jamie said. "I've tried to pry it out of her, but she wouldn't give me the details."

"That's surprising. You'd think that being around someone

like you, who is so open and sharing, who keeps *no* secrets from her, she'd blab her guts out."

"Get off it!" Jamie said. "I keep secrets for a reason. Tell me what you found out."

"As you know, Jared was the executor of Henry Bell's will and he overnighted the info to Hallie. But it seems that her stepsister, Shelly, opened the package, then began an elaborate scam to steal Hallie's identity. She even sent a copy of Hallie's passport to Jared but put her own photo on it. It was only by chance that Hallie came home early and found out what was going on. So now Jared is determined to help her out."

Jamie took a moment to catch his breath. "Her stepsister faked a passport?! Isn't that a federal offense?"

"Yeah, but Mrs. Westbrook said Hallie would never press charges. She's too nice a person." Todd paused. "I talked to half a dozen people on that road and no one had a bad word to say against your Hallie, but they certainly had plenty to say about her stepmother."

"You mean Ruby?"

"Yes. There were a lot of complaints about unmowed grass and loud parties. The neighbors said that Hallie used to come home from college on weekends to do yard work. And after Ruby and Hallie's father died . . ." Todd trailed off.

"What happened?" Jamie asked.

"Hallie quit college to take care of her stepsister. From what I was told, that first year was hell for everyone on the street— and they all agreed that the hell was caused by a teenage Shelly. I checked out the police reports and after the parents' deaths, neighbors called 911 six times because of all-night parties. Some of them involved gangs on motorcycles. There were a lot of warnings issued before the noise finally stopped."

"Poor Hallie," Jamie said.

"She's not told you any of this?"

"Some, but not much," Jamie said. "She mostly talks about her grandparents and how happy her life had been with them."

"You're with her twenty-four-seven and I've never heard you speak about any other woman the way you talk about her, but you know practically nothing about her. What are you *doing* with your time together?"

"Looking into some ghost story, and lately we've been cleaning." Jamie wanted to get back to the subject. "What did you find out about this Braden character?"

"You're *cleaning*?" Todd said in disbelief. "And ghosts? This is how you are courting this woman?"

"No one said anything about 'courting.'"

It was Todd's turn to be silent.

"All right! So I like her. I like her a *lot*! She's funny and smart and caring and—"

"And not bad to look at," Todd said.

"That too. Is this Braden coming here?"

"Yeah," Todd said, "he is. I'm not sure when, but in a few days. His mother had some very interesting things to tell me about her son."

"Such as?"

"That he just broke up with his latest girlfriend. She said this is the third one who's left him because Braden only goes after the unattainable."

"What does that mean?"

"Seems he pursues the girls in the highest heels, the ones who are clawing their way to the top. They use Braden, then leave heel dents on him when they climb up and over him."

"Good," Jamie said.

"I know what you're thinking, that if that's what he likes, he'll stay away from your Hallie. Want to hear the best news?" Todd didn't wait for an answer. "Mrs. Westbrook has been trying to get her son and dear, sweet Hallie together since they were kids."

"He's too old for her!" Jamie said.

"Not according to his mother. She thinks Hallie would make him a great wife and give her half a dozen grandkids. So what does your Hallie think of him?"

"I don't know," Jamie said softly.

"What was that? I couldn't hear you."

"I don't know what she thinks of him!" Jamie half shouted, then calmed. "All I know for sure is that Hallie calls him her friend and she wants the place spotless before he arrives."

Todd drew in his breath. "You're helping her clean up the house for her boyfriend?"

"He's not—" Jamie closed his eyes for a moment. "Besides being stupid about women, what else is this guy like?"

"Squeaky clean. Not so much as a parking ticket. Dad knows someone at the law firm where he works, so I—"

"You told Dad?! Please say you didn't tell Mom too."

"Sure I did. In fact, Mom's decided that her next book is going to be about a physical therapist who—"

"Spare me," Jamie said. "What did Dad say?"

"Braden Westbrook is soon to be made a partner in the law firm. The guy is a hard worker and as honest as a lawyer can be. Those rapacious women he goes after seem to be his only flaw. But his mother thinks that the way he was treated by this last one is going to make him change his ways. I don't know about that, but the day I was there, he was in Boston buying himself new clothes to wear on Nantucket. How are you doing in your sweats?"

Jamie didn't answer the question. "What's he look like?"

"A blond Montgomery."

"That's good," Jamie said. "Skinny, no muscles, washed out, bland."

"You keep telling yourself that. This guy looks great and has a good job. Just out of curiosity, have you told Hallie how much you like her?"

"Not yet," Jamie said. "It's too early and I need more time to work things out."

"I agree," Todd said. "Take all the time you need. I'm sure there are thousands of unselfish, funny, smart, beautiful girls like Hallie out there. And I bet that when the family starts arriving not one of the cousins is going to hit on her. What are Adam and Ian up to now? Or does she like bulk? Raine should fill that need. And what happens when Westbrook asks Hallie out to dinner and a moonlight walk on the beach? Is she going to want to stay home with you and clean things? Or talk about ghosts?"

"You're a real bastard, you know that?" Jamie said in anger.

"Just trying to get you to leave the past behind," Todd replied with an equal amount of anger. "You have a chance and I don't want you to blow it. If I found my Hallie, I'd go after her with everything I had."

"Yeah, well, there are extenuating circumstances. I—"

"Heard it all before," Todd said. "The way I see it, you have just days to make her look at you as something other than her cleaning partner. I'll call you tomorrow. No! You call me when you've done something about all this. Otherwise, don't bother." He hung up.

Jamie was angry after his brother's call, but when he got back to the house and saw Hallie, he nearly exploded. She was in the pantry, on one tiptoe on the top step of the little ladder, trying to reach something at the back of the uppermost shelf. She looked like she was a quarter inch away from falling.

"What the hell are you doing?" Jamie bellowed, then immediately regretted it. It was the voice he used on a battlefield and at home it had sent many a child running away in tears.

But Hallie seemed unperturbed. "I almost . . ." She stretched even farther. "Got it!" she said just before doing what looked like a one-footed dance on the stepstool. When she went to put her other foot down, she met vacant air.

As Jamie lifted his arms, his crutches clattered to the floor, and he made a leap, catching her about the waist as they fell. When the dust settled, Hallie was lying fully on top of him, her nose almost touching his. "If you needed a hug, you could have just said so."

Jamie laughed. "What were you doing up there? If I hadn't been here—" His eyes widened.

"What's wrong?"

In an instant, Jamie rolled over so Hallie was on the floor, then he scooped her up into his arms as though he was going to carry her out. It was a struggle with his leg in the long brace, but he made it.

When he started to walk, she called out, "Wait!" and he halted. "You can't carry me with your leg like that."

"I have to get you out of here!"

At his tone, she realized there was panic in his eyes. Just as she did at night, she put her hands on the sides of his head, her face close to his. "Jamie," she said quietly and with great sincerity, "tell me what's wrong."

Her words seemed to pull him out of his trance and he stared at her forehead.

Reaching up, she touched her hairline and her fingers came away bloody. "I think that box hit me in the head." He still looked worried. "Put me down and I'll get a bandage."

The light was coming back into his eyes. "There's so much dirt in your hair, it wouldn't stick. Come on, I have first aid supplies in the gym, and I'll fix that cut for you."

She could tell that he was embarrassed at the way he'd reacted, but she wasn't going to mention it. Was it her being hurt or the sight of blood that had bothered him?

They walked through the garden to the gym and Jamie had her sit on the end of a workout bench. Gently, he pulled back her hair and examined her scalp.

"Will I live?" she asked, trying to lighten his mood. He seemed very serious about what was an everyday accident.

"There's so much dirt on your scalp that it might get infected. I need to clean the entire area. Come with me."

She followed him outside to the end of the gym, where he opened a door she'd not noticed before and pulled out a folding chair.

"What is that?"

"An outdoor shower," he said. "For when you come in sandy from the beach. Sit here while I get what I need."

As soon as she sat down she closed her eyes. They'd been doing heavy-duty cleaning for a day and a half now. Plus there were Jamie's treatments morning and night. Add that to his two A.M. night terrors and she was being worn down.

She was half-asleep when he said, "Lean your head back and keep your eyes closed." To her absolute delight, he poured warm water over her hair. It felt heavenly!

"This is antiseptic shampoo. It doesn't smell great, but it works."

As the shampoo—which she didn't think smelled bad at all—turned to lather, he gently began to massage her head. When he got near the cut, which she knew wasn't very big, he blew on it, as though the shampoo might burn her. It didn't, but she didn't want him to stop.

He massaged around her ears, at the back of her neck, then over her scalp. His hands were strong—and accurate, she thought. As someone who'd had a lot of training in massage, she was aware that Jamie knew what he was doing. She started to ask him where he'd studied, but she knew he wouldn't answer. Besides, she was so totally enjoying his touch that she didn't want to interrupt it.

His hands went down around her neck, then to her shoulders. As his thumbs went into her trapezius muscles, she could feel tension leaving them.

It took several buckets of warm water poured over her head to rinse it. Then slowly, he began to comb out the tangles.

When he stopped, she sighed, sorry that it was over. She looked up at him.

"Would you do me the honor of going out to dinner with me tonight?" he asked.

Without hesitation, she said, "I'd love to."

"Then go put on something pretty and I'll meet you in an hour."

Hallie practically ran back to the house and up the stairs. Of course she shouldn't go, she thought. He was a client and it wouldn't be long before he left and she'd never see him again. But still, dinner out would be nice.

When Hallie had packed for Nantucket, she hadn't thought about what she was putting in the suitcase. At the time, between an inheritance and Shelly's latest trick, she hadn't been thinking clearly.

But Shelly'd had time to plan leaving with Jared. She had taken Hallie's suitcase and carefully filled it with her own clothes and a lot of Hallie's. When the plans had changed, Hallie had emptied her suitcase of what Shelly had packed and pulled her own garments from the pile. One item was a plain black sheath dress, silk, with little straps. It had been in the very back of Hallie's closet, saved for a special occasion that had never come. Right now Hallie was very glad she had the dress. Should she thank Shelly for pulling it out, she wondered, and almost laughed at the idea.

It took her a while to blow-dry her hair and she was almost sad to take away the reminder of Jamie's washing it. As she worked, she hummed every tune from *South Pacific*.

When she put the dress on, she was surprised that it was a bit loose. When she'd bought it, it had fit like it was painted on her.

She opened the little jewelry roll that Shelly had filled and found things she hadn't worn in years. She chose a plain gold chain and matching earrings.

When Jamie politely knocked on her bedroom door, she was ready.

"Wow!" he said. "You look great. Let's stay in and make out."

Hallie laughed. "I want dinner with wine, and you don't look bad yourself."

"Thanks," he said and let her go down the stairs before him.

When they were at the front door, she handed him the car keys, her eyes daring him to say no. He'd driven before and he could do it again.

As they pulled out, Hallie said, "Tell me about the wedding. How many of your family are coming?"

"A lot of them. Everyone loves Aunt Jilly. You'll be introduced to all of them, then you'll be quizzed on the names. But if you forget every Montgomery, that's understandable."

"Poor Montgomerys. But I was more interested in them individually, such as . . . I know, who's the smartest?"

"My dad and his brother. But that's just my opinion and don't tell either of them I said that."

"Nicest?"

"Without a doubt, Aunt Jilly."

"Best looking?"

"My brother Todd," Jamie said with a little smile.

"Okay," Hallie said. "Who is the most interesting?"

"That would be Uncle Kit. No question about it. In spite of the fact that he's a Montgomery, he's interesting because no one knows much about him, not his job, his personal life, nothing. All very mysterious."

Kind of like you, Hallie thought but didn't say. "What do you think he does?"

"He's a spy. All of us in the family believe that. One time he showed up at Christmas with two teenagers—a boy and a girl—and introduced them as his children. The kids were very sophisticated and accomplished. They could do anything, from sports to brain games. They were quite intimidating."

"Surely not in a gym. They couldn't possibly outlift *you*."

Jamie smiled. "You have raised my ego to the sky! But alas, it's my cousin Raine who's the winner on that score. We never saw the kids after that one Christmas. I think they thought we were barbarians."

"Even the Montgomerys?"

"Yes. Shocking, isn't it? You should see Uncle Kit with my mother. She quizzes him mercilessly, but he never tells her anything. We all believe her Detective Dacre, who is a retired spy, is based on him."

"Will your uncle Kit be at the wedding?"

"Who knows? Just look for tall, thin, lots of gray hair, and elegant. My mom likes to come up with things to see if he can do them, like archery and fencing and backgammon. He's never disappointed her yet."

Hallie laughed. "Your mother!"

"Yeah, I know." He pulled into the parking lot of the Sea Grille, turned off the engine, and looked at her. "She'll like you."

For a moment they sat in the car looking at each other and Hallie had an almost overwhelming urge to lean forward and kiss him. But then kissing Jamie was a familiar thing to her, as she did it every night.

She almost giggled at the thought of how shocked he'd be if she did kiss him. Smiling, she turned away and got out of the car.

Chapter Nine

"So where do you see yourself in, say, five years?" Jamie asked as he filled Hallie's wineglass for the second time. He wasn't drinking. His excuse was that he was the designated driver, but really he knew better than to mix alcohol with the medications he was taking.

Hallie smiled. "You sound like a therapist." She lowered her voice. "How do you *feel* about inheriting a house and a jet-setting patient?"

Jamie winced. "I wish Dad hadn't sent the plane," he said. "The weight of it has leaked onto me. How are your scallops?"

"Great. Fabulous. Are you trying to get me drunk?"

"Yes," he said with such a leer that she laughed. "What's your fantasy of your future?"

"I'm afraid I'm not very creative. I tend to like ordinary."

"What does that mean?"

She drank more of the wine. The beautiful restaurant, the beautiful man, and the wine were loosening her natural caution. Jamie was eating in silence and waiting for her reply. She'd never seen him in anything other than athletic clothes so his crisp shirt, the jacket that she was willing to bet was made for him, the creased trousers over the brace, made him look like something out of a dream.

She took a breath. "What most women want: a home, a husband and kids, a good job. See? I told you that I'm a very ordinary person."

"It doesn't sound ordinary to me. I thought women today wanted to climb the corporate ladder and become CEO of some billion-dollar company."

"Maybe they do, but it's never interested me. What about you? What do you want?"

He almost said, To regain myself, but he didn't. "Pretty much the same thing."

"Just in a mansion with marble hallways."

Jamie frowned. "My family isn't like that. We—" He stopped because he wanted the conversation back on her. "You now own two houses, so what are you going to do with them?"

Hallie groaned. "I don't know. I haven't had time to think about the future. I'd give the Boston house to my stepsister, but then she'd just sell it and—" She took a deep drink of her wine. She did *not* want to talk about Shelly! "Any suggestions?"

"Sell the Boston house and stay here on Nantucket."

"And support myself how? Besides, the house in Boston is heavily mortgaged. When I got it, it was in bad shape and I needed money to repair it. If I sold it, I'd clear some but not a lot. So how long could I live on the small proceeds and pay taxes on the Nantucket house? And you saw the prices at Bartlett's. This island is expensive."

"It sounds like you've thought about it a great deal. Surely they have need of physical therapists on this island. Or you could work on clients in the gym."

"It would take years to build up a private practice and what do I live on in the meantime? Why are you smiling?"

"I'm impressed by how practical you are," he said, but he was thinking that she was free. "You said you want a husband. Anyone picked out?"

"No, no one," Hallie said, but she looked away. This afternoon Braden's mother had called her.

"He's in a bad way," Mrs. Westbrook said, happiness in her voice.

"Oh?" Hallie asked. "Has something happened?"

Mrs. Westbrook gleefully told of her son being dumped and his resulting misery. "I'm sending him to you, dear Hallie. I'm hoping . . ." She didn't finish her sentence, but they both knew what she meant.

"A penny," Jamie said and again he was frowning.

Hallie emptied her wineglass and he refilled it. "A small house," she said. "That's what I'd want. Not one of those things with a three-story foyer and eight bathrooms. And you?"

"A big farmhouse with a porch where I can sit and watch it rain."

Hallie thought maybe it was the most personal thing he'd ever said to her. "And a garden with vegetables and flowers all mixed up. Did you know that if you plant basil near tomatoes, it keeps the bugs away? Or that's the theory anyway."

Jamie was nodding. "And we'll enclose it in a fence with sunflowers along the back."

"They draw birds that peck at the vegetables."

"Then we'll put up a scarecrow that will frighten them away."

"And I'd have a few chickens," she said. "My grandparents had hens and I gathered the eggs. I think it's good for kids to have chores and to know where food comes from. Have you ever seen a chicken up close?"

"Are you kidding?! My relatives are practically farmers. My aunt Samantha lives next door to us and she grows nearly every-thing our family and hers eat. I can shuck an ear of corn—and de-silk it—in less than a minute."

Hallie was looking at him with wide eyes. "I can't imagine you doing that. Jetting about, yes, but—"

"Does owning a jet stereotype my whole family? Look," he said seriously, "my father and his brother work with money. They buy and sell things and they're good at it, but they need to be near the various stock markets. They both had the wisdom to marry women who wanted homes and families, not high-society lives, so they all moved to Chandler, Colorado, to be near the relatives. But my dad and uncle need a way to get to work. Going from Chandler to New York on commercial air-lines takes a lot of time away from their families."

"So they bought their own plane," Hallie said. "Who pilots it?"

"My cousin Blair—but only on the condition that she not do somersaults in the air. At least not if there are any passengers."

Hallie laughed. "I like her already."

Jamie looked serious. "I'm not like what you think, nor was I raised as you believe. As a kid I had chores and responsibili-ties."

"So why aren't you at home in Chandler with them now? Why come to Nantucket to stay with a stranger?"

"I—" he began, but then a waiter came to take their empty plates away and he didn't finish. When they were again alone, he changed the subject. "It's working out well, isn't it? You and I are a good team."

Yet again, she thought, he wasn't going to reveal anything truly personal about himself. Suddenly, Hallie felt deflated. She hadn't realized it before, but dealing with a ghost story had provided the perfect distraction so she didn't have to think about the future. What *was* she going to do? Should she try to get a job on Nantucket and live in the beautiful old house she'd inherited? Or should she sell it?

"I think I've upset you," Jamie said, "and I didn't mean to."

"The truth is that I don't know what to do." Maybe it was the wine or maybe it was that Jamie seemed to want to hear what she had to say, but she wanted to talk. She surprised herself when she realized he was right, that she *had* thought about her future.

He ordered a chocolate dessert and two forks and while they shared, she told him what had been going through her mind. If she got a job on Nantucket, would it pay enough for the upkeep of an old house? If she sold it, what would happen to the artifacts in the tea room? "I feel an obligation to those things since they're connected to an ancestor of mine," she said.

"I bet Dr. Huntley would have some answers to these questions." He paused. "Chandler could use a physical therapist. It's cowboy country and there are lots of injuries. You could—"

"Be supported by your rich family?" she said with more anger than she meant. "No, thank you. I don't take charity. Are you finished? I'd like to go home now."

"Hallie, I'm sorry. I didn't mean—"

She stood up. "It's all right. I shouldn't have talked about my problems. This was a lovely dinner and I thank you. It was kind of you to do it."

Jamie paid the check, then they walked to the car, and Hallie was embarrassed. She'd revealed too much to this man who lived in a very different world than she did. He didn't have to worry about things like where he was going to get a job or whether or not to sell a house. And from the sound of his relatives, he didn't have a Shelly in the lot of them.

When they were in the car, Jamie said, "Does your friend Braden have a place in your future?"

She started to say no, but changed her mind. "Maybe. If I'm very, very lucky."

"Nice to know," Jamie said and he drove the short distance home in silence.

⚬⚬

When Hallie heard the first moan, she wasn't sure if it was hers or Jamie's. She was so tired that she could barely open her eyes and she almost went back to sleep. But a louder groan made her throw back the covers and stagger through to Jamie's room.

As always, he was thrashing about.

"Do be quiet," she said, but not in her usual tone of infinite patience and understanding. She was too tired to understand anything.

Dutifully, she put her hand on Jamie's cheek. "You're safe." She yawned. "I'm here and— Oh!" Jamie's big arm swooped out and pulled her into the bed beside him.

In a single motion, he turned onto his side and snuggled her up against him.

"Teddy bear time," she said and for about a millionth of a second, Hallie thought of struggling against him, but then she closed her eyes and went back to sleep.

⚬⚬

Hallie knew she was dreaming. She was standing outside the tea room, the doors were open, and the interior was beautiful. There were four little tables in the middle of the room, each one draped in divinely thin and floaty white cotton. At the side of the room was the big dresser, its shelves filled with dishes she and Jamie had found, only they were new and sparkling clean. In fact, everything was warm and inviting.

But what drew Hallie's eyes weren't the objects but the beautiful woman who was sitting on the window seat on the far side of the room. Hallie didn't think she'd ever seen anyone as pretty. Her dark hair was piled onto her head, framing every exquisite feature on her face. Hallie could imagine her on the cover of every fashion magazine published, and from the look of her body under that pretty silk dress, that included *Sports Illustrated.*

Hallie wanted to say something to the young woman, but before she could take a step, another woman, equally pretty, walked through her.

Hallie gasped in shock, but neither of the women seemed to be aware that she was there. This is a dream, she reminded herself, and stood at the doorway and watched and listened.

"I wondered where you were," Hyacinth said to her sister as she walked into their pretty tea room. She was halfway across before she saw the little man sitting in the shadows behind the far table. "Oh!" she said in surprise.

Juliana was on the window seat, staring out at the garden. She had on her wedding dress, a grayish-blue silk that exactly matched her eyes. "He was Parthenia's idea, and Valentina backed her," she said. "They insisted that I have a quick portrait done on my wedding day. Come and sit with me."

Hyacinth stretched out by her sister, her pale pink dress a complement to her complexion, and looked at the small, dark man as he set out pots of ink. "Does he speak English?"

"Not a word."

"Then his silence will be bliss," Hyacinth said. "The house is already so full of guests that I want to run away and hide."

Juliana wasn't fooled by her sister's lighthearted tone. They'd been together every day since Juliana was born, but tomorrow she was leaving the island to live with the family of the man who would soon be her husband. She opened her arms and Hyacinth put her head on her sister's shoulder.

The new positioning caused a flurry of angry-sounding words from the artist, but Juliana just waved her hand. He could draw them together or neither of them.

"How will I function without you?" Hyacinth whispered.

"It won't be for long. Leland said you're to come to us in the spring. He has a cousin who is to visit. I think Leland means to wed you to him."

Hyacinth laughed. "He plans to turn the tables on us? Now I am to be matched with someone rather than find a mate for another? But poor Father could not bear for both of us to leave him."

Juliana glanced at the artist, who had stopped complaining and was now sketching the two young women. "Do you think Father will show up in Boston with his great oar and pelt your suitors?"

"Probably," Hyacinth said. "I saw him just moments ago and I've never seen anyone look so forlorn. He was in a chair by himself and brushed away anyone who came near him."

"After the ceremony I must remember to spend time with him. I cannot give everything to Leland. Not yet, at least."

When Hyacinth lifted her head to look at her sister, the little man again started complaining. He wanted them to remain still. Turning back, she gave him her sweetest smile and he quieted.

"Do you love your Leland very much?" Hyacinth whispered. "With all your soul? To the end of time?"

"I do," Juliana said, then laughed. "I didn't at first, not like everyone thinks I did. Only you know the true story of that day."

"Tell me again," Hyacinth said. "Tell me a thousand times."

"Everyone believes it was love at first sight, but Leland . . ."

She waited for her sister to add to the story. They'd laughed about it many times.

"Leland had fallen asleep at his desk," Hyacinth said. "He was lying on a freshly printed woodcut."

Juliana smiled. "The ink had come off, and on his cheek was a picture of two geese and—"

"The word 'sale' written backward," Hyacinth finished.

"Yes," Juliana said. "His cheek was facing me, so only I saw it and I couldn't help staring."

"And everyone thought you'd fallen in love with him at first sight," Hyacinth said.

Juliana smiled in memory. "Especially Leland."

"But then he did fall for you the very moment he saw you."

"He says he did," Juliana said. "But whatever his true feelings, it gave him the courage to . . ." She took a breath.

"Kiss you in the pantry." Hyacinth sighed.

"I will always wonder if he would have been so brave if he'd ever felt Father's oar on his backside."

"That sent many of our prospective suitors running," Hyacinth said. "I still long for a man who dares to brave his wrath."

"There have been plenty of them," Juliana said. "Caleb Kingsley climbed up the rose trellis almost to your bedroom window before Father heard him and began the chase. Caleb can certainly run fast! He would have made you a fine husband."

"I'm not so sure. I think he and Valentina are the better match. She returns Caleb's grand emotions. I prefer a quieter life." Hyacinth took her sister's hand. "How will I have our tea parties without you?"

"How will I bear meeting all of Leland's relatives alone?" Juliana said. "They are such an elegant set. His mother got seasick just from the trip over to the island. And his sister asked how well I can play Mozart."

"*And what did you reply?*"

"*That I didn't know any Mozart, but I could play 'Lame Sally's Jig' on a brown jug.*"

"*You didn't!*"

"*No,*" Juliana said, "*I didn't. But I wanted to.*" For a moment she looked around at the familiar setting and thought of all the laughter and good times they'd had there. "*I will miss this room and this island every day of my life. Promise me something.*"

"*Anything,*" Hyacinth said.

"*That if something should happen to me, if—*"

"*No!*" Hyacinth said. "*Don't think like that on your wedding day. It's bad luck.*"

"*But I feel that I must say this. If all does not go well with me, bring me back here to this house, to this island. Let me rest here forever. Will you promise me that?*"

"*Yes,*" Hyacinth said softly. "*And I ask the same of you. We must stay together always.*"

Juliana kissed the top of her sister's head. "*We'd better go or Father will think someone has stolen us away, and get out his oars.*" She looked at the little man. "*Finished?*"

He nodded as he got up and put the sketch on the big dresser to dry. It was of two beautiful young women, sitting side by side, heads together, the window behind them. Beside the drawing of them was one he'd done earlier of the bridegroom.

The sisters, with the artist behind them, were nearly to the door when it was flung open by their friend Valentina. She was beautiful too, but in a colorful, flamboyant way, a striking contrast to the quiet loveliness of the two sisters.

"*You must get to the church,*" Valentina said. "*We're all beginning to think you two ran off with a couple of handsome mermen.*"

"*I'd rather have Leland,*" Juliana said.

"And I'm holding out for Neptune," Hyacinth said. "I like his trident."

Laughing, they all left the room. None of them noticed the way the wind caught the pictures on the dresser and lifted them flat against the backboard. When the door closed, the papers fell straight down behind the big cupboard, hidden from view. And later, in the tragedy of what happened that day, no one thought to look for the drawings.

When Jamie woke, he didn't know where he was. As now seemed to always be the case, he felt a sense of panic. Where was his gear? Where were his fellow soldiers? Where were the exits and entrances?

He flung out his arm, searching for what he needed. Why had he slept?! Why hadn't he made sure that everyone was safe?

When he heard a woman's soft weeping, he remembered Valery. He'd tried to help her, but a medic had held him down. "Hold on there, sir. You can't get up. Most of you looks like Freddy Krueger went to work."

"Sergeant!" someone yelled. "Zip it!"

Jamie kept trying to get up. It was his job to help, his responsibility. He owed them. They were his to protect.

He flailed about until someone shot him full of morphine and he passed out.

It took minutes before the panic subsided and he remembered that he was on Nantucket. He was surprised that Hallie was in his arms, but she wasn't the one crying. She was restless, her bare legs moving against his, and she seemed to be trying to say something, but he couldn't understand her words.

He wondered why she was in bed with him. Had she been telling the truth when she said she was frightened by the ghosts?

Damn! he thought. If he didn't take those blasted pills to help him sleep, he would have heard her. He certainly would have known when she needed help.

"Shhhh," he said, stroking her hair back. "Be quiet. I'm here and you're safe."

"Juliana," she whispered, her voice fretful. "Juliana has died."

She was dreaming of the ghosts, he thought, and he held her close to him. Maybe she was right and they should stay at Jared's big house. Maybe they—

He broke off his thought because there was a flash of lightning outside, and in the quick light he saw a young woman standing by the bed and looking down at them. She was extraordinarily pretty and wore a high-waisted dress that was the color of . . . What had Dr. Huntley said? Something about a storm. On her dark hair was a white veil. She was a bride.

For an instant, she smiled at Jamie, then nodded, as though telling him she was pleased with the way he was comforting Hallie.

"Juliana?" he whispered and held out his hand toward her. But in the next flash of lightning, she was gone. And with her went all of Hallie's restlessness, and she grew quiet in his arms.

For a few seconds Jamie was frowning, wondering what he'd just seen, but then a deep sense of calm came over him. For the first time in over a year, his mind filled with something other than the memory of guns and bombs and fear and . . . and death.

As his body relaxed, he began to see a house. It was two stories, with a deep porch across the front, and to the right was a glassed-in room. He felt himself floating, hovering above the earth, and he could see inside that room. It was off the master bedroom, and he knew Hallie had made it into a nursery. There were two cribs, but one was empty and for a moment, Jamie felt the all-too-familiar sense of panic. But, no, the second crib had two little boys, identical, just as he and Todd were. And just like them, these boys refused to sleep apart.

The vision, the dream, whatever it was, made Jamie feel the best he had since . . . He couldn't remember ever having felt so good. He pulled Hallie even closer to him, smiled at the way her legs entwined with his, and fell into a deep and peaceful sleep, the first he'd had in a very long time.

Chapter Ten

"He's asleep," came the loud whisper of a little boy.

"I told you he would be," his sister replied.

"Mom said not to wake him."

She looked around. "We could knock over that chair, and that wouldn't be us. Or we could—"

"Who's she?" asked the boy. He was pointing across Jamie to Hallie's head, which was barely visible above the covers.

"The exercise lady," said the girl, trying to sound as though she knew. She was three minutes older than her brother and she took the age difference quite seriously. When she saw a little flicker in Jamie's closed eyes, she knew he was awake, and she had to resist a giggle of anticipation. "She probably got cold. Jamie is really fat so she'd be warm near him. She—"

"Who is fat?!" Jamie growled, then with a twist pulled them both up into the bed.

The girl threw herself onto Jamie and he began tickling her, but the boy stepped over Hallie and lay down to stare at her.

"Shhhh," Jamie was saying to his little sister. "Hallie's trying to sleep. She's worn out from taking care of me."

The girl lay still on Jamie's chest and looked at him with a frown of concentration. "Did you fall on the floor and roll on her?"

A flash of guilt ran through Jamie's mind. When he'd first returned from the hospital had been the worst. Every noise, every quick movement, every closed-in space had set him off. But then he smiled at his little sister. "Only twice, and you know what? She *liked* it."

"If she likes you, she must be crazy," his sister said seriously.

"I'll get you for that." Jamie started tickling her again.

When Hallie began to wake, she thought maybe she was still in her dream. In her mind, there were homemade cakes and champagne that she knew had been brought over from France by one of the Kingsleys. And she could hear children laughing. Smiling, she opened her eyes to see a little boy who looked like Jamie staring at her. He had the most beautiful eyelashes. She smiled back at him.

But then Jamie's arm landed on her head just in time to keep another child from rolling on top of her. He moved onto his side so his whole body was pressed against Hallie's back, and she looked into the eyes of the two children who were both fixated on her.

Jamie began nibbling at Hallie's ear. She was still in such a dream state that she smiled at all of it, for surely none of it could be real.

"Are you in love with my brother?" the girl asked.

"I think she is," Jamie said. "She can't stay away from me even at night."

Hallie was coming awake. "Stop that!" She batted at his

head and twisted around to face him. "For your information, I'm in bed with you because—" She broke off, her eyes so wide they nearly touched in the middle.

"Good morning," came a deep male voice.

Jamie rolled onto his back, his eyes closed. "Tell me that's a recording and he's not really here."

Hallie's first thought was to get out of bed, but she had on only a beat-up old T-shirt, and besides, Jamie's heavy leg with the big brace on it was half thrown across her.

She managed to sit up, a child on each side of her, and they looked across the wide expanse of Jamie. What she saw were two truly gorgeous young men. They were both over six feet, broad shouldered and slim. They had on cotton shirts and trousers with a crease down the front. Their faces were like something off a runway show: chiseled, with long aristocratic noses, lips like on a Greek sculpture. One had thick, coal-black hair and eyes that were almost as dark. In the right clothes he would look like a pirate. The other one was equally handsome, but his hair was lighter, his eyes a golden brown. In a movie he'd play Captain America.

"Are they real?" she whispered to the little girl.

The men smiled, eyes twinkling.

"I guess," the girl said, unconcerned. "They're bad on horses, but that's because they're—"

"Let me guess," Hallie said. "They're Montgomerys."

The young men laughed. "Our reputation precedes us."

The darker one said, "I am Adam and this is my cousin Ian."

Jamie finally opened his eyes. "I thought you weren't going to be here until next week." He sounded annoyed.

"Aunt Cale wanted to see the old house they bought," Ian said, smiling at Hallie, who was trying to comb her hair with her fingers.

"Who's here?" Jamie asked.

"Everybody!" the little boy said as he stood up on the bed. "I'm Max and this is Cory. Jamie and Todd are our brothers."

Hallie took Max's hand so he wouldn't fall off the bed. She was still looking at the young men, smiling at them, when another man entered the room and she started blinking rapidly. He was a bit shorter than the others, but still tall, and built like a bear. His T-shirt clung to muscles that seemed to ripple even when he was standing still. As for his six-pack . . . she wasn't sure but he just might have a twelve-pack.

Finally, she looked up at his face. "Sweet" was the only word she could think to describe it. Short dark hair that had a bit of curl in it, blue eyes, a cleft chin.

Max yelled, "Raine!" and launched himself off the bed.

Without breaking his look at Hallie, the man caught the boy, then nestled him in the crook of his right arm. When he held out his left arm, the girl used Jamie's stomach to push off. Raine caught her, then held both children, who snuggled up to him, faces buried in his strong neck.

All Hallie could do was sit on the bed and look across at them. There were the two elegant, lean men on the left, and on the right was the big man holding the two beautiful children. And Jamie was stretched out on the bed.

"I think I've died and gone to Heaven," she whispered.

"Out!" Jamie yelled as he sat up. "The lot of you, get out!"

None of them so much as moved. "Are you and James a couple?" Adam asked.

"No, not really," Hallie said. She motioned at the bed. "This happened because we, uh . . . I mean, we . . ." She didn't want to embarrass Jamie about the nightmares, but neither did she want them to think there was an attachment when there wasn't. And all in all, the beauty of all four of the men was making her a bit incoherent.

"Out!" Jamie growled. "This minute."

With dazzling smiles, the three men left, and the children followed them.

When they were alone, Jamie turned to her. "Why are you in bed with me?"

She didn't want to explain anything. Instead, she threw back the covers and got up. "I need to dress. See you downstairs." She took off running.

Hallie took her time dressing. She got out the new clothes she'd bought at Zero Main and spent a lot of time with her hair.

While she was dressing, she remembered her dream of the Tea Ladies. Usually, dreams faded from memory, but not this one. She remembered every second of it. As she used her curling iron, she thought of the drawings that had fallen behind the dresser.

She had to see Jamie! Had to tell him about her dream and they had to pull the big cabinet out from the wall to see if the drawings really were there.

When she was dressed and started down the stairs, she could hear voices and laughter. Had more of the Montgomery-Taggert family arrived? But, no, the same beautiful men with the two children were in the kitchen, with one addition.

Jamie was sitting at the table looking as though he was working hard to control his temper. Beside him was a man Hallie had never seen before, but she already knew he must be a Taggert. He wasn't as tall as Jamie but did look somewhat like him, though he was heavier and not nearly as good-looking.

When Adam saw Hallie, he stopped talking and stepped back. Ian, then Raine, did the same thing. The children clung to Raine, watching Hallie in absolute silence. They formed a path so she could get to the table and the two men sitting there.

What in the world is going on? she wondered as she walked forward. Jamie wasn't looking at her.

When she reached the table she stopped. The new guy was looking up at her in question, as though waiting for something.

"Hi," she said. "I'm Hallie, and you are—?"

"Todd," he said and stood up to shake her hand. "I'm Jamie's brother."

After that, everyone started talking at once. Except for Jamie, that is. He got up on his crutches and without even a glance at Hallie opened the door into the pantry and went inside, shutting the door behind him.

Hallie wanted to go after him and tell him about her dream, but she was surrounded by gorgeous men whose only goal in life seemed to be to please her. She was asked what she wanted for breakfast. As they began to make it, she saw that her fridge had again been filled with food.

One by one the men told her about ailments and injuries they had and asked her advice on how to treat them. She was asked what she charged for a massage.

After breakfast the men—except for Todd and Jamie—escorted her to the gym so she could begin working on them. They were a happy trio and she enjoyed their company, but at the same time she kept wondering where Jamie was.

At lunch she managed to catch Cory as the child was running through the garden. "Where is your brother?"

"Which one?" the little girl asked. She had a wooden sword and was waving it about in the air. "I have five of them."

"Really?" Hallie asked. "Jamie. Where is he?"

"With Todd. They're always together."

"Could you please find Jamie and tell him we need to work on his knee?"

"He won't come," Cory said. "Todd won't let him." She went tearing off through the garden.

Hallie saw that the big red gate had been propped open so the family staying at the B&B could come and go easily. Ian told her that guests were also staying at Kingsley House, Toby's house, and at various hotels all over the island. He said all this as though it were something ordinary, but to Hallie, with her one and only non-blood relative, it was anything but. When she remembered Jamie's jokes about how he knew all about cousins and could supply relatives of any size, gender, age, etc., she couldn't help laughing.

At the time, Adam was on his stomach on her massage table, his long, beautiful body stretched out and covered only by a small white towel over his behind. He was a nice man, with a dry sense of humor, and he'd complimented her on how she'd helped relieve the tension in his shoulders.

"We saw the kitchen implements on the sheets outside," he said. "Did you find them in the house?"

Hallie's mind filled with all that had happened before finding the artifacts. It would be too much to tell about a couple of matchmaking ghosts and her vivid dream about them. Besides, that was something she and Jamie shared.

Instead, she told of the locked doors and how Dr. Huntley had given them the key and they'd found a dirty room inside.

Adam turned onto his back, again with only the towel over him. "And you and Jamie cleaned the place? Did you enjoy doing it?"

"We did," she said, smiling as she ran her oiled hands over his chest. He was in good shape, she thought, probably ran as well as did some sort of martial arts. His muscles were relaxed; he didn't hold the tension that Jamie did. He was an easy man to work on, to talk to, and probably to get to know.

But he wasn't Jamie.

After lunch—eaten outside with Adam, Ian, Raine, and the children—she set to work on Ian. He was in as good a shape as

Adam and as likeable. Whereas Adam had an intensity about him that was almost intimidating, Ian was all smiles and laughter.

At three Raine got on the table. By that time Hallie was frustrated from her failure to find Jamie. She hadn't seen him or his brother since before breakfast.

She smiled at the sight of Raine's big body. It was more like Jamie's. "Where is he?" she asked as she began trying to get deep down into his muscles. She didn't explain who "he" was.

"With Todd," Raine said. Of the three men, he talked the least, but she had an idea that he saw and heard the most.

"Is he hiding from me?" she asked, her hands paused in their work.

"My guess is yes," Raine said.

"And the lot of you are trying to keep me entertained so I don't notice?"

"Yes," he said simply.

Hallie wanted to think that she wasn't hurt by Jamie's behavior, but she was.

"Jamie has—" Raine began.

She knew he was going to say "problems," but she didn't want to hear it. "Bad manners," she said and felt a chuckle from Raine.

"Very bad," he agreed.

She did the rest of the massage in silence, mostly because she needed all her energy to dig into Raine's thick, heavy muscles.

The men insisted on taking her out to dinner and they all went to Kitty Murtagh's. It was like an old tavern and Hallie enjoyed herself, but she missed Jamie.

At that thought she wanted to bawl herself out. Every female in the restaurant was looking at her with envy. With the way the children went from her to Raine and back again, it looked like they were a married couple and the kids were theirs. In fact, more than once she caught Raine looking at her from under his lashes in a way that made little chills run up her spine. Of the whole group of gorgeous men she'd met, he was by far her favorite. She liked his quietness, his humor, and the way he listened. In other words, whatever about him was like Jamie, that's what she liked.

By the time they got back to the house, the men were discussing who was going to sleep on the cot downstairs. At first she thought perhaps they believed Nantucket was a dangerous place, but then she realized that they were worried about Jamie's nightmares.

Maybe they were being protective of him or maybe of her. Whichever it was, she didn't like what they were saying.

Against their protests, she ran them all out of the house. The two Montgomerys seemed ready to stay anyway, but Raine led them away.

When she went upstairs she hoped Jamie would be there, but he wasn't. The house was eerily quiet and she didn't like that. He had been there since the first day. It was *their* house, not just hers.

As she took a shower, she tried to get herself under control. She'd known from the beginning that Jamie Taggert wasn't for her. All day his cousins had mentioned schools and countries and events, even sports, that she'd only read about. Once Jamie's leg was healed he'd get on the family jet and she'd never see him again. At best, she'd get a Christmas card.

When she got out of the shower, she put on a pair of pajamas instead of her usual big T-shirt and headed for her bed. But she wanted to know if Jamie had returned. His bed was empty.

All her resolve left her. "Damn you, Todd!" she said aloud, then told herself to calm down. The main question was why she was so upset that Jamie wasn't there. It wasn't as though they were a couple. She'd told his cousins that and it was true.

She went back to her own bed and was asleep almost instantly. As had become a habit, she awoke at two A.M. and lay there listening, but she heard nothing. No moans or groans. She turned on the light and went through the sitting room to Jamie's bedroom.

His nightlight was on, but his bed was empty. On impulse she opened his closet door. Had he packed and gone back home to Colorado? Would she get a card from him saying thanks, he'd had a good time?

But his clothes were still there, mostly sweatsuits big enough to cover up even him, and the one nice outfit he'd worn to dinner.

On the back of the door was one of those big terry cloth robes and she put it on, pausing for a moment to snuggle it around her body. Barefoot, she went downstairs and it too was empty. He wasn't sleeping on the narrow cot.

When she noticed a light on in the tea room, she opened the door. In the far corner of the room was a tall, gray-haired man wearing an elegant blue silk robe and slippers. He was sitting on the old couch and reading.

"Ah," he said when he saw her, sounding as though she was the person he most wanted to see in the world.

"You're either a ghost or Uncle Kit," she said.

He put his book and reading glasses down and stood up. "How perceptive of you, and tonight I feel that I may be both of them. The tea is hot and I find the accompaniments delightful. Perhaps you'd join me."

"I would love to." She sat down on one of the chairs while he poured and served. Hallie tucked her feet under her and looked around the room. She hadn't really looked at it since she and Jamie had cleaned it. In the dim light from the table lamp, the room was quite pretty and very atmospheric.

She looked back at Kit. "I guess we should exchange proper introductions. I'm Hyacinth Lauren Hartley, better known as Hallie."

"And as you deduced, I am Christopher Montgomery, commonly referred to as Kit." He smiled. "Or Uncle Kit. There, now that that's done, why are you wandering about at this time in the morning?"

"Looking for Jamie. Why aren't you sleeping?"

"I'm sure my nephew is with Todd, but where they are I don't know." He put his teacup down. "As for my inability to sleep, may I confide in you?"

"Please do."

"First of all, I must apologize for trespassing. Sometimes I find the boisterousness of my family more than I can abide. When I was told that you had run everyone out of your house, I felt I'd heard of a kindred spirit."

Hallie smiled. He was a very handsome man, sixtyish, and there was something about him that made her feel safe and comfortable.

"I found the door to this room unlocked and came in here and slept." He nodded toward the window seat, where there was a pillow and a blanket. "But I was awakened by a dream of—"

"Let me guess," Hallie said. "Two fabulously beautiful young women with Playboy bunny bodies." She sipped her tea. "Just a guess."

For a second Kit looked astonished, then he laughed. "My life has been such that I'm not easily surprised, but you have done so. I am intrigued. Have you too dreamed of them?"

"Yes, but I've also heard their stories. Perhaps . . . ?"

"Perhaps I would like to hear? Oh, yes, very much."

It took Hallie nearly an hour to tell all she knew about the ladies. Kit asked a question now and then.

"Has Jamie heard from his mother about her research?"
"And you say it was a box that hit your head? What was in it?"
"Are the drawings actually behind the dresser?"

The answer to each question was "I don't know."

"How very interesting," Kit said when she'd finished, and

poured them more tea. "Don't you think it's also interesting that after over an hour the tea is still hot and the cakes and cookies are still plentiful?"

"It's always like that. We'd come into the house to find that our neighbor had set up a lavish afternoon tea for us. Jamie eats a lot, but there was always enough, and yes, the tea stayed hot." She looked at him. "I'm sorry, but I didn't allow you to tell about your dream."

"It was quite simple. There were two beautiful young women and one said, 'You must find Leland's cousin.' I felt she was speaking to me. That was all. The total of it."

"I wonder if that's the cousin Leland was going to introduce Hyacinth to?" she said, referring to her own dream.

"I'll have to ask Jilly to look into that. She's the family's genealogist. Ah, but wait, this is *her* wedding. No doubt she'll be quite busy. Have you met her?"

"No. I have been surrounded by men all day. Raine said they were keeping me entertained so I wouldn't notice that Jamie wasn't around. But I *did* notice!" She said the last with such vehemence that she was embarrassed. "Sorry. It's just that I need to treat his knee."

"Yes, of course." Kit was smiling. "May I give you some advice?"

"Please do."

"My family isn't for cowards."

She waited for him to expand on that comment, but he didn't—and she had no idea what he meant.

"Now, my dear," Kit said and his tone was dismissive, "I think we should try to get some sleep before dawn. I'm sure Cale's youngest hellions will escape and be here as early as possible. They seem to be fascinated with the 'exercise lady' who has all the young buck cousins coming over here."

"Just out of curiosity, are there any females in your family? Other than Cory, that is."

"Actually, there's a rather interesting assortment of females, and I'm sure they'll start showing up soon. And Hallie, dear?"

"Yes?"

"Perhaps we should keep this"—he waved his hand to include the room—"to ourselves as best we can. However, tomorrow I shall harness the brawn of a few Taggerts to move the cabinet to see what's behind it."

"And I'll find the box that hit me on the head."

"And I'll see what Cale has found out."

"But please remember that Jamie is in on this too," Hallie said. "He's to be told everything."

For a moment Kit looked at her as though trying to figure out something. "What do you like most about my damaged nephew?"

"Among other things, he makes me laugh."

For the second time, there was a look of astonishment on Kit's handsome face. "That is an excellent answer, and certainly one I wouldn't have predicted."

Chapter Eleven

By four that afternoon, Hallie was ready to lock the garden gate and put up a no trespassing sign. An endless stream of male wedding guests had come to her asking for appointments for treatments, advice about injuries, and massages. They had each paid her asking price and tipped her generously. But as far as Hallie could tell, they really just wanted to *meet* her.

Why?! she wondered. It wasn't as though she was ever going to be part of their family. Not that she'd mind that. All the men were very nice, good to look at, intelligent, educated, and very courteous. Except for Todd. She didn't like him *at all*.

She knew that some of the animosity between them was her fault. By the afternoon, her arms and shoulders were aching from one massage after another. At one point there were three young men sitting under the arbor, each one wearing nothing but a towel. They'd rinsed off in the outdoor shower, but rather than get dressed, they'd tied towels around their waists and waited for their turn on Hallie's table.

They were all so very polite that when she got to Todd, she was shocked by his attitude.

As soon as he stretched his nude body out on the table on his stomach, he said, "What are your intentions toward my brother?"

It was late in the day and she was tired. "To kidnap him and steal his jet," she said before she thought.

Hallie knew Jamie would have laughed at that. But Todd didn't. When she felt his muscles tighten under her hands, she sighed. "I have no 'intentions' of anything except rehabilitating his knee. He has now missed several sessions, plus his breathing exercises. He *needs* them!"

"What does that mean?"

Hallie frowned. Maybe his animosity came from jealousy. Todd wasn't as handsome as his brother or as well built, and she was beginning to think that he didn't have a whole lot of brains. She spoke slowly and distinctly. "Jamie hurt his knee skiing, he's had surgery, and he needs to get his knee working again. I was hired to help with that."

"I mean the breathing exercises," Todd snapped. "What are they for?"

Hallie rolled her eyes. "To help him breathe."

"Why were you in bed with him?" Todd asked, his tone that of the law enforcement officer she knew he was.

She had no doubt that he wanted to know about Jamie's nightmares. Last night she'd realized that his family knew of them, but there was something in her that didn't want to report on them. "Fabulous sex," she said. "All night long."

Clutching the single towel, Todd turned over on the bench, sat up, and glared at her. "I don't appreciate being lied to."

"And I don't appreciate your attempt to use me as a spy. We're done here." She grabbed a towel, wiped her hands, and walked away. One of the men asked her if she was okay, but she just kept going.

When she got to the house she went around to the side, to the tea room. Maybe it would be quiet in there.

Somehow, she wasn't surprised to see Jamie standing by a table that had one of the lavish teas on it. Had Edith come by in her little cart?

"Where have you been?" she shot at him, anger in her voice.

"You've had a bad day, haven't you?" When he saw tears come to her eyes, he leaned his crutches against the wall, opened his arms to her, and she went to him. He held her, her face against his chest, and she could hear his heart pounding. His big, hard body was like an island of calm in the turmoil of the last two days.

Much too soon, he held her away from him and looked at her as though trying to read her mind. "Come on," he said softly. "Edith brought us tea, so sit down and tell me what you've been doing." She didn't move and for a moment she thought he was going to kiss her.

But he didn't kiss her. "You look exhausted."

"Thanks," she said in sarcasm. "Looks like my hour with a curling iron was wasted."

Laughing, Jamie held out a chair for her. "Are you kidding? The cousins are raving about you. They think you're beautiful and smart and that you have magic hands."

Hallie poured the tea. "Your brother hates me." When Jamie said nothing, she glared at him. "You're supposed to say that he doesn't hate me, that he's . . . I don't know, cautious or something."

"It's more like he's protecting you from me."

"Would you please reassure him that I'm not *really* planning to kidnap you or seduce you or whatever just to get the family jet?"

Jamie nearly choked on one of the anise seed cookies he

liked so much. "Is that what you told him you were going to do?"

Hallie shrugged, then looked at Jamie. "More or less. Too much?"

"For him, yeah." Jamie was still laughing.

"Think he'll put me in handcuffs?"

"What an enticing vision," he said softly and gave her a look of such heat that the hair on her neck seemed to stand up straight.

"Jamie . . ." she whispered and leaned toward him.

Instantly, he moved away and his face changed. "So tell me who you've met."

It took Hallie a moment to calm herself. Okay, she'd missed him, but that was her problem, not his. He was her patient and maybe, possibly, they could become friends, but that's all there ever would be. "Your uncle Kit." She was pleased to see the surprise on Jamie's face.

"I didn't even know he was here."

"That's because you ran away somewhere. If you'd stayed here and let me treat you, you'd have seen all your male relatives. Tell me, how does your family reproduce without any women?"

The smile came back to him. "The women are drowning in wedding activities: cakes and flowers and who sits where and— I don't know. I told Aunt Jilly to come find you. I think it's all too much for her."

"Yes, do send her to me."

Reaching out, he smoothed a strand of hair out of her eyes. "I still want to know why you were in bed with me."

She thought quickly. "I heard a noise and when I went to see about it, you pulled me into bed with you. You'd worked me so hard that day I was too tired to get up." She stared at him, waiting for him to question her more.

Jamie took his time before he spoke again, seeming to decide whether or not to pursue that. "When did you see Uncle Kit?"

"Two A.M., in here. We had tea together. Seems he's been dreaming about the Tea Ladies."

Jamie's eyes widened. "Yeah? About what?"

Hallie opened her mouth to tell him all, but didn't. "I'm not telling you anything until I see you on the table. I want to look at your knee, and you're slumping to one side again. And—" She narrowed her eyes at him. "And I want your clothes off."

Immediately, he stiffened in the chair. "You haven't had your hands on enough men in the last few days?"

"Yes, I have, and they're all flawless specimens of mankind. I've never before seen such perfection. They don't need anything from me."

"But I do?" Jamie had his head down and his voice was low.

She put her hand over his. "Yes, you do. You carry a lot of tension in your body and I could *help* you."

Jamie stood up so abruptly that his chair fell backward and hit the floor hard. When the sound echoed in the room, he grabbed a crutch in a way that looked like he was about to defend the two of them from something.

Hallie stared at him in astonishment. "Jamie! Are you all right?"

It was a while before he seemed to know where he was. He picked up the other crutch and leaned on them. When he looked at Hallie, his expression was cold, distant. "I don't need *help*. I don't need pity. I don't need—" Breaking off, he quickly went across the room and left, the double doors slamming behind him.

Hallie was stunned. She had no idea what had just happened. What had made him so angry? Usually when she asked if he needed help he smiled and said yes. In fact, he pretended to need her help with his crutches, with walks around the garden, to go up and down the stairs. So why was he different now?

Todd! she thought. *He* was what had changed everything. As soon as he'd arrived, he'd scooped up his brother and taken him away. *Was* he jealous? Did Todd resent that Hallie and Jamie were . . . what? Becoming friends? But didn't Jamie say that his brother was the reason he was here?

Hallie sat at the table, feeling stunned. She didn't know what was going on. When she reached for the teapot, her hands were shaking, but then the tea was icy cold. "It's the way I feel," she whispered. She put her face in her hands and for a moment she let herself shed tears.

She looked about the pretty room. "I don't know if there are ghosts here, but I'd certainly like some help right now. Everything in my life is changing and I don't know if it's for good or bad. I like this man Jamie a lot. I tell myself he's not for me, but then I see him and . . . I don't know, I'm drawn to him."

She paused, feeling silly for talking to nonexistent people, but she couldn't seem to stop. "Dr. Huntley said that only people who have not met their True Loves can see you. Since I can't, I guess I have met him. He's Braden, of course. The man at the top of the heap. Incomparable and perfect."

There was only silence. But saying her feelings out loud had made her feel better. She took a few deep breaths, then stood up. As she glanced at the cold teapot and the uneaten food, she knew she should clean up, but she didn't. She just wanted to lie in a tub of very hot water and think about nothing at all.

When she went through the door into the kitchen, Raine was there. His face lit up when he saw her, and she couldn't help thinking how simple it would be if she turned her attention to him. Raine was pleasant company, gorgeous, etc.

But all she did was give him a weak smile and wish he'd go away.

He understood. "I'll clear everyone out," he said. "Rest. You've done a lot today."

"Thank you," she said and by the time she got upstairs she could feel the emptiness of the house.

She filled the tub with water as hot as she could stand and

stayed in it until it was cold. While in there, she reached a decision. She would forget the personal aspect of her relationship with Jamie and concentrate entirely on the professional one. She'd been hired by his family to rehabilitate his injured knee and that's what she was going to do.

Kit had said, "My family isn't for cowards," but she *was* being a coward. She was letting a bunch of very charming men distract her from her purpose of making Jamie better. And the worst of these distracting offenders was Todd.

As she dried off and put on her pajamas, she made a vow that tomorrow she was going to do whatever was necessary to get to work on Jamie. Neither his quick temper nor his brother's grouchiness nor the delightful interference of all his cousins was going to keep her from her goal.

By the time she got into bed, she felt much better—except for the loneliness of the empty house. Why did it seem so small when Jamie was there and so big when he wasn't?

Think professional! she thought as she snuggled down and went to sleep. But as always, she awoke at two A.M. and before she thought, she started to get out of bed. Then she seemed to see and hear the swish of a silk skirt, and as a great calm came over her, she lay back down.

When she awoke again, she looked at the clock and saw that it was almost six A.M. Usually, she would have gone back to sleep, but she was wide awake. "Jamie!" she said and got out of bed.

He worked out at this time so maybe he was in the gym now. She practically ran to the bathroom, hopped about on one foot as she put on underwear, then shorts, a shirt, and sandals. As she hurried down the stairs, she was tying her hair back in a ponytail.

She ran out the back door, across the dew-covered grass, and the first person she saw was Todd. He was outside the gym, wearing sweatpants and a T-shirt, and he was towel-drying his hair. He looked as though he'd just stepped out of the shower.

When he saw Hallie, his eyes widened, and he gave a furtive glance at the outdoor shower.

It didn't take much for Hallie to put it all together. Jamie and Todd had already finished their daily workout, Todd had showered, and now Jamie was in there.

Hallie headed toward the shower. She didn't know what she intended to do, but she was going to stop this nonsense right now.

Todd put his big body in front of her. "My brother wants privacy," he said in what could only be described as a growl.

She glared up at him. "Yeah? Well, I want to do my job! Move."

He was a big man and he stayed where he was. He was as determined to not let her pass as she was to get around him. They glared at each other, neither of them backing down.

It was Jamie who solved the problem. He threw back the wooden door and stepped onto the stone pavement. A towel was wrapped around his waist and the brace covered his right leg, but the rest of him was bare.

At last, Hallie saw what he'd been keeping secret. His body from the waist up to his shoulders, as well as his left leg, was a mass of scars. There were gashes and dents, places that had skin grafts. It looked as though he had been flayed with metal claws, his skin torn off in rows, then sewn back on.

At her first sight of the mutilation of what had once been a beautiful body, Hallie thought she might faint, or cry, or throw up. Or all of them.

Jamie was drying himself and she was hidden behind Todd, so he didn't know she was there.

"I'll take you back to the house," Todd said, his voice barely a whisper.

She looked at him and what she saw there made her want to slap him. There was a sneer of disgust on his face. He was assuming that Hallie would now want to run away. She didn't say anything, just quickly stepped around him and went to Jamie.

When he saw her, his face drained of color. For a moment his eyes dared her to say anything, but then he straightened and stared ahead at nothing.

As he stood at attention, she walked around him and looked at his wounds. Most were skin-deep, but some went down to the muscles. She couldn't imagine his pain during the injuries, the subsequent healing, and the rebuilding of his body.

When she got back to his front, he was still looking over her head. He seemed to be waiting for her to make the first move, but the emotion that was building inside her was overtaking her sympathy. She was remembering all the tricks and half-lies that had been played by him to cover what she was now seeing.

Reaching out, she put a single fingertip at the end of one long scar that ran from his shoulder to his stomach. "Soldier?" she asked.

"Yes." He didn't look at her.

A movement caught her eye. Adam, Ian, and Raine were coming through the gate. They had helped Jamie in his lies.

"You have one hour to get off my property," she said as she started toward the house. Todd was there, but she didn't look at him. She was walking fast, her steps full of the rage she was feeling.

Jamie caught her arm. "What do you mean?"

Hallie stopped but didn't look at him. "You heard me. Go away. I never want to see any of you again."

"I understand," he said. "I disgust you."

She turned back to him. "Don't speak to me in that tone! You have insulted me—insulted my professional abilities. You have humiliated me." She glared at him. "You have *betrayed* me." She started walking again.

He stepped in front of her, blocking her. "What are you talking about? How have I betrayed you?"

His scarred chest was directly in front of her. "What did you think would happen if I saw you? Saw *this*?"

"That you'd feel sorry for me." His voice was soft.

"Right. As I said, you have insulted my entire profession." She tried to step around him, but he wouldn't let her pass. She halted, her arms folded over her chest, but she wouldn't look at him.

"Hallie, please, I just didn't want you to . . . to . . ."

"To what? To be able to *help* you? Did you think I was one of those bimbos you meet when you're jetting around the world? But wait! That's a lie too, isn't it? You wanted me to think you were some rich playboy who took up space on the earth. You hid the fact that you are *a soldier*! Not knowing the cause of your physical problems has hindered me greatly."

She turned back to look at the four men standing to one side and watching them. They all seemed to be astonished by her reaction. "All of you helped him conceal this from me," Hallie said, so angry she could barely speak. "You gave me this job, then wouldn't let me do it. I want all of you gone. Now!" She started walking.

Jamie ran after her on his crutches.

When Hallie got to the house she didn't go into the kitchen. For all she knew there might be people in there. Instead, she went around to the side and threw open the doors to the tea room. Thankfully, it was empty.

Jamie was right behind her. "I never meant to hide anything," he said, his voice genuinely contrite. "I just wanted to be normal, that's all. My family treats me like I'm a delicate piece of glass that's about to shatter if they breathe too hard."

She turned to him. "Normal? You think this situation is *normal*?! You're isolated with your own private physical therapist. I needed to know about your injuries, but you played a childish game of hide-and-seek. Tell me what's normal about that!"

Jamie hobbled over to be closer to her. "It's not the physical therapist part that's the problem, it's just that you're so pretty, so desirable. From the moment I saw you I have been out of my mind with wanting you." He was smiling at her so very sweetly.

"So now I'm supposed to fall into your arms?" Hallie said. "Is that what you think I'm going to do? You admit you're willing to jump into bed with me and I am supposed to instantly forgive you?"

"Well, I did think it would make a difference if you knew and I thought . . ." He could see that every word he spoke was making her even angrier. For a second he seemed to hear Dr. Huntley's laughter at him, saying he'd never been "on the receiving end of a woman's rage over a man's prevarications." And it was true that he didn't know what to say or do to make her forgive him.

When he made a step toward her, she backed up. "Hallie, please let me explain," he said. "I thought—" He broke off because his three cousins were outside the window behind Hallie. They were holding up pieces of paper with words on them. Adam's said "Apologize." Ian had written "Grovel." And Raine's paper said "Tell her you're wrong."

"I'm sorry," Jamie said. "I was wrong. I thought of myself and that's all."

"Yes, you did!" Hallie said. "You were utterly selfish."

He took another step toward her, but again she stepped back.

"I just wanted some time away from pity, that's all," Jamie said and the words were from his heart.

"So you let me nearly go crazy wondering what was wrong with you? All because you thought I'd *pity* you?"

The men outside were nodding at this. "Yes, I did," Jamie said, his head down.

"You had no respect for my profession."

Outside, the men nodded in agreement.

"I'm really sorry and you are right. I didn't respect you or your expertise and I thought of no one but myself. It's just that—" He stopped when the men started vigorously shaking their heads no. Raine made the motion of zipping his mouth closed.

As Hallie looked at his nearly bare body, a tiny bit of anger left her. He still had on only the towel and the brace. Up close, the gashes and cuts were worse than they'd first appeared. "So what else is there? PTSD?"

"Yeah. I'm—" Jamie stopped talking.

"When the gate slams?"

"I go into a stance of defense," he said.

Hallie nodded. "Your fear to leave the grounds?"

"Crowds, strangers, places I don't know, they all . . ." He took a breath. This wasn't easy for a man to admit. "They scare me."

"What medications are you on?"

"For sleep, anxiety, depression." He paused. "But Hallie, since I've been with you, I've tapered off. You've been the best thing that's happened to me. You—" When he stepped closer to her, this time she didn't back away.

"Wait a minute! You told Dr. Huntley, didn't you? You told a *stranger* what you were going through but not me. No, you let *me* try to figure it out. I'm here to help you, but you wouldn't even take off your shirt. You . . ." He was only a few feet from her and the thought of what he'd been through was beginning to sink in. Anger was being replaced with tears.

"Hallie, I'm sorry," he said, his voice barely a whisper. "Really, I am. I just wanted you to see me as a whole man, not as damaged. I didn't want you to think of me as less than a man."

Some of her anger returned, but it was different. "Do you have any idea how stupid that sounds? You're more of a man than anyone I've ever met. You care about . . . about everyone. You're funny and smart and . . . I thought we were becoming friends. But you ran off with your brother and left me alone with your naked cousins."

It was sinking in to Jamie that she wasn't going to feel sorry for him. Todd had talked him into staying away for a couple of days to give them both time to think. But Jamie had agonized over her meeting men who weren't damaged by war and life. And she had reduced them to "naked cousins." He wasn't sure if he wanted to laugh or cry in joy.

He motioned for the guys to leave, then took a step toward her. "I did a stupid, selfish thing because I didn't know women like you existed. I assumed you were like everyone else and would be sickened at the sight of me." His heart was in his words. His pride, his very manhood, was there. To admit his failings was almost as painful as the wounds on his body. "Hallie, I have problems, deep ones, and I honestly don't know how to handle them. I can't sleep well without pills. I—"

"You don't sleep very well *with* them," Hallie said. "If it weren't for sleeping kisses, you would have fallen out of bed the first night I was here."

Jamie's eyes widened. "Sleeping kisses?"

"At two A.M. every morning I'm at your bedside trying to get you settled. The only thing that works are kisses and hugs. And sometimes sleeping with you like I'm your favorite stuffed toy. You're like a toddler. Except for—" She couldn't keep up her bravado. Reaching out, she put her hand on his chest, on the ridges and dips of the scars. Some of them were burns. "I could have helped you," she whispered.

"I know that now, but I didn't then." He touched her earlobe. "You're so beautiful, but I'm so . . . so repulsive. My cousins are perfect and I'm—"

"More interesting!" Hallie said. "They *are* perfect. They haven't a mark on their flawless bodies, but you . . . You've done something for other people and for your country. You . . ." She was fighting tears. "You're more of a man than they will *ever* be."

When Jamie held his arms out to her, there were tears in his eyes and she went to him. For a moment he held her as he had before, as friends, and her mind was on what he'd been through.

But as they stood there, bodies entwined, Hallie became aware that at some point Jamie's towel had fallen off. And he was ready for her. She could feel the hardness of him through the thin fabric of her shorts. It looked like some parts of him weren't damaged!

When she pulled away, she meant to make a joke. But the look in his eyes erased all thoughts of humor. It had been a long time since she'd had a boyfriend and Jamie Taggert was a *very* desirable man.

For a moment his eyes searched hers and she knew that "yes" was written in them.

Bending his head, he kissed her, but only for a second. He drew back and looked at her in shock. "I remember!" he said. "I remember the taste of your kisses."

She started to smile, but Jamie's passion took over. Within seconds, she was bare from the waist down and her shirt was open.

Never before had she experienced such desire, such energy and excitement. He moved her out of sight of the window, pressed her back against the wall, and pulled her leg up to his hip. She wrapped it around him.

He entered her with a force that she'd never felt before, and she gave a sigh. "Ooooooh." It seemed that every part of Jamie's body was big.

"Did I hurt you?" He sounded alarmed.

"Oh, yeah," she said, her head back against the wall, her eyes closed. "I might not survive."

He gave a low chuckle. "Me neither." He put his mouth on her neck.

Hard, deep thrusts sent chills of pleasure through her body. Desire—need—flooded her. He picked up her other leg so she was fully clasping his hips as he thrust into her again and again.

All thought, all sense of being a human, seemed to leave Hallie as she gave herself over to this man. Mind, body, soul became feelings, sensations.

With her upper back against the wall and her legs around him, she lifted her arms. The leverage made his thrusts even deeper.

When the end came, waves of pleasure and release went through her. She went from being a tower of strength to her body collapsing. If Jamie hadn't held on to her, she would have fallen, but his arms went around her and pulled her against his bare chest.

He took the few steps to the old couch and stretched out on it, his braced leg extended and touching the floor, with Hallie on top of him.

She still had on her bra and shirt but was nude from the waist down. As they lay there, his hand caressed her lower half, enjoying her curves.

As for Hallie, it took her a while to recover. She was floating in a delicious haze of sensations, and she couldn't seem to return to the world.

"All right?" he whispered.

"Yes." His chest was so very warm. It wasn't smooth, but she could feel the strong contours of it. She ran her hand over his ribs and down to his side, over the thick scars there.

Very slowly, she remembered where she was—and who she was. She had just broken a rule of her profession about sleeping with a client.

She didn't want to, but she made herself get off his big, warm body and sit on the edge of the couch, her back still touching him. There was a pillow on the floor and she pulled it onto her lap, then started to button her shirt—which was a useless endeavor as most of the buttons had been torn off. She saw one glistening on the floor by the wall where they'd just— She took a breath. There were things that had to be said and she dreaded his response.

"This can't happen again," she said softly. "We aren't—"

"Going steady?" he said cheerfully.

She looked at him in surprise. In her experience, when you told men there wouldn't be any more—even if it was mutual—they got angry. But Jamie was smiling at her. He was stretched out on the couch, one big, muscular arm behind his head, and he had a little smile on his handsome face.

She couldn't help a bit of a frown. "You agree?"

"I understand," he said. "You don't think there is any future for us, and I'm your patient. And besides, you have a guy from back home coming to visit any day. You don't want any complications."

"Right," she said. That was exactly what was in her mind, so why was it so very annoying when *he* said it?

"I have a question," Jamie said. "Did you finagle me into moving into the upstairs bedroom so you wouldn't have to wander around in the dark? Because of my nightmares, that is?"

"That's right."

"You made up the lie about being scared of the beautiful Tea Ladies just to save yourself the trek?"

Her frown left her and a smile began. "Yes, I did. I flat out told a going-to-hell lie, and my toes thank me for it. Actually, my whole body thanks me, since I spent the first night on the couch. I nearly froze!"

A look of such softness came to Jamie's face that she almost bent forward and kissed him.

"Thank you," he said. "Hand me the towel, will you? Unless you want to have some more friendship sex."

She knew what he meant, that he was ready again—and she didn't dare look or she just might climb back on top of him.

For a few moments their eyes locked and Hallie felt herself weaken. Even as she knew she shouldn't, she leaned toward him, her eyes beginning to close.

But abruptly, Jamie sat up, causing Hallie to nearly slide off the couch. His strong arm caught her as he moved out from behind her. She fell back against the couch and watched him walk across the room in all his naked glory. So there were a few indentations, she thought. Well, maybe more than a few, but they didn't take away from his beauty.

He wrapped the towel around his waist, then turned back to hand her her garments.

Hallie still hadn't moved. What just happened didn't seem to have affected him at all but it certainly had her. But then hadn't she always thought he was just a playboy who jetted around the world? Maybe he was used to this kind of thing. But today she'd found out he'd been a man who'd served his country and had nearly died from it. The two images didn't seem to go together. Who was the real Jamie Taggert?

"I'm going upstairs to put on some clothes," he said. "I don't like the kids to see me like this. You still want to work on me on your table?"

"Yes, of course."

"I'll meet you at the gym in an hour."

Before Hallie could reply, he went through the door to the kitchen and closed it behind him.

After she was dressed, she looked about the empty tea room. What an understanding man Jamie was! she thought. They'd been caught up in the moment and had sex. It was, of course, understandable, born out of a combination of emotions. For one thing, she'd just discovered what he'd kept secret, then she'd seen the evidence of his severe injuries, and they'd had an argument. Anger always got the blood flowing, didn't it?

All in all, it made sense. Any two healthy young people, with him wearing only a towel—which had slipped to the floor, no less—would have done what they did. It was natural. If it had been Jamie's cousin Raine, it would probably have happened.

Even as she thought that, she knew it wasn't true. She'd wanted Jamie from the day she'd looked out a window and seen him.

So it had happened and now it was done with. And as Jamie had said, Braden was coming in a few days, then they would . . . Who knew?

But if everything was all right, why did she feel like she wanted to yell at James Michael Taggert? Bawl him out? How could he just leave that way? He'd acted as though nothing had happened. He'd even spoken of turning her over to Braden.

Didn't their making love mean *anything* to him?! "Men!" she said aloud, then went into the kitchen. She closed the door behind her just a little bit too hard. No windows broke, but they certainly did rattle.

Upstairs, Jamie felt as well as heard the door slam with the force of a storm, and for the first time since he got out of the hospital, he didn't jump. Instead, he smiled. His worry had been her reaction to his body, but now that that was settled, there were no more obstacles. At least none that mattered. A blond Montgomery lookalike didn't even count.

Still smiling, he got into the shower. He wanted to be very clean for the coming massage.

Chapter Twelve

When Hallie got to the gym, Jamie was already on the massage table, face down, only a skimpy towel covering part of him. The sight of him put her mind back on her work and she was once again a professional. She began to run her hands over his back, assessing the scars and thinking how she was going to work on him.

"How did this . . . ?" She didn't complete her question.

But he knew what she was asking. "Humvee exploded. One leg and my head and shoulders fell under my buddy's body or they would have been sliced and diced too."

"And your friend?"

"Didn't make it."

"Is Valery . . . ?"

"The best of us. I couldn't go to her funeral, but later I talked to her husband and—"

"Shhhh," Hallie said. His body had begun to tighten, the muscles pulling into themselves. "No more talking. Breathe like I showed you and try to clear your mind. Think of a happy place."

"That tea room comes to mind."

She was glad he couldn't see her smile. "Think of something more peaceful. Maybe a childhood place with grass and sunshine."

When he started to relax, she knew he was falling into someplace far away. "There's a house with a porch," he whispered.

She began to work on him. "Just be calm."

She knew enough about anatomy to imagine what had caused his injuries and what had been done to repair the damage. That he hadn't bled to death was a miracle. The medical care must have been extraordinary.

There were places on his body that weren't fully healed and she managed to work around them, gently coaxing his muscles to release. Other areas were thick and hard with scar tissue and she wished she could have worked on him from the beginning, right after he was hurt. She might have been able to loosen the skin and kept it from welting.

But she thought Jamie wouldn't have allowed that then. She reminded herself that he was so stubborn, it was only by accident that she was working on him now.

She spent over an hour working on his back before she felt she'd done all she could. Her arms were aching, but she wasn't about to stop.

"Turn over," she said, and did what she could to help him. The brace made his movements awkward.

"Thank you," he said, his eyes closed.

She knew what he meant, as she was beginning to feel the tension leave him.

As she unfastened his brace and began to work on his injured leg, she had an idea that the story he'd told of his knee injury was a sugarcoated version. Had he panicked at some sound and forgotten he was on skis? Dived for cover and landed on his knee?

His eyes were closed and she wasn't going to ask him.

She refastened the brace and started on his other leg, noting his injuries and working with them.

When she felt him beginning to sleep, she knew her treatment was starting to work. His face was relaxing. He was falling asleep without the use of any pills! That she had accomplished this made her feel as though she'd just climbed a mountain.

When she finally finished, she'd been working on him for nearly two hours. She was weak, shaky even, from exertion. It had been a very long morning. She'd jumped out of bed very early, then had the trauma of finding out about Jamie, then . . . then . . .

Smiling, she ran her hand over his cheek. If anyone deserved rest, it was this wounded soldier.

Stepping back, she put her hands on her lower back and stretched. She'd like to go to the house, but she didn't dare leave him alone. His big body filled the table. If he had one of his nightmares, he'd roll off and hit the ground.

She looked around for someone to watch him, but there was no one in the garden. Yesterday Ian said the family was going to a beach so that's probably where they were. She was about to pull up a chair when the red gate opened and in walked a man she'd never seen before. He looked older, with gray at his temples, and he was built like a bigger version of Jamie. The word "bull" came to mind. Obviously, he was one of the Taggerts.

He saw her right away, as though he was looking for her. Smiling, she motioned for him to come over.

When he got closer, he asked in a deep rumble of a voice, "Need some help?"

"Could you please watch Jamie while I go inside?" she said in a whisper. "Let him sleep and don't do anything to wake him. If he starts, uh, dreaming, do something nice, like sing him a lullaby. But whatever you do, do *not* let him fall off this table."

The man was looking at her oddly, as though he was trying to figure her out.

Hallie was walking backward toward the house. "But you probably know all this, don't you?"

"Not all of it," he said. "Go. I'll take care of him."

She was reluctant to leave. "You can't step away for even a minute. When he starts thrashing about, he's fast and he's strong."

"I won't let him fall. I promise," the man said and for the first time, he smiled. "Now go before he wakes up and wants you to give him a mani-pedi."

Laughing, Hallie turned and ran to the house.

"Dad," Jamie said when he woke up. His father was sitting on one of the wooden chairs and reading a newspaper. Jamie realized a blanket was covering him and he was still on top of the massage table. "I think I dozed off."

"For over an hour," his father said. "Half the family's been over here to gawk at you. I almost couldn't keep Cory from climbing on you."

Jamie ran his hand over his face. "Did I . . . ?"

Kane knew his son was referring to the nightmares. "It was a mild one. This girl Hallie seems to be good for you." Kane was watching his son, trying hard not to let the fear show in his eyes. He'd nearly lost his son in a war, and since Jamie had returned, every day Kane worried that Jamie's grief and guilt and all that he'd been through would overwhelm him. Kane had read too much about the suicide of young soldiers to dismiss the possibility.

"She is," Jamie said, but didn't elaborate.

But Kane saw the way his son's face softened, the way he was looking around to see if she was there. When Jamie tried to sit up, Kane had to resist the urge to help him. And when the blanket fell away, he couldn't repress a wince at the sight of his son's scarred body. This isn't what you envisioned for your child when you diapered him and held your hands out for his first step.

Jamie saw the grimace and pulled the blanket up to cover himself.

"You want to tell me about her?"

"No," Jamie said. "Not yet." He kept looking around the garden.

"She took a nap," Kane said. "Your mother went up to check on her and she was stretched across the bed asleep. I have a favor to ask of you."

"About what?" Jamie asked, his voice cautious.

"Take care of your aunt Jilly tonight. We're all going out to dinner and I think it might overwhelm her. We arranged that you and Hallie would have her and Uncle Kit over for dinner. Something quiet."

They both knew Kane was lying. A full family dinner, probably in some restaurant where they'd reserved every table, would be too much for Jamie. Kids screaming and running around, adults laughing, glad to see one another, would be as loud as a battlefield.

"Sounds good," Jamie said, but he didn't meet his father's eyes. "When's the groom going to get here?"

"As soon as he can. Speaking of grooms, Graydon's wedding is tomorrow morning. Some of the kids are setting up a screen in Kingsley House. You want to go there or have a setup put in here?"

Jamie had to look away and swallow a few times before he answered. He knew that his family meant well. Their constant, never-ending care and concern for him were based on love. He knew that and appreciated it. However, the last few days with Hallie, being yelled at, being told to *do* things, had been the best he'd felt since he was pulled out of the wreckage of an armored vehicle.

"Put in a set here," he said at last.

"Todd said—"

"Don't send him," Jamie said quickly.

Kane's eyes widened. Since they were born, the twins had been inseparable. The only argument they'd ever had was when Jamie said he was going to serve his country. Todd had gone berserk, shouting at his brother, saying that he was a fool and that he could be *killed*. It had taken three Montgomerys and a Taggert to hold Todd down, while Jamie just stood there, unbending in his resolve. "Todd will want to see the wedding with you."

"Yeah, I know," Jamie said and there was a flush on his cheeks. "But he and Hallie don't get along. He keeps testing her."

"He thinks she's a gold digger?"

"He thinks she'll leave me when she gets tired of my . . . of my . . ." He couldn't finish or meet his father's eyes.

"What do you think?"

"That if she's smart, she'll run away." He was scratching one of the scars over his rib cage.

"I think that if she's smart she'll overlook a few mosquito bites and see my son underneath."

"Thanks," Jamie said and met his father's eyes.

"Are you hungry? Your mother yet again packed your refrigerator full of food. She's becoming great friends with Dr. Huntley's wife, Victoria. I think they're going to collaborate on a book. A sort of murder mystery cum ghost story. Your mom found a lot of info about your Tea Ladies ghosts and gave it all to Kit."

Jamie nodded. He knew what his dad was doing. He was

putting Jilly and Kit, the calmest people in the extensive family, together with his injured son. It was certainly well meant, but Jamie couldn't suppress the resentment he felt. He *needed* to be singled out, but that didn't mean he *wanted* to be. Poor, pitiful, damaged Jamie.

"That all sounds great," Jamie said as he got off the table. "Hallie and Uncle Kit had some meeting at two A.M. and now they're friends."

"Did they?" Kane asked as he handed his son his clothes. "But Kit doesn't talk to anyone."

"Everybody talks to Hallie and everybody likes her," Jamie said, sounding almost defensive. He had his back to his father and didn't see the smile that reached down to Kane Taggert's very soul. This girl was putting life back into his son, and for that Kane was deeply grateful.

"So I've heard. Raine can't shut up about her."

"What does that mean? Two sentences?"

"Four!" Kane said and they laughed, the tension between them broken.

When Jamie was dressed, he flexed his shoulders and back. "I feel better after Hallie's massage. You should let her work on you."

"I think I'll give her a break. It seems like every male in the family has been over here. Come on, let's go see what your mother left for us to eat." He put his arm around his son's shoulders and they walked back to the house.

"Hi," Hallie said as she saw Jamie enter the kitchen. After her nap, she could think more clearly—and right now she was re-membering Jamie holding her against a wall. "Feel better?" she managed to ask.

"Much," he said.

Hallie started to say more, but behind him came the big man. "I think you've met my dad."

"I have," Hallie said as she shook his hand. "But I didn't realize who you were. Mr. Taggert, would you like something to eat? But then I think it's your wife who fills our refrigerator."

"Or Edith and her golf cart," Jamie said, and he and Hallie looked at each other in a shared joke.

"I'd love something," Kane said and sat down at the table. He took a chair against the wall and settled back to watch his son and this young woman whom most of his family had been praising to the skies.

He'd wanted to meet her the first day they'd arrived, but his wife, Cale, had nixed that.

"She'll know you're studying her, judging her," Cale said.

"I just want to meet her, that's all. No judgment."

"Ha!" Cale said. "You want to see if she's worthy to be around your wounded son. You'll be like Todd and make it into a criminal investigation. The poor girl will run away."

"And you wouldn't question her?" Kane said, sounding more angry than he meant to.

"I would scrutinize everything about her!" Cale shot back. She was quite small and her husband was very large, but she had *never* been intimidated by him. "I'd watch her like she was under a magnifying glass." Her voice was rising. "If she said even a word that wasn't kind and loving and gentle and caring to our Jamie, I'd tear her eyes out. I'd—"

Kane pulled her into his arms. "It's okay. We'll both stay away."

Cale was trying to calm down. "Jamie and Todd have talked every day and I don't know what the girl is doing, but Jamie *likes* her." Since his injuries, they'd paraded half a dozen truly fabulous young women before him. "Brilliant Beauty Queens," the family called them. Vassar graduates who'd given them- selves pocket money by modeling. But Jamie had been so uninterested that Cale had consulted his doctor about any sexual injuries he might have. But, no, that part of his body was unscathed.

Kane had been furious when his wife told him what she'd done. Thankfully, Jamie didn't find out.

Repeatedly, the family had been told to wait, to give Jamie time to recover. When Todd told them of his idea of taking Jamie away from his family's loving home, away from their care and concern, everyone had fought him. But Todd had a couple of doctors on his side. Only after the family agreed to allow it had Jamie been told.

At first he'd said yes, but as the day to leave approached, he'd started to back down. But somehow, Todd and Raine had persuaded Jamie to go.

So now Kane was getting his first look at this girl. She was quite pretty and as curvy as a snowman. As he watched Jamie and Hallie at the sink, he couldn't help thinking of the tall skinnies Jamie's family had paraded past him. It looked like when it came to taste in women, it was like father, like son.

Hallie put a tray of vegetables and dip on the table, and as Kane munched, he saw the way the two of them moved about the kitchen. Their voices were low, but then they didn't seem to need many words, as they worked well together.

There was an interesting moment after Jamie said something and Hallie laughed. They were standing at the sink, inches apart, their backs to him, and they looked at each other. Such electricity passed between them that Kane paused with a carrot halfway to his mouth.

Somebody's been in the cookie jar, he thought, then reached for his phone. He wanted to tell his wife that Jamie's long spell of celibacy had been broken.

But when Hallie turned and asked if he'd like iced tea or lemonade, Kane took his hand off the phone. "Tea," he said and leaned back in his chair, unable to get the grin off his face.

"What have you two been doing?" Kane asked when they were seated across from him.

Jamie knew his father well and when he looked up, his eyes had a bit of a glint in them. Kane met his son's eyes for only a second, and his smile widened. It was a silent message between them.

Hallie started telling about Edith and the elaborate teas she brought them and how the woman talked to the lady ghosts.

At first Jamie was quiet, letting Hallie tell the story, but when she got to Dr. Huntley's visit he joined in.

Kane sat back, listened, and smiled. He wasn't much interested in the ghost story—though he knew his wife was—but he was very, very happy to see his son so animated.

When they ran out of salad dressing, Jamie got up and retrieved a bottle from the fridge. It didn't seem to mean anything to Hallie, but it was monumental to Kane. After Jamie came home, wrapped in bandages, his wounds healing, there had always been someone nearby to get whatever he needed. Now he was on crutches, his leg in that big, cumbersome brace, but he was doing his own fetching. Neither he nor Hallie seemed to think his physical problems were an excuse for him to sit and be waited on.

"I nearly forgot," Hallie said. "We have to move the dresser in the tea room." When Jamie sat back down, she took his crutches and leaned them against the wall.

"Why?" Jamie asked.

She looked startled. "I just realized that I haven't told you about my dream! I saw the ladies. After I told Uncle Kit about it, he said we have to get some Taggerts to move the dresser to see if what I dreamed was real."

"You told my uncle but not *me*?"

Kane took a big bite of his sandwich to keep from laughing at his son's tone of disbelief, and maybe even some hurt at being left out.

"It was that morning when I woke up in your bed and the kids were jumping on us, then your naked cousins showed up. I was so dazzled by them that I forgot all about the dream. If you hadn't—" Breaking off, she looked at Kane. "Sorry. They weren't really naked. Not then, anyway."

Kane raised his hand. "Don't mind me. Say what you want."

Jamie was glaring at Hallie. "You could have told me later. You could have taken a break from your harem and told me about your ghost dream."

"*You* were hiding out with your brother, remember? I couldn't *find* you! I asked everyone where you were, but they wouldn't tell me. I *still* don't know where you were."

"Busy," Jamie said. "So what was your dream?"

"I'm not going to tell you now. I'm going to wait until tonight and tell everyone."

"But you just said that Uncle Kit has already heard it."

"Yes, but I got an email from him saying he was reading the research material your mother brought and that at dinner tonight he'd tell us about it. And he says your aunt Jilly is taking a break from wedding activities to look more deeply into the Hartley family tree. Tonight she's going to tell us what she found out. I am certainly looking forward to the dinner. What do you think we should cook? Scallops? They're local."

Jamie was staring at her in open-mouthed astonishment. "Uncle Kit gave you his email address?"

"Yes. Don't you have it?"

"No, I don't. He is a *very* private person."

For a moment the two of them looked at each other as though they were going to get into a serious argument. Kane thought maybe he'd have to step in, but then the two young people started laughing.

"So now you're going to run off with Uncle Kit?" Jamie asked, teasing.

"No. I'm after Raine. Think I could sweet-talk him into moving that big dresser?"

"I could—"

"Oh, no, you can't," Hallie said. "You could injure your knee again and my arms are still sore from a morning of working on all of your incredibly tight muscles. You're not going to use any muscles while I'm around."

"I thought you liked my tight muscles." His meaning was clear.

"Not on a massage table! Right now we need Raine and another one of your bull-sized relatives to move that cabinet." With a gasp, she turned to look at Kane. "Sorry. I didn't mean to disparage anyone." Her face turned red.

"At least we Taggerts are good for something," Kane said as he got up. "Jamie, get your phone and tell Raine to come over here and we'll see what we can do about the furniture. Hallie, come with me and show me this thing." He looked from one to the other. "If you two can bear to be parted, that is."

"I can walk and text at the same time," Jamie said as he reached for his crutches, obviously not wanting to be left behind.

But when he stumbled, Hallie said, "Give me the phone." He did and they went into the tea room.

Chapter Thirteen

*K*it arrived with Raine, who was carrying a big file box. The three Taggert men looked surprised when the tall, elegant man kissed Hallie on both cheeks. "You look well, my dear," Kit said.

"I had an interesting morning," she answered and ignored the little snort Jamie gave.

"So I heard." Kit nodded for Raine to put the box on the coffee table. "Should we empty the cabinet before it's moved?"

Kane gave a snort identical to his son's. "I think we can manage it fully loaded." He looked at Raine and the two big men easily moved the huge old dresser away from the wall, then stood back. "It's yours," Kane said to Hallie, meaning that she could look first.

Leaning against the wall they'd exposed were two pieces of old paper, one about ten by twelve, the other half that size.

Whatever was on them was hidden from view. The fact that they'd been there, untouched, for over two hundred years didn't surprise Hallie. Her dream had been so vivid, so clear, that it was as though she'd lived it.

When she picked up the papers, an envelope fell forward. On the front, in beautiful copperplate writing, was the single word "Kit." In one movement, she hid the envelope under her shirt, then got up and put the papers face down on a tea table.

As the men moved the dresser back in place, she caught Kit's eyes and he understood that she had something to show him. As he walked past Hallie, she surreptitiously slipped the envelope to him.

When they'd all gathered around the table, Hallie said, "Is everyone ready?"

"With breath held," Kit said.

Hallie turned the large one over first. The ink drawing was exactly as she'd seen it in her dream. Two beautiful young women were stretched out together on the window seat, one with her head on the other's shoulder. Their pretty dresses draped about them, nearly encasing them.

The artist had caught what looked to be sadness in their eyes. But then that was understandable. On Juliana's wedding day, they'd known it was their last moment together in the same house. The next day, Juliana was to leave with her new husband. What they didn't know was that within a week, death would separate both of them from everything they loved.

Hallie looked at Kit in question and he nodded at her. Yes, these were the young women he had seen.

"And what is that one?" Kane asked.

Hallie flipped over the other paper—and gasped. It was a drawing of her father. He was wearing a high-collared shirt and his hair was longer than he used to wear it, and he was very young, but it was most certainly her dad.

"Whoever he is, he looks like you," Jamie said. "You have the same eyes."

She looked at the others standing around the table and each one nodded in agreement.

Hallie picked up the drawing. "I guess this is Leland Hartley, my ancestor." She looked at Jamie, his father, and Raine, noting the resemblance among them. Her father had been the only blood relative on his side she'd ever seen, but here was evidence of someone else related to her.

When she looked at Jamie, he seemed to understand. This discovery needed privacy.

"Okay, that's enough," Jamie said. "Everybody out."

"I agree completely." As Kit started for the door, he nodded at the big box by the couch. "I think you'll find the contents of that interesting." He left with Raine.

Kane paused by his son. "Your mom will send dinner over later, so you two don't have to worry about that. Enjoy yourselves." With a warm smile at both of them, he left the tea room.

Hallie looked at Jamie. "He doesn't think you and I are . . . uh, together, does he? I mean, he doesn't know that this morning we—" She couldn't say what was in her mind.

Jamie didn't want to lie, nor did he want to confess, so he said nothing.

But Hallie understood. Yes, he knew. Embarrassed, she stepped out the door. "I think I need to clean up the gym, so I'd better go." But the sky suddenly opened and rain pelted down on her. She ran back in and shut the door behind her.

"You're wet," Jamie said. "Stay here." He went into the kitchen and returned with a stack of dry kitchen towels, put one over her hair, and began to rub.

"I need to go upstairs and change," she said.

Suddenly, Jamie did *not* want her to leave the room, didn't want either of them to leave it. He pulled the folded blanket off the window seat and wrapped it around her shoulders. Rain was coming down hard outside and they could hear it lashing against the windows. It was a fierce summer storm.

When Hallie shivered, Jamie put his arm around her. "This looks like it may be coming down for a while. How about I build us a fire and we go through the box Uncle Kit brought over? And you can tell me about your dream that seems to have been real."

Hallie put the towel around her neck. "I think that's a great idea. Do you know how to build a fire?"

Jamie couldn't help shaking his head in disbelief. "Of course. I've watched the butler do it many times."

Her eyes widened.

"We don't have a butler and I'm from Colorado. I can build a fire on top of snow."

"Really?" She sat down on one end of the couch, wrapped in the blanket.

"Watch and learn," he said. It took him only minutes before the fireplace was going strong. The wind hit the old windows, making them rattle, but it was cozy and warm inside, and the light from the fire was cheerful.

Hallie leaned back against a pillow and stretched her legs out. For some odd reason, her clothes no longer felt wet. "This is nice."

When Jamie sat down on the opposite end of the couch, she drew her knees up. Reaching out, he pulled her feet onto his lap and began to massage them.

"I don't think this is appropriate," she said and started to draw back, but he held her feet to him.

"Let me get this straight," Jamie said. "This morning you had me buck naked on a table with only a towel the size of a washcloth over my behind, and your hands were all over me.

Inside my thighs, well below my navel, everywhere. And that's not even counting when we were all over each other. But now I'm not allowed to touch your *feet?*"

Hallie couldn't help laughing. "I guess when you put it that way, I can't say no. And besides, it does feel good." He was stroking her feet, his strong hands caressing them, and she closed her eyes.

"You're not used to people doing nice things for you, are you?" he asked.

"I guess not."

"Your stepsister didn't do anything to thank you for all you did for her?"

It was Hallie's turn to give a snort. "No, that's not something Shelly does. Can you reach the box Kit brought?"

Once again, Jamie knew he'd been told to back off. "Sure," he said. "You mind if I take off this sweatshirt? It's heating up in here."

At her nod, he pulled the heavy garment over his head. Under it he had on a plain white, short-sleeved T-shirt, which allowed the scars on his arms to show. When he reached over to get the box, she could see the outline of more scars on his back.

"Do you cover up with long sleeves just for outsiders?" she asked.

"No!" He pulled the lid off. "I have to cover up around my family. If I don't, the aunts get teary and start asking if they can get me anything. The uncles pat my shoulder and say this country is lucky to have men like me."

"And your cousins?"

"They're the worst. They say, 'Jamie, why don't you sit there and watch us have fun?' Or 'Our game of Ping-Pong won't be too loud for you, will it?'"

Hallie was trying not to laugh. "Ping-Pong?"

"Well, maybe not that particular game, but I'm sure not invited to play rugby with them."

"But somebody got you to go skiing."

"That was Todd. Tough love that put me back in the hospital."

"Sounds like your family was right to coddle you. But then the skiing is what got you *here*." She wiggled her toes on his lap.

"Yeah, it did. So maybe I owe my brother. Just please don't tell him that." Jamie leaned forward as though he meant to kiss her.

But Hallie pulled back. "So what's in the box?"

"Just papers. You know, you wouldn't be nearly so cold if you moved to my end of the couch. I'm a very warm person."

"I'm not cold at all. I want to see what Uncle Kit brought us."

"Speaking of him, what did you slip my uncle when you two thought no one was looking?"

"You saw that?!"

"Of course. So what was it?"

She told him of the envelope with Kit's name on it. "Do you think that tonight at dinner he'll tell us what was inside it?"

"If he does, it's only because he's mad about you."

Hallie laughed. "I don't think so, but thanks for the compliment."

As Jamie held the box up, they looked inside it. There was a thick envelope on top and under it were a lot of loose papers, most of them photocopies.

"Shall we divide things?" Hallie asked. "You take the envelope and I'll take the papers?"

"No. We can do it together. No more secrets."

"I like that," Hallie said. "So what's in the envelope?"

He unlooped the string from around the two dots. "I bet this is from Aunt Jilly."

"I don't see how she could do this. If she's getting married in just a few days, wouldn't that be her major interest?"

"She's never liked the chaos of big family events. Raine's mother is here and she could organize a war. Aunt Jilly probably gave her a helpless look and Aunt Tildy took over. Then Aunt Jilly probably hid somewhere with a computer and did a lot of searching—and was happy doing it." He pulled out the papers. "By the way, whoever gets Raine gets his mother."

"After watching him move that heavy dresser, it might be worth it. I thought that T-shirt of his might rip apart. The Hulk come to life!" She gave a dramatic sigh.

"Did you?" Jamie said, then gave a stretch and lifted his arms above his head, making his biceps double in size.

Hallie pretended she didn't see him, but the room suddenly grew warmer. She tossed the towel from her neck and let the blanket slip down. Holding her hand out, he put a folded paper on it.

It was a genealogy chart like the one she'd seen on the plane coming over, but this one branched differently. Instead of just going down through her father to Hallie, this chart went to another side of the family.

Hallie sat up straighter. "Am I reading this right?" She bent forward to show Jamie. "This says I have a relative, a *living* one." She pointed to the entry. "He's also named Leland and he's thirty years old."

Jamie was staring at her. He couldn't grasp the concept of having no known relatives.

"*Is* he a cousin?"

He took the chart and looked at it. "You two share the Leland Hartley who married Juliana Bell, so yes, that makes you distant cousins."

"Wow!" Hallie said as she fell back against the couch. "I wonder what he's like? Where he went to school, what he does for a living." She gasped. "Maybe he's married and has *children*! I could be an aunt."

He didn't have the heart to point out that the man's kids

would also be her cousins. But then in his family "aunt" and "uncle" were often courtesy titles.

Jamie picked up a paper from the pile on his lap. "Let's see. The Leland Hartley in this generation grew up in Boston and graduated from Harvard with a degree in business. Afterward, he worked on a farm for three years so he could— Hmmm, I can't seem to make this out." He was teasing her.

Hallie took the paper out of his hand and read aloud. "He's a landscape architect. He travels all over the U.S. and designs parks. He's not married, no children." She looked at Jamie. "He has a website for his business."

Jamie was truly enjoying her wonder and excitement. "Too bad he's so ugly."

"What?!"

He handed her a photo Jilly had run off from the website.

Leland Hartley was a very good-looking young man. And what's more, he looked like a younger version of her father. The hair and clothes were different, but the two men were nearly the same. She looked up at Jamie.

"He looks enough like you that he could be your older brother," Jamie said.

For a moment there were tears glistening in Hallie's eyes. "I want to meet him. After your leg heals I'll go back to Boston and . . ." She didn't finish because she didn't want Jamie to think that his rehabilitation was hindering her.

"See this?" He held up a big cream-colored envelope. "Know what it is?"

"No. Should I?"

"It's an invitation to Aunt Jilly's wedding. There's a note from her and she suggested that you write a letter, include a copy of this chart, and invite your newly found cousin to the wedding."

It took Hallie moments to realize what he was saying. "That's a wonderful idea! Oh, Jamie! You are great. Your whole family is fabulous." Bending across the papers spread out on him, she put her hands on each side of his face and kissed him hard, then got up.

"You can do better than that," he said.

Hallie was standing in front of the fireplace and didn't seem to hear him. "Where will he stay? If he can come, that is. He might be on a job and can't make it. Or maybe he wouldn't be interested in meeting some distant cousin. Should I tell him about the ghosts? No! Definitely not. He'd *never* come if I told that. Maybe . . ." She looked at Jamie.

Jamie was smiling at her enthusiasm. "I know! I'll sic Mom on him. She'll call him and tell him about you and she'll get him to come. She's very persuasive."

"She'd do that? For me, I mean?"

There was so much to answer in that question that he didn't know where to begin. Hallie had made Jamie laugh, and for that he knew his mother would do anything for her. "Yeah, she'll do it. But she'll want to hear every detail of the story, so be prepared."

Hallie put her hands behind her back and began to pace.

Jamie smiled as he watched her, amused by the deep frown of concentration she was wearing. But after a few minutes his smile began to fade. He could afford to laugh about this idea of wanting a family because he had one in abundance. But what would it truly be like to have no one?

When he was in Afghanistan, the thought of family and home kept him going. At every mail call there were letters from his family. His parents wrote constantly. His mother's letters were full of funny, loving stories about everyone. His siblings, even little Cory and Max, had sent him drawings, gifts, and food.

When he saw that some people with him never received any mail, he'd sent a plea to his mother to get the relatives to write to them. Within a week, Montgomery-Taggert letters were coming in by the bagful.

Jamie watched as Hallie picked up the paper that told about her one and only cousin and read it again. She seemed to be memorizing it, studying it, trying to get a real person out of it.

He remembered what Todd had told him about her stepsister, and Hallie had made some rather horrific offhand comments about her life after her father had remarried. What had happened to her?

As he watched Hallie, he realized that her wounds weren't visible, as his were. She didn't have to wear long sleeves to cover the scars, but right now he was thinking that it was possible she was as deeply scarred as he was.

He pulled his phone out of his pocket and punched the button for his mother's number. She answered instantly.

"Jamie!" Cale said, her voice on the verge of panic. "Are you all right? Do you need me? I'm just next door. Tildy has me buried in ribbons, but I'll gladly leave. I can—"

"Mom!" Jamie said, making Hallie stop pacing and look at him. "I'm fine. I feel better than I have since— Anyway, yes, I'm great."

Hallie sat down on the end of the couch and watched him.

"I know you're busy," Jamie said, "but I have some urgent business I want you to do. Did you see that Aunt Jilly found Hallie's relative?"

"No," Cale said, her voice serious. "What's going on?"

"I want you to bring him here. Now."

Hallie drew in her breath.

"Can she hear me?" Cale whispered.

"No," Jamie said cheerfully. "Not at all."

"You said 'relative' singular and 'him,' also singular. Is there just one—besides that stepsister I heard about?"

"Yes, Mom, you're exactly right." Jamie gave Hallie a thumbs-up. If there was anything on earth his mother knew about, it was rotten families. He'd only met people from her side once and it had been a disaster. A sister had threatened to write a tell-all book of lies about Cale if she didn't pay millions. Jamie didn't know what his father did, but the sister went away and was never heard from again. "You think you could get this guy here for the wedding?"

"If it's possible, I'll do it." Cale lowered her voice. "But first I'll make some calls and find someone who knows him. After I verify that he's a good guy, I'll send the jet to pick him up."

"Brilliant," Jamie said. "Let me know everything as it happens."

"Of course I will. And Jamie, dearest, how are you really and truly?"

"It's what you wished for." He was looking at Hallie and smiling.

Cale drew in her breath. "That you're beginning to heal?"

"Yes, you have it right."

"Okay," she said. "I'm now going to go somewhere and cry, then I'll make some calls. Oh, no! Here comes Tildy. I have to hide. Jamie, I love you more than you can imagine." She clicked off.

He put his phone down and looked at Hallie. "He'll be here as fast as my mom can get him here. Which means he'll probably knock on the door at any second."

Hallie was calming down. "I'm sorry for getting so excited about this. It's just that I never dreamed this could happen. My mother's family only seems to give birth to single children, no siblings, and my dad grew up as a ward of the state."

It came to Jamie to make a joke about that being a blessing, but he didn't. He wanted her to tell him what had happened with her stepsister, but at this point he knew better than to ask her directly. "You have any girlfriends you want to invite to the wedding? The big meal is a buffet, so there's room for more people." He handed her some papers from the box. The rain was coming down hard and the fire felt good. Her legs stretched out beside him, her feet by his hip. His uninjured leg was beside hers, but the braced one was half on, half off the couch. He shifted so their legs were together, then pulled the blanket over them.

Hallie looked like she was about to protest, but when a flash of lightning lit up the room, she didn't. "This is some storm. I wonder why we weren't warned about it on the news?"

"Dad says that storms on Nantucket aren't for sissies."

"That looks to be correct. Anyway, I have no special girl-friends to invite. A few work friends but not that BFF."

Jamie picked up a copy of an article from the local newspaper dated 1974 and told Hallie of the first lines. A young couple on their honeymoon had been staying at the Sea Haven Inn. The wife went to the police and said her husband had been talking to two women at the house next door and they'd told him to get a divorce.

"Listen to this!" Jamie said and began reading aloud. " 'When the police investigated, they found that the room where the husband said he'd had tea with the young women was securely locked and when it was opened, the inside was filthy.' "

Jamie showed the page to Hallie. There was a grainy black-and-white photo of the tea room and it was just as dirty as it had been when they'd first seen it.

Hallie took the page and continued reading. " 'When questioned, the husband told the police that the beautiful young women he'd had tea with were ghosts. He said they only appeared to him because he'd not yet met the woman he would love with all his heart. He said he needed to be free so he could search for her.' "

"This was on their honeymoon?" Hallie said. "No wonder his wife was furious!" She read more, telling how the owner of the house, Henry Bell, had denied the existence of any ghosts. He said the room was locked when he bought the house, and since he didn't need the space, he'd left it locked. "Do you think Henry was telling the truth?" Hallie asked.

"I think he was lying through his teeth," Jamie answered.

"I agree. I do think Henry was in love with them." She put the paper down. "I just remembered the embroidery we saw. It was on the porch and you took a photo of it."

Their eyes met and in the next second, Hallie was running through the house to get it while Jamie looked on his phone for the photo. When she didn't come back right away, he called for her, but there was no answer. He called twice more but still no answer.

A bright flash of lightning was followed by a crack of thunder so loud the old house seemed to quake. Hallie's disappearance, the lightning, then the noise, were too much like what Jamie had experienced on the battlefield. He rolled off the couch and hit the floor hard. He couldn't remember where he was, but he *had* to get out of there!

He was crawling across the floor on his stomach, his braced leg dragging behind him, and keeping his body low.

Hallie came into the room carrying a heavily laden tea tray, a bag over her shoulder. "Look what Edith dropped off. Sorry I took so long, but I couldn't find the tray. Jamie? Did you fall?"

When she set the tray and bag on the dresser and looked down at him, she realized that he wasn't himself. He was like he was during his nightmares, awake but not awake.

"Jamie!" she said. "It's me, Hallie. You are safe." But he didn't respond. And he was crawling toward the blazing fireplace! She put her hands on his shoulders and pulled back, but he kept moving. "Jamie!" she shouted, but again there was no response. What could she do? "Help me," she whispered aloud. Jamie was now inches from the fire. "Please help me know what to do!" she cried out.

Suddenly, she stood up straight, her shoulders back. "Soldier!" she yelled. "Halt!"

He stopped moving.

Hallie turned on the two floor lamps to put as much light as she could in the room. When she looked back, Jamie had collapsed onto his stomach, his face buried in his arms. She knelt down at his head and stroked his hair.

"Go away," he mumbled. "I don't want you to see me like this."

She sat down beside him. "I'm not leaving."

He turned his head away from her. "Get out of here!" he shouted. "I don't want you!"

Hallie didn't move. "You can yell at me all you want, but I'm not leaving."

"I told you to get out!" His voice was a growl.

She still didn't move but just sat there beside him and waited. She knew he was embarrassed; she could feel it. It was like something that filled the room. Waves of regret and sorrow, fear and helplessness, were all around them.

Jamie turned onto his back, his hands on his chest, which was still heaving.

Hallie just waited. If she'd learned no other lesson in her life, she was very well acquainted with patience. Since she was eleven and her father had come home with a new wife and a pretty little stepdaughter, Hallie'd had to cultivate patience. It was a seed that had been planted on that first day and it had grown with the rapidity and strength of Jack's beanstalk.

It took a while for Jamie's breathing to quieten, for his heart to stop pounding. She saw a tear in a corner of his eye.

How awful it must be to be a man, she thought. To always be burdened with having to be strong, to show no weakness. A loss of strength made him think he was less than who he was supposed to be. Weakness took away who he *was*.

Finally, Jamie turned his head toward her. Just a bit, but it was enough for her to know that he was himself again.

She didn't say anything, just patted her lap in invitation.

He didn't hesitate as he put his head on her lap and his arms around her waist. "I'm—"

She put her fingertips over his lips. She did *not* want to hear an apology.

For a while he held on to her so tightly that she almost couldn't breathe, but she didn't try to loosen his grip. Instead, she just stroked his hair and waited for him to relax. When she felt his arms begin to loosen, she said, "Edith left us some tea. Want some?"

He took a while before he answered, then he nodded. She waited for him to sit up, and when he did, she wasn't surprised that he wouldn't look at her. When he tried to stand up, he stumbled and almost fell. Hallie's instinct was to help him, but she didn't. Instead, she got the big tray of tea off the dresser and put it on the coffee table. Jamie sat down on the couch.

"Look at this." Hallie opened the bag and tossed him the embroidery hoop. "See the difference?"

Jamie still hadn't looked at her, and she could see he was having trouble focusing on the embroidery. "It's still the same."

"That's what I thought at first too, but look again."

He picked up his phone and compared it to the picture he had taken that first day. "This is yellow." Finally, he met her eyes.

"Right. The first one we saw had birds on it, but this one is of daffodils. Here are the birds." She handed him a pillow.

Jamie put both on the table. "You know, this is a bit creepy."

"Very," she said and handed him a cup of tea with six different types of cookies on the saucer.

He took a drink, then said, "Hallie, I . . ." He couldn't seem to find words for what he wanted to say. "I don't hurt anyone," he said at last. "If I'd ever come close to hurting anyone, I wouldn't have allowed myself to be here alone with a young woman." He took a breath. "It's just that sometimes I don't know where I am." He paused. "I didn't mean the things I said."

Hallie nodded in understanding. "I know." She could tell that he didn't want to say any more about it. But that was all right because she too had things she didn't want to talk about. She gasped. "The box! We forgot the box."

"What are you talking about?"

"The one that hit me on the head. Remember? You freaked because you thought I was bleeding to death and you washed my hair. I turned into Meryl Streep fighting for her Kikuyus and—" She looked at his blank face. "It's a girl thing. I'll go get the box, but you stay here. Okay?"

"Yes," he said softly. "I'll stay right here and wait for you. Just this time don't take too long."

She wasn't sure, but she thought maybe he was making a joke about what had just happened.

She went to the pantry but didn't switch on the light. Instead, she leaned back against the wall and put her hands over her face. That had been truly *scary*! She'd not known how to help him. Stand back and let him get over it by himself? Or step in and *do* something?

When she closed her eyes, she seemed to hear the words "In every war, the soldiers are different. This one responds to love."

Her eyes flew open, but no one was there. But she knew who had "spoken." The same voice had told her which bedroom to choose, had told her to give a soldier orders, and was now giving her advice.

"Hallie!" Jamie yelled.

"I'm here," she answered back. "I'll be there as soon as I find it." When a bit of lightning highlighted the old box as though a spotlight had been turned on it, she rolled her eyes. "Why am I not surprised? And I bet that tea is still piping hot."

When she heard what sounded like the laughter of two young women, she hurried out of the pantry.

Chapter Fourteen

"Are you okay?" Jamie called.

"Yes," she answered and picked up the box. She sniffed a bit and put on a smile. She wasn't going to let Jamie see how much he'd upset her.

As she rounded the corner, Jamie was coming toward her on his crutches. But before he could say anything, there was a knock on the door. "Fun's over," he mumbled. When he nodded at the box, she shoved it way back on a shelf of the dresser, and Jamie opened the door.

It was Ian. "I have been given instructions to equip this room with a properly set table for dinner tonight. Dr. Huntley and his wife had dishes and silver sent over from Kingsley House. You two need to get dressed." Ian stepped inside. "It's a sauna in here! Did you have a fire going?"

"Yeah," Jamie said. "With the storm, it was cold in here."

"Storm?" Ian said. "We've been on the beach today and it was so sunny we nearly fried. We went through a dozen tubes of sunscreen."

"Maybe it was a localized storm," Jamie said.

Ian unhooked the double doors and threw them both open. Outside the grass was dry; there wasn't a drop of moisture on the paving stones.

Hallie was just behind Jamie and staring in disbelief. "Interesting."

"Whatever you two have been drinking, you should share it," Ian said. He looked out at the garden. Raine and Adam were coming toward them carrying big boxes, and behind them was an older woman.

"Is that Aunt Tildy?" Jamie asked.

"None other."

Jamie turned to Hallie. "We have to get out of here as fast as we can run."

"But I want to meet her," Hallie said even as Jamie got behind her and began pushing.

"Unless you want to tell every secret you've ever had, especially about your stepsister and the passport, you'll get out of here before Aunt Tildy arrives."

Hallie took time to blink twice, then began running toward the stairs.

"Dinner in an hour," Ian called after them. "And we set up the TV in the living room while you two were braving the big bad storm. Did the thunder keep you from hearing us?"

Hallie stopped at the top of the stairs and looked at Jamie. "We're either both crazy or . . ."

"Or the ladies played some game on us," Jamie answered.

"I don't know about you, but I prefer crazy," Hallie said.

"I agree. So what was in the box?"

"I didn't have time to look. I need to get dressed. If your cousins are bringing over china, is this thing formal?"

"Put on the black dress you wore to dinner. But you should know that if Uncle Kit's involved, he may show up in a tux. And Aunt Jilly might—"

"Why didn't you warn me about this? I should have started getting ready two hours ago. Damn!" She ran to her bedroom to get in the shower.

Minutes later, as she was frantically trying to get the curling iron to work on her hair, Jamie knocked on her bedroom door.

"Are you dressed?" he asked.

"Enough." She had on her underwear and a bathrobe.

Jamie came in, wearing the clothes he'd worn when they went out to dinner. "You don't need to do that to your hair. You look great with it pulled back flat."

"Nice to hear but not really true," she answered. "Oh, no!" Her cell phone was ringing.

Jamie took it off her nightstand and looked at the ID but said nothing.

"Who is it?"

Silently, he handed her the phone. In big letters it said BRADEN. "It's probably his mom." She put down the iron, took the phone, and stepped into the sitting room. "Hello?" she said tentatively.

"Hallie?"

"Braden! How are you? And how is your mother?"

"Everyone is fine. Do you have a moment?"

"Of course. My time is yours."

Jamie was standing in the doorway. "We need to go down and greet our guests," he said rather loudly.

"You're not alone," Braden said. "And you have guests? Is that someone I know?"

"No, you've not met him," Hallie said while frowning at Jamie and motioning for him to go away.

But he sat down in a chair, his hands on his lap, looking as though he meant to stay there.

Hallie turned her back on him. "I was told that you're coming here to visit."

"Yes," Braden said, "I am. Hallie, I have to tell you something and I hope it won't upset you. I wanted to hear both sides of what went on between you and Shelly so I spent some time with her. I even took her to the office with me."

"Oh," Hallie said and sat down heavily on the window seat. "Let me guess. You think she went about it the wrong way, but she has a valid reason for what she did."

Braden gave a laugh. "No, I haven't changed."

Hallie's smile deepened. "Has she put my house up for sale?"

"No, and she's not going to!" Braden's voice was firm. "But she made a pass at my boss."

"She didn't!"

"Oh, yes," Braden said. "She most certainly did. Anyway, Hallie, I have some paperwork to clear up at the office, then I'll fly out to Nantucket and we can talk. But honestly, is it all right for Shelly to continue living in your house for another week or so? She got a job at a restaurant so she can feed herself, but she can't pay the mortgage. Once this is settled, I'll get her out."

"Let her stay. I'll make the payments from here. Whenever you can come, let me know. I have a guest bedroom and—" She broke off as she looked at Jamie, who was glaring at her. "I'll be here," she finished.

"Hallie, I so look forward to seeing you again. Maybe when I'm there it won't all be work. Maybe we can play some."

"I'd like that," she said. "I'd like that very much."

They said goodbye and hung up. Hallie sat there for a few moments, holding the phone in her hands and thinking about what had just been said. Maybe they could *play* some?

She came back to the present when Jamie got up and started to leave—and she realized she'd just given his bedroom away. "I didn't mean to—"

"That's all right," he said. "He's your friend and you want him to be more. You think I should wear a tie tonight?"

"No," she said. "Jamie, I—"

When he turned to her, his face was cold, withdrawn. "Hallie, we all have pasts full of secrets. When your friend arrives, I'll get out and he can have the bedroom next to you. And oh, yeah, this morning when you and I . . . you know, don't think about it. It would have happened with anyone." He went to his bedroom and shut the door behind him.

Hallie started to knock. They needed to talk! But she looked at her watch and realized she had only minutes before she had to be downstairs to greet their guests.

She had trouble reaching the long zipper of her dress, but she managed it. When it was on, she was shocked to see that the dress was downright big on her. She could grab a handful of silk at her waist.

Jamie was waiting for her at the landing and he was still wearing that cold look.

"Oh, for heaven's sake!" she said. "Are you in some jealous fit because I talked to another man?"

"Talk?! It's more like you oozed to him. 'Oh, Braden,'" he said in falsetto, "'you're so strong and smart and I'm just a helpless little thing.'"

Hallie tried not to laugh. "You *are* jealous. For your information, I have known Braden Westbrook my entire life. He gave me piggyback rides when I was a toddler."

"And how old were you when you started planning your wedding to him?"

"Eight," she said before she thought.

"My point exactly," he said smugly.

Hallie's hands made fists at her sides. "I have a right to talk to anyone I want to in any *way* I want to and you have *no* right to—"

"I hate to interrupt here," said a deep, smooth voice from

the bottom of the stairs, "but your guests are on their way." Ian was looking up at them in curiosity. With a bit of a smile, he walked away.

"We can finish this later," Jamie said as he motioned for her to go down ahead of him.

"There's nothing to finish," Hallie said under her breath. "Braden is—" She stopped when she saw the tea room. The furniture had been rearranged so there was a round table for four in the center, draped with a snowy linen cloth. The dishes on it were Herend, winking in the light of the many candles that were set about the room. The air was fragrant with food, wine, and flowers. "This is truly exquisite," she said and smiled at Adam, Ian, and Raine, who were beautifully dressed and standing to one side.

"We are here to serve you," Adam said. His dark eyes were made for candlelight. If a Regency romance novel came to life, Adam Montgomery would be the hero.

"All of you will be here tomorrow to watch the wedding, won't you?" She took a step toward him.

"Out!" Jamie said. "We can serve the food ourselves."

"If you need us . . ." Raine said as he walked toward the doors.

"Go!" Jamie said. "We don't need any of you." He shut the doors behind them.

"What is *wrong* with you?!" Hallie said.

"Where do I begin? I was in a war and the vehicle blew up and—"

"Don't you even think of blaming your bad mood on a war! This has nothing to do with—"

"Am I interrupting?" Kit asked from the doorway. "I was told to come in."

"Please do." Hallie turned away from Jamie.

Kit stepped back to allow a woman to enter before him, and Hallie had her first sight of Jilly, the bride. She was a very pretty woman, her face soft, ethereal even. She was thin and wearing a dress of gauzy fabric that suited her pale skin.

"If you'd rather, we can come back another time," she said, her voice as soft as her face.

"No, it's fine," Hallie said. "Jamie's just being a jerk." Immediately, she put her hand over her mouth. "I'm sorry! He's your nephew and—" She wanted the floor to open and swallow her.

Jilly laughed. "He can be." Smiling, she affectionately ruffled Jamie's hair. "Todd is worse."

"Isn't he!" Hallie said, then rolled her eyes. "I *am* sorry. I'm really putting my foot in it tonight."

Kit made formal introductions. He was dressed in a dark suit, no tie, and from the quick way he glanced about the room she thought he was casing it. She wasn't surprised when his eyes landed on the box she'd slipped onto a dresser shelf.

"Would you mind if I used your facilities?" Jilly asked. "And Hallie, maybe you'd show me the way."

"Of course." She led the way past the dark living room. She was startled to see the big flatscreen TV that had been set up at the end of the room, with chairs facing it. How in the world had she and Jamie not heard this being put in? But then the thunder of the storm—the one that didn't happen—must have covered the noise.

She waited for Jilly to finish in the bathroom, but then she heard what sounded like retching. She softly tapped on the door. "Are you all right?"

When Jilly opened the door, her face was without color.

Hallie took over. She sat Jilly on the side of the tub, got a washcloth, and soaked it in cold water. "How about we get you to the hospital?"

"No," Jilly said. "It was like this the last time. I'll be fine in a few minutes. Just let me sit here."

Hallie filled a glass with water and handed it to her. Did this woman have something physically wrong with her? An illness? Maybe she . . . Hallie stepped back to wring out the cloth. *It was like this the last time,* she'd said. "When are you due?" Hallie asked.

Jilly gave a sigh. "About seven months from now. No one knows, not even my soon-to-be husband, Ken."

Hallie frowned at that.

"No, it's not like that. He's in Lanconia right now. He's known Graydon's bride since she was a baby. I was going to go too, but their wedding was moved forward because Toby is pregnant—and only family knows that."

"Toby is the bride?"

"Yes," Jilly said. "She finally drove Graydon to the limit of what he could resist and . . ." Jilly waved her hand. "It's a long story, but our wedding dates ended up very close together and I used that as my excuse not to go with Ken. If I'd told him that I was expecting, he wouldn't have gone."

"And he would have missed the wedding." Bending, Hallie put her hands on Jilly's neck and began massaging it.

"If even one person in my family suspects my condition, it will spread like a forest fire. And Ken will be hurt that he didn't hear first."

"We'll just have to keep it a secret until he returns. It'll be between you and me. And tomorrow I'll put you on my massage table and get rid of the tension in your shoulders." She looked Jilly in the eyes. "Everything will be all right. In fact, why don't you stay here tonight? If you're having morning sickness in the evening, it won't take much for anyone to guess what the problem is." She could feel the tension in Jilly loosening. "We'd better go back or the men will worry." She rinsed out the cloth.

"What were you and Jamie arguing about—if I may ask?"

"I was talking to an old friend on the phone and Jamie got quite unpleasant." She looked at Jilly. "Do you think he was jealous?"

"Probably," Jilly said, then caught Hallie's hand. "Thank you. Thank you for this and especially for making Jamie display a normal emotion. For years now he hasn't really been back with us. Does that make sense?"

"Perfect sense," Hallie said, "but I'm still not going to put up with it."

Jilly was frowning. "I don't think you know about Jamie's problems, about—"

"His seizures? His nightmares? His fears of ordinary daily occurrences? Oh, yes, I know all about that and I understand them. It's just that I have some problems of my own. I've spent too much of my life being controlled by other people and I'm *done* with it."

For a moment Jilly looked shocked, then she smiled. "Oh, my goodness! I think that whatever you're doing, it's working. Shall we return?"

When they got back to the tea room, Jilly turned down a cocktail and Hallie got her some orange juice. Jamie was still frowning and watching Hallie's every movement.

Jilly went to stand by Kit. "If that boy loses her, it will be the worst thing he's ever done in his life."

"I agree completely," Kit said.

⌒⌒

"Why are you here?" Todd asked his brother.

It was the morning after the dinner party and Jamie was sitting by the swimming pool at the house of a man named Roger Plymouth. They had no idea who the guy was, but they'd been told that he was in the wedding in Lanconia and that's why the house was empty.

The six bedrooms were all full of the Montgomery-Taggert bachelors who'd happily agreed to a vacation on Nantucket to attend Aunt Jilly's wedding. But then the Montgomerys always agreed to go anywhere there was water, and the Taggerts had come because Jilly was theirs.

Right now all of them were either at Kingsley House or at Hallie's getting ready to watch Graydon's wedding on TV. Todd was dressed and holding car keys as he prepared to leave. But Jamie had on a big pair of swim trunks and was sitting in the sun. He knew his wounds benefited from the ultraviolet rays, but he didn't show his scars around anyone except his brother. And Hallie, he thought.

"What?" he asked Todd.

"I asked why you're here. Dad had the TV set up at Hallie's house so you two could watch it in private. But you came here late last night and now you're just sitting there. The wedding won't wait on you."

"Hallie invited half the Montgomerys and all the Taggerts to come to her house. At least it seems like that many." Even Jamie thought he sounded sulky.

Todd put the keys in his pocket and sat on a chair in the shade. "I'll stay here with you. In case—"

"In case what?!" Jamie said. "In case I *need* something? In case a plane goes overhead and I freak out at the noise and land face down in the pool?"

Todd had had a couple of years to get used to his brother's mood changes: smiling one second, enraged the next. He was unperturbed, but then he knew that the girl was Jamie's problem.

"The old me would have gone after her."

Todd looked at the sun glistening off the pool water. "I'm not sure about this, but I don't think this girl would have given the old you the time of day."

"What does that mean? That she prefers half men?"

Todd was keeping his own temper down, but it wasn't easy. "Is that why she kicked you out of the house last night? Because you're a wounded soldier?"

"Of course not! Hallie's not like that." Jamie took a breath. "Jilly wasn't feeling well, so Hallie suggested she stay there with her, in the quiet. It was good advice. Kit used Hallie's car to drive me out here."

"What happened at the dinner last night? Anything bad?"

"No," Jamie said. "It was all good. Uncle Kit and Hallie seem to have formed some sort of alliance over the Tea Ladies. Hallie described her dream and Uncle Kit told about seeing them and I told of seeing one of them."

"You didn't tell me that you saw a ghost." Todd's voice was sharp. It wasn't easy for him to keep his opinions to himself. This girl Hallie seemed to be pulling his brother away from him. It was as though the twin bond was being stretched so far that it just might break. War hadn't snapped it apart, but this pretty girl from Boston might cut the tie.

The problem was that Todd didn't trust her. He knew his brother was falling for her, but Todd didn't think she felt the same way about him. She liked him and she hadn't been repulsed by the sight of Jamie's wounds, so that was in her favor. But he didn't sense any real depth of feeling coming from her.

Earlier this morning Todd had called Uncle Kit and asked what the hell had so angered his brother. "He's back to where he was months ago. What happened?!"

"I think it's just a case of the green-eyed monster," Kit said. "At dinner Hallie mentioned that she'd had a call from a guy named Braden and that he was coming to visit. I wouldn't have thought anything about it, but young Jamie's face swelled up so red he looked like some poisonous fish. He really should work on controlling his emotions."

Todd thought so too, but he wasn't going to side with anyone against his brother.

"Do you know who this Braden is?" Kit asked.

"Vaguely," Todd said. As a law enforcement agent, he wasn't going to tell what he knew about anything. "I'll see you later today." After he hung up, Todd thought about what he did know about Braden Westbrook. When Todd had visited his mother, she'd gone on and on about how she so very much wanted her son to marry Hallie.

"Everyone complains about mothers-in-law," Mrs. Westbrook said, "but no one thinks what we mothers have to put up with. I'm scared my son will marry someone like . . . like Shelly."

"What does Hallie think of your son?"

"She thinks no one knows, but Ruby—that's Hallie's late stepmother—and I used to agree that if Braden said, 'Hallie, jump into that volcano for me,' she wouldn't hesitate. *That's* the kind of mother I want for my grandchildren. Do you know what I mean?"

"I do, yes," Todd said.

He hadn't told his brother of the conversation, but he certainly remembered it.

His worry was that Hallie was very good at her job and that to her, Jamie was just her client. She cared about him and would do anything she could to help him heal, but it ended there. On the day she'd seen how deeply injured Jamie had been, she'd mainly been concerned that he'd insulted her *profession*.

Todd feared that when Jamie's knee had healed and he could walk again, Hallie would consider her job done. She'd kiss him on the cheek, tell him goodbye, and look to the next patient. Add that to what Jamie had already been through and Todd wasn't sure his brother would ever recover.

"Stop thinking so hard and leave," Jamie said. "Go enjoy yourself. I'll be fine here. Actually, I'd like some down time. I'll sit in the sun and let it heal me."

Todd looked at his brother. "You want me to go to the house and report back to you, don't you?"

"Yeah," Jamie said and gave a bit of a smile.

Todd stood up. "I'll take one of the cars Plymouth said we could use, but I'll leave the Range Rover for you. Keys are in the kitchen."

"I won't be there," Jamie said. "I don't want to ruin everyone's good time."

"You won't," Todd said, but he knew it was no use arguing. "Just so you know, though, if Raine makes a play for her, she's on her own. I won't tackle him even for my brother."

Jamie gave a bit of a laugh, then waved his brother away.

Chapter Fifteen

*H*allie awoke with a sense of panic. She hadn't gone to Jamie at two A.M.! She was halfway out of bed before she remembered that he'd left with Uncle Kit after the dinner.

It was still early so Hallie lay back in bed, snuggled with her pillow, and thought about the dinner. It had turned into an evening of the Tea Ladies, as each one told all that he or she had experienced.

Jilly was a wonderful audience. She expressed shock or delight at everything that was revealed.

Hallie described her dream and showed the drawings that had been behind the big cupboard. "Have you ever heard of anything like that?!" she asked.

"Actually," Jilly said, "Toby and Graydon . . ." She trailed off. "No, nothing."

Jamie told of seeing the beautiful young ghost and of hearing

"Juliana has died," but he didn't say that it had been Hallie who'd whispered it. That led to Jamie and Hallie telling Caleb's story of why the young women were ghosts.

"I'd like to read the documents that tell the story," Hallie said.

"I doubt there are any," Jilly said.

The other three looked at her in interest, but she just smiled. "Kit said something about a box you found."

Hallie got up and pulled the old wooden box off the shelf and set it down in the middle of the table. "I didn't open it. Jamie was—" She broke off. There was no need to mention Jamie's panic attack.

But to Jamie, they were family. "She didn't have time to open it because I was coming apart and crawling across the floor in panic," he said. "Same ol', same ol'."

Kit and Jilly gave him a look of sympathy—and that bothered Hallie.

"The oddest thing about Jamie's attacks is that hugging and kissing are the *only* things that soothe him. I'm beginning to wonder if they're real."

Hallie was still standing and for a moment the three of them looked at her in shock. Kit was the first to laugh and Jilly followed. Jamie picked up her hand and kissed the palm.

After that, anything left of his bad mood was gone.

At dessert, Kit showed the card that had been inside the envelope with his name on it. FIND THEM was beautifully handwritten on it.

They passed the card around, but no one had any idea what it meant. "Find who?" Hallie asked.

"Who are you missing?" Jamie asked, but Kit said nothing.

The box was full of recipes, and they seemed to cover centuries and the world.

"Look!" Hallie said to Jamie as she held up a yellowed card.

"This is for those cookies you like so much." Her statement led them to talk about the wonderful teas Edith left for them.

"They're very high calorie," Hallie said, "but we eat them anyway."

"Doesn't look like it's hurting you," Jamie said. "That dress used to be tight."

"I know. I think it's all the work on your naked cousins. Digging into Raine's muscles probably used a couple thousand calories."

Jamie groaned. "See what I have to put up with?"

Out of the corner of her eye, Hallie saw Kit and Jilly smile at each other.

All in all, it had been a lovely evening—and Jamie had agreed with the idea of his dear aunt Jilly staying the night. Kit said he'd drive Jamie to a house where he could spend the night.

"I'll see you tomorrow for the wedding," Hallie said as they parted at the door.

"Yeah," Jamie said hesitantly. "Maybe." Before she could ask what he meant, he turned to Kit. "We better go."

Kit took Hallie's car and drove Jamie away, and Jilly stayed behind. Hallie took one look at her and sent her upstairs to bed.

"But I should help clean up."

"No, you shouldn't," Hallie said and stood there waiting as she went upstairs.

When Jilly was out of sight, Hallie returned to the tea room and began to put things away. The house was eerily quiet and she couldn't help wishing Jamie was there. He'd make jokes and the chores would be easier.

She was halfway finished when she sat down on the couch and put her head in her hands. It had been a long day! Seeing Jamie's scars, running away from him, and feeling so very angry, then . . . then feeling his lips on hers, his naked body against hers. Later, being together on the couch, legs entwined, the storm outside, the fire inside. She remembered his attack and how helpless she'd felt, but at the same time he'd made her feel needed.

She looked around the room. The fire was dead, most of the candles were out, and the plates on the table were empty.

Why had Jamie been so angry about Braden? Surely, Jamie knew that here and now was temporary. It was all a fantasy. The romance of the old house with its beautiful ghosts, the gorgeous young men wandering about, the scrumptious meals that seemed to appear out of nowhere . . . None of it was *real.*

She couldn't help thinking that it was like her life with her grandparents. It had been happy and fun and carefree. But it had all ended in a single day.

She had no doubt that when Jamie's knee healed he'd leave too.

Getting up, she paused at the table. She was too tired to do any more. She'd clean it in the morning. She blew out the few remaining candles and went upstairs. Ten minutes later, she was sound asleep.

Now it was morning and she wished she could stay in bed, but she heard water running and knew Jilly was up. She should see if she was all right.

Hallie quickly dressed and went through the sitting room. The bedroom was open and Jilly was just climbing back into the bed.

"I agree," Hallie said and Jilly nodded to the other side. Hallie went around to the far side and stretched out on top of the covers by Jilly.

"I think this is the first morning that having another baby has felt real to me," Jilly said.

"You didn't plan it?"

"I'm forty-three. No, I didn't."

Turning their heads, they looked at each other and smiled.

"You're making me remember my daughter," Jilly said.

"She's at college now and has little need for her mother. And you?"

"I don't remember my mother, but I had a young, energetic grandmother and that was enough. Will Ken be happy when you tell him?"

"Ecstatic. He and his first wife, Victoria, have only one child. Have you met either of them?"

"No. I just seem to meet tall, beautiful men who take their clothes off at the first sight of me."

Jilly laughed. "Except for Jamie."

Hallie groaned. "Getting his clothes off was an ordeal! I wanted to strangle Todd. Why does he dislike me so much?"

"He's just protective of his brother. When Jamie told him he was going to serve a tour in Afghanistan, Todd nearly went crazy. He was terrified of losing Jamie."

"But isn't Todd in a profession where he gets shot at?"

"If you're asking me to explain male logic," Jilly said, "I can't do it. Todd's wanted to be a policeman or a sheriff since he was a kid. Every Halloween he wore the same costume. When he was little, Cale bought him the whole set of Mayberry videotapes. He watched them and Jamie watched cartoons."

"Not videos of being a soldier?"

"No," Jilly said, "and I think that's part of why Todd was so upset. He's a very orderly young man. He doesn't like surprises." She looked at Hallie. "Are you ready for today?"

"I guess so. I haven't thought about it. Jamie and I have been so wrapped up in the ghosts that we've barely talked about his cousin's wedding. It seems like a lot of work to set up TVs so they can stream it. I guess the bride and groom hired professionals to do the video."

Jilly lifted on her elbows to look at Hallie. "You don't know, do you? No one has told you?"

"I guess not, since I have no idea what you're talking about."

Jilly lay back down. "If they weren't so big, I think I'd paddle my nephews. Where should I begin? During World War II, J.T. Montgomery married Princess Aria of Lanconia and they became king and queen. When their son was forty, they turned the throne over to him."

Hallie was watching Jilly in shock as she was beginning to see where this story was going.

"Graydon Montgomery, the groom, is J.T.'s grandson."

"Oh," Hallie said. "Oh."

"Exactly," Jilly answered. "It is a *royal* wedding. Graydon will be the next king of Lanconia and Toby will be the queen. And no one told you of this?"

"Not so much as a hint."

"I can understand. To them, Graydon was just one of the kids in the summers. The family switches back and forth from Maine to Colorado. Mostly we just leave the doors open and keep food out and the kids run wild. A bit chaotic, I guess."

"It sounds heavenly," Hallie said, her mind still on the big wedding. "I invited Adam and the rest of them over to see the wedding here. How many do you think will show up?"

Jilly took a moment before answering. "They'll be respectful of Jamie so there won't be too many."

"Just the big guys who can physically deal with him if . . . if something happens?"

"Yes," Jilly said. She was looking at Hallie's frown. "Please tell me what you're thinking."

"No wonder Jamie snaps at his cousins," Hallie said. "He must know why it's only big, strong, healthy young men who hang around him. And the two little ones who can be taken away so they don't see. I guess that's why the men showed up the morning the kids climbed in the bed with us." She closed her eyes.

"You were in bed with Jamie?" Jilly asked.

Hallie waved her hand. "Not like that. I was a leftover from his nightmares." She was thinking about what she'd just learned.

"Hallie, I don't mean to turn motherly on you, but if you and Jamie do become sexually active, you need to be sure to use protection."

"He has an STD?"

"No, that's not possible. The hospital checked everything about him and since then there haven't been any . . . Sorry to give out confidences. No, the problem is that we Taggerts seem to be extraordinarily fertile. I'm a living example. Cale swears her youngest two came because she and my brother shared a spoon. It's none of my business, but sometimes in the heat of a moment people can be overcome and forget things."

Hallie let out a sigh. "Right. Towels fall to the floor and there's all that warm, golden skin."

"I do understand," Jilly said. "A man steps out of a shower and he has a face full of whiskers and suddenly you're glad you just washed the bathroom rug because it's up against your back."

"What is it about men's muscles that have a direct connection to a woman's knees? Flex a bicep; bend a knee."

"Ken can look at me over a cup of coffee and I'm on my back. It's as though my mind takes a holiday."

"I figure it's procreation," Hallie said.

"If we women didn't enjoy how men look and all we could do was *listen* to them, no babies would ever get made," Jilly said.

Hallie laughed. "I think you're right."

Jilly said, "Not to be nosy, but have any towels fallen around you?"

"Uh . . ." Hallie began.

"Is anybody here?" came a male voice from downstairs. "We have food."

"And beer," came another voice.

Hallie sat up on the bed. "Take your time getting dressed. I'll deal with the men."

"Your face just lit up," Jilly said. "Who are you hoping to see downstairs?"

Hallie started to answer truthfully, but then said, "Max," and ran from the room. She went to her own bathroom and put on makeup that she hoped would look like she wasn't wearing any. She reached for her curling iron but didn't pick it up. Instead, she pulled her hair back into a ponytail. "Pulled back flat," as Jamie called it.

Raine was waiting for her at the bottom of the stairs and smiling up at her. What a sight to wake up to! Men's muscles and women's knees, she thought. "Good morning," she said.

He put his hands about her waist and swung her down the last two steps. "Good morning. Aunt Cale talked to your cousin, Leland, and he's going to come to Aunt Jilly's wedding."

"That's wonderful," Hallie said. "Please thank her for me."

Adam stepped around Raine. "These were baked last night. Tell me what you think." He held out a cookie to her, but when she tried to take it, he moved it away. She bit while he was holding it.

Ian came from behind her. "Try this." He held up a glass for her to drink out of. It was a fruity white wine.

"Delicious!"

"Hallie!" screamed Max and Cory as they ran at her at full speed.

Raine grabbed a collar of each child and only released them when they stopped running.

When Hallie knelt, they both hugged her. "Mom said we could stay only if you said it was okay," Cory said.

"More than okay. But you have to tell me who everyone in the wedding is. I don't know anyone."

Adam and Ian had left, but Raine was still standing there smiling at her.

"Some of the people we don't know," Cory said seriously.

"Uncle Graydon is a Montgomery, but he doesn't live in Maine." She said this as though it were a very strange thing.

Max leaned toward Hallie's ear. "Jamie isn't here," he whispered.

"Does that make you sad?" Hallie whispered back.

"Yes. Our brother almost died. We saw him in the hospital and Mom and Dad cried a lot."

Cory stepped away and Hallie drew the little boy into her arms. "Jamie's better now, isn't he?"

Max pulled away to look at Hallie, his little face close to hers. "My mom says you make Jamie laugh and she loves you for that."

"Does she?"

"Max!" Cory yelled. "Dad sent cupcakes and he said not to tell Mom." The two children went running.

Hallie stood up and looked at Raine. "I lost out to chocolate sprinkles."

Raine leaned over and kissed her cheek. "All of us thank you," he said softly, then stepped back. "Come on and let's eat, then we'll watch a Montgomery get married."

He sounded as if he couldn't believe such a thing could happen. "Sometimes when you kiss a frog you actually do get a prince," she said.

Raine laughed. "I don't know about the prince part, but you have the frogs right."

For the next hour everything was so busy that Hallie didn't have time to think. Another Montgomery, named Tynan, and a Taggert named Roan showed up, both of them young and beautiful. Part of Hallie was annoyed that none of the women came.

When she asked about them, Roan said, "I think they're doing their nails and hair. We decided to leave them to it."

Adam leaned over and whispered, "He's young. The women

are doing shots of tequila and reading naughty books. They banished us. We can't live up to their fantasies."

Hallie was still laughing at the image when Jilly came downstairs. "I think I'll go to Kingsley House. My brothers set up a private screen for Kit and me and a few other quiet-loving people. You can go with me, if you want."

"No, I'll stay," Hallie said.

Jilly looked at her hard. "If it's Jamie you want, my guess is he won't show up. There's too much noise and too many people for him. You could go to where he's staying, but you'd miss the wedding."

"I'd like to see it."

"Aunt Jilly!" Ian said, then picked her up and whirled her around. "Are you going to dance with me at your wedding?"

"And me?" Adam said as soon as Ian set her down. He began to dance her around the room. He led her through the big pantry and into the tea room.

Hallie followed behind them and was pleased to see that someone had cleaned up from last night's dinner. The tables were pushed back against the wall.

Raine took Hallie in his arms and began to dance her round and round. For someone so big, he was certainly light on his feet. Music came from somewhere and Hallie was passed from one man to another. She was laughing and enjoying every second of it!

"The wedding's about to start," someone called and they all went to the living room—except for Jilly, who escaped out the side doors.

Hallie was escorted to the sofa directly in front of the big-screen TV. Adam was about to sit on one side of her and Raine on the other, but the kids made a flying leap and took their places.

"Brats!" Adam murmured. "Isn't it your bedtime?"

"It's morning and I can outride you," Cory said.

"And I can outswim you," Adam said as he sat down beside her. He kissed the top of her head—then wiped his mouth. "You have sand in your hair."

"Keeps the boys away," Cory said.

"I'll have to remember that trick," Hallie said.

"Wouldn't work for you," Raine said softly, his eyes on the TV.

"Roan!" Adam bellowed over the back of the couch. "Popcorn." He looked at Hallie. "Only thing kids like him are good for."

"I can't think of any other use for him," she said.

"Look! It's Graydon," Cory yelled, pointing.

On the screen was a photo of two extraordinarily good-looking people. Graydon was tall and dark, while his bride, Toby, was tall and blonde.

"They're beautiful," Hallie said.

"He's a Montgomery," Ian said with pride.

He got popcorn thrown at him.

They spent nearly an hour watching guests arrive at the huge Lanconian cathedral where the wedding was being held. The announcer told the names of diplomats and ambassadors as they arrived. When there were personal guests, everyone made comments and explanations.

"That's Dr. Huntley!" Hallie said, then her eyes widened. "Who is the woman with him?!"

"That's his wife, Victoria," Adam said in a low voice, and the room suddenly went silent.

Victoria Huntley was a striking woman. She had on a green suit that hugged the fabulous curves of her body. A perfect little hat perched on top of her magnificent red hair.

"She's a knockout," Hallie said. When no one commented, she looked around her. Every male in the room—including Max—was staring at the woman in wide-eyed, open-mouthed appreciation.

Hallie and Cory exchanged a look of disgust. Cory picked up the remote and turned off the TV. "Oops."

When the men started yelling and racing to get the TV back on, Hallie and Cory high-fived each other.

Beside them, Raine and Adam were silently laughing.

Hallie saw Todd enter through the kitchen. He nodded at her, but he said nothing as he went to the back of the room and sat down on the old desk chair.

When Hallie saw Jared and his wife on TV, she was shocked. Alix was pretty, but she also looked smart. Not what Hallie had thought a famous architect would have for a wife. When Alix turned sideways, Hallie saw that she was pregnant.

"Another one," Hallie said, mostly to herself.

But Raine heard her and for a moment he looked at her as though trying to figure out what she meant. He looked back at the TV and just before he put a piece of popcorn in his mouth, he said, "Is Aunt Jilly feeling better?"

"Yes, she is," Hallie said.

Raine didn't look back at her, but from the way he smiled, she had an idea that he'd guessed about his aunt. She and Raine now shared a secret.

When the guests were at last seated, the groom and his brother arrived. They were both wearing dark blue uniforms, resplendent with gold buttons and braid on their shoulders.

"Men in uniform," Hallie said with a sigh.

"Jamie has a uniform," Max said.

"I guess he does," Hallie answered, smiling at the image.

Graydon and his brother, Rory, were joined by another man who was very tall, with skin the color of honey and thick black hair. He had a way of walking that was truly majestic.

"That's Daire," Raine said. "He's Lanconian."

"Beautiful country," Hallie said in admiration.

The three men walked down the long aisle to the front of the magnificent cathedral. The flowers were so abundant, Hallie could almost smell them. Next came the two bridesmaids, one a tall woman with long black hair, the other shorter and very pretty.

"Lorcan and Lexie," Adam said. "Lexie and Toby were roommates in the house at the end of the lane."

The camera panned to a tall, dark-haired man in the audience. He was so good-looking that Hallie drew in her breath. "Who is *he*?"

For a moment, no one answered. "Lexie's husband," Adam said. "Roger Plymouth."

Hallie nudged Cory. "What do you think of him?"

Cory shrugged. "Nicholas is better."

Hallie looked at Adam in question.

"He's a Montgomery cousin, Aunt Dougless's son. He's not here."

"Too bad," Hallie said with an exaggerated sigh. She glanced about the room at the men surrounding her. "I guess I'll have to make do with you trolls."

There were groans of pain, as though she'd wounded them, and Hallie laughed. It was nice, she thought, to *belong*. Even if it was temporary, it was wonderful to be part of a real live *family*.

They showed the bride arriving in a carriage with big glass windows, adorned with thousands of little blue flowers. It was so pretty that everyone in the room was silent.

The carriage stopped before the cathedral doors and Toby stepped out.

She had on a simple dress of white satin covered with delicate lace. The TV announcer said it had been handmade by members of the Ulten tribe of Lanconia. The dress had long sleeves and a high neck. It would have been chaste if it hadn't fit Toby's excellent figure so perfectly. Diamonds glittered on her head, her face covered by her veil. Her train was so long that it took her two bridesmaids minutes to pull it out of the carriage.

A handsome older man stepped out of the shadows and offered his arm to her.

"Is that her father?" Hallie asked.

"Yes," Raine said.

Adam leaned across Cory. "Toby's mother was so shocked when she was told of her daughter's royal engagement that they had to call an ambulance to revive her."

"I think Toby looks like a princess," Cory said.

"Me too," Hallie answered.

Everyone was quiet as the two bridesmaids, then Toby walked down the aisle. When the bride reached the groom, even through her veil, her smile of love could be seen.

Hallie sighed. "She certainly does *like* him and I think he might start crying."

"Montgomerys don't cry!" Tynan said.

Raine leaned over to Hallie and said softly, "Taggerts do."

"Raine, you're . . ." Hallie couldn't think what to say but just smiled at him. Only when the ceremony began, did she turn away.

Some of what the gorgeously clad officiant said was in Lanconian, but not understanding the words didn't take anything away from the beautiful ceremony. Hallie put her arm around Cory and the two of them sighed as they watched. As for the men, they were silent. It seemed to be a universal protocol that a royal couple wouldn't be filmed kissing, but as soon as they were declared man and wife, everyone in Hallie's living room started cheering.

Adam picked up Cory and danced around with her, while Raine put Max on his shoulders.

"I am now a princess," Cory yelled.

"And I'm a knight," Max shouted.

"Really," Roan said, "*do* we get titles?"

Hallie didn't know if he was joking or not, but it felt good to be part of the celebration. The TV was turned to blaring so the sound of the church bells in Lanconia was nearly deafening.

Ian took Hallie's hands and began doing a sort of polka around the room with her. Between him and how hard she was laughing, she was dizzy. As he swirled her past the doorway, Hallie saw two beautiful young lady ghosts standing there and watching them—and they didn't look happy. It was just a flash, but Hallie thought it was almost as though they were warning her of something.

Ian went around full circle, and when she came back to them, the doorway was empty. Surely, she must have imagined seeing them.

"The reception is next," Adam shouted as he took her from Ian. "Private camera. Just for us. Want to see the cake? It's ten feet tall."

"I would love to!" Hallie yelled back. She didn't know what speakers had been installed, but they were so loud she felt like she was in the midst of the cheering crowd in Lanconia. "Are there any black sheep in your family? Or are all of you perfect?"

"Ian!" Adam shouted. "Hallie wants to know if we have any misfit family members."

"Ranleigh," Ian said as he whirled away.

Adam nodded. "Definitely Ranleigh."

"When can I meet him?" Hallie said, laughing.

Adam started to reply, but suddenly, everything went silent. The TV was still on, but the sound had been muted. Everyone stopped dancing, laughing, talking.

"Is this for Dr. Huntley's wife again?" Hallie asked as she looked up at Adam. "I think I'll tell her husband on the lot of you. He will . . ."

She trailed off because everyone was looking past her toward the front door—where just moments before she thought she'd seen the Tea Ladies. Hallie dropped Adam's hands and slowly turned toward the doorway, fully expecting to see two semi-transparent ghosts standing there.

Instead, she saw Jamie. He was leaning on his crutches and when his eyes met hers, he smiled.

Hallie didn't understand what was going on. Everyone was still frozen in place, still staring at Jamie.

She left Adam and went to Jamie. "You're just in time to see the wedding reception." She nodded for him to follow her, but he didn't move.

Roan finally broke the silence. "Jamie," he said so very nicely, "can I get you a chair?"

"Take my seat," Ian said.

"What do you need?" Raine asked.

Their voices were subdued and slower than they usually spoke—and she couldn't figure out why. Todd was still in the back, near Jamie's old desk, and his eyes seemed to be a combination of concern and helplessness.

When she looked back at Jamie, she at last understood. In their daily activities, they were normal around Jamie. But now the chaos made them concerned about how he'd react. They had shut down all laughter because of what he'd been through.

While their love and care for him were evident, it still made her stomach heave to see them isolate him as they were doing.

"I think I should leave," Jamie said and he turned toward the door.

Hallie didn't know what she could do to stop this, but she damn well *had* to do something! She put her lips by Jamie's ear. "You turn tail and run away and I will never give you another massage."

When he looked back at her he had a bit of a smile. "Can't risk that, now can I?"

"No, you can't." She was looking at him hard, using all she

had inside her to will him to stay. It hurt to see him ostracized like this!

Adam stepped back so Jamie could get to the couch. Hallie watched them, so caring, so concerned, so gentle and nice—and she was so angry she wanted to shoot them. Not even Shelly with all her deep selfishness had *ever* made Hallie this angry.

She couldn't sit down. Instead, she went to the kitchen. She needed to get away from them.

She stopped at the old countertop, her hands braced against it, and stared out the window. She was shaking all over as anger ran through her. How could they *do* that to him? Jamie had made jokes about his family treating him like glass, but it hadn't really sunk in. She'd laughed at the images he'd brought to mind. But what she'd just seen wasn't funny.

Behind her, she heard the TV come back on, but the sound was turned way, way down. Old people's homes *down*. Don't wake your dad *down*. Don't send Jamie into a panic attack *down*.

"They want more potato chips," she heard from behind her and knew it was Cory's voice.

Hallie had to take a few deep breaths before she could turn around to look at the child. She was standing there holding a big empty bowl and looking up at Hallie with almost fear in her eyes.

"Are you mad at Jamie?" Cory's lower lip trembled.

Hallie took the bowl from her and set it on the table. "No. Not at all. But I'm *very* angry at everyone else in that room."

Cory blinked at that, then smiled. "That's okay. I get mad at them all the time. But if you yell at Jamie he might get sick again."

"Does everyone always get quiet when Jamie comes in?"

"Yes," Cory said, then lowered her voice to a whisper. "Sometimes Jamie can't remember where he is."

"I know," Hallie said, "but I think he's better now." She stood up straight. From what she'd heard, Jamie had been back from the war for a long time and he had improved a great deal. But they were still treating him as though he'd come home from the hospital yesterday. If only she could *show* them that he no longer needed what they were doing for him—at least not to the extent of silence.

When an idea came to her, she tried to stamp it down. What she was thinking of doing could backfire, and if it failed, it could make Jamie's life worse. It might reinforce the awful— but caring—way his family treated him.

On the other hand, she thought, maybe it could help. She looked down at Cory. "Are you any good at making noise?"

"My dad says I'm the best there is," she said.

Hallie nodded. "I want you to get Max in here. I have a job for you two."

Cory didn't hesitate as she ran to get her brother.

By the time they'd returned, Hallie had pulled three big metal pans and spoons out of the cabinets. She handed one of each to the children and kept one for herself.

"I'm going to stand in the doorway and when I hit the pan with the metal spoon, I want you two to do the same thing. I want you to yell and scream and bang and pound and make as much noise as you possibly can. Do you think you can do that?"

Max's eyes were wide. "But Jamie will get scared."

Hallie went to her knees in front of him. "Remember you told me your mom said that I had made Jamie better?"

"Yes."

"Then I need you to trust me on this. Will you do that?"

Max hesitated, but he nodded yes.

As she went to the doorway, Hallie's heart was pounding in her throat, but the scene in the living room made her more sure of what she was about to do.

The happy atmosphere in the room was gone. The TV was

on but turned so low that it could barely be heard. Everyone was sitting stiffly in his seat and staring at the screen. No one was laughing and any comments were made in the quietest tones possible.

Worse was that Jamie had left the couch and was near the front door. Todd was behind him. He was leaving so the others could enjoy themselves. He was putting others before himself.

And damn the lot of them! Hallie thought. She took one more breath then yelled, "Hey, Taggert!"

The sound echoed in the quiet room and every man looked at her, but Jamie knew her words were for him. When he turned, for a flash of a second she saw the loneliness in his eyes. He was surrounded by people who dearly loved him, but he was as alone as a man could be.

She locked eyes with him—and hers pleaded with him to trust her.

Jamie looked puzzled, not understanding what she was trying to say. Todd put his hand on his brother's shoulder, urging him to leave, but Jamie stood there, not looking away from Hallie.

As she lifted the big pan and the metal spoon, she didn't break eye contact with him. When she hit the pan, the noise was so loud that even she winced—as did everyone else, including Jamie. But he didn't move.

"What the hell are you doing?" Roan said, and took a step forward. Raine put his hand out and held his young cousin back.

Jamie stood his ground, watching Hallie, trusting her.

Behind her the twins took great delight in making a lot of noise. Banging, yelling, stomping.

Hallie kept her eyes on Jamie's as she slowly walked forward, the children behind her. They were a little parade.

The others in the room didn't make a sound, just stood there and watched.

When she was inches from Jamie, she stopped and dropped the utensils with a clatter at his feet. Behind her, the children halted, silent as they waited for whatever Hallie did next.

The quiet reverberated in the room. Hallie and Jamie just stood there, looking at each other, not speaking.

But Jamie knew what she was doing and the gratitude on his face brought tears to Hallie's eyes.

Raine was the one who broke the silence. "Jamie, I'll arm wrestle you for the seat next to Hallie," he said in a normal voice. Not one that was unnaturally quiet, not a voice used with an invalid. Just a normal male challenge.

Jamie's eyes were still on Hallie's. "I'd be afraid I'd break your arm."

Adam said, "Would somebody turn up the damned TV? I can't hear it over all the noise Jamie is making."

In the next second the TV was turned back up. Not to blaring, but loud, and Ian put his arm around Jamie's shoulders and led him away. "How about a beer?"

"With all my meds?" Jamie said. "I'd start seeing flying monkeys. You have any colas?"

Hallie stood where she was for a few moments. Jamie looked back over his shoulder at her but then was overtaken by a gaggle of cousins. The twins wanted to do more banging, so they were told to go find their father and make him crazy.

It was all so deliciously, divinely *normal*. Just exactly what Jamie had said he wanted.

Hallie managed to walk back to the kitchen and once there her legs gave way and she collapsed onto a chair. Her whole body was shaking. It could have backfired. She could have traumatized Jamie forever. She put her head in her hands.

"Your instinct was right," said a voice from across from her. It was Raine.

She didn't remove her hands. "I could have failed horribly." Her voice was full of the tears that were threatening to come.

He put his hands on hers, pulled them down, and she looked at him. "But you didn't fail. And you weren't acting blind. You know him. You've spent a lot of time with him. You made an educated guess based on *him*. Not on a textbook case but on one man in one situation."

Hallie blinked back the tears. "I guess so."

"I know so." Raine was still holding her hands. "You did something great for all of us."

"How is he?"

Raine leaned the chair back, looked around the corner, then set the chair back down. "He's laughing. He and Adam are watching TV and arguing about some really dumb thing a Montgomery is doing."

"That's wonderful," Hallie said, but she could feel the tears starting.

Raine stood up and pulled her up with him. "I am ordering you to go out and get some fresh air. Walk into town and buy yourself something pretty. You deserve it."

"Thank you," she said. "Do you think he will—"

"Tell me you're not going to ask how Jamie will be without you."

Hallie smiled. "I guess not."

"Go on. Go out through the tea room and no one will see you. The wedding is being recorded so you can see it later." There was an eruption of laughter from the living room and Raine smiled. "When it's quieter in here."

Hallie nodded, then left the house through the tea room.

Chapter Sixteen

*H*allie wandered around town, past beautiful little shops full of jewelry, clothes, and furniture. Part of her felt like she was floating. She had taken such a very big chance with Jamie. That she'd won seemed to be beside the point.

She kept telling herself that she must never, ever, *never* do anything like that again, but as Raine had said, this had worked because she *knew* Jamie.

As she looked in the store windows, she kept thinking about him. What clothes would he look good in? What would he like to see her wearing?

A window display of shoes made her remember his jokes about the flats she'd bought the day Dr. Huntley visited. Candy reminded her of how much he'd liked the chocolate-covered cranberries she bought him.

Actually, there didn't seem to be anything that didn't remind her of him. This morning when he'd arrived at the house she'd wished everyone would disappear so she and Jamie could watch the wedding alone. It would be just the two of them as they'd been in the first days.

But his family was nice. Overwhelming, yes. Invasive, maybe. Jamie had warned her about them, had said that if they got to be too much he'd send them away. But it had been fun to laugh with them. Dance. Celebrate. Participate in their happiness.

After Jilly's wedding they'd all leave again, and she and Jamie would have their house back.

No! she told herself. After the wedding, they'd leave, then she'd return to working on Jamie's body. But when he was well, he too would leave.

Then what? Hallie thought. She'd met so few Nantucketers that she'd be alone on an island, her job of treating one person finished. Her roommate would be gone. The only thing she'd have left was an old house with a couple of ghosts.

All in all, it was a daunting prospect and she needed to decide what she was going to do. Her first thought was to talk with Jamie about it, but how could she do that? Ask him what she was going to do with her life without him in it?

Not quite!

At the edge of the water, she went to a seaside restaurant, sat outside, and ordered a glass of tea and a salad.

"Hello," came a woman's voice.

Hallie looked up to see a pretty woman, older, with blonde hair and blue eyes. She'd seen her somewhere before and it took her a few moments to realize where. "Book covers."

"Yes. I'm Cale, Jamie's mother. May I sit with you?"

"Please do," Hallie said. "I've already ordered, but I could get you something."

"Maybe some tea." She signaled the waitperson. "Raine said he sent you away, so I've been looking for you. I'm sorry I haven't been over to introduce myself, but we thought it would be better to give Jamie some space. We all tend to hover over him. I think we made the right decision."

"He's done well."

"Because of you," Cale said.

"He's a strong man and he's done most of the work himself."

"I'd heard you were modest, but this is beyond the call. Any physical therapist could have done the bodywork, but you've worked on the underlying problem."

As Hallie's salad arrived she thought about being gracious and saying thank you. This was Jamie's mother and one of the bestselling writers in the world. She was a bit intimidating.

Hallie decided on the truth. "I can't take full credit for his success because everything I did was by accident. There were times when I thought he was going to drive me insane. What I had to go through to get his clothes off was a nightmare!"

"Was it?" Cale asked as she sipped her tea. "Tell me every word."

When Hallie started talking, she couldn't seem to stop. She started at the beginning, with Jamie's refusal to undress, then his nightmares and the "sleeping kisses" she'd used to calm him down.

"He was like that as a child," Cale said. "He was the most affectionate boy there ever was. Todd was always more reserved, but Jamie loved to cuddle."

As Hallie took a drink of her tea, she thought, He still does. "Why did he go to war?"

"The million-dollar question," Cale said. "The one we all asked him so many times. It boils down to social conscience. He felt that he has so much while others have so little. He wanted to share his good fortune."

"That's what I guessed. He really is the kindest man I've ever met."

"Is he?" Cale asked, acting as though she was calm, but her mother's heart was doing flip-flops. She loved nothing better than hearing that her children were seen as the magnificent beings she knew them to be.

"I guess you heard what happened earlier."

"Yes," Cale said, "I did. In full, glorious detail from Cory. She thinks you're wonderful, and she usually thinks adults are, at best, overrated. But she loves her brothers very much. When Jamie was near death I feared that we'd lose her too."

"I'm sorry for that," Hallie said. "It must have been so awful for all of you."

Cale was watching her. "From what I hear, you haven't had such an easy time lately either. Jared told me about your stepsister."

Hallie leaned back in her chair as the waitress took her plate away. "That problem is being taken care of."

"If you hadn't come home early and discovered what was going on, it might have been your untrained stepsister with my son. I don't like to think about that."

Hallie laughed. "Shelly is beautiful and always lands on her feet. Jamie would have managed well enough with her."

"I don't think you're right," Cale said.

"But you've never met my stepsister." Hallie didn't want to talk about Shelly anymore. "How's the wedding coming? Oh, no!" She looked at her watch. "I promised Jilly a massage today and it's getting late. She *needs* one."

"Because she's pregnant?" Cale asked.

"No one's supposed to know that."

Cale smiled. "If the Taggerts are good at nothing else, they're exceptional at making babies, and we know when one's due. My mother-in-law told me I was carrying twins when I was four weeks along. I laughed at her. I said I was too old and I'd had my children. But as you've seen, Cory and Max are here."

"And aren't you lucky?"

"Oh, yes," Cale said. "I am lucky in all aspects of my life. I see you have a few bags with you, but would you mind doing some shopping with me? There's a jewelry store just down the street, all handmade items, and I'd like to see it."

"I'd love to, but I need to see Jilly."

"When I left she was going for a nap, and she doesn't know it, but Ken is on his way here. He'll be able to relax her even better than you can."

"I'm sure he can," Hallie said, smiling. "But if you have her number, I'd like to call her."

"Certainly," Cale said, and mentally added "conscientious" to the list of traits for this young woman.

Jilly's daughter answered the phone and said her mother was sleeping but that Jilly would be fine with the massage being postponed. Hallie paid her check and she and Cale left together.

"I like her very much," Cale said to her husband over the phone. Hallie was in a dressing room trying on an outfit to wear to the wedding. "She talks about Jamie *all* the time."

"That's understandable since they've been more or less living together for some time now," Kane said.

"Jamie lived with Alicia for two *years,* but I never heard her say that Jamie liked anise seed cookies, or that he wanted a house with a porch. And the sight of a chicken that wasn't butchered and on a plate would have sent her running."

Kane rolled his eyes. "Okay, I got it. Everyone in the family knows you hated Alicia. She's gone, so there's no more worry about her marrying Jamie. Cale, my dearest wife, can't we leave it up to our son to choose who he wants to live with?"

"Men are idiots about women. Remember how you—?"

"Not again!" Kane said. "That was nearly thirty years ago."

Cale took a breath. "Yeah, I know and I've forgiven you, but I still worry. Todd's being even quieter than usual and that worries me too."

"I think you should step back and let the kids figure out their own lives."

"I guess you're right. Do me a favor, will you? Ask Kris if she brought that lace Dolce dress she wore last Christmas. If she doesn't have it with her, get someone to overnight it. I think it would look great on Hallie and she can wear it to Jilly's wedding."

"You aren't buying Hallie a lot of things, are you?"

"No, I'm not. I didn't even pay for her lunch, but then I think if I'd offered to, Hallie would have refused. She has a very independent spirit."

"Interesting," Kane said. "She has an independent spirit and a lying, cheating, thieving sister. Sound like anybody else we know?"

Cale grimaced. "Be glad I'm already married to you because if the offer came up again, I'd probably say no."

"That's not what you said last night."

"Sex yes, conversation no."

"Sounds good to me," Kane said.

"Yeah, well—I have to go. Hallie's coming. And keep the yes to sex in your mind."

"Always do," Kane said as he hung up.

Hallie truly enjoyed shopping with Jamie's mother, and it was a brand-new experience for her. Before her grandparents left, Hallie had been too young to care a lot about clothes. Anything that was pink and sparkly suited her.

After they left, clothes shopping had been left up to Ruby. That had consisted of Ruby saying "Maybe we can find something in the husky department that will fit you." Back then, Hallie had been normal-sized, but compared to the very thin Shelly, she was almost big.

Being with Cale and hearing her opinions about what looked good on Hallie and what didn't was wonderful. They were in their third shop when two beautiful young women walked past the store.

"It's Paige and Lainey," Cale said. "Mind if we ask them to join us?"

"I, uh . . ." Hallie hesitated. The girls were tall and thin and almost as beautiful as Shelly. She didn't want to try on clothes around *them*!

Cale seemed to understand Hallie's hesitancy. "They're nice girls. Trust me," she said over her shoulder as she went out the front door and returned with the two young women.

When they were inside and she got a closer look at them, Hallie couldn't help gaping at them. "You're Adam and Ian."

The girls laughed. "Exactly right. Adam is my brother," Lainey said, "and Ian is Paige's brother."

Hallie was looking at them in curiosity. "If you two look so much like your brothers, does Raine have a sister who looks like him?"

The three women nearly exploded in laughter. "Raine has a younger brother and that's all. No sisters."

"I think that may be good," Hallie said, and there was more laughter.

She'd thought that shopping with Cale was fun, but it didn't compare to being with the young women. It was another new experience for Hallie. After Ruby and Shelly had arrived in her life, there had been little money. Her grandfather's income from the home bookkeeping service he ran was gone, and with the garden flattened, their food bills—mostly takeout—skyrocketed. Add that to Shelly's endless lessons and the clothes she needed for auditions, and there wasn't a lot left over.

Now, for the first time in her life, Hallie could afford new clothes. But what was most fun was the giddy laughter of the women. Cale stepped back and watched as the girls moved through the stores, looking at everything.

"Hallie," Lainey said, "this would look great on you. Try it on." It was a pretty cotton dress with a tight, low-cut bodice.

"I've never worn anything like that. The top isn't exactly modest."

"That's the point," Lainey said.

Paige agreed. "If I had your rack, I'd wear sundresses in the snow. And I'd bend over a lot."

Hallie still hesitated.

"Jamie would like it," Cale said, then smiled when Hallie snatched the dress from Lainey's hand.

"That's right," Paige said. "Alicia used to wear—" She stopped at the looks Lainey and Cale gave her. "Jamie will love it."

Hallie was behind the curtained dressing room. "Who's Alicia?"

"Old girlfriend," Lainey said. "Long, long time ago. So what do you think of my brother Adam?"

"Intense," Hallie said as she stepped out in the peach-colored sundress with the little knit jacket. It was indeed quite low cut, but it looked very good.

"Isn't he?" Lainey said. "I'm always telling him to lighten up. You *must* buy that. It was created for you."

"Cory said Adam was dancing around your house," Paige said. "That doesn't sound like him."

"Everybody was celebrating the royal wedding," Hallie said.

Paige paused while holding up a very cute leather jacket. "Even Jamie?"

"No dancing for him," Hallie said, "but I think after I left he stayed to watch the reception on TV." She was going through the racks and looked up to see the two young women staring at her.

"With all those people around?" Lainey asked. "I know they're family but still . . ."

"Tell them what you did," Cale urged. "Cory called it the Pan Parade."

"I didn't hear about that!" Lainey said, sounding shocked.

"I was scared to death," Hallie said, then told the story from the beginning.

"What did you do when you realized it was the sight of Jamie that had made everyone stop?"

They kept shopping as Hallie talked. She didn't leave out how frightened she'd been or how it all could have backfired. And she told them what Raine said afterward.

When they were on the street, Lainey and Paige walked in front, with Cale and Hallie behind. "You seem to like Raine a lot," Cale said.

"I do. He's been kind to me and he's a very perceptive man." Hallie saw that Cale was frowning. "But he's not Jamie," she added.

Immediately, Cale's frown disappeared and she slipped her arm through Hallie's. "Want to come to Kingsley House tonight for dinner?"

"Thank you for the invitation, but I need to work on Jamie's leg." She wasn't sure if she should say that she was looking forward to a quiet evening at home. While the day had been exciting, now she wanted to tell Jamie about everything that had happened and . . . well, to just be alone with him.

"I understand," Cale said. "I have just one more errand. I have to buy my eldest sons some clothes. They both packed too little. Too bad you don't have time to help me choose some things. I could buy for Todd and maybe you could pick out some clothes for Jamie."

"Oh!" Hallie said, her eyes wide. "I think I could manage that. Jamie has practically nothing here, mostly just workout clothes. He needs some nice, casual shirts and a few buttoned cottons. Blue is his color. Not navy but a brighter blue. And he could stand a couple of cardigans to wear in the evenings. I saw some heavy white cotton ones he might like. Plain but good quality, that's what he'd like. And he needs socks. Maybe we could get—"

Cale turned away to hide her grin. Oh, yes, mothers loved people who loved their children.

Jamie was stretched out on the couch in the tea room, his arm across his face, his head on the pillow that had been made from the bird embroidery. It had taken a while, but he'd finally rid the house of relatives and he was enjoying the quiet. Now if Hallie would just return from wherever she was, everything would be perfect. Raine said he'd sent her off to do some shopping and give her some time away from taking care of all of them.

At that thought, Jamie smiled. Hallie *did* take care of people. Whether it was working on a Montgomery's tennis elbow or digging into Raine's lats, Hallie was always helping someone.

This morning had been horrible for him. After Todd left Plymouth's house, Jamie had been torn between wanting to put himself between Hallie and his male cousins, and staying where he was. Hallie had won out.

When Jamie got to her house, things were worse than he'd expected. All of them were dancing. His slick Montgomery cousins were waltzing Hallie around like they were at some formal ball.

If that weren't bad enough, the noise nearly killed him. They'd installed the kind of speakers used in rock concerts, so bells were ringing, people shouting, music blaring. Jamie's mind began to go round and round. Todd saw him from across the room and was about to run to his brother's aid.

But then Ian saw Jamie in the doorway and instantly muted the TV. Everyone knew what that meant: Fun-killer Jamie had arrived.

He pivoted on his crutches to get the hell out of there, but first he wanted a look at Hallie. He wanted to tell her that he was there and if she needed him . . . But who was he kidding? She was dancing and having a great time. She didn't need to be reminded of her burdensome wounded soldier.

He was turning to leave when she told him he couldn't go. But a glance at his cousins and he knew he *had* to leave. How could they have a good time if Jamie was there?

Hallie persuaded him to stay, but everyone was so subdued that he couldn't take it. He got up to leave.

When he saw Hallie in the kitchen doorway with a big spaghetti pot and a spoon in her hand, he had no idea what she was doing. Cooking for everyone? But her face was more serious than he'd ever seen her. It was as though her eyes were trying to tell him something—but he had no idea what it was.

At her first bang on the pot, he understood what she was doing. She and the sprouts made lots of noise but it hadn't bothered him in the least. It was unexpected noise and cacophonies where he couldn't tell where all the sounds were coming from that sent him spiraling.

He kept his eyes on Hallie's as she walked toward him, bashing away on the big pot, the kids trailing behind her like noisy little ducks.

When she got to him, he wanted to kiss her. Wanted to take her in his arms and kiss her with all the thanks and appreciation and gratitude he was feeling. She had *never* treated him as though he were about to break. She'd never been frightened by his attacks. Never . . .

He was standing there, eyes locked with hers, when his cousins took over. Ian nearly dragged Jamie to the couch, while his other cousins made their stupid whose-is-biggest comments.

Jamie went with them because he wanted to show them that he could participate, like he used to, but he also wanted to find Hallie.

But by the time he could excuse himself from being in front of the TV, Hallie was gone. He'd ended up sitting in the back beside his brother, eating popcorn and watching his princely cousin use a sword to cut a giant wedding cake.

Every few minutes he'd looked around to see if Hallie had returned, but she hadn't. After a while, he and Todd went to the gym to work out. Raine joined them and they stayed there for hours.

When Jamie returned to the house, Hallie *still* wasn't there. He showered, put on clean clothes, and went downstairs to get something to eat. No tea was set up and he missed it. No, actually, he missed sitting there with Hallie. What the hell was she *doing*?! Where was she?

He began to feel so agitated that he knew he had to calm down, so he went into the tea room. It's where he'd spent so much time with Hallie, where they had shared laughter and . . . and one intimate, too-quick time together.

He stretched out on the couch, the same one the two of them had sat on together and talked of ghosts while a cozy fire burned in the fireplace. A knock on the door made his heart leap. Was she home?

As he started to get up, the door opened and he saw his father.

"Hi, Dad," Jamie said and lay back down.

"I know that look," Kane said, smiling. "I'm not the girl."

"No, I'm glad to see you. Everything okay?"

"Yes," Kane said as he sat down in a chair near his son. As always, he scanned his son, glad all his limbs were there, glad he was alive. "Your mom went into town to search for Hallie."

"Does she know what she looks like?"

"Sure. She saw your Hallie asleep, remember?"

"She's not mine," Jamie said. "Not really."

"That's what I want to talk to you about."

Jamie's eyes were closed. "I know how babies are made and I *will* respect her in the morning."

When Kane said nothing, Jamie knew he'd stepped over the line. "Sorry. It's been one hell of a day."

"So I heard. Your little sister told us every detail. She's very happy that she no longer has to tiptoe around you."

"When did she ever?" Jamie sat up on the couch and was surprised at the seriousness on his father's face. He'd seen this particular expression only a few times in his life. One time was the night before he left for war. "What is it?"

Kane took a breath. "You know the story of how your mother and I met?"

"Sure. I've heard it a thousand times. You took some women on a trail drive and she was one of them. Mom says she fell in love with Todd and me first. You came later."

Kane smiled in memory. "That's true. She was so mad for you two that I was afraid she was going to kidnap you." He paused. "Has she ever told you about the other women who were there?"

"Oh, yeah. She used to make Todd and me laugh about them. A former cheerleader and an herbalist and another one. I can't remember what she did."

"It doesn't matter. I think that if I'd gone to counseling back then I would have been diagnosed with PTSD—if it was a name then. I was still grieving over your biological mother. At least that's my excuse. One of the women on the drive looked like my late wife and I went after her with no holding back. I was a charging bull. Nothing, not common sense or intelligence, got in my way."

This was all new to Jamie and he tried not to show his surprise. "Not even Mom?"

"Especially not her. It took me a long time to see how much your mother meant to me. You can't imagine how close I came to losing her."

"But you did the James Bond act with the helicopter. Mom said it was the epitome of romance."

Kane put up his hand. "I had to do something big to cover my stupidity. But before that I had to get to the point where I swallowed my pride and admitted I had made a wrong choice. When I finally regained my senses, your mother was there. I still believe that I only got her because she's a writer."

"How do you figure that?"

"If a gorgeous creature like her had been out and about instead of locked up with her books, another man would have snatched her up."

Jamie smiled, but he'd heard the story from his mother's side, about how she was miserable while she waited for him. She'd thought he didn't *want* her. Jamie's head came up. "This is about Hallie, isn't it?"

"I'm trying to teach you from my mistakes. You need to *say* something to Hallie. Don't put it off. Don't let it hang in the air."

"Isn't this kind of fast?" Jamie said. "Hallie and I've known each other a very short time."

"True, but I've seen you two together and—" He paused. "It's your life and I've always sworn to leave the interfering to your mother. But in this case, I wanted to give my opinion."

"The truth is," Jamie said, "I'm not sure I'm what any woman should have to deal with. Not yet. But thanks to Hallie, I'm making rapid progress. Maybe when I'm a whole person again, I can think of, as you say, 'speaking' to a girl."

"That makes sense," Kane said. "As soon as you get back to being who you used to be, you should talk to Hallie. Tell me, do you still think champagne is a food group?"

Jamie groaned. "Dad, that was one time and one night. I was a kid smarting off. I've been through a lot since then. There's been school and war. Remember them?"

"I do. Do *you* remember them?"

Jamie frowned. "I've got the scars to show for one of them."

"You sure think a lot of those scars, don't you?" He stood up. "I gotta go. My *wife* and my *children* need me."

"Subtle, Dad. Really subtle."

Kane went to the door. "Your mother taught me to say what I needed to when it should be said. If you want to come over tonight, we're all having dinner at Kingsley House. We decided to spare the restaurants the family's presence."

"I think Hallie and I will stay in tonight. We have some things to talk about, and—" He broke off at the knowing look on his father's face.

"A girl who'd rather stay home with you instead of partying. Not exactly what the old Jamie would have liked, is it? See you tomorrow." He left, closing the door behind him.

Jamie flopped back against the couch. "See what I have to put up with?" he said to no one—but then he figured the Tea Ladies were there.

He picked up the box of research Jilly had collected and began to flip through the photocopies. A picture fell onto the floor and he picked it up. It was a glossy magazine photo of a very pretty engagement ring. Very simple, very elegant, and he thought Hallie would like that.

In the next second he tossed the photo onto the coffee table. "Et tu, girls?"

As he stretched out on the couch and began to read, he was sure he heard dual giggles.

Chapter Seventeen

By the time Hallie got home it was after six. She had so many bags to carry she could hardly walk. Cale had offered to send some of the "boys" to help her, but Hallie said no. She really hoped that Edith had shown up with her little cart full of food-from-around-the-world, so she and Jamie could eat and talk.

She wanted to tell him who she'd met that day and ask him about the other family members she'd heard mentioned. And she might bring up Alicia and ask who she was. And Hallie looked forward to showing him the clothes she'd chosen for him. She might even be persuaded to model what she'd bought for herself.

Hallie thought about how they'd go out to the gym and she'd take Jamie through his exercises. She'd check to see how his knee was healing.

And maybe a towel would once again fall to the floor.

When she got to her front door, she was surprised to find it locked. She looked in her purse for the key but couldn't find it. When she lifted the brass dolphin knocker and gave it a couple of bangs, no one came to the door, and she didn't see any lights on in the house.

She gathered her pile of shopping bags and went around to the side of the house. Just as they'd been told, the doors into the tea room were temperamental. Sometimes they would open with a light turn of the knob, but sometimes they were locked tight.

She was glad to find that this time they were not only unlocked but one of them was standing open a few inches.

"Is this an invitation?" she laughingly asked the resident ghosts as she went inside. "Or are you just helping with all these bags?"

She put them on the floor by the couch and turned on a table lamp. On impulse, she dumped all Jamie's new clothes out and began spreading them over the furniture. There were sweaters, shirts, and even trousers that she'd chosen with the help of Cale.

"He can roll these sleeves up," she'd said to his mother.

"Jamie won't like that," Cale said. "His arms . . . He wants them covered."

"I think he should get over that, don't you?"

"Yes," Cale said, smiling. "Think we could get him into a pair of sandals?"

They looked at each other and shook their heads. No way, they agreed. For Jamie, it was barefoot or shoes and nothing in between.

When Hallie heard a sound coming from the kitchen, she went through the pantry. As with the side doors, the door into the kitchen was half open. Hallie was about to step inside when she saw Todd. He was standing as Jamie sat down at the table and leaned his crutches against the wall.

"All I'm asking is that you be cautious with Hallie," Todd said. "Don't mistake gratitude for love."

Whatever else he was about to say, Hallie didn't want to hear. She took a step forward to show herself, but the door into the kitchen moved, as though it meant to close. The movement was so disconcerting that she stepped back into the darkness of the pantry.

"I'm not confusing anything," Jamie said. "I like her a lot. You saw what she did today. It was more than all those counselors I went to did."

Hallie had no interest in hearing what Todd had to say, but she *did* want to hear Jamie. She leaned back against the shelves and listened.

"To be fair to all those highly trained specialists," Todd said, "a lot of time has passed since then."

"But Hallie—"

"I agree," Todd said, cutting his brother off. "Hallie is a great physical therapist. What she does is almost magic, and her grasp of what needs to be done is brilliant. I don't dispute any of that. What worries me is that she might see you as just a patient. Will she still like you when you aren't freaking out at thunderstorms?"

"Who says I will recover?" There was anger in Jamie's voice.

"You will," Todd said. "That's not the problem. You know that I was all for her, but now that I've seen her . . . I don't know, there's something missing. I think she's falling in love with our family, not *you*. You should have seen her today when the wedding was on. She was flirting and sharing secrets with Raine so much anyone would have thought they were a couple. I'm not disparaging her as a person. I just think she hasn't made up her mind about who she wants." Todd paused for a moment. "Hallie's had a life with almost no family. She desperately wants a family like ours. Right now, what I'm seeing is that she might take any one of us who asked for her hand in marriage.

Or maybe she's set on Braden." Todd's head came up. "You haven't had sex with her, have you?"

"That's none of your business."

"Great," Todd said sarcastically. "I hope you used protection. Where is she, anyway?"

"Shopping with Mom and some of the girls." Jamie's voice was heavy.

"Then she'll be back soon," Todd said. "She'll want to tell you how great our family is. I better get out of here. She doesn't like me."

"Right now, neither do I," Jamie said.

"Just think about all this, will you? You're a prize catch and I just want to be sure who the fisherman is."

"I think you should leave now," Jamie said.

"Okay, I've had my say and I won't mention it again. I'll see you tomorrow."

Hallie was still leaning against the shelves. She heard the back door open and close, then after a moment she heard Jamie get up and go outside.

It was a while before she could push away from the shelves and walk back into the tea room. The clothes she'd so joyously spread out for Jamie to see were still there. When she picked up a sweater, her hands were shaking.

Had she really made a fool of herself in front of his family? She remembered dancing with them, laughing—and the massages! Had they all thought Hallie was just trying to worm her way into their beautiful, *rich* family?

She folded Jamie's clothes and neatly piled them on the couch. Todd said he thought she was so desperate for a family that she'd accept any man who asked.

And Raine! Even Cale had asked what was between her and Raine.

Hallie picked up her shopping bags. On the top was the

pretty sundress Lainey and Paige had chosen for her. Had the girls laughed at her too?

She walked to the door at the far end of the room. It was closed.

"Okay," she said aloud, "I heard what you wanted me to, so now let me out of here."

She wasn't the least surprised when the door opened by itself.

"Thank you," she said and went up the stairs to her bedroom, closed the door, and locked it.

Thirty minutes later, she was in bed, wide awake. The joy of the shopping trip was gone and all she could think about were Todd's words. What made her so deeply angry, what hurt the most, was that Todd was right. She *was* desperate for a family. She *had* been flirting with Jamie's relatives. She hadn't recognized it until now, but she realized that every moment since meeting them, she'd imagined being part of the big Montgomery-Taggert family.

But Todd was also wrong. She liked Jamie the best. From the first day they'd met, they'd worked together, talked and laughed as though they'd known each other forever. His injuries were the least of it. His laughter, his concern for others, all that was what she liked so very much.

As for Todd saying she'd marry *any* of them, that certainly wasn't true. Adam was too remote. Hallie thought a woman would have to work too hard to really get to know him. Ian had the air of someone who would be happiest living in a tent on a mountainside. Raine . . . Well, there wasn't anything wrong with Raine.

Except that he wasn't Jamie.

As for Todd, she did *not* like him. How could he be Jamie's brother? They didn't even look alike. And the more she was around him, the less attractive he seemed.

But Hallie knew that what she thought about them wasn't the problem. It was how *they* saw *her.*

Throughout her life, she'd always had goals. The only time she came close to giving up was when she learned that her father had allowed her college fund to be spent on Shelly's many lessons. It had been a dreadful scene. Ruby had cried and said that when Shelly was a famous actress or singer or model she'd repay everything. "You'll get it all back," Ruby said, tears glistening in her once-pretty eyes.

Hallie had been devastated. As usual, her father dealt with the turmoil by getting in his car and driving away. As he went out the door, he mumbled, "Sorry, Hallie. I thought the money would be replaced by now." She knew that Ruby had talked him into believing that Shelly was always just a day away from great success. But then Ruby knew enough to never let him attend any of Shelly's lessons.

But Hallie had seen and heard them. Shelly couldn't carry a tune, her acting was flat, and she was stiff in her dancing lessons. She couldn't even master the runway walk in her modeling classes. It was Hallie's opinion that the harder Ruby pushed, the worse Shelly did at every lesson—and furthermore, Hallie thought Shelly failed on purpose.

One time, when Hallie was driving her stepsister home from a session, she said, "If you don't want to take all these lessons, then you should tell your mother so."

"I guess *you* would do great at them, wouldn't you?" Shelly said nastily. "Are you hiding some fabulous singing voice?"

Hallie'd just sighed. It was no use trying to talk to Shelly about anything.

On that horrible day when she'd been told that the money that had been put aside for her college tuition was gone, Hallie had gone into shock. Her dad left right away. Ruby was holding Shelly as though to shield her, her eyes daring Hallie to say something negative.

But Hallie knew that going into a rage wouldn't put the money back in the bank. She went outside and without even thinking about what she was doing, she went across the street to the Westbrook house.

Only Braden was home. By that time he was in law school and had a girlfriend. He answered the door to Hallie but barely glanced at her.

"I've got something on the stove," he said.

She followed him to the kitchen and sat down on a stool at the counter. She was too stunned to be able to speak.

Braden slid an omelet onto a plate. "I came home unexpectedly, but Mom still left for the weekend," he said. "Looks like the honeymoon stage is over. I'm having to fend for myself. The worst thing is that I only know how to cook omelets so I've been eating them twice a day." He put the plate in front of Hallie. "There. Eat it."

"I can't. It's . . ." She was afraid to speak for fear she'd start crying. "If your mom isn't here, I'd better go."

"No," he said firmly. "You and I have to eat because we need our strength for what's coming."

She looked at him.

"I know I'm not Mom, but you're going to tell me every word of whatever Shelly and Ruby did to you this time."

Hallie stared in horror. "I can't . . ." she whispered.

"Can't talk to a friend? I don't believe that. Are you old enough to drink coffee?"

"I'm eighteen."

"Are you?" Braden said. He had his back to her as he made a second omelet. The toaster popped up. "Could you get that? And put a lot of butter on mine. I need the energy for when I tell you what my girlfriend did to me."

Hallie got off the stool and went to the toaster. "What did she do?"

"Nope. You first, but I bet I can top whatever you have to tell."

"My dad let Ruby and Shelly take the college fund my grandparents set up for me. I don't know how I'm going to pay for school."

Braden halted with a plate in his hand and stared at her. "Hallie, that's serious. Is all of it gone?"

"Every penny."

"Did your dad leave?"

"So fast that he's probably in Texas by now."

Braden shook his head. "That's some family you have. Come on, let's take this into the study. We have to figure out how to get a brain like yours into school."

She followed him down the hall and they spent hours figuring out what Hallie was going to do. Braden made calls and looked online.

In the end, Hallie didn't get to attend the school she'd dreamed of, but she did go to college. And she did so well there that she qualified for a partial scholarship for the second year. But the summer after her first year, her father and Ruby were killed in a car accident and Hallie had to put her education on hold to take care of Shelly.

The sound of Jamie on the stairs brought her back to the present. In spite of his crutches and the brace, he made little noise. He went into his bedroom and she heard the shower running. There was a bit of quiet, then she heard him go downstairs.

A few minutes later he was again on the stairs, but his gait was hesitant. Her first thought was that he'd reinjured his knee, and her impulse was to run to him.

But she didn't move.

When he tapped lightly on her door she didn't respond, but

then it was as though Todd's words were screaming in her head. Playing over and over.

"Hallie?" Jamie said. "I made us some tea. It has lots of milk in it, the way we like it."

Don't be a coward, she told herself, then she got out of bed. She grabbed her robe from the back of the closet, put it on, and opened the door.

To her dismay, Jamie was shirtless. He had on gray sweatpants that were barely hanging on to his hips. A tiny tug on the drawstring and they'd fall to the floor. In spite of all his scars, he looked so good her heart started pounding. If Todd's words weren't in her head, she would have dragged him back to bed with her.

But she didn't. Instead, she smiled pleasantly and took both mugs of tea from him. "How did you manage to get up the stairs on crutches with these in your hands?"

"Juliana and Hyacinth carried them up for me."

She didn't laugh, and when he took a step forward as though he meant to go into her bedroom, Hallie slipped past him to the sitting room. She sat down on the window seat, put one mug on the sill, and began sipping from the other.

She saw the frown he gave as he turned and took the other end of the seat. "Aren't you cold like that?" she asked.

"I'm still sweating. I did two workouts today. The first one was with Todd and Raine."

My enemy and my supposed lover, she thought but didn't say. "I'm sorry I didn't work on your knee today."

"What you did this morning was the best therapy I've ever had."

"I guess I'm good at my job." She heard the underlying anger in her voice.

"Are you okay? Did something bad happen?"

"I think I'm a little homesick," she said. "I guess being around your family makes me miss my own. My dad's birthday is in a few days and I really miss him. He and I used to drive from Boston to Fort Lauderdale to see my grandparents. We'd spend a week at a time with them."

"Did you?" He sounded surprised. "You never talk about your father or your stepmother, or Shelly."

"I guess I don't. Maybe it was because my mother had passed away, but it made my dad and me closer. He bought me my own cell phone when I was just five and he called me every day. When I got older, he included me in his work. By the time I was ten I was pretty much his secretary."

"Isn't that asking a lot of a child?"

"I loved it!" Hallie said. "It made me feel needed. He'd call and say someone had a question about some drug. He knew I'd have read all the info on it so I had the answer. My teachers used to laugh at the way I rattled off the scientific names of prescription drugs. There was an anti-drug campaign at my school and I was called on for advice."

"I had no idea," Jamie said.

He was leaning back against a cushion and he looked so very good. There wasn't an ounce of fat on him. The only light was from the open door into her bedroom, and it showed the curves of his muscles. How easy it would be to put her mug down and slide forward. She knew how his skin would feel under her hands.

But, no, the words that were in her head were stronger.

He ran his hand over his bare stomach. "You know, I think I've lost weight too." When Hallie didn't remark on that, he said, "What about Ruby?"

Hallie gave a little laugh. "She was a character! She never cleaned anything, couldn't cook, didn't understand the concept of organization, but she was *fun*! If it snowed, she'd drag Shelly and me outside to build a snowman and we'd drape it with every piece of costume jewelry Ruby had. Our snow lady would have four-inch-long rhinestone earrings and a tiara."

Jamie was looking at her in surprise. "I got the idea that things in your family were different. What about your stepsister?"

Hallie took a moment to answer. While she could sugarcoat Ruby and her father, she knew she wasn't creative enough to gloss over Shelly. "We learned to live together," Hallie said. "But then I always had Braden and his mother nearby, and they made it bearable."

"Braden seems to have been a big part of your life."

Hallie saw the way Jamie's jaw muscles tightened at the mention of the name and she was glad of it. "Yes, he was. Whenever Shelly pulled one of her tricks on me, Braden was there to make me laugh. He'd tell me how smart I was and how people liked me so very much. He's a truly honorable, caring man."

"I guess you'll be glad to see him when he gets here," he said softly.

"I look forward to it very, very much." When Hallie glanced at Jamie she saw what looked like pain in his eyes. If she hadn't heard what Todd said, she would have told him that even when she was an adult, Braden always treated her as a child.

But she didn't reassure Jamie. Instead, she waited in silence. If there was the possibility of anything permanent between them, wouldn't he *say* something? Even if it was just a hint?

But Jamie said nothing.

Hallie put her empty mug on the windowsill and got up. "I need to go back to bed. Thank you for the tea. It was very thoughtful of you."

"You said you were homesick, but the people you love are . . . gone. So is it Braden who you're homesick for?"

"I guess so," Hallie said, even though it was a lie. But letting him think that was better than Jamie believing what Todd had said—that she was desperate for his family. What a terrible word. *Desperate.*

She paused at her bedroom door. "I have a favor to ask of you."

"Anything," he said.

The look in his eyes made her want to go to him. It was a kind of emptiness that she'd seen flashes of, but it had never lasted long. Now it seemed to be there permanently. "Could you ask your family to stay away tomorrow?"

Jamie's eyes brightened. "You want us to stay here alone, just the two of us? I'd like that too. We could—"

"No, that isn't what I meant. All this"—she waved her hand to indicate the house—"has made me think about things. I'm a single, unattached female with good credentials. I can live any-where in the U.S. No! In the world. So I'm going to try to get a really fabulous job in some place that's glorious. Do you think I could get your father to write me a recommendation?"

"Yes. Everyone in my family will write letters praising you. My uncles know people who can help you find a job—if that's what you want." His voice had a tone of resignation to it, as though he knew he'd just lost something important.

"That's a very kind offer, but no thanks. I'd like to be hired on my own merits, not because I know the right people. I was thinking that in a week or so you'll have healed enough that you'll no longer need twenty-four-hour supervision. Once you leave, I'll be free to go and do anything. See the world." She smiled at him as sweetly as she could manage. "I owe all of your family. You've made me see possibilities. Goodnight. See you tomorrow."

He didn't say anything, just looked at her.

Hallie went into her bedroom and shut the door behind her. As she leaned back against it, she couldn't help the tears that came to her eyes. She'd wanted to know if there could be any-thing more than work between her and James Taggert, and now she knew. It looked like his little jealous fit about Braden had been just that. A male marking his territory.

It had been a spur-of-the-moment idea to apply for a job somewhere. What had she expected him to say? "No, don't leave. Stay here and let's get to know each other better?"

How ridiculous that was!

But as much as Todd's words had hurt—especially about her father—Hallie also remembered what he'd said about her work. Maybe she wasn't good enough to be part of his illustrious family, but she was good at her job. "Magic" and "brilliant" were the words Todd had used.

She got back into bed and turned out the light, but she didn't sleep. She waited until she heard Jamie go to his own bedroom. His walk was slower, as though his leg was hurting him. Only when she heard the clink of his crutches as he dropped them did she start to settle.

"Are you happy now?" she whispered into the dark, meaning her words for the ghosts in the house. "So much for matching people up."

She felt like crying, but then she began to feel very calm. When she'd first heard that the Tea Ladies showed themselves only to people who'd not yet found their True Loves, she'd immediately thought that hers was Braden. All she had to do was make him see that she was all grown up and he'd realize how compatible they were. They'd had a lifetime of sharing laughter and good times. They knew each other, understood each other. So why not keep on with it?

"Is that it?" she whispered. "I was getting too close to Jamie? I was forgetting Braden? Are he and I True Loves?"

She couldn't remain awake. As she heard the swish of a silk skirt, sleep overcame her. She didn't awaken at two A.M. and if Jamie had a nightmare, she didn't hear it.

Chapter Eighteen

*H*allie put the papers she'd printed out down on the desk and leaned back in the chair. Her shoulders were stiff from sitting in front of a computer for most of the day. When she woke up this morning she'd made a plan to be as cool as possible to Jamie. She'd be professional but nothing else. No joking, no teasing, just do her job as best she could.

Jamie had done what she asked and his family had stayed away, so all day it had been just the two of them.

In the early morning she'd worked on his knee. No full massage, but she'd manipulated his leg deeply. She could feel that a lot of the tension had come back into his body, but she didn't work on it.

Only once did he refer to her near silence.

She was directing him in some gentle leg lifts and she could see by the sweat on his forehead that he was in pain. He didn't complain. What he said was "If you want to talk, I'm here."

In answer, she gave him a cool look but no words.

Ever since they'd met, their attention had been on him—and rightfully so. His war injuries, the skiing accident, his fears, all took precedence.

But today had been about Hallie. Whatever his personal feelings about her applying for a job were, he'd put them aside and helped her. He called people and got information. His uncle Frank had had a few good suggestions.

"The trouble is that I have so little experience in physical therapy," Hallie said as she looked at her updated résumé. "Massage, yes, and I worked part-time at the hospital with a great teacher, but . . ."

"You need to include what you did for your father," Jamie said.

"How do I put that on my résumé? Do I tell that when I was fourteen the principal called me in to ask about the drugs they'd found in an illegal search of the kids' lockers? Kids were putting oxy in bottles labeled for allergy medicines."

She looked at Jamie, her eyes wide.

"Think your principal would write a recommendation for you?"

"A glowing one." She turned back to the computer. "Thanks," she said.

All day Jamie stayed in the room and read one of his detective novels. It seemed natural to discuss with him whatever she was writing or finding on the Internet.

"What about San Francisco?" she asked. "I could apply there."

"Beautiful city. Hard driving on the hills, but a nice place."

"Portland sounds good. Or maybe I should go south. Maybe Arizona. Or California."

"They'd all be lucky to have you," he'd said and gone back to his book.

Only once did he again suggest Colorado. "My family would love it if you lived there."

Every word Todd had said came to Hallie and her face showed it.

"Okay," Jamie said, his hands up in surrender. "I get it. You've had enough of us."

"Your family is lovely," Hallie said, "but I want to make it on my own." When Jamie just nodded, Hallie thought how astounding it was that you could spout a current cliché and be believed. Every TV show and movie had some smart-talking girl saying she wanted to make it on her own, so when she said the same thing, no one seemed to question it.

But Hallie didn't actually want to be on her own. She would love to have help and get a job someplace where she knew people. How could she do it all by herself? Get an apartment, furnish it, meet people, make a social life as well as a professional one? Or could she stay on Nantucket and try to meet people here?

But she didn't let Jamie see any of her doubts.

By evening she'd sent out over two dozen emails of inquiry. She'd asked people for letters of recommendation, asked institutions about possible jobs, and had even printed out a few pages of places to live in some glamorous cities. But the thought of leaving her house in Nantucket made a wave of sadness pass through her.

At dinner—prepared together—Jamie reminded her that Jilly's wedding was tomorrow. "You want to go with me?"

"I'm not sure I should go," Hallie said.

"Mom sent over a dress for you to wear. She said it's really pretty."

"I can't accept—"

"It's a loan," Jamie said, sounding agitated. "Not a gift. It belongs to one of the cousins and you can give it back to her after tomorrow." He put his hand on hers. "Hallie, please tell me what I or my family have done to offend you."

She pulled her hand away. "Nothing. All of you are perfect. You are beautiful to look at, interesting personalities. There's not a flaw in any of you."

"Okay," he said. "Just know that Aunt Jilly will be hurt if you're not there. What happened between you two the night she and Uncle Kit came over? She's called me twice asking about you."

"Nothing happened." She couldn't meet his eyes. Maybe the females in his family knew about the pregnancy, but few of the males did. And until Hallie knew for sure that Ken had been told, she wasn't saying a word.

"I see," Jamie said and got up from the table.

"You don't want any dessert?"

"No, thanks," he said. "Just leave all this and I'll clean it up later. I'm going to the gym for a while."

Of course Hallie didn't leave the cleanup to him. After the kitchen was tidy, she thought about what to do. The big TV was still in the living room and she could watch it, or she could go into the tea room and read the research Cale had assembled.

But Hallie couldn't bear to go into that room. Jamie's clothes were still in there, piled on the sofa, and she didn't want to see them. The clothes she'd purchased for herself were still in bags in her bedroom.

As always, when Jamie wasn't around, the house seemed big and empty. Like my life, she thought, but then brushed the thought away.

By nine Jamie still hadn't returned to the house. Hallie was tempted to go out to the gym, but she didn't. Instead, she went upstairs and got into bed, planning to read one of the novels on her eReader. Instead, she fell asleep so deeply that she didn't hear Jamie come up the stairs.

A pounding woke her. At first she didn't know what it was and she lay there for a few seconds before she realized it was someone at the front door. "Jamie!" she said, thinking that something was wrong with him. She leaped out of bed and ran to the stairs.

But Jamie was already halfway down, clutching the banister, his crutches nowhere to be seen. When he turned to her, his face was white, and she knew what he was thinking, that something horrible had happened to his family.

"Stay back," he said. "I'll handle this."

"Your family wouldn't knock," she said as she hurried past him and flung the door open.

A young man she didn't know, college age, was standing there. The goofy grin on his face made her realize he'd been drinking. "He said he was staying at the Hartley house. We had a hard time finding the place." His words were slurred. "If you're Hallie, he says he loves you."

"Who says that?" she asked.

Jamie was behind her and opened the door wider. He was taller and could see over the boy's head. Behind him were two more college boys holding a man upright. He was in his thirties, rumpled suit, dirty blond hair, and was clearly feeling no pain. "How much has he had?"

"A lot," the boy replied. "He said he wanted to go back to college and do everything all over again."

"*Who?!*" Hallie asked again.

The boy stepped aside.

"Braden!" Hallie ran to him.

"Hallie," Braden said, smiling, his eyes half closed. "You are beautiful. I don't remember you ever before looking this good." Grinning, he looked at the three boys around him. "Didn't I tell you she was great?"

"Yeah, you did," the first boy said appreciatively, then looked at Jamie. "Can we leave him with you?"

"Take him upstairs to the bedroom on the left," Jamie said.

"But that's your room," Hallie said.

"I have a feeling you'll want to be near him tonight and there's no place for you to sleep downstairs."

"But you—" She stepped aside to let the young men toss Braden's luggage in, then push-pull him up the stairs.

"Don't worry about me," Jamie said. "Take care of your friend."

Part of Hallie was pleased at Jamie's words, but part of her was annoyed. What happened to that delicious jealousy of his?

"And put on some clothes!" he added.

Hallie glanced down. Her big T-shirt exposed her bare legs. When she walked up the stairs in front of Jamie, maybe she swayed her hips just a tiny bit more than was necessary.

She went to her bedroom to pull on jeans and apply a bit of makeup to her sleepy face. It was Braden! He was here!

When she got to the hall, the college boys were just coming out of the bedroom. "That guy sure knows his stuff," one of them said.

"Braden?" Hallie asked. "Did he give you some legal advice?"

"Him? No." They were laughing. "He told us to stay away from women forever."

"He's had a hard time lately," Hallie said. "Do you guys need a ride somewhere?"

"No, we're walking." They went down the stairs and paused at the bottom. "He's too old to go drinking. You better keep him home with you."

"I'll do that, thanks," Hallie said. They left and she went into Jamie's bedroom.

Braden was in the bed, half sitting up and grinning.

"He threw up outside," Jamie said, "so he should be better tomorrow. We got his clothes off and put one of my clean shirts on him. He still stinks, but I wasn't going to hold him up in a shower and wash him." He looked at her. "Or maybe you'd like to do that."

"I'll pass on that, but thank you for doing this. I hate running you out of your bed. You want to use mine?"

Jamie took a moment to answer. "I'll accept that invitation when you're included in it." He stepped back from her. "I'll leave you to it. See if you can get some more water inside him. But then I'm sure you know that." He left the room.

"Hallie," Braden said as soon as they were alone.

"How are you?" she asked as she bent over him. Jamie was right: He *did* stink.

"I've been better."

She went into the bathroom, got a washcloth, soaked it in cold water, and took it back to put on his forehead. She considered pulling up a chair, but it would be too short for the bed. Instead, she climbed up beside him, sitting on top of the covers.

Braden's eyes were red and seemed to be floating around in his skull. He took her hand in his and kissed the back of it.

Hallie leaned toward him and smoothed his hair back. It was a beautiful golden blond. When he was younger his hair had been almost white. His mother loved to tell how her son had been cast as an angel in every school play. For Hallie, it felt good to touch his hair, his face, his neck.

He kissed her palm. "I've made a mess of it."

"Of what?"

"My entire life."

She gave a little laugh. "Far from it. Your mom says you're about to make partner and that you're the youngest one in the firm to do so."

Braden waved his hand. "That's me. Best lawyer Boston has. I win all my cases. It balances out my personal life, where I lose everything. Did you know that I've proposed marriage to three women?"

"Yes," she said.

Braden groaned. "Of course you do. Mom told you. One turned me down, the other two said yes but later dumped me. I should buy engagement rings in bulk. I'll put in a standing order with the jeweler. With the number of them I buy, I should invest in a diamond mine."

"They didn't return the rings?" Hallie asked.

"The last one did." With a sound of pain, he pointed toward his jeans hanging over a chair. "Look in the pocket."

Hallie got off the bed and searched the pockets until she found the ring. It flashed in the light of the room. There was a diamond in the center surrounded by what seemed to be dozens more little diamonds. They surrounded the larger stone, went down the sides and halfway around the band. "Gaudy" was the first word that came to Hallie's mind.

"Did—what was her name? Zara?—choose this?"

"Yes, she did," Braden said.

"I think Shelly would love it," Hallie said as she got back on the bed beside him.

He groaned. "That's your ultimate condemnation."

Hallie was toying with the ring. "You said you took Shelly to work with you."

"I did. But if I tell you the truth about that, you'll hate me."

She picked up a bottle of water from the bedside table and held his head as he drank. "No, I won't."

Again he kissed her palm. "Why can't I marry someone like you?"

"I have no idea," Hallie said seriously. "In my opinion, that's one of the great mysteries of the universe."

Braden pulled back to look at her, blinking to clear his eyes. "You're different. Something's happened. You've changed."

"Maybe getting out of the house where I grew up has let me see some things differently."

He was staring at her. "You look really good. I mean really *really* good."

Hallie could feel herself blushing. "Everybody and every-thing looks good when you're drunk. So what happened that would make me hate you?"

Braden turned away. "I used Shelly, just plain *used* her."

"Sex?" Hallie was trying to sound coolly sophisticated, but her nails were biting into her palms.

"Lord, no! What do you take me for? I used Shelly to make me look less like a failure. I put her in a pair of four-inch heels, a Chanel suit, and took her to work with me to show her off. I wanted Zara to see that I wasn't suffering because she threw me over for a bigger diamond, a bigger house, a bigger *life*." He let out his breath. "But it all backfired on me. Shelly came on to one of the partners. When he told me what she'd done, he said that if I wanted to make partner I needed to get another kind of woman for a wife. He said I should get someone to run a home for me, to entertain clients. Someone I could have kids with." He looked at her. "He meant someone like you, Hallie."

She laughed. "I'm the girl next door. Only men from else-where marry us. We're exotic to them."

He took her hands in his. "I've thought about you these last few days. You're perfect. You always have been. And I've al-ways loved you. You know that, don't you? And you're a saint. You took care of your whole family without one complaint."

"I never stopped complaining. Ask your mother. She dried my tears." Hallie started to get off the bed, but Braden held on to her hand.

"You have the ring?"

She handed it to him and he slipped it onto the ring finger of her left hand. "Think about it, will you?"

"I think this is the best drunken marriage proposal I've ever had."

His eyes were beginning to close. "Have you had many pro-posals? I ask because I pass them out like party invitations. Marry me, have my kids, live in a four-bedroom three-bath, have date night on Fridays, come watch me coach Little League. Why are women today so repulsed by that?"

"I have no idea," Hallie said honestly as she got up, took the washcloth off his head, and tucked him in.

"Let me hear you say yes," he murmured. "I've had too many nos lately."

"Yes," she said. "You won't remember any of this in the morning, so I accept. Now, sleep well and you can go to the wedding with me tomorrow."

"Shelly said her wedding colors would be purple and green. Does that sound good or not?"

"Why were you and Shelly discussing her wedding plans?" Hallie asked, but Braden was asleep.

"What the hell do you have on?" Jamie said through clenched teeth when Hallie walked into the kitchen the next morning.

She glanced down at her jeans and T-shirt, not understanding what he meant. "I'll change before the wedding. I hope you will too." He had on sweats and a long-sleeved T-shirt that, as usual, covered most of his body.

Jamie pivoted on his foot, took her left hand in his, and held it up. "What is this?"

The big engagement ring sparkled in the early morning light. "Oh. That. I couldn't get it off. Are there any more of those cranberry muffins? I think Braden might like them."

She tried to step around Jamie, but he wouldn't move, just stood there staring at her.

"Are you planning to *marry* him?"

Hallie gave a little laugh as she sidestepped and went to the refrigerator. "Maybe. He asked me and I said yes, so that could mean I will. But on the other hand, he was drunk. If you'd stayed longer he might have asked you."

Jamie stood in the middle of the room, glowering. "If you think this is all a joke, why do you have that ring on?"

Hallie was rummaging in the fridge. She needed to buy groceries. Now that she had two men to feed, she should buy a lot. When she closed the door, Jamie was standing there.

"Hallie?" he said with exaggerated patience. "What's going on?"

She saw a basket with a big napkin in the center of the table. It held an assortment of muffins. There was also a full teapot. When she sat down and began to eat, Jamie took the place next to her. He was waiting for her to speak.

She sighed. Obviously, he wasn't going to give up. "Braden's had a hard time lately. Well, maybe not just recently but ever since he was in college. I guess you could say he's been very unlucky in love."

"You're saying that a bunch of women dumped him so now he's going after you?"

"Yes, I mean no. He was upset last night, that's all, and he showed me the ring that had been returned to him."

"And you put it on?"

"Actually, he slipped it on my finger. I tried to take it off before I went to bed but it stuck and I couldn't get it off this morning either." She held out her hand. "What do you think of it?"

"Garish. Flamboyant. Not like you are. Mind if I try getting it off?"

"Be my guest." He pulled her up and led her to the sink, where he spent nearly half an hour working to remove the ring. He tried bar soap, liquid soap, Crisco, butter, and bacon grease. None of them budged the ring.

Through all of it, Hallie kept smiling. She liked standing so close to Jamie, liked his concentrated effort to get the ring off.

"I think my finger is swollen," she said, "and until the swelling goes down, the ring will stay there."

"There's a toolbox in the—"

"No!" she said and curled her hand up. "Could we please just have breakfast? What time is the wedding?"

"Ten. I showed you the church. After the ceremony, we're all moving to Alix's chapel for the reception. There are big tents there."

"It sounds great. Will there be dancing?"

"Into the night. Tell me about you and Braden. Is he why you were sulky all day yesterday?"

"I wasn't sulky! I just wanted—" She was not going to be put on the defensive. "Braden is my friend and he's always been there for me. Whenever something bad—or good—happened in my life, Braden was there. I wouldn't even have gone to college if it weren't for him."

"What did he do?"

"It's a long, boring story, but if it weren't for him I probably would have gone from high school to working in a burger joint. But besides the big things, Braden held the back of my first two-wheeler. When a toy broke, Braden fixed it. One time when I was in high school, he heard that I'd gone out on a date with some kid he knew and Braden came to get me. He knew that my date often bragged about what he did with girls in the backseat of his dad's car. I was really mad at him then, but later the boy nearly raped a girl. Braden saved me. See? He and I have a long history together."

"It sounds like my little sister and me," Jamie said. "I took her on her first ride on a horse. I walked her pony over her first jumps. I've become an expert at putting heads back on dolls. I can even rebraid the hair of a Barbie."

"But you two are related. It's different with Braden and me."

"It seems so," Jamie said, "if he asked you to marry him. You two set a date yet? Choose your wedding colors?"

She got up from the table. "You're being a jerk and I don't want to talk about this any longer. Tomorrow I'm going to the local hospital to talk to them about temporary work." She put her dishes in the sink.

He went to stand beside her. "You can't be thinking of moving back to Boston to live in some perfect little house with him. Is that really what you want? No ghosts floating around? No bothersome naked cousins? No man who freaks out when a car backfires?"

"Stop it!" Hallie said. "Braden is—" She wasn't sure how it happened, but suddenly their anger turned into passion.

Jamie pulled her into his arms and kissed her. At first the kiss was hard and she pushed at him. But his big body against hers made her pull him closer. His lips on hers softened and the kiss deepened. His tongue touched hers.

Hallie forgot who she was, where she was. Only this man and this moment mattered.

When he lifted her and set her on the table, she didn't protest. His hands went under her shirt and her bra unsnapped. He took his lips away only long enough to pull her shirt over her head so she was bare from the waist up. In the next second, his shirt came off.

His beautiful chest, scarred as it was, was against her breasts, his hot, bare skin next to hers.

Hallie's heart was pounding, her breath coming fast. His lips were on her breasts, her neck, then back up to her waiting mouth. All she wanted in the world was to get the rest of their clothes off.

"Hallie?" came Braden's voice. "Where are you?"

It took long moments for her to realize where she was and who was calling her. She pushed at Jamie, but his eyes were glazed, as though he were in another world.

"Jamie!" Hallie hissed. "Let me go!" She pushed hard at him. "In here," she called to Braden as she ducked down and slid off the table away from Jamie. She grabbed her T-shirt and hurried into the pantry. It was only when she was in there that she realized her new lacy black-and-pink bra was still in the kitchen, hanging by a strap on the back of a chair.

She peeped around the door to Jamie. He was pulling his shirt on over his head. "Pssst!" she said and pointed to her underwear.

Jamie started to reach for it, but Braden appeared in the doorway.

"Good morning," Braden said.

Jamie put himself between the blond man and the chair. Behind his back, he lifted the bra.

"How are you feeling today?" Jamie asked as he moved sideways across the kitchen toward the pantry.

"Not so good but better than I thought I would. Is there any coffee? And where is Hallie? This is her house, isn't it?" Braden wiped his hand across his face. "I don't remember too much from last night, but I did see her here, didn't I?"

"Sure you did. She stepped outside. Let me get her." Jamie went into the pantry, closed the door behind him, and held out the bra to Hallie. "He doesn't even remember last night, but you're wearing his ring!" he whispered.

"Turn around," she whispered back.

"We were just about to make love for the *second* time, and now I'm not allowed to *see* you?!"

"Sex on a table or against a wall isn't making *love*. It's two people who have been doing without for a long time in a situation where they can't control themselves."

"I've been 'controlling myself' for over two years and I've been in lots of easier situations than this one."

Hallie turned her back on him and removed her T-shirt. She put her arms through her shoulder straps of the bra and tried to fasten it in the back. But her hands were shaking so badly she couldn't do the clasp.

"Here!" Jamie said angrily. "Let me." He quickly put the hooks and eyes together.

She turned back to face him. "You're good at that, aren't you?" she said just as angrily.

He was staring at her breasts in the bit of lace that had been designed to lift and enhance. It was doing its job very well.

"I have cousins," he said softly.

"What does that mean?"

"Girl cousins cut their teeth on boy cousins. I've fastened so many bikini tops I couldn't count them." He looked back at her eyes. "That's what relatives do. They help each other."

Hallie pulled the T-shirt over her head. "I guess that's supposed to mean you think Braden and I are related. Well, we're *not*. Would you move so I can go to him?"

"Of course. Go back to the rebound guy who gives you a used engagement ring that you don't even like."

"Once again, you're being a jerk." She had her hand on the doorknob as she looked back at him. "You wouldn't tell Braden about . . . about us, would you?"

"About our extreme sexual attraction to each other? That every time we get too close, clothes go flying? Is that what I shouldn't tell him?"

Hallie couldn't help herself and laughed. "However color-fully you state it, just don't tell him, all right? Whatever you think, Braden is real to me."

"And I'm not?" Jamie asked softly, all his anger gone.

"You and your whole family are a fantasy. Will you promise me?"

Jamie closed his eyes for a moment. "Yeah, I'll keep my mouth shut. Anything else you want from me? Blood on a contract?"

"You are too much! Just behave yourself and don't hurt Braden."

"Hurt him?" Jamie said. "What makes you think I'd—?" But Hallie had left the big pantry and closed the door behind her. He leaned back against the wall and closed his eyes. He *did* need to get himself under control.

There was a sound, as though something on the shelves had moved. He opened his eyes and saw that by the door into the tea room, a little wooden butter mold had fallen to the floor. When he picked it up and put it back on the shelf, he saw the piles of clothes on the couch. He could tell the clothes were for him and he guessed that Hallie had brought them back from her shopping trip.

Why had she left them in the tea room? Why hadn't she shown them to him?

All he could figure out was that she was very angry at him about something, but he had no idea what. All day yesterday, every time he got too near her, she jumped away. She had stayed intently focused on trying to find a job somewhere in the U.S. If he so much as mentioned that he might possibly like to spend time with her past when his knee was healed, she bit his head off.

Jamie had backed down, pretended to read a book, and just answered questions. He refrained from saying, "I have PTSD. What's your excuse?" He didn't think Hallie's bad mood would allow her to laugh.

But that evening, the arrival of a drunken, stinking, blond lawyer had turned her into a pot of melting honey. Instantly, her snapping turtle persona was gone and in its place was an ooey-gooey, eyelash-batting girl who nearly swooned at the sight of a skinny, pale guy with regurgitated beer down the front of his shirt.

Jamie was sure his own actions got him some high marks in Heaven. He had helped his rival get into bed, checked his vitals, and even got the boys to help clean him up a bit.

All for Hallie.

Jamie picked up a sweater off the couch. It was exactly the

kind he liked: good quality but not flashy. The complete opposite of that hideous ring that was nearly welded to Hallie's finger.

"You two did this, didn't you?" he said aloud to the spirits in the room. "You're two well-meaning old biddies who want Hallie to get a whole man, not a damaged one like me. That's what this is about, isn't it?"

Jamie threw the sweater back onto the couch. "The hell with the lot of you!" He turned on his crutches and went out the door. He needed to get dressed for his aunt's wedding and as soon as it was over he was going home. Back to Colorado, where only horses stamped a man's heart to the ground.

In the tea room, two beautiful young women looked at each other and smiled. In their experience, sometimes you had to light a fire under a man to get him to do what he should.

Chapter Nineteen

"Hallie," Braden said when she entered the kitchen. He'd showered, washed his hair, and put on one of Jamie's sweatshirts—which hung on him. "I was beginning to think I'd dreamed you last night."

"No, I'm very real. Want some coffee? There are muffins on the table."

"Actually, I am hungry, but I don't see the muffins."

Hallie looked up from the coffee pot and saw that the basket was gone. She looked under the table, but it wasn't there either.

"Wind blow them off?" he asked.

"Something like that. How about some toast?" She had to turn away so he wouldn't see her blush. Jamie tossing her onto the table must have sent the whole basket flying somewhere.

"Hallie, you look great. Have you lost weight?"

"I think so, but I don't know how. There's a B&B next door

and the owner's mother brings us lavish teas with cakes and cookies, and we eat every bite."

"The 'we' refers to you and your client? Is he the big guy I just met? On crutches?"

"Yes, that's Jamie. He got you into bed last night."

"I'll have to thank him."

Hallie put a plate of buttered toast in front of him.

"That's an interesting ring you're wearing," Braden said.

Hallie tugged at it but it didn't move. "Sorry. I couldn't get it off. Jamie tried but no luck." She poured him a cup of coffee. "I'll stay away from the salt today and it'll come off."

"I think it looks good on you. I didn't, by chance, ask you to marry me, did I?"

Hallie smiled as she cracked eggs into a bowl. "'Fraid you did, but I won't hold you to it."

He didn't say anything until Hallie handed him a plate of scrambled eggs and bacon and sat down across from him with a cup of coffee.

"I took the slow ferry to the island, the one that brings cars over," Braden said. "I wanted time to do some thinking."

"Did you?" She sipped her coffee. "About you and Zara? Or your job?" She wasn't going to remind him that he'd told her last night what the partner at his law firm had said about getting a wife and kids.

"Neither. I was thinking about that old adage of doing the same thing over and over and expecting a different result. That's what I do. I fall for these knockout, gorgeous women who care only about my future prospects. Not about me but about what they can get from me. The minute they find someone who seems to be moving up the ladder faster, they leave me behind like a snake shedding its skin."

"That's some comparison."

"Am I shocking you? I guess since I've always seen you as a

little girl, I used to dull down my conversation. But you don't look like that now. You are one hot babe."

Hallie laughed. "Thanks."

"Anyway, all the way over on the ferry I was thinking about you and me. I'd like for us to get to know each other better—but in a different way. Do you think that's possible?"

What he was saying was wonderful, a dream come true. But at the same time, something about it bothered her, though she couldn't put her finger on what, exactly. Maybe it was the word "gorgeous." He said he usually liked "knockout" women, but now he wanted to go another route—and that seemed to mean Hallie. It looked like she was a woman he was *sure* wouldn't dump him.

"Did you know I took those papers out of the trunk of your car?" he asked.

Hallie was so deep in her thoughts that at first she didn't know what he meant. But then her eyes widened. If the papers she was to deliver to her boss had been in the trunk where she'd put them, she wouldn't have gone back to the house to get them. If she hadn't returned, she wouldn't have found out that Shelly was trying to steal a house that had been willed to Hallie.

"I knew Shelly was up to something," Braden said. "She borrowed a fancy tea set from Mom. I couldn't imagine any of Shelly's boyfriends drinking tea out of a porcelain cup. I thought you should look into what was going on, so I ran across the street and took what looked to be an important package out of your car and put it inside the front door. I watched and saw Shelly pick it up."

"Why didn't you just tell me what you suspected?"

Braden shook his head. "Hallie, dear, if I'd told you Shelly was up to something, you would have stayed away until midnight. Both you and your dad always ran away from Shelly. You still do."

That was news to Hallie. "Do I? I always thought I stood up to her."

"Sometimes, I guess." He didn't meet her eyes. "Now that I've been on the receiving end of her selfish little tricks, I better understand what you endured." Braden reached across the table and took Hallie's hand in his. "I wish I'd helped more when you were a kid."

"You couldn't have done anything, and you helped me a lot." She smiled. "Don't forget that if it weren't for you I wouldn't have gone to college. And now I owe you for all this." She gestured toward the house. And I wouldn't have met Jamie, she thought but didn't say.

She pulled her hand from Braden's. "I'm going to a wedding that starts in about an hour and a half. You can stay here or come along. Did you bring any nice clothes?"

"I'm a lawyer, so of course I brought suits. I just have no idea where they are."

"I'll go look," she said, but Braden caught her arm.

"Hallie, I'm making a mess of what I'm trying to say, but I want you to think about you and me. We could have a good life together. I've thought about nothing else for the last few days and I think it could work. You're already part of my family."

"Braden, this is all so sudden and unexpected. I don't know what to say."

"I know, and that's my fault. I should have had sense enough to see what was right in front of me. But I didn't. Will you promise to think about this? And later we can talk. I won't leave until we do."

"All right," she said. "I promise. But I have to get ready now."

"Sure. I look forward to spending time with the new you. I think we could work something out."

He sounded like he was negotiating a contract. She gave him a bit of a smile, then hurried from the room. Right now she couldn't think about what Braden was saying. All she could think about was seeing Jamie. Their fight had upset her. How was *he* feeling?

She went up the stairs, but Jamie wasn't there. The bed had been made and a big leather hanging bag was spread out on it. She knew without asking that it was Braden's. She could almost hear him saying that the expensive piece of luggage looked like something a lawyer on his way up would carry. Braden had always valued image.

Jamie wasn't anywhere upstairs. It looked as though he'd gone to the wedding without her. Ahead of her, she corrected herself. She couldn't blame him for wanting to be with his family.

It was only when she went back to her bedroom and opened her closet door that she saw the dress. No, actually it was The Dress. She'd only seen garments like it on movie stars. It was short, with a scoop neck, sleeveless, simple really. But it was far from simple. It was made of an unusual pale pink lace, kind of crocheted, kind of embroidered, all under a very fine net.

Hallie'd said she didn't want to wear anything from Jamie's family, but that was before she saw *this* dress. She knew without trying it on that it would fit. It wouldn't have before she came to Nantucket—too many late night doughnuts and not enough exercise—but now it would.

On the floor was a pair of cream-colored high heels with a rhinestone ornament across the toe. Manolo Blahnik was written inside them.

For a moment Hallie thought about ignoring the outfit. She'd bought a perfectly respectable navy-blue dress to wear to the wedding.

But then she saw the Dolce & Gabbana label inside the dress and that did it.

She made a quick trip downstairs to tell Braden his luggage was there and that she was going to get dressed. "Meet you in an hour," she called as she ran back upstairs. She went to the bathroom, wrestled with a curling iron, and managed to put her hair up on her head. Little tendrils fell down beside her face.

One thing she'd learned from being around Shelly was how to pile on the makeup. She had one of those little kits of eyeshadows and she used every one of the earth colors. Blush followed base, then she outlined her lipstick.

When her hair and face were done, she went to the bedroom and stripped down to her skin. She was glad she had pretty, white, matching underwear.

The dress felt as good on as it looked. It had been lined with some silky fabric that slid over her skin. And it fit perfectly—as did the shoes. There was a little white beaded clutch on a shelf and Hallie quickly put her keys, credit card, some cash, and a lipstick in it.

She was almost afraid to look in a mirror. When she did, she saw a different person than the one who usually stared back at her. Braden was right. Something had changed in her.

There was a soft knock on her bedroom door and she immediately thought, Jamie!

But she found Braden standing there wearing a dark suit. She had the great satisfaction of seeing him inhale sharply, and he seemed to be speechless.

Hallie turned full circle. "How do I look?"

"You . . ." Braden could do little more than stare. "Stunning," he said at last. "Are you really the little girl with skinned knees who lived across the road from me?"

"One and the same." Oh, but it felt good to have a man look at her as Braden was doing! It was a kind of power she'd never felt before. Men used to say, "Hallie, do you know if your dad has a hammer I can borrow?"

But right now Braden was looking at her the way men looked at Shelly. "Can I get you something?" they asked her. "Can I do something for you?"

"Shall we go?" Hallie asked, her voice as demure as she could make it.

"I would be proud to escort you," Braden said and held out his arm to her.

The sidewalk in front of the church was full of people, all beautifully dressed.

Suddenly, Braden halted, holding her to him. "Hallie, that's Kane Taggert and next to him is his brother, Michael. And the man on the left is Adam Montgomery senior."

"Really? I bet he's Adam's dad. I'll have to introduce myself." She started forward, but Braden didn't move.

"Hallie, you don't seem to realize who these people are. They own things. Big things. We've been trying to get the Montgomery-Taggerts to our firm for years. To handle just one percent of their business would make us. If *I* brought them to the firm, I could write my own ticket."

Hallie realized what he was saying. "I'd prefer that you didn't do any business today. They're nice people, not clients to be won." When she looked at Braden, his eyes seemed to be glazed. "There's Uncle Kit. I have to talk to him. Why don't you . . . ?" Kit was walking away. "I'll see you inside," she said to Braden and left him as she hurried to the church.

"Hallie, my dear, you look quite lovely," Kit said.

"Thank you. I have a favor to ask of you."

"Anything." They started up the church steps.

"Would you please find Raine and ask him to stay with Jamie today? Jamie's in a bad mood and I'm afraid the noise will cause him some problems."

"And our strong young Raine can get Jamie out before he is embarrassed?"

"Yes," Hallie said, grateful for his understanding.

"How very kind of you, especially since it's my guess that Jamie's agitation is caused by the rather remarkable ring you have on."

Hallie held up her hand. "Awful, isn't it? It's not mine, but I can't get it off."

"The question is how it got on your finger in the first place."

"I accepted a marriage proposal, but it wasn't real." She nodded toward Braden, who was earnestly talking to Jamie's father—who was scowling. "Oh, no. I have to rescue Braden before a Taggert steps on him."

Kit laughed. "I am assuming that he's your fiancé. What I'd really like to know is why you don't tell Raine yourself. Has something happened between you two?"

Hallie's smile disappeared. "Let's just say that someone thinks I'm too friendly with Raine."

"And of course that would be Todd. You are having some problems, aren't you?"

"Yes," she said.

Kit tucked her arm into his. "Why don't you sit by me? I'll be sure young James is taken care of and I will do my best to see that no one grabs your fiancé by the collar and throws him out."

"Thank you," Hallie said, and truly meant it.

Once they were inside the beautiful old church, Kit stepped aside for a moment to talk to an older man Hallie'd never seen before. "It's all been taken care of," Kit said when he returned. "And now we may enjoy Jilly's beautiful wedding."

Kit led her to a third-row bench. He sat on the aisle, with Hallie beside him. The church was filled with roses of pale colors: cream, pink, yellow. There were tall vases of more roses in the front, all of them making the church smell divine.

Braden slipped into the pew beside her. "I met all three of them," he said under his breath as he pretended to read the wedding program. "I don't think they're going to move their business to my firm, at least not yet. But I've made a connection." He turned to look at her. "Hallie, I had no idea you knew people like this."

She had to work to keep from frowning at Braden.

As the guests arrived, she said hello to everyone she'd met. Lainey and Paige told her the dress looked great on her. Adam asked her to save a dance for him. Ian said he wanted to introduce her to his parents. Raine looked at her and gave a little nod, letting her know he'd received her message, but he said nothing.

Twice Hallie turned around to see if Jamie was there, but he wasn't. Kit patted her hand. "Jamie is staying away until everyone is in their seats. He's taken care of, so you can quit worrying."

Hallie fiddled with the ring, pulling at it, but it still didn't budge. Beside her, Braden was twisting around to look at the guests.

"May I?" Kit asked and lifted Hallie's left hand. He examined her finger, massaging it a bit. He pulled on the ring once, but it didn't move. "If I believed in such things, I'd say it was witchcraft."

"I agree," Hallie said. "But I don't understand *why*. Am I supposed to marry Braden?" She glanced at him. He was turned half around as he watched Kane and Cale walk down the aisle to their seats.

Kit bent toward her. "The family gossip is that you've been in love with this young man since you were a child."

"And I'll bet that gossip came from Todd. I'd like to—" She gritted her teeth, unable to finish.

"Would you like me to give you some boxing lessons?" Kit was teasing.

"Oh, yes," Hallie said. "I'd like to be strong enough to— Oh, well. What about you? Done any searching?"

He reached inside his suit jacket and withdrew the card

they'd found behind the dresser, the one that read FIND THEM in the same old-fashioned writing she'd seen on the envelope. "The only question remains *who* I am to find," Kit said.

When the music began to play, Kit put the card back in his pocket and Hallie sat up straight.

Braden turned toward the front. "Who's the old guy next to you?" he whispered to Hallie.

"He's the man Ian Fleming modeled James Bond on and he can kill with a single blow, so behave yourself."

Braden looked shocked at her words. "Who *are* you?" He was looking at her as though he'd never seen her before.

"I think the genuine me is coming out," Hallie said, then turned her attention to the front of the church where a woman had started singing.

There was a bit of a lapse when the solo was finished, before the choir began. A man, tall, with brown hair and blue eyes, stopped by the pew.

"Are you Hallie?" he asked softly. "I just wanted to introduce myself. I'm—"

"Leland," she said. "You look like my dad. Please sit with us." She motioned for Braden to move aside, but he protested.

"Leland is my cousin," Hallie said, and reluctantly, Braden moved so Leland could sit by Hallie. She couldn't help staring at him.

"And you look like my dad's sister," he said. He saw the ring on her finger. "You're engaged."

"Wow. More family. But, no, I'm not engaged," Hallie said.

"Yes, she is," Braden said from the other side of him.

Leland looked over her head to Kit.

"Our Hallie is a very popular young lady," Kit said.

The music began again and there was no more talk.

Minutes later, the groom and Jared came from the side to stand at the front. As Jared looked around the audience, he smiled at Hallie.

Braden leaned across Leland. "You know the famous architect too? Who's next? The president?"

"Shhhh," Hallie said and leaned back against the pew.

Leland was looking at her questioningly, but Hallie just shrugged. Kit's eyes were sparkling in amusement.

When the music for the bride began, everyone stood up. Jilly's dress was extremely simple: high necked, long sleeves. But the fabric was embellished with long rows of tiny silvery sequins. As she passed by, people gasped when they saw the back of the gown. It was covered with a transparent mesh and showed off Jilly's beautiful, toned back to well below her waist.

"Now, *that's* a gown!" Hallie said.

Kit smiled. "Our Jilly has always had a bit of fire in her."

"When I—" Hallie cut herself off. She had an idea that if she even mentioned marriage, Braden would comment on it. What in the world was *wrong* with her?! Everything she'd ever dreamed of was happening, but all she felt was a sense of gloom.

She couldn't help it, but she yet again looked toward the back of the church. Sitting in the last pew, near the aisle, with Raine beside him, was Jamie. He was staring at her and frowning, but Hallie smiled at him, glad that he was safe. Suddenly, her feeling that something was missing disappeared.

She turned back to the front and looked up at Leland. When he smiled at her, it felt good. He was her family. All around were Jamie's relatives, but this man, Leland Hartley, was related to *her*.

He seemed to understand what she was thinking. He reached into his inside jacket pocket and pulled out a card. It was an old photograph, probably early 1900s, of a pretty woman wearing a costume with a tall lace collar. It looked like something Elizabeth I would have worn. Beneath it was printed EMMELINE WELLS.

"Your great-grandmother," Leland whispered.

If the pastor had not started speaking, Hallie would have bombarded him with questions. As it was, her hands held on to the card tightly. She'd never known anything about her father's family and there had been grandparents only on her mother's side. To suddenly see how she belonged in the world was touching something deep inside her.

"She's almost as pretty as you are," Kit whispered, making Hallie smile.

She gave her attention to the beautiful ceremony.

"How are you doing?" Raine asked as he sat down beside Jamie, whose chair was up against the tent wall. After the ceremony, the guests had been transported to a piece of land owned by the Kingsleys, where Jilly's new husband's daughter had designed a beautiful chapel. Jilly had wanted to be married there, but it wouldn't hold even half of her big family. She'd settled on being married in the church, with the reception near the chapel.

"Great," Jamie said, his leg stuck out before him, his crutches in his hand as though he were ready to leave at a moment's notice. "The woman I love is wearing another man's ring and dancing with every man here."

"Interesting description of her," Raine said. "Have you told her how you feel?"

"Hallie's so nice she'd probably marry me out of sympathy."

"I don't think you're right," Raine said. "Hallie has a mind of her own and she doesn't do things she doesn't want to. She won't dance with me."

Jamie snorted. "She tends to like those skinny ones. Every Montgomery here has whirled her around."

"And so have the Taggerts," Raine said. "It's just *me* she

refuses. I thought she and I were becoming friends, but today she won't even look at me. I wanted to tell her that our secret is out, but she turned away before I could say it."

"What secret?"

"Aunt Jilly is expecting. All the women knew, but the men were in the dark."

"I knew," Jamie said.

"Yeah, well, you don't count."

"Todd said you two had a secret between you, but you wouldn't tell him what it was."

"You know Todd. If he'd known, he would have gone to Aunt Jilly and asked her if she was taking her prenatal vitamins. Jilly wanted to tell Ken first. Anyway, did you meet Hallie's cousin?"

"She brought him over. Seems like an okay guy, and he's making Hallie happy, so that's good."

"But what about the other one? The childhood sweetheart?"

Jamie turned a face of fury to his cousin. "He's not that! He's just . . ."

"Just what?" Raine asked. "That ring Hallie has on looks pretty real to me. Did you know she and this guy were so serious?"

"No!" Jamie said so loudly that several people turned to look at him in concern. "I have to get out of here before everyone starts whispering in fear of upsetting the damaged soldier." He stood up with his crutches.

"I'll drive you," Raine said.

"I can drive! I'm perfectly capable of taking care of myself."

"You're not getting behind a wheel when you're as angry as you are." When Jamie looked like he was going to balk, Raine said, "I'd hate to have to knock you out and carry you over my shoulder."

"Try it." Jamie spoke with such challenge that Raine laughed.

Three kids ran past them, one of them nearly knocking Jamie's crutches out from under him. Raine grabbed a bag from one of them, who kept on running.

"Have some candy," Raine said and held out the bag. "Maybe it'll sweeten your temper."

Jamie knew when he was being ridiculous. He reached into the bag, withdrew a handful of lavender M&Ms with tiny pictures of the bride and groom on them, and popped them into his mouth. "Okay, you drive."

"Good choice," Raine said and minutes later they were at Hallie's house.

The quiet was wonderful to Jamie and he sat down at the kitchen table, while Raine rummaged in the fridge for sandwich makings. Raine put jars and bags on the table and got Jamie a knife and some plates so he could sit and make the sandwiches.

"Maybe I've been around Aunt Cale too much, but this thing with Hallie is a bit of a mystery," Raine said. "What made her go from liking me one day to refusing to look at me the next?"

"I don't know. I leave solving mysteries to Mom and Todd," Jamie said.

"By the way, where is your brother?"

"He was called back to work to handle one of his cases. He flew out early this morning."

Raine dished coleslaw onto plates. "So I'm on my own in trying to figure this out. Maybe Hallie's had enough of our family and wants to get away from them. Remember Adam's last girlfriend? She said being around our family was like living in the middle of a sports team. She wanted nothing to do with us. Maybe Hallie's starting the breakaway with me."

Jamie put pickles on top of slices of turkey. "Todd thinks Hallie likes our family more than she does me. He thinks Hallie is so desperate to have a family that she'll take any of us so she can have all of us."

"What else does Todd think?" Raine asked, an eyebrow raised.

"He worries that I like her but that she doesn't like me—except as her patient."

"I think your brother is full of crap," Raine said as he sliced a tomato. "When Todd said all of this about Hallie, did he say anything about me?"

"Yeah. He said you two were flirting so hard during Graydon's wedding that he wanted to throw a bucket of water on you, and also that you two had some secret. I guess that was about Aunt Jilly."

"And now I know why Hallie wouldn't dance with me."

Jamie looked at Raine. "But that would mean she knew what Todd said. You don't think the Tea Ladies told her, do you?"

"Ghosts told her?" Raine said. "You've been here too long! I think Hallie overheard your idiot brother spouting off. Where were you when this happened?"

Jamie's eyes widened. "The clothes!" he whispered, then grabbed his crutches and went through the pantry. The new clothes that Hallie had chosen for him—his mother had told him the whole story—were still on the couch.

Raine was holding something out to Jamie. "I found this on the floor by the door to the kitchen." It was Hallie's set of keys to the house and the car Jared had lent her. The key ring had a charm on it with 1776 and the word BOSTON.

Jamie dropped down on the couch. "She *did* hear. She must have heard every word Todd said."

Raine picked up a stack of sweaters, moved them to the end of the couch, and sat down next to Jamie. "This is bad. Someone has to tell Hallie the truth. Personally, I think Todd should apologize to her. As for me, I'm going to tell her— Where are you going?"

When Jamie didn't answer, Raine followed him into the kitchen. "I think I'm missing something. You've been so angry today that you've looked like a gargoyle, but now you're grinning. Why?"

"I thought Hallie was staying away from me because . . ." He took a breath, then looked at his cousin, who could see relief in his eyes. "Because she wanted to let me know that she didn't want a man as badly damaged as I am. That she didn't want to deal with a man who sometimes can't figure out where he is. But that's not the problem."

"What is?" Raine asked.

"She's just mad at me. Old-fashioned girl anger. She heard my brother say some bad things about her and she's in a snit. Furious at me." He shook his head in wonder. "This is *normal*. I can handle normal."

"Yeah?" Raine asked. "And how do you plan to do that?"

"If you remember, I used to be a player. I'm going to show her how I feel about her."

Raine picked up his sandwich and bit into it. "I sure hope that big ring she's wearing doesn't make more scars on you."

Jamie took a drink of Coke from a can. "Good point. Maybe first I should clear up some things with Braden the Greedy. This morning Dad was so mad at the guy that if it hadn't been for Hallie, he would have tossed him off a pier."

Jamie went to the door. "I feel the overwhelming need to eat some wedding cake. How about if we go back and tell Aunt Jilly how much we wish her all the happiness in the world?"

Raine stood up, sandwich in one hand, drink can in the other. "Only if you drive."

"I can't do—" Jamie broke off. "Sure. Why not?"

Smiling, Raine followed his cousin out the door.

Chapter Twenty

*H*allie was standing near the doorway and watching the dancers. Braden was doing some old-fashioned disco moves with both Lainey and Paige and seemed to be in heaven. Every now and then he'd look around for Hallie and give her a thumbs-up.

She was glad he was having a good time. She'd talked on the phone to his mother twice since she'd been on Nantucket and knew that she was worried about her son.

"I'd like to do something horrible to *all* those girls!" his mother said. "How could they be so cruel to my son? Of course it doesn't help that he chooses such dreadful women. Oh, Hallie, why can't Braden see what's been right in front of him all these years?"

Hallie knew that meant *her.* Why didn't Braden have sense

enough to see that just across the road was a young woman who'd never give him any problems? If Hallie got married, she'd never be unfaithful. She'd have two or three children and be a devoted mother. When they were older she'd go back to her highly respectable job and . . . and, well, be perfect.

Perfectly boring, she thought as she waved to Braden. She'd never before seen him in low spirits. In high school he'd been the president of the senior class, and he'd been popular in law school too. No one who knew him was surprised that he was up for partnership in his prestigious law firm when he was so young.

As Braden said, only women gave him problems—and Hallie's stepsister seemed to have been the last straw. She had been the one who'd made Braden so desperate he decided to go with a sure thing—meaning the girl he'd known since she was born. Hallie couldn't help but feel responsible for this last blow to Braden. She was the one who got him involved with Shelly. Damn! But why couldn't Shelly have behaved for even one day?

When a familiar arm slid around the front of her shoulders, for a moment she forgot everything and leaned her head back against Jamie. He kissed the side of her neck.

In the next second, she jumped away and turned toward him, angry. "What do you think you're doing?"

"Saying hello," he said with an innocent grin. "Did you get any cake?"

"No. Your relatives have kept me on my feet all day." She was frowning.

"And those look like such comfortable shoes."

She wanted to stay angry at him but couldn't. "Even my toenails ache."

Jamie held up a set of car keys. "How about if I drive us home and I give you a foot massage?"

"Ecstasy," she said. "Better than sex."

"That's because you haven't been to bed with me yet."

The look in his eyes took Hallie's breath away for a moment. "There's no 'yet' and I can't leave with you. I'm here with Braden."

Jamie glanced at the dance floor. "He doesn't look like he's suffering." He caught Adam's arm as he walked by. "Keep the boyfriend busy, will you? I'm taking Hallie home. Give him lots of cousins and mention the word 'heiress' often."

"Will do," Adam said, then bent and kissed Hallie's cheek. "See you tomorrow."

Jamie stepped back to let Hallie go ahead of him.

Turning, she tried to get Braden's attention. She should tell him she was going to leave. No, she *should* stay there with him. Jamie telling Adam to say "heiress" was a low blow—but unfortunately true. Just minutes ago Braden had said the word in connection with Paige.

When Braden saw her, she made a motion toward the door and he blew her a kiss. He seemed to be okay with her leaving. She waved to Leland and he smiled back.

Jamie held the door to the big tent open for her. "Braden's not exactly worried about your running off with another man, is he?"

"I don't think he sees you as competition."

"Then he's a fool," Jamie said.

Outside, she followed him through the many parked cars to a big black Range Rover. He opened the door for her, then stood back. It was a very high step up to get into the vehicle, and Hallie's skirt was quite short and her heels very tall.

"I don't think I can do this," she said. "Mind giving me a hand?"

"No," Jamie said. "I just want to watch."

"What's gotten into you tonight?"

"Can't a man be a man?"

She didn't understand what he meant and turned back to

trying to figure out how to get into the big car without her skirt riding up to her waist.

Finally, Jamie took pity on her. He leaned his crutches against the car, put his hands on her waist, and lifted her up to the car seat. "Better?"

"Yes," she said and turned around while he got in the driver's side. On the console was a white bakery box. "What's this?"

"Wedding cake. I thought we'd go home, open some champagne, and have some. Sound good?"

When she didn't answer, Jamie turned toward her. It was late afternoon and the sunlight through the trees was nice. As always on Nantucket, the weather was divine. He knew that the air hadn't been cleared between them. "Did you overhear my brother?" he asked, his light tone gone.

Hallie's first instinct was to say no. It wasn't polite to eavesdrop. But she didn't lie. "Yes."

"And that's what you've been angry about?"

She gave a shrug.

Jamie reached over to take her hand. "First of all, my brother said all that, not me. Second, it's his job to never believe anyone, and third, he's very protective of me. He's worried that I'm going to die at any second. He'd like to lock me away from everyone just to keep me safe."

"Everything he said is true," Hallie said softly.

"About Raine?"

"No! I like him but not like that," Hallie said, then realized Jamie was teasing her.

"I'm glad because Raine has been crying a lot." Jamie started the car and began backing out.

"Has he? Did you let him cry on your shoulder?"

"Are you crazy? If he rolled on top of me, I'd be crushed. I'd be back in the hospital with my whole body in a cast."

Hallie was trying not to laugh. "I guess I'll just have to let him cry on *me*."

"So he'd crush *both* of us at once?" Jamie sounded confused.

Hallie's laugh came out. "Oh! I've missed you." She stopped herself. "I mean—"

"It's okay," he said. "I've missed you too. I think some of the happiest times of my life were when you and I were alone in our little house. That's the kind of thing soldiers fight for."

Hallie looked out the window at the pretty buildings they were passing. Nantucket was so beautiful that it was like something created by heavenly creatures. Maybe it was the atmosphere, but she calmed down. "Braden says I've changed and I think I have."

He was maneuvering the big vehicle down the narrow Kingsley Lane. "Changed how?"

She waited for him to park, then get out and come around to her side. Reaching up, he put his hands on her waist and lifted her down.

For a moment they looked at each other, faces close together, and it seemed natural that they kiss. Jamie bent his head toward hers, but Hallie turned away to get the box of cake out of the car.

He didn't seem to mind as he followed her to the front door.

"Locked," Hallie said. "Just like last time." She told him of when she'd come home from shopping and her keys were missing and the door was locked. "I think I was meant to go into the tea room. I think . . ." She looked at him. "I think they wanted me to hear what your brother said."

"And that led to you having that ring on your finger? Are you still trying to get it off or are you going to leave it on there?"

When she looked at him, she saw the seriousness in his eyes. "Right now Braden needs to have some security in his life. He doesn't need to have his backup girl, the one who's always been there, tell him she doesn't want him either."

For a moment she saw anger flash across Jamie's eyes, but it was gone quickly. "That makes sense. Can I walk you down the aisle at your wedding?"

She narrowed her eyes at him. "If you're trying to be funny, you're not succeeding." Turning, she headed for the tea room doors.

"I never joke about the wedding of the woman I love."

At his words, Hallie slowed her steps, but she didn't stop. Just as before, one of the double doors into the tea room was half open. On the coffee table was one of Edith's luscious teas. "Look," she said to Jamie and opened the door all the way.

"I don't know about you," he said, "but I'm starving. Raine cleaned out the fridge and the Montgomerys, picky eaters that they are, ate everything at the wedding."

Hallie was glad he was back to joking and wasn't saying more about being "in love" with her. Right now that was more than she could handle.

The couch still had clothes piled on it. Jamie tossed a stack of sweaters onto a chair, sat down on the couch, and patted the seat beside him. "So what's your cousin like?"

Hallie gave a sigh of relief that he wasn't going to be serious and sat down beside him. This was like he had been, before everything became complicated with the arrival of relatives and a man who was kind of, maybe, her boyfriend. "Leland is great," Hallie said. "We escaped everyone for nearly an hour and walked all around the property. He told me about his job and how he's sick of living in hotels. He wants to settle some-where and— Oh! I forgot. He said he stopped by here and left his suitcase and a box full of info for me." Hallie started into the house through the pantry, but she found the box on one of the shelves. She picked it up and carried it back to the tea room and put it on the floor by the coffee table.

"Try this," Jamie said and held up a little sandwich for her to bite into. He ate the other half.

"That's delicious. What is it?"

"Some kind of sea creature. I'm better with beef. So what's in the box?"

As they ate, Hallie went through the contents. There were letters, an old scrapbook of newspaper articles about a man who was touted as one of the greatest actors of all time, and several theater tickets. In the bottom was a little bouquet of dried flowers wrapped in a silk handkerchief.

Hallie read aloud while Jamie fed her. "Mmmm, look at this," she said, her mouth full of wedding cake. "Miss Emmeline Wells married Mr. Drue Hartley on the twenty-second of July in 1912. They're my family."

Jamie leaned forward and kissed the corner of her mouth. "You had icing right there and I couldn't find a napkin."

"There's one on your leg."

"So there is. What did Leland say about your ancestors?"

"Uh . . ." Hallie was having trouble recovering from his kiss. "Oh, yes. Drue was the youngest child and when he was nineteen he fell madly in love with a pretty young actress. His father, who was a very wealthy businessman, gave his son a choice of the family or pretty little Emmeline."

"And he very wisely chose the girl," Jamie said. "And that choice eventually gave birth to you. Did I tell you how much I like that dress on you?"

"No, you didn't. But everyone else did. Braden said I could only wear it because I've lost so much weight. I don't know how I've done it since we eat such high-calorie food."

Jamie picked up the papers that were on the couch between them and put them on the floor so he could move closer to her. "He certainly does think a lot about weight, doesn't he?"

"What are you doing?"

Jamie ran his hand down her bare arm. "So what's your cousin planning to do?"

"I don't know. He's as unattached to family as I am. That's why he dropped everything to come here to meet me. He may . . ." She trailed off because Jamie had put his hand on her waist and was kissing her neck.

"I've missed you every second we were apart," he whispered. "I wanted them all to leave so we could be together."

She leaned her head back to give him greater access to her throat.

He whispered as he kissed her. "I missed all our talks, our sharing time and food. I missed knowing you were in a bed close to mine. I remembered when I woke up with you in my arms."

He was kissing her chin, her cheeks. His hands clasped her face and he kissed her closed eyelids.

"I don't think we should do this," Hallie said, but her voice lacked conviction.

Holding her face, he waited for her to open her eyes and look at him. "Are you going to marry a man who thinks of you as a consolation prize?"

"No," Hallie said and with that answer, she felt a great relief come over her. She didn't want to disappoint Braden or his mother, but she really couldn't go through with it. "No, I'm not."

Jamie started to put his lips on hers, but a clatter made him draw back. He looked on the floor and there, sparkling up at him, was the big engagement ring. It had fallen off Hallie's finger. He picked it up and held it between his thumb and forefinger. He started to say something, but Hallie took it out of his hand and put it on the table.

"Okay, that's it," she said. "I've heard enough about your lovemaking. I'd like proof of life."

Smiling, Jamie took her hand in his, grabbed a crutch, and made it to the stairs. He let Hallie go up first.

Once they were in the bedroom, she felt a little nervous. What now? she wondered. More up-against-a-wall? Or get into the bed?

But Jamie took over. He sat down on the edge of the bed, his knees apart, and pulled her to him. He turned her so her back was to him and slowly unzipped her beautiful dress. He kissed her skin as each bit was exposed, his hands sliding around her bare waist, then down over her hips.

Gently, he pushed the dress forward, over her shoulders, then down until it puddled at her feet.

Turning her around, he pressed his face on her bare stomach, kissing it, then put his arms around her, holding her close to him.

Hallie bent down, her face in his hair. She'd touched him in massages, but this wasn't the same. "I've missed you too," she whispered.

He looked up at her, smiling, and when she bent to kiss him, he abruptly pulled her off her feet to land on the bed in a flurry of covers.

"Now I have *you* on your back," he said in a way that made him sound like a cartoon villain.

Hallie laughed and started to unbutton his shirt.

He brushed her hand away. "Nope. It's your turn to be naked in front of me."

"What a terrible idea," she said, blinking rapidly at him.

Jamie began kissing her neck, his hands roaming over her body. She still had on her pretty white underwear, but he didn't remove it, just ran his hands over all of her, feeling, caressing. "I've thought you were beautiful since the first day I saw you," he said as his kisses moved downward.

He certainly did seem to know what to touch and how to do it, she thought as his hands and lips moved over her body. She wasn't sure when the last of her clothing came off, but she was nude before him and he touched her body. His hands caressed her inner thighs so that she opened her legs for him. His lips on her breast made her arch her back.

When she was ready for him, she found that he had protection with him and he put it on.

When he entered her, she clung to him, loving the weight of his big body. He still had on his shirt and she could feel the buttons on her skin.

The size of him, the weight, the pure masculine smell of him, nearly drove her to a frenzy. She came before he did and he held her to him, caressing her back. Just holding her tightly to him, letting her feel the release in her body.

Gradually, he began his long, slow strokes inside her, waking her in a way she'd never felt before. It was as though something deep within her was coming alive.

She gave herself over to it, let herself feel only this man and this moment.

"Jamie," she whispered.

"I'm here," he said, his lips against her ear. "I'm always here."

His shirt came off and she felt his hot skin near hers, felt the ridges of the scars. Her hands on his back went over the bumps and dents—and they made her smile. This was Jamie. This unique, fascinating man was Jamie.

When he came, he fell against her, holding her to him. As he lay in her arms, his body limp, relaxed, she had a feeling of power. He *needed* her. For all his strength and size, all his masculinity, with her he could release all that. With him, it was a matter of trust and possibly love.

They slept for a while, wrapped up together, so close they were like one being. In the early morning, Jamie became restless. A nightmare. As always, Hallie soothed him with kisses. He settled, but a moment later he woke up.

"Did I do it again?"

"Yes," she said, smoothing his hair back from his face.

"I may never recover," he said softly. His naked body was close to hers, his leg over hers, and she could feel the tension that was beginning to build in him. His tone was light, but she could feel that what he was saying meant a lot to him.

"I know."

"No, you don't," he said. "I may always be plagued with nightmares. I can't imagine that I'll ever be tolerant of loud noises. If I hadn't wanted you so much, I would *never* have gone to a family wedding. All those doorways and people and noises and—"

She kissed him. "I know. It's all part of you."

"The scars inside me will always be there. Years may dull them, but they'll never go away. I can't live like other people; I have to make concessions."

Hallie wasn't sure, but she thought maybe he was talking about the two of them being together past when his leg healed. She didn't have a reply to that but just kissed him some more.

"I like your answer," he said. "Your turn to be on top."

Smiling, he rolled onto his back while holding her up, and set her down on him. He was ready for her.

Hallie woke to the sound of water running. The door to her bathroom was open and she saw Jamie in front of the mirror. He had just a towel around his waist and he was shaving.

He saw her in the mirror. "You finally woke up."

She stretched luxuriously, not bothering to keep the sheet over her naked breasts.

Jamie paused in shaving to watch her. He finished, dried his face, then went to sit on the side of the bed.

"You in just a towel," she murmured as she ran her hand over his arm. "That's what got me in trouble the first time."

He kissed her, but when it became deeper, he pulled back. "I don't know how you want to handle this, but Adam just sent a text. Your boyfriend will be here in a few minutes."

She was kissing his neck. "Who is that?"

"Glad you don't remember," Jamie said as he stretched out beside her.

Suddenly, Hallie sat up. "I forgot about Braden!"

"Understandable." Jamie reached out to pull her down beside him, but she rolled to the far side of the bed and got out.

Jamie's shirt was on the floor and she picked it up, put her arm in one sleeve, and turned the other one to the right side as she ran to the bathroom. "I forgot all about him," she said through the door. "Where did he sleep? Oh, no! You don't think he jumped in bed with one of your cousins, do you? His mom will *kill* me. I'm supposed to take care of him but I didn't. This is terrible."

Jamie was stretched out on the bed, a stack of pillows under his head. "No to all of it. Boyfriend is safe and virginal."

Hallie looked around the door at him. "You can laugh about this, but Braden is my responsibility. I'm going to have to tell him that even his backup girl won't marry him. And how do you know he's safe?"

"From about a dozen text messages. Adam wrote that he took both Leland and the boyfriend—"

"Please stop calling him that."

"*Ex*-boyfriend to Plymouth's house. With Todd gone, they had an empty bedroom."

"Your brother left?" Hallie said. "Too bad. I would have liked to say goodbye to him. Maybe Uncle Kit can teach me some special goodbye boxing moves just for your brother."

Jamie chuckled. "Just so you know, Todd would *never* hit a girl back."

"Good to hear." She left the bathroom wearing her robe. "You made me forget everything last night."

"Did I?" Jamie opened his arms to her.

She went to him, snuggling beside him, and they began kissing. Her robe opened and his hands began to explore.

"Hallie? Are you here?" she heard Braden call from downstairs.

She pushed away from Jamie. "I have to go." When he didn't release her, she pushed harder. "I have to see to Braden."

"Tell him you're busy."

She gave such a big push that she would have landed on the floor if Jamie hadn't caught her as he got out of bed. "He can't know about us. Not yet. I have to break it to him gently. He's had too many heartbreaks lately." She put her hand to her forehead. "I just remembered I promised Leland that this morning I'd walk around Nantucket with him. And some of your family is leaving today and I have to say goodbye. You should too."

"I had all the family I can bear yesterday. How long before you can get rid of cousin and boyfriend?"

"Leland leaves this afternoon, but Braden . . . I don't know. He's a mess right now and he's my friend." She went to the stairs to call down to him that she'd be there in a few minutes. "I have to get dressed," she said to Jamie as she hurried past him. "Do me a favor and go mess up your bed so Braden thinks that's where you slept."

"I don't like lying," he said.

She put her hands on his back and pushed him toward the door. "You love lying when it gets you what you want. Now go! And put some clothes on."

"Boyfriend might freak at the scars of a soldier?" He said it as though he were a martyr.

Hallie stopped and looked at him. "No, because you are so magnificently beautiful that Braden will feel awful."

"Yeah?" Jamie asked, smiling.

"Go!" she said as she went into her closet. For a moment she stood there and breathed deeply. She wanted time to think

about all that had happened, to go over everything in her mind:
Jamie, Braden, finding a family, Jamie, Todd, and oh, yeah,
Jamie.

"Don't let this get messed up," she said aloud and didn't
know if she was praying or talking to the resident ghosts who
always seemed to be near. "Let me *keep* this. Please."

She didn't have time for more thought. People were waiting
for her. She grabbed clothes and pulled them on.

Chapter Twenty-one

Jamie was in the gym and working to concentrate. He was so angry that he had to remind himself not to sling the weights around. Years of training from his dad and uncle were strongly in his mind. "Form is everything," his uncle Mike always said. "A wrong move and muscles can detach."

What was making it so difficult now was that in a few minutes he was to meet Hallie's "boyfriend" for a "chat." That's what he'd said at breakfast.

Hallie had been in a hurry to meet her newly found cousin and to say goodbye to some of the older members of Jamie's family. Braden, sitting quietly at the table, had begged off. He said he had too bad a hangover to go anywhere. He just wanted to stay at the house.

Jamie was at the sink when Braden came up behind him—something that was guaranteed to set Jamie off—and said he wanted to have a private "chat" with him. "About ten? And please don't say anything to Hallie. This is just between us men."

All Jamie had been able to do was nod silently in reply. Throughout breakfast, through cousins arriving to pick Hallie up, Jamie had thought about the coming meeting. Was this guy going to ask for help in getting Hallie? Would he play on Jamie's sympathy so he felt as sorry for him as Hallie did?

When the house was empty, Jamie went to the gym to try to work off some of the nervous energy that was building in him. But he kept looking at the clock, dreading what was coming, but also wanting to get it over with. Whatever the guy wanted, Jamie knew he'd do what was best for Hallie.

At five minutes to ten, Braden showed up at the door. He had on clean, crisp clothes, while Jamie's loose workout gear was soaked in sweat.

"Go ahead and finish," Braden said. "I'll wait."

Jamie put down two sixty-pound dumbbells. "No. We'll do it now." He sounded like he was facing a firing squad. He nodded toward the arbor and the two chairs there, and Braden followed him.

Once they were outside, Braden sat down, and Jamie wished he'd taken the time to shower and change. On impulse, he pulled his sweaty shirt off over his head and sat down, naked from the waist up. It wouldn't hurt to intimidate the enemy.

When Braden saw Jamie's bare upper half with all its scars, his eyes widened. "Oh, man! You look like a survivor of the gladiator ring. I read about your injuries, but that's not the same as seeing them." He was studying Jamie's chest and shoulders, stomach and arms. "Thank you," he said. "Thank you for what you soldiers do for our country. But then none of us can thank you enough. Mind if I shake your hand?"

This wasn't what he'd been expecting, Jamie thought as he

held out his hand and shook Braden's. His buildup of anger was being replaced with confusion. "What do you mean you read about me?"

Braden settled back in the chair. A bit of sunshine hit his face and he closed his eyes to enjoy it. "I couldn't let Hallie stay here with some guy I knew nothing about, now could I? Sergeant Bill Murphy says hello and that if you ever need anything, he's ready."

"You want to tell me what's going on?" There was a bit of a threat in Jamie's voice.

Braden smiled. "You have a little sister. When she starts dating, will your family do some checking on her boyfriend?"

"Hallie is *not* your sister."

"Might as well be," Braden said, unperturbed by Jamie's temper. He looked across the garden and smiled in memory. "I was six when her parents brought their new baby home from the hospital. When Mom and I walked over to see her, Hallie reached up, grabbed my finger, and smiled at me. Everyone made a big deal of it, saying she was much too young to smile, but it never changed. For all her life, whenever she saw me, she smiled."

Jamie couldn't control his sneer. "So now you want to *marry* her?"

"About as much as you want to marry your little sister." Braden took a breath. "I picked that ring up at the airport. Ugly thing, isn't it? I knew Hallie would hate it. By the way, years ago she told Mom she'd like to have an oval diamond."

"If you don't want to marry her, then why did you ask her?"

"To release her," Braden said. "You see, when Mom called me in hysterics and said that if I didn't get here fast I was going to lose Hallie to her client, I knew it was time to change things."

"Change them how?"

Braden took a moment to organize his thoughts. "Since her

dad was always gone, the only real security Hallie had was Mom and me. And you know how girls are. If they see you as a rescuing hero, they think they're in love with you." He looked at Jamie. "Until you. I knew from Mom's voice that this was different, so I used the resources at my law firm to do some research on you. Dr. James Michael Taggert is spoken of highly. Sergeant Murphy said you saved his leg. He told me how you volunteered to go on some of the most dangerous missions with the men and women. You wanted to be there at the moment they needed your medical expertise."

Jamie shrugged. "It's what needed to be done."

"Not quite! You could have gone to work in some plush clinic or had your dad buy you a wing of a hospital. But you chose to go into the army and save our soldiers."

"I'm not a hero, if that's what you're implying. You said you came here to release her."

"I wanted to let Hallie know that it was okay to love someone else. And to do that, I knew she had to stop seeing me as the epitome of all that was good in mankind. She had to see me as I am, a man with a whole lot of flaws. How much did your young cousins laugh at my dancing?"

"A lot." Jamie looked at Braden. "Are you saying that all of this has been an *act*?"

"Yes," Braden said. "So tell me, how have I done? Have I been obnoxious enough? Hitting your dad up for possible business at a wedding was the low point. He looked so angry and he's so *big* that sweat was running down the back of my shirt. Then his brother joined him and I was so scared I wanted to run away, but I held my ground."

Jamie was listening in astonishment. "What about that first night? Were you really drunk?"

"Give me *some* credit," Braden said. "I can hold my liquor. Two beers and those kids were sure an old man like me was drunk—but it was one of them who threw up on me. Anyway, I knew that a sober me could never pull off asking Hallie to marry me. But I couldn't let her go through life thinking I was the one who got away. And also, I wanted to see you two together. One sight of the big drippy way you two looked at each other and I knew where your hearts were. So how was my acting?"

"Excellent," Jamie said. "I believed it all."

"I thought about being an actor, but then my dad died and I knew I had to get a real job. Support the family, that sort of thing. Though if my law firm ever finds out I alienated one of the heads of the Montgomery-Taggert clan, I'll be out on my ear. I'll be begging on the street corner."

"You don't have to worry about that," Jamie said. "I'll take care of it." He was looking at Braden. "This was a noble thing you did."

"Yeah, I know," he said. "What's going to be hard is when I tell Mom. She deeply and truly wants me to marry Hallie, but it wouldn't work. I actually am a workaholic and Hallie's so self-sacrificing she'd never demand anything of me and—" He shrugged. "I'd make her miserable."

He looked at Jamie. "I never meant to tell you or anyone the truth." Braden paused and when he spoke again, there was no laughter in his voice. "I only told you this so you'd trust what I'm about to tell you. Shelly texted me that she's arriving at around seven this evening. When she gets here, Hallie is going to freak out. Come apart. My guess is that she'll tell you that she never wants to see you again, that she wants you to get out of her life forever."

"Because of her stepsister? Why?"

Braden was quiet for a moment. "Hallie will think that if you see Shelly in person, you'll drop her in favor of her stepsister." When he saw that Jamie didn't understand, he continued.

"You know those Victoria's Secret shows on TV? If you put some wings on Shelly, she could walk down the runway beside those girls and fit right in."

"So?" Jamie said.

Turning, Braden smiled at him. "Good answer. The problem is that Hallie won't believe you because Shelly stole every boyfriend she ever had."

"Bastards!" Jamie grumbled.

"Yeah, well, at seventeen you don't have any brains. Shelly would show up wearing about two ounces of clothing and the boys would go crazy. And by comparison Hallie was downright plump—or at least that's what Ruby used to say. The contrast between the girls was dramatic. But last night Hallie sure looked good in that dress. What did you do to get her in such great shape?"

"I got her away from people who see her as second best," Jamie said.

"Ouch!" Braden said. "I just wish you weren't right. Men love Hallie, but they lust after Shelly."

"Not me," Jamie said. He was looking at Braden in speculation. There was something about the way he said Hallie's stepsister's name that set Jamie on edge. "Can I take it that you don't think of Shelly as your little sister?"

Braden let out his breath. "When she was growing up, I never paid much attention to the kid. But then one day I came home to visit and there was this girl—five eleven, maybe six feet—outside Hallie's house wearing a bikini. You ever look at a woman and get dizzy with lust?"

"I nearly passed out when I met Hallie."

"Good. I like that. She deserves it. Anyway, that's what I felt when I saw Shelly at sixteen." Braden took a moment before speaking, as though trying to decide whether he should reveal the truth or not. "I'll tell you something nobody else knows. All these women since then—the ones who keep dumping me—the truth is that I understand why they do. To me, they're just weak copies of Shelly, and they sense that."

"So why not go after her?"

Braden shrugged. "What would it have done to Hallie if I— her knight on a white horse—went after her stepsister like all the other guys did? And then there's my mom. She's had years of hearing all the mean, petty things done to Hallie by Shelly. I couldn't do it to either of them."

"A lot of men wouldn't have cared about any of that," Jamie said.

"And you were in a Humvee when you could have been safely in a hospital being a doctor. We all have things that make us earn the title of 'man.'"

"Yeah, we do," Jamie said. "I've never been able to get Hallie to talk to me about her stepmother and she's said little about Shelly—except that she felt like a donor who had to give body parts to her stepsister."

Braden laughed. "That's a good one. I've always loved Hallie's sense of humor. Did she tell you what happened to the garden?"

"No, but I'd like to hear the story." Jamie's voice was earnest.

"Okay, but first you have to understand that Ruby had an ambition that ate the earth—and it was *all* wrapped up in her pretty daughter. About a year after they moved in, Ruby decided she wanted a big in-ground swimming pool. But Hallie's grandparents had a glorious garden in the back. They fed their own household and shared with neighbors. When the grandparents said no to the pool, Ruby was very calm, and they thought the matter was settled. But they underestimated her."

"I'm afraid to ask what happened," Jamie said.

"The grandparents took Hallie away for a weekend and

when they returned, the garden was gone. Bulldozed flat. Even the cute little playhouse Hallie's grandfather had built for her had been destroyed."

"What did Hallie's father say when he saw it?"

Braden shook his head. "Talk about a coward! Mom called him The Runner because he fled from all confrontation. He stayed away for six weeks. Mom said that the Hartley household was a war zone. In the end, they all agreed that they could no longer live in one house. The grandparents decided to move to Florida. They just wanted the dad's permission for Hallie to go with them. But Ruby said no, so Hallie had to stay." Braden was quiet for a moment, then he looked at Jamie. "Can I give you some advice?"

Jamie hesitated, but considering what this man was willing to do for Hallie, yes, he'd accept advice. He nodded.

"Tell her you're a doctor."

"Hallie knows that."

"I don't think she does. When she called my mother and raved about you, she didn't mention it. If Hallie'd told her you were a doctor, Mom would have hit me over the head with it. She thinks doctors are above lawyers on the ladder of helping humanity."

"We are," Jamie said, "but you guys rescue us from the predators."

Smiling, they looked out at the garden.

After Braden left, Jamie stretched out on the old couch in Hallie's living room and tried to keep his mind on the latest issue of the *Journal of the American Medical Association* that his mother had brought for him. She was adamant that he keep up with his training as she hoped that he'd soon go back to his profession. She and his dad had offered to build him a clinic near their house in Colorado. "Or in Maine," they'd said. The idea was that he'd feel more secure if he treated only people who were related to him.

Until now—until he'd met Hallie—he'd turned down their offers without a second thought. But now he was thinking about it.

His mother called him as they were leaving Nantucket.

"Hallie is here and everyone is kissing her goodbye," Cale said from the airport. "Everyone likes her so very much."

"You can stop hinting," Jamie said. "I like her too."

"How much?" Cale asked quickly.

Jamie started to make a quick retort about that being his own business, but instead, he smiled. He knew everyone had seen how much better he was doing since he'd met Hallie and they wanted the best for him. "I like her the ultimate amount. Is that what you wanted to hear?"

"Yes," Cale whispered. Jamie knew his mother was fighting tears and he gave her time to calm herself. "So when are you going to let her know this?"

Jamie rolled his eyes. "Leave something to me, will you?"

"I know, sweetheart," Cale said, "but I'm a mother so I worry. I'm afraid Hallie might decide she's in love with that man Braden. She doesn't seem to see what he's really like! Your dad was furious for half of Jilly's wedding. I almost couldn't get him to calm down. Braden said—"

"Mom!" Jamie said loudly. "It's okay. Hallie isn't going to run off with Braden. When I get back I'll tell you about him. He's a really good guy and you're going to love his story."

"I doubt that," Cale said. "I think he— Oh, no. Your dad's about to throw me in the back of a truck."

It was a running joke in their family that when their dad wanted his wife to hurry up he said he was going to toss her into a truck, something he'd done long ago.

"I love you," Cale said. "And *talk* to Hallie!"

"I will," Jamie said, "and I love you both."

He clicked off the phone and tried to go back to his magazine, but he kept listening for Hallie's return. He was dreading telling her that Shelly was on her way to Nantucket. If there was anything Jamie knew about, it was irrational fear. In theory, he knew that a room with lots of doors in it wasn't something to fear, but that didn't stop him from standing against a wall and watching. Who knew what was going to run through a door at any second?

Logically, Hallie had no reason to fear her stepsister, but that wouldn't keep her from doing so. Someday maybe Hallie could feel secure enough to stand up to Shelly, but for now Jamie was going to do what Braden had done for so many years and protect Hallie. He was going to put himself between the two women and do whatever was necessary to make Hallie feel safe.

When Jamie heard a car door slam, he was on his feet in seconds and at the front door before it opened.

Hallie threw it open. She was drenched! "The sky opened up just as I got out of the car."

Jamie dropped his crutches onto the stairs and held out his arms to her.

"I'll get you wet."

He didn't lower his arms and she went to him, the two of them holding each other close. Her head was on his chest and she could hear his heart beating.

"I went to the airport with them to say goodbye. Uncle Kit left with your parents, and Leland caught a flight to Boston."

He kissed the top of her wet hair, then began leading her up the stairs as she kept talking.

"I hardly know Lee, but we had so many things in common. He's an only child like I am. I'm going to meet the family at Christmas, but Lee and I made plans to spend Thanksgiving together."

Jamie led her to the bathroom door, got a towel, and began drying her hair.

"Uncle Kit said he'll join us. I think the huge celebrations of your big family are too much for him. He said he's going to make the pies. And Lee is going to make the dressing."

Jamie unbuttoned her wet shirt and pulled it off her.

"That leaves me with the turkey and vegetables and bread to do." She looked at Jamie. "Unless you want to help."

"I get dibs on yams and green beans," he said as he unfastened her trousers and helped her step out of them.

"So I get the turkey." Hallie's teeth were beginning to chatter. "What's your favorite bread?"

"Brioche," he said as he led her to the bed and pulled back the covers.

"Mine too." She started to get into the warmth of the bed, but Jamie stopped her as he removed her two pieces of underwear.

Naked, she looked at him and he pulled her into his big, warm arms.

"Did you miss me?" he whispered.

"Yes. Every minute. I think I talked about you a bit too much."

Jamie stepped away from her long enough to remove his own clothing, then slid into bed. "What makes you think that?"

"Adam said he hadn't noticed that you'd grown seven feet tall and made Superman look like a wimp."

Smiling, Jamie opened his arms to her and as their bodies clung to each other, they began kissing.

It was Hallie who pulled away and pushed him onto his back. Her lips began to trace the scars on his body, kissing them, caressing them. Today his mother had told her how Jamie's former girlfriend Alicia had been sickened at the sight of Jamie's damaged body. She was repulsed by the scars and grafts, the indentations where parts of skin and muscle had been sliced away by flying pieces of metal.

But Hallie thought Jamie was beautiful. Her lips moved over him, across his chest, his arms, then lower and lower until she reached the center of him. Undamaged and perfect, she thought, but then she was beginning to see all of him that way.

When she took him in her mouth, he gasped, his head back, his eyes closed.

Minutes later she moved back up to his neck, to his mouth.

He moved her onto her back and began to make love to her, taking his time with her body as he slowly took her to new peaks of pleasure. When he entered her, she was more than ready for his long, slow, deep thrusts.

When he collapsed against her, Hallie held him, his head against her breasts, and stroked his hair as she thought about the day. Her morning had been great and she'd loved laughing with Jamie's cousins. At the airport she'd been teary as she said goodbye to people who'd become her friends. Jamie's mother had hugged her hard and his father's hug had lifted her off the ground. "Thank you," he said, then he'd abruptly set her down and run up the stairs to the plane.

Uncle Kit had kissed her hand. "We shall meet again soon," he said.

It had been hardest saying goodbye to Leland. "Thanks-giving!" he'd called to her as he got on the plane.

She stood there with Jamie's cousins and watched the jet take off, then they turned to Hallie. She knew what they were asking. What did she want to do now? "Home," she said simply. She wanted to see Jamie. They drove her back to Kingsley Lane and she was so anxious to see Jamie that she opened the car door while the vehicle was still rolling. Then, just as she got to the door, a quick summer storm nearly drowned her.

"Warm now?" Jamie asked, their bodies wrapped around each other.

"Yes," she said.

He lifted onto one arm to look at her. "Something's bothering you."

"Nothing is."

"You can tell me," he said.

She took a breath. "Please don't be jealous, but I just thought of Braden."

He kissed her sweetly. "I'm not jealous of him anymore. Tell me what you're thinking."

"Of this. Of you and me. I'm going to have to break Braden's heart. It's just that he isn't who I thought he was."

Jamie turned onto his back and put her head on his shoulder. "Tell me," he said.

"I guess I've always seen Braden through a child's eyes," Hallie said. "But then he's always been so very good to me. Even when he was a teenager and a big shot at our school, he always had time for the little kid that I was. Sometimes the other football boys would laugh at him for giving me a ride home or asking me about my homework or fixing a toy for me. But Braden was *always* glad to see me."

"And now?"

"Now I'm going to have to tell him that yet another female is turning down his marriage proposal. Oh, Jamie! He was so awful at the wedding! It was embarrassing to see him with your dad and your uncle Mike. I was so annoyed by him that when Leland showed up, I had him sit between Braden and me. I tried to be nice, but at the reception, all Braden could talk about was how glad he was that I was bringing the connection of your family to him. He said it was like my dowry."

"He was obnoxious, wasn't he?"

"Yes!" Hallie said. "That's the perfect word. Why didn't I see this when I was growing up?" She put her hand over her eyes. "The *worst* thing is going to be trying to explain to his mother. She and I . . . This sounds ridiculous, but we used to talk about how I'd grow up and marry Braden and she'd be my mother for real."

Hallie looked up at Jamie. "What am I going to tell her?"

"Tell her that she has raised a son who is a man of honor. That he is willing to sacrifice what he wants in life so he doesn't hurt other people. Tell her that she should be very, very proud of him."

"Wow!" Hallie said. "What in the world did you two talk about this morning?"

"Just guy stuff." He wasn't going to answer that question and betray Braden's trust. He started kissing her neck as his hand moved downward.

But Hallie moved away from him. "We have to get up because I need to work on your knee." She got out of bed, picked up his T-shirt off the floor, put it on, and went into the bathroom.

"You seem to like wearing my clothes," he said as he piled up pillows behind his head.

"And you seem to like going without them."

"Beauty such as this shouldn't be covered."

She looked at him in the mirror. When she'd first met him he'd been so embarrassed by his scars that he didn't want anyone to see them. But now he often pulled off his shirt—and every time he did, Hallie felt like melting. She no longer saw the scars, just the beauty of the man underneath them. "I agree completely," she said, smiling at him.

"I think my leg is fine for today. You should come back to bed."

"Absolutely not. The only thing your brother likes about me is that I'm good at my job. I don't want to lose that accolade."

"Why did you stand there and listen?" Jamie sounded more annoyed than he meant to.

"Ask Juliana and Hyacinth. I think they wanted me to hear."

Hallie went back into the bedroom. Jamie was stretched out on the bed wearing nothing but the big brace on his leg, a sheet corner across his middle. He was certainly glorious to behold! Honey-colored skin over muscles from the neck down. Abs that rippled. Thighs like tree trunks. He was like a god of old come to life.

"Hallie," Jamie whispered.

Somehow, she managed to turn away and step into her closet.

"Damn Todd!" she heard Jamie mutter as she pulled out a clean T-shirt.

"Hallie?" Jamie said and there was a serious tone to his voice. "This morning Braden said something strange to me. He said he didn't think you know that I'm a doctor. I told him that wasn't true because Jared gave you my medical file—didn't he?"

That astonishing bit of information made Hallie feel like someone had knocked the wind out of her. She leaned back against the closet shelves to give herself a moment to recover. When she'd been given his medical report she'd been so upset over Shelly trying to steal her house that she couldn't keep her mind on what she was seeing. But whatever the cause, no, she didn't know that about him. Part of her felt angry that this had been hidden from her. Or maybe she was angry at herself for not figuring out something so very fundamental about this man.

But she wasn't going to go the route of anger. She looked around the doorway at him. She well knew that humor worked best with him. "You mean you can get a *job*? Earn a living? That you aren't going to live off a trust fund set up by some relative who probably had *two* jets?"

Jamie groaned. "You sure know how to wound a guy. I'm so hurt I may have to go back to the hospital."

"You can't perform surgery on yourself?"

"Actually, I did sew up this one. It wasn't very deep, so I

took care of it." He ran his hand across a scar that ran down the side of his left arm. "It happened a few weeks before the explosion. I was afraid that if anyone saw it, I'd be sent home."

Hallie moved back into the closet so he wouldn't see her face. Suddenly, her joke didn't seem very funny. She could even envision Jamie sewing his own wound. She stepped back into the bedroom. "So. You have any other big secrets?"

Jamie knew that this was the moment when he should tell her that Shelly would be there in about three hours, but he couldn't do it. As much as he didn't like to admit it, Braden seemed to know Hallie well and he didn't want her to "freak out" as he'd said she would. Smiling, he put his hands behind his head. "You don't seem to have noticed that Todd is my identical twin."

Hallie scoffed. "Todd is four inches shorter than you are and has a roll around his middle. You should get him to go to a gym sometimes." She sat down on the bed beside him, and as she ran her hand over his chest, her face was serious. "Do you think you can work in a hospital?"

He knew she was referring to his PTSD. It was better but certainly not cured. "No," he said honestly. "Not yet, but I might be able to manage part-time in a small clinic. It would have to be in a place with few doors and few patients and—"

Hallie kissed him. "One day at a time. Eventually, you'll be able to do it all."

"Will you be there with me?"

She started to say yes, that she'd follow him wherever he went, that she couldn't imagine a life without him, but she didn't say that. She wasn't going to put everything inside her on the surface. Not yet anyway. She got up and with laughter in her voice, said, "If that's an invitation, where's the champagne?"

"It's coming. You like oval diamonds, right?" he said.

Hallie stared at him. She'd thought he meant dating past when his leg was healed, that they'd get to know each other in a more ordinary way, that sort of thing. But he seemed to mean something more permanent. "Yes, I do," she said softly, then turned away. "I, uh . . ." She couldn't think what to say. "I'll meet you in the gym," she said at last and hurried down the stairs.

Chapter Twenty-two

An hour later, Jamie was just stepping out of the outdoor shower beside the gym when he saw her. There was no mistaking who she was. Shelly was just as Braden had described: very tall, thin, with lots of blonde hair that stood out around a very pretty face.

What wasn't pretty was the way she was looking at him. He had on only a towel and the brace, an outfit he'd been wearing often lately. But the way this woman was looking at him made him feel, well, naked. Exposed.

He'd seen men look at women in that way, their eyes moving up and down, measuring their physical attributes like they were racehorses.

But Jamie couldn't remember a woman scrutinizing him in that way. His first instinct was to cover himself, but he didn't. He stood up straighter, his shoulders back, feet together.

Her eyes came back up to his and what he first saw there was anger, but then she changed and gave a little smirk, as though he wasn't worthy of her attention.

In an instant, she turned on her high heels and went toward the house, where Hallie was.

Jamie's only thought was that he *had* to get to Hallie before this woman did. He had to protect the woman he loved.

But when he took a step forward, he tripped on a stepping stone and went down hard on his uninjured knee. When he tried to get up, his brace caught on the stone and entangled him. His towel was on the ground a foot away and when he reached for it, a gust of wind caught it and sent it sailing.

Cursing, he struggled to get upright without a crutch, then looked down at himself. He couldn't burst into the house with no clothes on. He managed to hobble back to the gym and grab his sweatpants. When they caught on the back of his brace and he couldn't pull them up, his cursing grew angrier and louder.

It seemed to take forever to get his pants on and pull a T-shirt over his head. He grabbed his crutches and started for the house. The back door was locked. He banged on it and yelled to Hallie but no one came to open the door. Maybe they went upstairs, he thought and went around to the front door. It was also locked.

He had to go nearly full circle before he saw that the tea room doors were unlocked and he went inside. When he heard voices, he quickly went through the pantry to the kitchen door and looked inside.

Shelly was sitting at the kitchen table and Hallie was pulling things out of the refrigerator and putting them before her stepsister.

The scene made Jamie frown, but he understood about families and habits. When he and his brother were together, they seemed to know what each other was going to do before it was done. But Jamie hated seeing Hallie wait on Shelly.

He stepped forward, meaning to go into the kitchen to stop it, but the door closed in his face. When he tried the knob, it was locked. As he'd done outside, he knocked on the door and called for Hallie to open it from her side, but nothing happened.

It took Jamie just seconds to get across the room to the other door into the house, but it too was locked.

He gritted his teeth in frustration. He had no doubt that the two spirits of the house were doing this. "Is this what you did the day Hallie overheard Todd and me in the kitchen?" Jamie asked aloud, but there was no answer.

He hopped across the room on his crutches, back through the pantry, and as he knew it would be, the door was open a few inches. It looked like he was supposed to watch and listen, the darkness of the pantry hiding him from their sight.

Jamie looked at Shelly sitting at the table. He'd heard so much about her beauty that he was curious. He'd seen the professional photos she'd sent him and he'd thought she looked good but in a cool, remote way that didn't appeal to him.

Now as he looked at her, he thought of the old saying that beauty was in the eye of the beholder. Maybe Hallie and Braden saw Shelly as breathtakingly beautiful, but to Jamie she was far from it. She was tall and thin, shapeless really. His professional eye saw that she'd spent too much time in the sun. She wasn't going to age well.

Jamie thought Hallie was much prettier. He loved her curves, the shape of her face, the way she smiled at everyone. Hallie's hair was thick and soft and he knew it always smelled good, even when she was sweaty in the gym.

As he looked at the two women, he couldn't see why anyone would think Shelly was the pretty one. To him, Hallie beat her stepsister in all aspects of mind, talent, beauty, and personality.

Inside the kitchen, Hallie was doing her best to listen to Shelly. She'd been preparing a late lunch for herself and Jamie when Shelly had shown up. Like some black magic, she just seemed to appear in the Nantucket kitchen.

And once Hallie saw her, it was as though all the sunshine disappeared. It was like the doors and windows suddenly locked and the pretty little house became a prison. She hadn't seen or heard from Shelly since the day she'd come home and Jared had been sitting in her living room asking Shelly to sign some papers.

Hallie kept putting things on the table. Better that than sitting down and trying to talk with Shelly. She could argue for hours at a time, but all Hallie wanted was to get rid of her fast. Please, please, she thought, let Jamie stay outside. Don't let him come in here and see Shelly. Hallie didn't think she could bear seeing the two of them laughing and talking, flirting. Doing the things all men did with Shelly.

"I came here to work things out with you," Shelly was saying. "But then I'm always apologizing to you."

"You have *never* apologized to me," Hallie said and was instantly annoyed with herself for taking the bait Shelly was dangling.

"I'm sure that's the way you see it. For once, could we just talk and not fight?" she said, looking around. "This is a nice house, but it will take a lot of work to get the garden up to what your grandparents had. I guess that's what you plan to do."

"Shelly, what do you want?"

She gave a great, dramatic sigh. "I can see that nothing has changed; you're still hostile. All right, I will tell you. I honestly didn't think you'd mind if I took on the responsibility for this old house. You're always saying that I never help you with anything, but when I did offer to help, you acted like I'm a criminal. I thought you liked where you lived. You never hid the fact that you've always been madly in love with Braden. It's all I heard while I was growing up. It was embarrassing watching you make a fool of yourself over him."

Hallie knew that what Shelly was saying about Braden was true. It was quite possible—probable even—that if she'd received the package from Jared first, she would have sold the Nantucket house unseen.

Shelly opened a container of olives and nibbled one. "I really thought you and Braden would end up together. That's what his mom and you plotted, didn't you?"

Hallie sat down at the table and looked at her stepsister.

Shelly continued. "Never in my life would I have believed that you'd ever leave Braden. I thought you'd die in that house, just waiting for him to return and notice you."

"So you're saying that you wouldn't have tried to steal this house if it hadn't been for my caring about Braden?"

"Caring!" Shelly said. "It was more like an obsession. Face it, Hallie, you're not exactly the adventurous type. You lived in one house all your life. Even after all that schooling you had, you got a cheap job nearby just so you wouldn't have to leave him. You just sat there and waited for Braden to return and sweep you away to some future you dreamed about."

Hallie had her head down. Shelly's words were so true that she was beginning to feel awful. But then this was the way it had been since her father came home and announced that he'd married a woman who had a daughter. Her dad said Shelly was going to become Hallie's best friend.

But that had never happened. Instead, she'd found herself "talked to" by Ruby, lectured about how Hallie should give Shelly more and more and more. When Shelly was older, she'd done her own talking, turning things around so that Hallie was always in the wrong.

Yes, Hallie had been obsessed with Braden, but now she realized that she'd needed that dream of a happy future in order to survive.

Sometimes there are moments in people's lives when they suddenly see things differently. Call it an aha moment, an epiphany, whatever. It's a time when a person breaks. As Hallie looked at her stepsister, she decided that she'd had enough. She was no longer going to be afraid of her stepsister. If Shelly turned on whatever she did to attract men and if Jamie followed her like all the other males did, so be it. Hallie had had *enough*!

"You're right," she said to Shelly and there was a tone in her voice that she knew she'd never before used with her stepsister. It was the one that made reluctant patients get on the table. There was kindness, but it was backed by an unbreakable firmness.

"You're right that I was afraid of . . . adventure, as you call it. After you and Ruby took over my family, I was scared of leaving the only security I'd ever known. In your drive to win no matter what, you and your mother made what had once been a peaceful home into a battlefield. You drove my grandparents away and made my father hate to return."

Shelly was looking at her in surprise. Hallie didn't usually fight back. Ruby had taken all that out of her. But Shelly quickly recovered. "It's this guy who's turning you against your own family, isn't it? I guess he's the one you lost all the weight for." Her words were sly, as though she knew something Hallie didn't. "I saw him outside. He's so torn up most women wouldn't want him. But he's rich so I don't blame you for going after him."

Hallie didn't lose her temper at the accusation, and most important, she didn't go into defense mode. "If that's what you want to believe, go ahead."

A wave of anger went across Shelly's perfectly made-up face. Hallie knew that in the past that look meant her stepsister would take some revenge. A toy, a computer, a new piece of clothing, something would be ruined—and of course Shelly would deny having done it.

"Look, Hallie," Shelly said in a voice that others would hear as caring, "I'm younger than you are, but I've seen more of the world. Do you think this guy with his messed-up body will want you after his leg heals? You think his rich family won't snub you? One thing I've learned is that wealthy people only marry other rich people. Believe me, I've *tried* to change that, but it doesn't happen."

"And if someone who looks like you can't get a rich man, there's no hope for me, right?"

Shelly glared at her. "You always twist whatever I say, don't you? You're always so clever! But I know more about men than you do and I'm just warning you, that's all."

Hallie was calm. "Shelly, I don't know what's going to happen in my life, but I'm not worried about it. You see, I'm finally beginning to realize that I'm worth something. I'm good at my job and I've met people who genuinely like me, and that's made me feel the best about myself that I have since I was a kid." When Shelly started to speak, Hallie put up her hand. "And as for Jamie, I'm in love with him. Deeply and totally in love with him."

"You think that matters to a man as rich as he is?" Shelly was very angry. "I don't care how much weight you lose, he'll still leave you. When his leg heals he'll walk away and you'll never see him again."

Hallie stood up and looked down at her stepsister. "That's his choice and if he does, I'll survive it. It'll take me a long time to recover, but I will. And the next time I won't be afraid that you're going to show up and take a man away from me. Shelly, you may be beautiful on the outside, but the inside of you is quite ugly." She took a breath. "Braden is on the island and I'm going to ask one last favor of him. I want him to come get you and take you someplace far away from me. I've had all I'm going to take of your belittling me. And I am never again going to be afraid of what you can do or say to me."

Turning, Hallie walked out the back door into the garden.

She was shaking all over, but she felt very good. Right now, all she wanted was to see Jamie.

She was almost to the gym when he came up behind her and picked her up. She clung to him.

"I heard it all," he said, holding her tightly. "The ladies locked me in the tea room, but I'm glad because I saw you, heard you. You were wonderful. Stupendous. I am so proud of you." He was kissing her neck. "Deeply and totally in love with me, are you?"

Hallie laughed. "You weren't supposed to hear that."

He pulled her away to look in her eyes. "I understand things now, and I'm glad you didn't believe all that about me. Let's go out to dinner and drink champagne and celebrate."

"What about your meds?"

"I haven't taken a pill in two days."

"Really?"

"Yeah, but don't tell my doctor that. I'm sure I'll be back on them again."

"And who is your doctor—and so help me, if you tell me it's Raine, I'll start screaming."

"It's not. It's his—"

"I've had all the surprises I can take in one day," Hallie said as she kissed him.

"Then let's go eat, drink, and be merry." He took her hand in his.

"Wait!" Hallie said. "I have to call Braden and tell him to come get Shelly." Suddenly, she halted. "I don't have to take care of Shelly anymore, do I?" She looked at him in wonder. "Since I was eleven years old, I've had to look after her. In my household, she came first in everything. Even when she was in California trying to become a movie star, I had to send her money. Once I had to—" She broke off. "But all that's over. I don't know how to describe it. Nothing has changed but everything has. I'm done."

"Good," Jamie said, "but rather than leave her alone in the house, I already called Braden. He'll know how to take care of everything."

"You think so?" Hallie was surprised. "I want to hear what you two talked about this morning. What made you go from being jealous every time his name was mentioned to singing his praises?"

"We just talked is all. Where is that ring you had?"

"Last time I saw it, it was on the coffee table in the tea room. You want me to get it?"

"No!" Jamie said. "I just got out of being locked in that room and I saw Shelly go in there. Hallie?" His face turned serious. "I don't mean to be a scaredy-cat, but let's turn this house over to the Kingsley branch of the family. I think they're more used to ghosts than my side is."

"Yes, let's," she said. "Now, where are you taking me for dinner?"

"A picnic in bed?" he suggested.

Laughing, Hallie put her arms around his neck and looked at him. "Is any of this for real? You, your family, all this talk of us and we and the future? Will it last?"

"Yes," he said. "It's very real. I'm not going to run off as soon as my leg heals, and you've seen that my family adores you. Your stepsister certainly has a backward view of the world. She doesn't seem to consider that her mercenary attitude is what gets her tossed aside. Let's go to dinner and talk about our future. Like that idea?"

"Yes," she said, "I do."

"Interesting choice of words," he said and they laughed.

Chapter Twenty-three

By the time Braden got to Hallie's house he was in a seriously bad mood. Jamie had called him and told of the encounter Hallie had with her stepsister.

"I've never heard anything like it," Jamie said, his voice loud and angry. "She tried to make it sound like she was stealing in order to *help* Hallie."

"Yeah, that sounds like her. Ruby used to do that. She told Hallie's dad she had the garden bulldozed because the grandparents were getting older, the garden was too much for them, and they needed to take up swimming for their health. Shelly's just doing what her mother taught her."

"Yeah, well, she's not going to do it to Hallie ever again. Next time—if there is one—I'll be there."

"So why did you stand back and just listen this time?"

"It would take too long to explain," Jamie said. "I have to

go find Hallie. But come get that girl or I'll throw her in the street."

"What am I supposed to do with her?" Braden asked, annoyed.

"Get her to sign papers saying she'll stay away from Hallie. And Braden?"

"Yeah?"

"Thanks again for all you did for Hallie when she was growing up."

"You're welcome," Braden said. "But I warn you that if you don't take her to visit my mother often, she'll put a curse on you."

"Gladly," Jamie said and clicked off.

For a while Braden sat in the chair by the pool and thought about not going. He was staying in a house that belonged to a man named Roger Plymouth and he liked it very much. He'd never tell Hallie, but he hated that old house she'd inherited. He liked new and modern.

For a moment he allowed himself to imagine not going to pick up Shelly. Just leave her there, let her find her own way off the island. She got here by herself, so she could get herself back to the mainland.

But Braden knew he wouldn't do that. He'd take care of Shelly for Hallie and for his mom.

Slowly, he got up and went into the house to change into jeans and a shirt. The bad thing about having put on his act to turn Hallie off was that he'd alienated the entire Montgomery-Taggert family. There were half a dozen of them staying in the house for a few days after the wedding, but they wanted nothing to do with Braden. He'd been left alone while they went to beaches and shops and all the other delights of the glorious island of Nantucket.

To Braden's mind, *all* of this was Shelly's fault. If Ruby

hadn't been obsessed with her daughter, Hallie wouldn't have needed protection, which meant that now . . .

As Braden got into his rented car, he made himself stop thinking in that direction. The truth was that he was angry at Shelly for what had happened at his office.

He'd had a friendship with Hallie all her life, but he'd paid little attention to the stepsister. As a child, she'd looked at him with big blue eyes, a teddy bear clutched to her, and rarely said a word. But then, Ruby said enough for both of them. She constantly yelled at little Shelly to come inside or she might hurt herself.

One time Braden asked Hallie if the kid was accident prone.

"Nah," Hallie said. "Scabs mess up the photos."

At the time, Braden figured the kid just liked having her picture taken. It wasn't until later that he realized Hallie meant the photos taken at all the modeling agencies, TV auditions, whatever Ruby came up with. She and Shelly would drop Hallie off at school, then get on the commuter flight to New York. Hallie would return to an empty house and a bowl of canned soup for dinner.

He hadn't paid attention to Shelly until he saw her in a bikini—and after that he stayed away from her totally. Inviting her to work had been an impulse.

That day, he'd enjoyed her company. When they'd gone to a mall to buy her clothes, she'd asked him a lot of questions about his work, and he was surprised to find out that she understood everything he told her.

Braden's original goal in taking Shelly to work was to throw his ex, Zara, into a jealous fit. But by the time he and Shelly got to his office he'd forgotten about that.

At the office, she'd been charming to everyone. She was so tall and beautiful that she was a bit intimidating, but she soon set people at ease. As for Zara, she and Shelly had hit it off like best friends, talking about clothes and shoes and the earrings Zara was wearing.

When one of the partners demanded that Braden go over a brief right then, he'd been annoyed. But Shelly had assured him that she'd be fine on her own.

He'd just finished when the partner who'd dumped the work on him flung his door open and bawled him out about Shelly. Seems she'd slipped into his office and made lewd suggestions to him, had even unbuttoned her blouse in a suggestive way.

Braden had been livid! He'd apologized profusely, then gone to find Shelly. When he saw that the silk blouse he'd bought her was missing a button, his anger made him unable to speak.

All the way back to Hallie's house, he didn't say a word to her, and barely slowed the car to let her out.

Now, he parked in front of Hallie's Nantucket house, then got out and slammed the door loudly.

What was he going to do with Shelly once he got her out of here? Take her back to Plymouth's house for the night? She'd probably come on to one of the Montgomery men.

When Braden found the front door locked, he got even angrier. He knocked but there was no answer. He went around the house, tapping on windows, but all were locked and silent. Finally, he reached the far side and saw double doors. One of them was standing open.

Just as he touched it, there was a crack of lightning followed by a boom of thunder and rain started coming down hard. He barely made it inside before he got soaked.

It was dark in the room and when he flipped the switch, nothing happened. "Great!" he muttered. Lightning showed another door and the windows, but when he checked, they were all locked. He was trapped inside the room.

"This is ridiculous!" he said aloud and picked up a heavy metal vase. He was going to throw it through the window and get out that way.

"It won't work," said a voice behind him and Braden gasped.

Still holding the vase, he turned to see Shelly sitting on a small couch in a corner of the room. She had on jeans and heels and the Chanel jacket he'd bought for her. She looked fabulous.

But her good looks only made him angrier. He threw the vase at the window hard. It hit the glass and bounced off onto the window seat, then rolled onto the floor.

Behind him, Shelly lit a candle. "I told you it wouldn't work. I've thrown six things at that window, but the glass won't break."

"That doesn't make sense."

"I read that half the houses on Nantucket are haunted so it's my guess that there are ghosts here and they're protecting Saint Hallie. But then everyone does, don't they?"

"Why not?" Braden said. "She needs it."

"Of course. Dear, persecuted Hallie. She's only loved by everyone who meets her. I guess you know she's thrown you over for some rich ex-soldier."

Braden was rattling knobs and he put his shoulder to a door, but nothing moved. Outside, the rain was pelting down hard. He went across the room and plopped down in a chair across from Shelly. "What did you do to Hallie *this* time?"

"Tried to get out of being sued."

"Funny thing about the law. You steal something and you get punished."

"And Hallie's loving entourage will see to that, won't they? Tell me, will I go to jail?" When she looked at him, he saw that she'd been crying.

"A little late for remorse, isn't it?" He got up and tried the door again, but it didn't budge.

Shelly held up the ring Braden had bought in the candlelight. "This from you? For Hallie? She turn you down?"

Braden didn't like the way she put that, but he wasn't going to explain his motives. "What makes you think that?"

"Just a guess. Did she know how cheap it is?"

Braden sat down again and glared at her. He wanted to yell at her. How could she have done that at his office? Did she think the man was going to leave his wife for her? Or that he was rich enough to keep a mistress?

Shelly looked up from the ring. "Why?" she whispered. "What happened that made you so angry at me at the office?"

He couldn't keep from sneering. "Did you think I wouldn't find out? Hedricks told me how you came on to him."

For a moment, Shelly closed her eyes, then she got up and got her bag off the big dresser. She opened it, pulled out a business card, and handed it to Braden.

"So? You got Hedricks's card."

She was still standing in front of him and she turned the card over. Handwritten on the back was an address and a phone number.

It took him a moment to realize what they were. The address was of the corporate apartment, the one used by out-of-town clients. He didn't recognize the number.

"If you call it, you'll find that it's your boss's private cell number."

"How did you get this?"

Shelly sat back down on the couch, looked at the candle, and didn't answer him.

But Braden had a lawyer's brain and he figured it out. He'd seen the way Hedricks looked at Shelly when she was introduced. At the time, he'd felt nothing but pride. Later, the man had sent Braden away to do work and that's when he must have done whatever caused Shelly to lose a button.

"How did you get away?" Braden asked softly.

"I told him no in a way that let him know I meant it," she said. "I've had a lot of experience doing that."

All the anger left Braden and he fell back against the chair. "I'm really sorry."

"Good," Shelly said. "Maybe you'll remember that when you're trying to get me sent to prison."

Braden winced because all day he'd worked to do just that. He'd spent a lot of time thinking about how he could persuade Hallie to press charges against her stepsister. "Why?" he asked.

"Why did your boss see me as an easy mark? I don't know."

The rain was slashing outside and the darkness of the room with the single candle made them seem isolated, just the two of them.

"That's not what I mean," he said. "For all those years, I saw and heard what went on in the Hartley house, but it was all from one side. I've seen you do mean things to Hallie. You buried her toys. I saw you pour grape juice on her new dress. You bent the spokes on her bicycle. Why?"

When Shelly looked up, there was something deep in her eyes, a kind of emptiness. "No one knows this, but I don't know how to ride a bicycle. I used to watch you and Hallie riding together and my jealousy nearly devoured me."

"What did *you* have to be jealous of Hallie about?" He was incredulous.

Shelly snorted in derision. "You want to hear the truth? The *real* truth?"

"Yes, I do."

She took a moment before speaking. "No one seemed to understand that my mother was obsessed with using my looks to make money. How I *looked* was everything to her. While Hallie was *liked*. Loved even." Shelly got up from the couch and began to pace.

"I was jealous of Hallie from the second I went to live in her house. She had grandparents who adored her. They cared about her so much they grew food in the backyard. But my mother was dragging me around to auditions for everything she could find and I was lucky if I got a candy bar for dinner."

She stopped to glare at Braden, who was sitting there listening intently.

"Mom didn't bulldoze their garden to put in a swimming pool. She did it because she knew it would make the grandparents so angry that they'd leave. They were beginning to say things like 'Oh, Ruby, let the child stay home. I made a nice butternut squash soup.' I *wanted* to stay home. I was hoping that maybe they'd start liking me as well as Hallie.

"Mom saw it all, so the garden had to go. And of course when the grandparents left, they wanted to take their beloved Hallie with them, but Mom said no. Hallie was free babysitting."

Shelly took a breath. "Yeah, I did rotten things to Hallie. I remember one day Mom was yelling at me because I couldn't memorize lines from a Shakespeare play. Hallie was on her computer with her grandparents in Florida. They kept saying how they loved her and missed her and couldn't wait to see her again. That night I went into Hallie's room and poured Diet Coke on her keyboard."

Braden was watching her with interest.

Shelly took a breath, her hands in fists at her side. "Then Mom and Dad died when I was still a minor. After that, I was at Perfect Hallie's mercy. She quit college and took on lots of jobs so I wouldn't be put in a foster home. All I heard was what a martyr Hallie was. While *I* was reviled. *I* was the one who'd caused poor, dear, sweet, lovable Hallie to have to give up her career.

"So, yeah, I acted out. Between no longer being under my mother's thumb and having to live with Saint Hallie, I went wild. I admit it.

"The day after I graduated from high school, I told Hallie what I thought of her. I left with some no-good dirtbag just to make her angry. I went to L.A. and tried to get jobs in movies, but I wasn't any good."

"So you returned home," Braden said.

"Yeah, I did, and people rushed to tell me every wonderful thing Hallie had done, then they asked me what *I* had achieved. And the answer to that was a big fat nothing."

She paused for a moment. "And then one night I was watching TV and Hallie was, of course, at work, and an express envelope was delivered. I put it on a chair and it fell down the side and I forgot about it. A couple of days later, when I saw the corner of it sticking up, I panicked. I thought Hallie would throw me out on the street. I only opened it to see how much trouble I'd be in for not giving it to her right away."

Shelly took a few breaths to calm herself down. "When I read that she'd inherited a house from a guy she'd never even met, I went crazy with anger. It was all so deeply *unfair*. Why did she get everything *good* in life?!

"I didn't think about what I did. I wrote Jared that I was Hallie and I had lots of degrees and I would gladly accept the house. It threw me when he told me some rich guy wanted me to do physical therapy on his son, but what was I supposed to do? I couldn't back down, so I agreed to take him on as a client. Hallie's such a do-gooder, I figured that once I was there I could get her to write me out a plan for how to work on the guy.

"Most of all, I saw the whole thing as my once-in-a-lifetime chance to take another path. Just for a while I'd pretend to be Hallie, a person who never screwed up, who never got weak-kneed at the sight of a guy in black leather sitting on a big Harley. I'd have a highly respected career—and I'd be *liked*. Loved. *Just like Hallie is.*

"But it all backfired and I may be sent to prison. Yet again, Hallie is the good one and I'm bad. But then she probably won't prosecute me even after I tried to steal an entire house from her! What does it take to knock her off that holy cloud she lives on?!"

Braden was staring at her. He'd never heard this many words

from Shelly—and her anger had taken away his. "I think we should ignore the rain and get out of here."

"All right," she said.

When Braden tried the doorknob, it turned easily and outside the rain had stopped. He led the way to his car across grass that was quite dry and opened the door for Shelly. When he got in, he paused for a moment to look at her. Even though he'd known her since she was a kid, he was feeling that he didn't know her at all. "Mind if we get carryout and go back to the house where I've been staying? I think we should talk more. All right?"

"I'd like that," Shelly said and smiled at him.

Chapter Twenty-four

Hallie kept looking at Jamie as she worked on his knee. He was lying on the massage table and staring up at the arbor. Neither of them was speaking.

But then last night they'd done a lot of talking. They'd ended up buying food at Bartlett's, then driving back to the chapel. It was a quiet place and that's what they needed.

The building was beautiful in the fading light. They walked past it to sit on the sand by the water.

Hallie was still feeling the effects of her confrontation with Shelly and she didn't know if she was happy or sad about it. What happened now?

Jamie sat down with his braced leg stretched out and he took care of the food while Hallie began to talk. He wanted to hear her side of her life. He didn't tell her what he and Braden had spoken about.

Hallie's side of the story was softer than Braden's version. Between the two, Jamie was able to see what had been a very lonely childhood.

But what he liked was that Hallie carried no bitterness or hatred about it all. She just wanted it all to *stop*. She especially wanted to quit worrying that Shelly was going to steal her boyfriend.

"You mean me?" Jamie asked. "I'm the bargaining chip?"

"You are," she said. "If you and I are . . . you know."

That led into a discussion of their future, and they agreed that they'd like to try being together.

"I'd just like to stay here for now," Jamie said, "here on this magical island."

"Me too," Hallie said.

They made love on the beach. Slow, sweet love. Gentle, quiet, enduring love.

Afterward, they lay in each other's arms and looked at the stars, saying nothing, but both of them thinking about the future and where they would go from there.

It was late when they left and drove home. They slept together, cuddled, wrapped up in each other. And when Jamie's nightmares began, Hallie was there to soothe him.

In the morning they went about their usual routine, but they kept stealing looks at each other. Was this the person they would spend their lives with?

Hallie received a text message from Braden.

SHELLY IS WITH ME AND I'M TAKING HER
HOME TOMORROW.

After she read it to Jamie, he made a call to Raine. The last of the Montgomery-Taggert family had left the island and were on their way home.

Jamie clicked off the phone. "I think you should be told something, but I'm not sure how you're going to take it." He told Hallie that Shelly and Braden had spent the night together. Night as in one bed.

"Oh," Hallie said and sat down on a chair at the kitchen table.

"Are you okay with this?"

"Sure," she said. "It's just a bit of a shock." She looked at him. "But, no, it's not. Not really. Braden never treated Shelly as a little girl, at least not after she reached puberty. What's that look for?"

"Raine said Braden asked him an odd question. He wanted to know if Raine knew where to buy a set of motorcycle leathers."

Hallie and Jamie looked at each other and laughed at the vision of a lawyer in black leather with silver studs.

Jamie told Hallie of his talk with Braden and how he'd looked after her all her life. Jamie recounted Braden's attraction to Shelly but that he'd held off for the sake of Hallie and his mother.

"He did all that for *me*?" Hallie asked in wonder.

Jamie could see what a shock it all was to her and that she needed a way to relieve the stress. "Let's hit the gym."

Hallie groaned. "How did I get stuck with a doctor-jock?"

"I'm not sure, but I think a couple of ghosts did it all. You and me, and maybe Braden and Shelly. Raine said that Braden kept talking about a storm last night that locked him and Shelly together in the tea room."

They looked at each other and laughed.

And now Jamie was on the table and Hallie was finishing with his knee. It was nearly four P.M.

After Jamie got dressed, they walked back to the house together. There, sitting on the kitchen table, was one of the lavish teas, with food piled high and a steaming pot of tea.

"Edith, I love you," Jamie said as he washed his hands, Hallie beside him.

"I enjoyed your relatives' visit, but I'm glad to get back to normal," Hallie said. "We need to thank Edith for all this and do something nice for her."

"Shall we give her a trip away from her angry daughter-in-law?" Jamie suggested.

"I wonder how Betty and Howard did with all your relatives staying there? Especially the children."

"I'm sure the Montgomery kids were perfectly polite, but Mom said Cory discovered the way into the attic and found a box full of magazines with naked men on the covers."

"Ooooo," Hallie said. "Will she share?"

"I think that—" He broke off at a knock on the back door. "Speak of the devil, it's Betty."

He went to the door, Hallie just behind him.

"Hello," Jamie said as he opened the door. "It's good to—"

"Have you seen my mother-in-law?" Betty demanded. "Has she been over here to see those damned ghosts of yours?"

"We haven't seen her," Hallie said, "but she brought us another fabulous tea from your beautiful inn."

"We should pay you for them," Jamie said. "Tell me what you charge and Hallie and I will repay you. Plus a delivery fee."

Betty frowned. "What are you two talking about?"

"The teas Edith brings over," Hallie said. "But maybe you don't know about them. Sorry, but as Jamie said, we'll pay for them."

"Tea?" Betty said. "Delivered to you by my mother-in-law? Brings them over often, does she?"

"Yes, fairly regularly," Jamie said, leaning on his crutches.

"Remember the last time I was here?" Betty asked and they nodded. "The next afternoon Howard and I sent Edith to Arizona to visit her daughter. She just got back this morning and she's already disappeared. I don't know who's been bringing you food, but it wasn't her."

"Then who was it?" Hallie asked, puzzled. She stepped aside so Betty could see the table with the opulent tea set up. There were a couple of tiered trays full of sandwiches and cookies, cakes and pastries.

"As you can see," Jamie said, "there's a lot of food and the big pot of tea. Maybe someone else from your inn is delivering it."

Betty looked from one to the other. "You two are as crazy as my mother-in-law. There is nothing on that table but a bunch of empty dishes." She put her hand on the door. "I think my mother-in-law should go back to Arizona. It's saner there." With a shake of her head, she left, closing the door firmly behind her.

Jamie and Hallie looked at each other, then very slowly turned toward the table.

Moments before they had been hungrily eating the wide variety of foods and drinking tea that never grew cold.

But now they saw empty dishes. They were sparkling clean, but then they had often washed and stacked them, ready for whenever Edith came by and picked them up.

There was no food and no steam coming from the teapot.

When Jamie and Hallie looked back at each other, their eyes widened as they realized that for weeks they'd been eating nothing. And without saying it aloud, they knew that each feast had been prepared by hands that no longer existed.

Hallie was the first to speak. "So now we see why I lost weight."

For a moment Jamie looked as though he didn't know what to say, but then a bit of laughter escaped him.

"The Ghost Diet," Hallie said. "Think it will catch on?" She too began to laugh. Within seconds, they couldn't hold back. They fell into each other's arms and their laughter filled the house.

And inside the tea room, two beautiful young women smiled at each other. Yet again, they had helped True Love find itself.

Epilogue

Three months after Jilly's wedding, an email from Shelly came through. Hallie drew in her breath. "She and Braden have set a wedding date for next January and she wants me to be her maid of honor."

"What are you going to do?" Jamie asked.

"Decline, of course. She only asked me so I'd do all the work for the wedding while she does nothing. Absolutely not."

"Having relatives isn't all fairy tale happiness," he said. "I think you should give yourself some time to think about what you want to do."

Hallie thought that was good advice, so for three days she thought about nothing else. The first day she felt only anger. Of course she'd refuse! How dare Shelly even ask? But by the second day Hallie began to consider the repercussions of her actions. If she did attend Shelly and Braden's wedding, would it be with a heart full of anger? Did Braden deserve that? Would she cry with Braden's mother about the horror of his marrying someone like Shelly?

By the third day Hallie knew she had to make an effort at attaining peace. She left Jamie in Nantucket and flew back to her house outside Boston. Things there were worse than she'd imagined. Braden's mother was despondent to the point of depression. She was sure that her son was ruining his life—and she told him so often. Braden was working sixteen-hour days to keep his mind off the problems of his personal life. And according to him, Shelly was living in fear that at any minute he was going to break up with her. Nothing he said reassured her.

Hallie decided she *had* to help Braden and his mother. First of all, she spent hours talking with Braden. She wanted to be sure that he loved Shelly and wasn't just infatuated with her looks. She heard of his long-term love, and he told her about Shelly's side of her childhood hurt. It took a couple of days and many telephone talks with Jamie, but Hallie adjusted to this new knowledge.

Hallie thought about sitting down with her stepsister and having a heart-to-heart talk. But what would that be like? Bringing up years of accusations? "You broke my doll!" "Your grandparents loved you but not me!" "You stole my boyfriend!" "You got to play when we were kids, but I didn't."

No, that would accomplish nothing.

After some very long talks with Jamie, then with his aunt Jilly, Hallie decided to use the coming wedding to bridge some of the gaps between people.

Hallie went to Braden's mother and put on the show of her life. She took half a dozen bride magazines with her and, crying rather copiously, said that Shelly wanted her to plan her wedding, but Hallie didn't know how.

Within ten minutes, Mrs. Westbrook was organizing a wedding. It took Hallie two days before she managed to get Shelly into her place. She and Braden's mother became obsessed with flowers and cakes and gowns and even the crystals on the shoes. When Shelly told her future mother-in-law that she'd dearly love to have a baby right away, the bond was sealed.

In the ensuing peace, Braden called Hallie and said, "I love you."

Hallie laughed. "So did you decide on peonies or roses?"

"Who cares? Really, Hallie, Mom and Shelly are shopping together and making baby plans and—" He took a breath. "Thank you."

"What I did was nothing compared to what you and your mom did for my life. Are we friends?"

"Forever," Braden said.

As soon as she clicked off, she called Jamie. "I'm coming home tomorrow."

All he could say was a heartfelt "Yes!"

As she flew back to Nantucket, she knew she was leaving behind a lifetime of anger and resentment. She didn't think she and Shelly would ever be true friends but neither would there be deep hatred. There would be shared holidays and exchanges of triumphs and failures. Somehow, they would manage to leave the past behind.

That night, as she lay in bed with Jamie, she told him everything she was feeling.

"It's all normal in families," he said.

As winter approached, Hallie and Jamie began talking about their futures. They'd made no decisions about where to live or if Jamie could go back to medicine or how Hallie was going to work. Should she set up a private clinic? Work for a hospital? It was growing colder on the island and they knew that many stores and services would soon be closing. There wouldn't be a lot of work for Hallie.

One night they were sitting on the bed, each with a computer on their lap. "Holy—" Jamie said, his eyes wide.

Hallie looked at him. "What is it?"

He turned his laptop to face her. On the screen was a photo of a house with a deep porch and a glassed-in room.

"Is it the one from your dream?"

"Yes," Jamie said and they exchanged looks. "It's *exactly* the one I imagined."

Without saying anything, they both knew who was behind this. After months in the house, they no longer commented on what the Tea Ladies did. They'd had Caleb and Victoria Huntley to dinner twice and Caleb had talked about the ladies as if he'd known them personally. When Jamie and Hallie spent a long weekend in Colorado with his family, Caleb had asked if he could house-sit. Later he said he'd had a lovely visit with the ladies.

By that time Hallie and Jamie were so used to things being moved, needlework that finished itself, doors that opened and closed by themselves, that they didn't question a mere conversation.

Leland had visited once and Hallie had loved getting to know him better. When Leland showed up, he had a box of information about what happened to his ancestor after he'd been made to leave Nantucket. It was the story of a man with a broken heart that never fully healed.

The three of them spread all the documents out on the tables in the tea room, turned out the lights, and left them there. The next morning everything had been neatly stacked on one table, but a photo of a portrait of Leland as an old man was missing. There was a card beside the papers. In pretty, old-fashioned handwriting, it said

THANK YOU,

JULIANA HARTLEY

Jamie and Hallie thought the card was very sweet, but Leland said, "I need a drink."

For the rest of his visit, Hallie and Jamie refrained from mentioning the resident ghosts.

Hallie looked at the picture of the house on the computer screen. "I like it. What does Uncle Kit say about it?"

Jamie read the email. "He's bought a big old house for himself in a small town in Virginia. He says that when he saw this house—and it's for sale—he thought of you and me."

He read more of the email. "Ah. Here it is. I knew Uncle Kit had an ulterior motive. He says the town has only one doctor. It did have two, a father and son, but last year the father died. Now the son is having to work long hours on his own and he needs help."

He looked at Hallie. "Uncle Kit says this town is near a big lake with many houses on it. According to him, there are lots of injuries to people who sit all winter, then in the summer think they're still teenagers. He says a physical therapy clinic would do well there."

Jamie's eyes were intense. "What do you think?"

"I like the idea very much," she said. "What about you? Think you're ready to be a doctor again?"

"I think maybe I'm ready to try. Part-time, anyway." Pausing, he looked at her. "If you'll be there to help me, that is."

"Yes," she answered, her eyes serious. "I will go with you wherever you want to go. Or stay here with you."

For a moment they looked at each other, then their computers were pushed aside, and they were in each other's arms.

They knew that wherever they went, whatever they did, they wanted to do it *together.*

Acknowledgments

I'd like to thank my dear trainer, Mary Bralove, for her expert advice on physical therapy. She told me and showed me what to do. Thank you!

As they have through several books, my Facebook buddies stuck with me through the daily ups and downs of writing this novel. From coming up with character names to venting about copyeditors, they were there. Thank you very much.

I want to thank my beloved editor, Linda Marrow, who listens and laughs and endlessly encourages me.

I have a new publishing house, Random House, and I want to thank everyone there. They are always kind and considerate and helpful.

In researching this book, I read a lot about PTSD—and cried through all of it. There are not enough thanks in the world for our soldiers, for our wounded warriors. We owe you everything!

Please join me on Facebook and hear the truth about writing.

By the way, the story of Cale and Kane is in a short story, "Matchmakers," in *The Invitation.* Caleb's story is in *True Love,* Graydon and Toby are in *For All Time,* and J.T. and Aria are in *The Princess.* The story of Dougless and Nicholas's father is in *A Knight in Shining Armor.*